The Noble Fugitive

HEIRS OF ACADIA
-THREE-

The *Noble Fugitive*

T. DAVIS BUNN
ISABELLA BUNN

BETHANYHOUSE
Minneapolis, Minnesota

The Noble Fugitive
Copyright © 2005
T. Davis Bunn and Isabella Bunn

Cover design by The DesignWorks Group, Inc.

Scripture quotations are from the King James Version of the Bible.

Published by Bethany House Publishers
11400 Hampshire Avenue South
Bloomington, Minnesota 55438

Bethany House Publishers is a division of
Baker Publishing Group, Grand Rapids, Michigan.

Printed in the United States of America

ISBN 0-7642-2859-5 (Paperback)
ISBN 0-7642-0093-3 (Hardcover)
ISBN 0-7642-0094-1 (Large Print)

Library of Congress Cataloging-in-Publication Data

Bunn, T. Davis, 1952-
    The noble fugitive / T. Davis Bunn, Isabella Bunn.
        p.   cm. — (Heirs of Acadia ; 3)
    Summary: "Historical drama and romance set in Venice and the English countryside of the 1800s. Two lives become intertwined despite the burdens of their past. A place that once seemed only a dreaded detour becomes a sacred venue for the unveiling of God's Providence"—Provided by publisher.
    ISBN 0-7642-0093-3 (alk. paper) — ISBN 0-7642-2859-5 (pbk.) — ISBN 0-7642-0094-1 (large print pbk.) 1. Children of the rich—Fiction. 2. Italians—England—Fiction. 3. Tutors and tutoring—Fiction. 4. Women domestics—Fiction. 5. Venice (Italy)—Fiction. 6. England—Fiction. I. Bunn, Isabella. II. Title III. Series: Heirs of Acadia ; 3.

    PS3552.U4718N63 2005
    813'.54—dc22
                                                                      2005018200

For all the years of love, encouragement,
and graciousness,
this book is dedicated to

Becky Bunn,

wonderful mother and mother-in-law.

T. DAVIS BUNN is an award-winning author whose growing list of novels demonstrates the scope and diversity of his writing talent.

ISABELLA BUNN has been a vital part of his writing success; her research and attention to detail have left their imprint on nearly every story. Their life abroad has provided much inspiration and information for plots and settings. They live near Oxford, England.

*with Janette Oke   †with Isabella Bunn

Prologue

July 1832

The bosun's whistle piped the darkest hour of the night. Serafina quietly rose from her narrow bed and lit a candle. The world beyond Serafina's porthole seemed painted with a despair that nearly choked off her breath. Yet not even this could stop her.

Swiftly Serafina donned a modest frock of grayish blue, like the sky before sunrise. The dress was unadorned save for the double row of ivory buttons rising from the matching cloth belt to her neck. She wore no jewels because she had none. She brushed her hair carefully and tied it back in a silk ribbon matching her dress. Her shoes were dark leather and sturdy, but she did not put them on.

She inspected her impression in the tiny mirror attached to the wall above her stateroom basin. She hardly recognized her own face. Somewhere along the way, she had changed. There was a subtle shift in the way she held herself. Her mouth was set in firmer lines. Her eyes no longer seemed to shine as they had before. Serafina turned away with a sigh. There was nothing to be gained by looking back or wishing for events to have been otherwise. They were as they were.

She straightened the bed linens and set the letter for her parents on the pillow. Her determination mingled with the pain she was causing. The words inside the folded paper burned her mind with tragic finality. *I am leaving and will not return.*

Serafina slowly lifted the door latch and slipped from the cabin. Just across the narrow passage were her parents' quarters. She paused to listen but heard nothing beyond their closed door.

Elsewhere the ship was alive with quiet bustling. She could hear the crew padding about on bare feet. Officers spoke in the hushed tones of people aware that others slept. Serafina carried her shoes in one hand and a small case in the other. Her dark cloak, with the cowl pulled far over her face, hid her slender form and features. She moved swiftly through the passage and up the stairs.

As she stepped out to the deck, a cold wet wind sliced across the waters. She tightened her cloak and pulled the hood down farther. Somewhere far to the southeast, a kindly summer sun rose upon her beloved Venice. Here in the Portsmouth harbor, however, the weather remained chill and damp and hostile.

Fortunately she did not have long to wait.

"All right, missie." The sailor dropped quietly from the rigging to stand beside her. "Let's be seeing it."

Serafina set down her case and fished in the folds of her cloak for the coin. She held out one of the stolen gold ducats where it caught the light. "Just as I promised."

"It's smaller than a sovereign, but I reckon it'll spend good enough." His hand was black from gripping the tarred ropes. "Let's be having it, then."

"When I am on the rowboat and headed to shore." Serafina made the coin vanish. "That was the agreement."

"Agreements change," he said, his grin made evil by the gap where his front teeth should have been.

"Perhaps I should call for an officer." Her voice sounded much more confident than she felt.

"Do that and you'll find yourself back in your cabin swift enough," he hissed, but he also backed off a step. "Then you'll sail for America with the rest of us."

Her body felt trapped within talons of fear. But she did not yield. "I will pay only when I am safely on board the small vessel."

The sailor scowled and wheeled about. "This way, and keep silent."

Serafina followed the man as he crept around to where the last of the supply boats were moored at the side of the larger ship. Her heart was in her throat, both over the possibility of being spotted and the sailor doing wrong by her. But he moved with catlike swiftness straight for the lower mid-deck, scouting in every direction.

When they arrived he glanced over the railing and whistled once very quietly. Then he stood with hand outstretched.

Serafina glanced doubtfully over the side. The longboat rested calmly in the lee of the sailing ship. Two sailors held the craft steady against the ship's side and peered up at her. "How am I to get down?" she asked.

"On the sailors' ladder, and be quick about it." The sailor unfastened the railing's catch, swinging one portion out like a waist-high door. He then lifted his curled half fist before her face. "You'll pay me now."

She dropped the coin into his palm. Instantly the man whipped about and vanished. Nervously she leaned forward and dropped her case and her shoes to the outstretched hands. The boat seemed very far down from where she stood. A man in the longboat hissed words she did not understand, but the urgency was clear enough. She turned around and gripped the unsteady rope ladder with both hands. Step by tremulous step she eased herself down, the wind catching her skirts with a force that made her gasp.

Somewhere overhead an officer called to his men. Serafina hesitated, fearing the alarm was about to be raised. A pair of hands, tough as old oak, reached up and gripped her calf. She kicked them off. The man below might have chuckled.

She took the ladder's next rung. The descent seemed to last for ages. Finally her toe touched the boat's rail, and another hand reached for her arm. This time she allowed herself to be guided onto a plank seat.

As soon as she was settled, the two seamen pushed the long-boat away. The vessel reeked of the load of fresh vegetables that it no doubt had just delivered. They fitted their oars into the locks and pulled hard for land. The man in the bow said softly, "My mate tells me you'll pay for your passage in gold."

"A gold ducat when we arrive," Serafina agreed as she bent to slip into her shoes. She was surprised at how firm and low her voice sounded to her own ears, nothing like the sprightly tone she was accustomed to hearing. The sorrow she carried was no doubt aging her.

"There goes your ship now," the man said, pointing toward the stern with his chin.

Serafina turned quickly. She stifled a sob at the sight of the sails unfurling and the ship's anchor creaking up from the seabed. The officers on the foredeck were silhouetted against the first hints of the gray dawn. A bosun piped his mates aloft, as mournful a sound as ever she had heard. Her heart cried out words her mouth could not form, calling for her mother and father. She could watch no longer.

The oarsmen made a swift crossing of the inland harbor, and soon the longboat was fast against the dockside. One man helped her climb onto the stone jetty while another held her case at his side. "Our payment?"

She leaned over to hand him the coin. Half of her money was gone now. "Where can I find a carriage to Bath?" she asked, trying to keep the tremor from her voice.

"Couldn't say about travel to the Wessex region, missie." He pointed toward an inn at the harbor's far end, where light glowed from all the ground-floor windows. "But the post coach for London leaves from there at daybreak."

She thanked the men and started across the dock. A few workmen were about, rolling giant water casks toward a waiting craft. Otherwise the port was still. Her footsteps echoed loudly off the buildings at the harbor's edge. Up ahead a horse whinnied as bridles were fitted into place. A pair of gulls traced their way across the gradually strengthening light. She stopped a moment and watched them soar and swoop off across the water. In the far distance, sails were melting into the sea.

"I have no family and no friends," she whispered. Her shiver was as much from within as against the cold.

She started up the rocky port lane toward the inn. She did not allow herself to turn again as the ship carrying her parents westward vanished beyond the horizon.

Resolutely she focused upon the lamplight flickering over the inn's stable doors. Up ahead, her future awaited. As well as her beloved Luca.

Chapter 1

Serafina found it very hard to be the youngest. Everyone was always telling her how fortunate she was to be a Gavi, one of the oldest families of Venice. Most left unsaid that her mother was lucky to have become Alessandro Gavi's second wife. Serafina's father was one of Venice's leading *doges*, the merchant families who had ruled the water-bound kingdom for more than a thousand years. Her mother's family was far less grand. They were mere landholders from the Dolomites. But the year after Alessandro's first wife had died, he had met the lovely Bettina and married her. Serafina's father was sixteen years older than her mother. Two of Serafina's half sisters were already married and had children of their own. They treated Serafina with utter indifference, almost like an unwanted houseguest. But the youngest half sister, Gabriella, was another thing entirely. Gabriella, a few years older than Serafina's seventeen years, took every opportunity to make life miserable for her.

But Serafina would not have described her life as unhappy. She loved her parents and willingly sought to obey and please them. She loved their villa fronting Venice's Grand Canal. She could spend hours hanging over her bedroom's balcony railing, watching the water and the boats and the birds. She particularly loved the sunsets. For she had an artist's heart, like Luca. And because of Luca she yearned for this sunset most of all.

Serafina sat on the iron bench attached to the wall behind her balcony. Her view was over the Rialto Bridge and the promenade on the canal's other side. She could hear the crowds and observe the gondoliers setting down their passengers. But she was invisible to those below. Her father was very proud of this protected balcony, sometimes called a widow's ledge. He claimed it was of Arab design, originally brought west by the first crusaders. When Serafina had been a child, she had imagined being a damsel trapped in an evil lord's tower, waiting for her prince to come and rescue her. And now her childish dream was becoming a wondrous reality. She shivered with delicious anticipation.

She leaned over to the balcony's railing and observed the bolder ladies walking arm in arm with their paramours. The setting sun cast a gemstone glow over all the buildings. Truly she could imagine herself captured within a mythic realm, one from which only a great hero could rescue her. Or a handsome army officer with an artist's heart. Someone just like Luca.

From the bedroom next to her own, Serafina could hear Gabriella quarreling with her mother. Gabriella was engaged and close enough to her wedding day to challenge her stepmother. Gabriella's shrill voice carried through her open window. "I won't do it, do you hear?"

Serafina's mother sounded almost as sharp. "The whole city hears you! But this changes nothing!"

Gabriella's laugh was not a pleasant sound. "Why should I spend time with the little child?"

"Serafina is a child no longer, as you well know. She is seventeen and soon to become engaged herself!"

Serafina winced at that shrill reminder. She was indeed just days from becoming betrothed. Roberto was the son of another wealthy merchant, but he was thirty-two! An old man, in her estimation. Serafina had heard other merchant princes comment that the marriage was a union worthy of Venice's *consiglière*, the title her father carried.

The single issue over which Serafina quarreled with her parents was men. Her parents had grown weary of the constant train of suitors. Serafina felt as though she had been courted by every bachelor from Venice to Milan. But none had proven the least bit interesting to her.

Serafina's parents had grown increasingly impatient. She was seventeen, and it was time she was wed. Roberto was not unattractive. He was well presented and spoke with the languid musicality of Venice's elite. And his family's holdings stretched all the way to Vienna and Berlin. This suitor would do splendidly, they told her in no uncertain terms.

In truth, Serafina had not so much accepted the engagement as stopped paying much attention. The day before Roberto had presented himself, Serafina had met Luca. A fact Serafina kept most secret. Though her parents indulged many of their youngest daughter's whims, Serafina was well aware that Luca was not a man of whom they would approve.

Her mother demanded, "I want you to take your sister with you!"

"First of all, she is *not* my sister. And second, who are you to be insisting on anything?"

"I am your mother."

"You have never been my mother! You are my father's wife. You . . ."

Serafina heard the hurt in her mother's voice. "Please do finish your thought."

"Why, so you can fly off to Father and tell him what I've said and done?"

"Why shouldn't I? You are behaving in an utterly improper manner."

"Oh, I can hardly wait until I am out of this house and free of you and your wretched daughter."

"Why do you speak like this? What have I or Serafina ever done to hurt you?"

Gabriella did not reply. But Serafina knew too well what the girl was thinking. She had heard Gabriella speak with her sisters of how Bettina had usurped their mother's position. One of Gabriella's favorite topics was how infatuated their father had grown with Serafina, the daughter of his winter years. How dangerous Serafina was to their position. Especially because of her beauty.

As long as Serafina could remember, people had commented upon her loveliness. Venice's young dandies had followed her in packs since she turned twelve. But such words as they flung her way had meant nothing. Until they had been spoken by Luca.

Serafina heard her mother continue, "I have tried my very best to make this a happy home, a place where you and your sisters would feel welcome—"

Gabriella's voice echoed as she raced down the central stairs. "Why shouldn't we be welcome here? It was *our* home long before *you* ever came." The slamming front door boomed through the entire house.

Hurriedly Serafina reentered her bedroom, seated herself, and picked up some handwork. She had to distract attention from her balcony. Her mother knocked and opened the door. "May I come in?"

Bettina Gavi was from the alpine village of Campobello. Bettina was not an Italian name at all, but Austrian. Venice had become a principality of the Austro-Hungarian empire less than a hundred years earlier. But the Dolomite region had been held and lost a dozen times and more over the past thousand years. Though they claimed to be Italian, Bettina's family spoke German at home. She had insisted that Serafina learn the language as well. Serafina's sisters had complained bitterly and refused to sit with the tutor. But Serafina had loved the challenge and the way the lessons brought the world beyond Venice closer. Her mother had taken note of Serafina's gift with languages and hired additional tutors. Serafina soon became fluent in English and spoke passable French.

But it was not merely a gift for languages that mother and daughter shared. Bettina Gavi was a fairly tall woman and full figured. Both mother and daughter had hair the color of flax, a shade beyond blond. When the sea winds blew hard, her father claimed to see woven threads of sunlight in Serafina's tresses. Just as he had when he fell in love with her mother.

Serafina's sisters were all olive-complexioned like their father and his first wife, with sharp Venetian features and hair so dark it turned indigo in the sunlight. They were handsome women, all of them. But they also bore the mark of their heritage, eighteen generations of traders and merchants and holders of princely power. Their appearance only made Serafina appear even more feminine.

"I had thought perhaps you might like to take a turn with me," Serafina's mother said.

"No thank you, Mama."

"But it's going to be such a lovely sunset. Why should we not take a promenade together?"

Mother and this daughter had always enjoyed a special bond. Serafina found a unique delight in the closeness between herself and her parents. The fact that her plans for the evening went directly against this caused her great turmoil. No matter how often she told herself it was right to do as she intended. The closer the hour approached, the more excited she became. Yet her sense of guilt and dread increased as well, until she felt almost torn in two.

Bettina, as usual, was attentive enough to observe the shadow pass over her daughter's features. "What is it, Serafina?"

"Nothing, Mama. I'm fine." Oh, how she hated lying to her mother.

"You look flushed. Are you feverish?" She laid a hand upon her daughter's forehead. "You seem all right."

Serafina resisted the urge to tell her mother not to treat her like a child. Which of course was part of the problem. Night after night, Serafina had mentally argued through a dispute that in truth would never happen. Just one look at her mother's face was enough to convince her that Luca would never be accepted in this house.

Yet not even her love for her parents, or her parents' love for her, could turn Serafina away from her course. Or from the future this course held.

"You heard us quarreling, I suppose." Bettina Gavi seated

herself on the cushioned window bench beside her daughter. "You know why Gabriella treats you as she does. Her fiancé has a roving eye. He watches you like a hawk whenever you cross his vision."

Serafina was well aware of the impact her beauty had on young men. "But Gabriella has treated me badly since I was a baby."

"Because you, my darling daughter, have always shone as though the mountain light were captured in your face." Serafina's mother had a northerner's complexion, fine as stone-milled flour, and every emotion shone clear for all to see. "When you were still an infant I carried you into the market, and people would be drawn to you as if I offered them free honeycombs. You smiled, and grown men cried out with astonishment and delight. Nothing made your sister angrier than hearing people discuss your beauty."

"You have never spoken to me about Gabriella before."

"And I hope never to speak of it again. There is nothing to be gained from dwelling on the weaknesses of kin. Even so, it is true. She envied you from your birth." Bettina hesitated, then added almost in spite of herself, "It used to break my heart to see how cruel she was to you."

The bells of Saint Mark's Cathedral struck the hour before sunset, when the afternoon light angled tightly above the church and shadows over the canal waters were strongest. Serafina started. She had become so involved in her mother's words she had entirely forgotten the time.

"What is the matter, my daughter?"

"It is nothing, Mama." The repeated lie tore at her. She was a good daughter. She had never before knowingly gone against her parents' wishes. Though her heart fluttered tight in her chest, she managed to keep her voice steady. "I'm fine."

Bettina took on a girlish tone. "Come, let us buy ices from the vendor and stroll across the square and cherish all that is good in this world."

Serafina felt her heart tugged mightily by her mother's invitation. But the day was set upon another course. One to which Serafina would hold.

"Thank you, Mama. But I really would like to be alone with my thoughts just now." She picked up her embroidery and pretended to concentrate upon the design. But her mind was far, far removed from her family's home and the safety it offered.

Serafina watched her mother cross the room and depart without looking back. The sound of the door clicking shut seemed to drive a nail into her heart. Never had she felt so ashamed. So guilty.

Or so excited.

Truth be told, Serafina loved the evening promenade more than almost anything in her water-circled city. Here in Venice time was a guest, the locals liked to say, and not a ruler. Walking the streets at evening, it was possible to believe this was indeed true.

In these final hours of the Venetian day, the ancient palaces of colored stone seemed as delicate as Murano glass. Pillars looked translucent, too fragile to hold up the imposing façades. Normally Serafina would be begging her mother to come outside with her. But this was the hour when her mother was usually the busiest, supervising the evening meal and readying the house for Alessandro Gavi's return. For Serafina to have refused her mother's invitation was very strange indeed.

Serafina gripped her hands in her lap and wished the arguments raging in her mind and heart would end. She stared at the canal beyond her balcony and recalled another time of conflicting emotions. The summer she had turned eight, she had gone into the kitchen in the quiet hour after lunch, when even the servants were slumbering through the worst of the summer heat. Her mother had been seated at the kitchen table with a faraway look to her eyes. Tears had streamed down Bettina's face. They had caught the light streaming through the kitchen window, making her pale complexion shimmer.

"Mama?"

Her mother started and breathed a long shaky breath. She spoke not to her daughter but to herself. "God heard me after all."

"What is the matter, Mama?"

"Nothing, now." She opened her arms. "Come here, my child. Let me look at you."

Serafina did as her mother requested. But as she climbed up into her mother's lap, seeing the tears up close caused her to cry as well. "I'm frightened."

"Shah, my dearest one. Calm yourself." Her mother held Serafina in one arm and with the other hand wiped away her tears. She smiled, or tried to. "There, you see? All better."

But Serafina felt pierced by the sorrow that still stained her mother's features. "You're so sad, Mama."

"Yes. It happens sometimes. But it will soon pass."

"But why, Mama?"

"A woman's foolishness, nothing more." Yet saying these words caused fresh tears to course down her cheeks. "I am just being weak. And silly. You mustn't pay me any mind."

But Serafina had been infected by a sorrow far deeper than anything she had ever felt before. Her mother held her for a time, stroking her hair. Serafina wept and would not be consoled. Finally her mother said, "I will tell you a secret, but you must promise not to speak about it to anyone."

She sniffed and smiled. "I love secrets."

"Don't I just know it. You must promise, mind."

"I won't tell anyone. Not even Papa."

"Especially Papa!" Her mother gave a small laugh. "Very well. I was crying because I missed my home."

"But this is your home."

"I mean the home of my childhood. I was missing the hills."

"The place where Grandma and Grandpa live?"

"Just so. Where I lived when I was your age." She turned her face back to the sunlight. "The light is purer there, or so people claim. The summer heat is always spiced with wind blowing across the eternal ice. The water tastes different, as does the bread, the cheese. It is said the mountain folk have hearts and wills carved from their mountain stone."

Serafina listened as much to the dreamy nature of her mother's voice as the words. "That's no secret, Mama. Grandpa tells us this every time we go to visit them. He says I have a mountain woman's will. And when I tell him I can't because I'm still a child, he just laughs."

Again her mother seemed to draw herself back from a far distance. "You are far too perceptive for a child your age."

"I want to know the secret."

"Very well, and I shall tell you, my golden-haired beauty." She stroked Serafina's face, yet it looked as if her vision was once more drawn to what Serafina could not see. "When I was seventeen, I fell in love with a man."

"With Papa?"

"No, my child. With another. A shepherd. A mountain man."

"But you love Papa."

"Yes. With all my heart. But I was a foolish young girl then. To have wed this other man would have been a terrible mistake."

"So why were you crying?"

"Because, my darling child—" a tremor ran through her mother's frame—"this date was to have been our wedding day. And because I still have a bit of the foolishness in me, I thought of him. For the first time in so many years I cannot even count them, I thought of him."

"Do you miss him very much?"

"I can scarcely remember how he looked. And what does that matter?" She wiped away tears that deepened her voice. "He would be married now, and old. Perhaps even . . . No, I shall not dwell upon that."

Her mother turned her solemn gaze toward Serafina. "I sat here and I prayed for God to remind me why I am here and how blessed I am to be in this place and this home. And then in you come, with your dancing spirit and your angel's hair. My darling child, I was brought to this place so that I might love your father. And have you, heart of my heart. And be a part of this wonderful world."

Being eight years old and shunned by her older sister, Serafina found a certain satisfaction in how her mother did not include her sisters in this moment. "I won't tell anybody our secret, Mama. I promise."

Serafina's attention was drawn back to sunset's soft veil drawn over the water and the palaces. She sat very still and listened with all her might. Suddenly her intent was rewarded with a quiet whisper of sound.

She had not yet heard the front door close, signaling that her mother had departed. So she did not do what she wanted, which was to fly to the balcony railing and lean over and watch this new visitor do the utterly impossible. The side of the house fronting the canal was now veiled in shade, while all about it glowed the fiercely setting sun. Unless one was looking very carefully, it would have been impossible to notice a person scaling the smooth wall. Unless one was a young girl on the cusp of womanhood, who knew the visitor came to steal away her heart.

$$\mathcal{C}hapter\ 2$$

That particular Monday morning was hot even for Trinidad in July. The early hours were better for trade, and by sunrise Port of Spain's streets were already bustling. John Falconer wore the dark woolen broadcloth expected of a tradesman doing business with the governor's officials. In the rising heat the suit weighed heavy on his frame. But this was a minor irritation against the fact that his best mate had gone missing. John Falconer feared the man had been captured and questioned. If so, Falconer's own hours drained as fast as sand in a broken hourglass.

He checked his pocket watch. He was not due at the governor's customs house for another hour. Falconer waited upon the cathedral's front steps, hoping against hope that his friend might appear. Falconer ran the largest chandlery, or ship's merchant, on the neighboring island of Grenada. Some considered Falconer's the finest establishment of its kind in the West Indies. Local planters bought from him as well, and conversed as they did their business and drank his coffee. Which suited Falconer just fine. He was not interested in profit. He was after information. He had been a very rich man at one time. The money had brought him nothing save a reason to come crashing to his knees.

Trinidad was both a new island and very old. The explorer Christopher Columbus had landed near where Falconer now stood on July 31, 1498. Columbus had found the island teeming with natives. The next Europeans did not arrive until some fifty years later. Finally in 1783 the Spanish king opened the island to colonization. By that time native wars between the Amerindians and the Caribs, and diseases brought by the occasional ship, had reduced the island's population to less than a thousand. French colonists flocked to the island, such that by the time the British conquered Trinidad in 1797, the population had increased to almost thirty thousand. Eleven thousand of these were French, a thousand were Spanish, and the rest were African slaves.

The capital's main square held a large old cathedral, one that had traded denominations and names as the island had passed from one colonial power to the next. Now that the island was English, the church was Anglican, though the bell towers were built in the Spanish style and the altar frescos were French. The capital of Trinidad was built in a sheltered valley, with steep hills behind and the Caribbean's finest port stretching out ahead. From his position on the church stairs, Falconer could look out over the city's central square to the ships nestled comfortably at anchor. He searched the streets and shadows until he spotted a pair of the governor's soldiers eyeing him with suspicion. John Falconer was not a man who could go unnoticed for long. He slowly moved away.

Then a childish voice pierced the morning's heat. "Look, Mama!" The young boy tugged on his mother's hand. "A pirate!"

"Shush, James. Don't point."

"But he is! See the scar? I wonder why the soldiers don't arrest him!"

The mother blushed scarlet as she pulled her boy away. "Forgive him, sir. He means no harm."

"None taken, ma'am." Falconer doffed his hat politely and smiled at the boy. Many had told Falconer that his scar rendered any smile futile. Despite a curious nature, the young boy shied away.

Falconer knew what the mother saw. He was tall and broad about the shoulder. His legs were like ship's timbers and his hands remained half curled, ready for drawing sword or pike or whatever weapon was at the ready. His seaman's skin was blasted by salt and burned by sun. There was no sword upon his belt nor knife in his boot. But he had worn both for so long people seemed to sense the possibility. Or perhaps it was the air of danger that no amount of prayer or gentleman's attire could dispel.

Falconer felt the soldiers' gaze upon him. He could think of no better way to show he posed no threat than squatting before the boy and saying in his mildest voice, "I'm not a pirate, lad. But I've faced them, sure enough."

The boy's eyes rounded and he stiffened against his mother's attempts to draw him on. Finally his mother relented, and the boy said, "You fought Captain Blackbeard?"

Falconer had to laugh, for he had been raised on the very same tale. "You're off by a century and more, lad. I may be old, but not that ancient. No, my pirates were off the Horn of Africa. You know where that is?"

"No, sir."

"It's six weeks' sail into the sunrise." He pointed out over the harbor. "Head south by east until you escape the storms off the Cape of Good Hope by racing into the southern ice flows."

"But the cold lies to our north, sir."

"Aye, that's true enough, lad. But if you go very far south you hit Antarctica. The waters there are as rough and as cold as any on earth. Around the Cape and north again, into the Mozambique Channel and the trade winds. Islands there are big as countries. With smaller ones abounding—so many they aren't even named. The pirates lie waiting there for the trade ships. Venetian and Spanish merchants travel west from the Spice Islands, bearing gold and pepper and teas, their holds so full they wallow fat and slow in the water."

"Come, James," the mother tried again. "We mustn't take up the gentleman's time."

"Oh, sir!" The boy heard nothing save what Falconer had to offer. "Were the pirates so very fierce?"

"Aye, that they were. Mussulmen came out of the sun when it was westering and we were weary from another day watching and waiting. They use low-lying vessels that are hard to spy, with lateen rigs. You know a lateen sail?"

"Forgive me, sir." Since speaking to her son had no impact, she addressed herself to Falconer directly. "We really must be away."

He rose to his feet and doffed his hat a second time. "Of course, ma'am."

"Bid the nice gentleman farewell, James."

The boy could not help but ask a final question. "Is that where you gained your scar?"

"James, really. That is not proper."

"No offense, ma'am." But the woman was not listening. The boy must have sensed his mother would not be stalled further, and he allowed himself to be pulled forward. But not before he straightened to attention and shot Falconer a worthy salute.

Falconer smiled and touched his forelock with one finger. This caused the lad to beam like the sun and go skipping away. Falconer watched them depart, his heart pierced by the absence of anything so fine as a future and a son.

When he turned back, the soldiers had sauntered on their way, certain he was not a threat. For once, Falconer wished it was the truth.

The church's interior was cool in the manner of a cave and smelled of incense from the morning service. Two priests Falconer did not know moved about the nave, shifting a load of books. Falconer sat in a pew and placed his hat on the seat beside him. He made the sign of the cross and bent forward, gripping the back of the pew in front of him.

It was only in such places that he studied himself, for John Falconer was a man of action. Like most men who lived by deed and not word, he was not given to dwelling much on his own internal state. But these old churches, musty from the centuries of psalms and prayers, affected him deeply. He looked at his own hands and saw the calluses caused by grasping sail and tiller and sword. He imagined his leathery skin stained by the blood of others. No matter how often he assured himself that the blessed Savior had died for men such as him, Falconer remained inwardly wounded by all the errors of a violent and gutted past.

He closed his eyes and prayed in his customary terse manner. His words came with difficulty because he felt so humbled by a God who welcomed him, even him. As always, Falconer first apologized. If only he had come to know God sooner. If only he had been a better man. If only . . .

He then prayed for his mission. And his few friends. The ones bonded to him by shared cause and passion and faith.

As though in response, Falconer sensed someone approaching. He might now be a changed man, one who sought eternal truth, but his senses remained honed by a life of battle and adventure. This man who approached knew Falconer and his ability to sense danger. He gave a seaman's whistle, a quick note sent aloft in fog or between mates in the fury of close-hand battle. Enough to tell friend from foe.

Falconer remained as he was, head bowed over the pew ahead, as the man settled into the seat beside him.

The man was a former shipmate called Felix, now serving as curate at a church in the town's poorer section. The curate's parishioners were drawn largely from freed slaves, small farmers, sailors, and laborers. The hands that came to rest alongside Falconer's were accustomed to hard work and harder storms. The face that rested upon his knuckles was clearly carved from fierce years. But Felix's features burned with a light that Falconer envied, for the man's faith had always seemed purer than his own. Ever since this man had led Falconer through his first feeble and fumbling prayer.

Falconer could confess anything to Felix. Even the murmured words, "I saw a likely young lad in the square. I found myself wishing I was a better man, someone deserving of a son. Someone a mother would not run from."

The curate continued with his prayer, then leaned back and crossed himself. "You are too hard on yourself, my friend. You always have been. Finding God has changed this not one iota. The trait defines you."

"You did not see how the mother dragged her boy away from me."

"As a proper woman would from any stranger." Felix stilled further discussion with an upraised hand. "I have news."

Falconer studied his friend and grew certain the news was foul. Which could only mean one thing. "Jaime?"

"He is dead." The curate crossed himself once again. "May God take His servant swiftly home."

Jaime was not his given name, which hardly mattered in a land where many new Christians asked to be renamed by the priest. Such newcomers to the Savior hoped by leaving their name, they would also leave behind their past. And if not their past, at least their memories.

Jaime was a Carib Indian, a tribe so fierce the entire southern seas now bore their name. Two centuries earlier, the Caribs had emerged from the Amazon Basin and sailed from island to island, wreaking havoc wherever they landed. The other tribe native to Tobago was the Amerindians, a mild and friendly race. They had been decimated by the newcomers, who in turn had been wasted by disease. Many of the Caribs who survived were still cannibals.

Jaime's tribe had been lost to smallpox when he was still very young. He had worked as a fisherman, a farmer, and a smithy. But mostly Jaime had been a bandit along the roads between Port of Spain and the British fortress of Picton.

Since the curate had led him to the Savior, Jaime had also served as Falconer's spy.

Falconer again bowed his head and said a prayer for yet one more soul sent on ahead of him. He felt an uncommon burning to his chest. He had so very few friends.

Felix let him be for a time, then said, "The official word is that bandits are plying the northern Paria roads again. For those who know Jaime's past, they claim it was a fitting end."

Falconer coughed lightly to clear the blockage in his throat. "They will use this as an excuse to close the road."

"It has already happened. Two garrisons of soldiers patrol the roads leading to Pitch Lake, and another two have been sent to Rio Claro and Sangre Grande."

Which meant the governor's men must have decided that Jaime was not the only one endangering them and their secrets. "I must move swiftly to learn what Jaime discovered," Falconer said.

"You must do nothing." The curate hissed his urgency. "What if they already suspect you?"

"My merchant status should protect me."

"Don't talk utter nonsense. Jaime was acting on official church business. Which means they will stop at nothing to keep us from divulging their secrets."

Falconer studied his friend, the man who had done what no one else ever could. The curate had spoken to his soul and shared with him the gift of eternity. Even now, with a third of their little band gone and the danger surrounding him, the curate showed no fear whatsoever. Only concern for his one remaining friend. Falconer asked, "What would you have me do?"

"Leave," Felix urged. "Take the next ship leaving harbor. Make your way to England."

"But our case is not fully made!"

"What good will knowing more do if we all perish?" The curate's grip was rock solid upon Falconer's arm. "Do you have the documents at hand?"

"Buried by the tree where I tethered my horse."

"Take them and flee!"

"And you?"

"If I am seen to depart, all will know what is about. But you travel throughout these waters as part of your business."

"I can't leave you—"

"And I'm telling you, my joining you would risk everything." The curate leaned closer. "I have never given you an order. Not one in all the years. I have asked many things but never commanded. But I am charging you now. Retrieve the documents and depart. Go to England. Find someone we can trust with what we know, someone who will help you fit together the final pieces. Then make your case before Parliament."

"But the only people I know in England are tavern keepers and wenches! I haven't been there since——"

"You will go and you will ask and you will be certain before you move." The longer they talked, the more insistent became the curate's tone. "My own contacts are ten years old. Who knows whether they have been turned. We hear rumors of such and see the same happening here. You must take great care and move only when you are certain."

"Certain of what? And of whom?"

"The only name I am sure of is William Wilberforce. This man can be trusted. But take care not to bring danger onto Wilberforce's head! He is old and very ill, so I'm told. And many have abandoned him. Take great care in how you approach him. In the meantime, do nothing, *say* nothing, until you make this contact. Only him can you trust, and those to whom he points you."

Slowly Falconer shook his head. "I am the man of action. I follow your lead. We have succeeded thus far because of your wise head."

"And I tell you again. You are too hard on yourself. You refuse to accept what all others see. You must——"

The rear doors boomed open. The noise was all the warning Falconer required. He slipped from his seat and crouched upon the floor.

The curate rose to his feet and stepped into the central aisle. Falconer lowered himself to his belly and slipped under the next pew. Hopefully the newcomers' sudden dash from sunlight to the church's gloom would grant Falconer precious seconds to disappear.

As Felix stepped toward the wide open doors, one of the intruders called, "Who's that there?"

"A simple curate, good sir. Coming to offer you God's greeting in His holy place."

"A curate, eh. Never did understand the term. Meant to be only half a priest, are you?"

"I entered the service late in life, sir. And school was never a place where I felt welcome."

"Then you and I share that, at least." Boot steps scraped forward. "Wait, I know you. You're that fellow from the church north of town. My overseer is churched by you."

"Robert," the curate offered, giving the name a French intonation. "A fine man."

"He was, until you filled his head with such stuff and nonsense as would choke a horse. Now he won't carry a whip and he insists upon my slaves resting one day a week. He's after them being churched as well."

Falconer knew the planter's voice, having heard it any number of times. He had even sat next to him once at the governor's table, guests at a banquet the governor had given the previous winter. The planter, with a girth as large as his voice, was known as a hard man, the sort who was certain every opinion he held was not only the right way, but the *only* way. Which was very dangerous, as the planter held the power of life and death over 457 slaves. Falconer knew such numbers because he had made it his business to know.

Putting together a list of slaves and their owners was not what placed Falconer in danger. Owning slaves was not a crime anywhere in the British empire. But the *trade* in slaves had been outlawed for a quarter of a century. No person could be captured, traded, or sold into servitude. Or so the law said.

Falconer knew differently. As did his mates. It was their gathering of evidence to prove trafficking in slaves still existed that made John Falconer a threat. The day Falconer's enemies identified him as the man who could testify against them would be his last. Just as had happened to Jaime.

"All God's children deserve a chance to see the light, sir," the curate replied. "Even your slaves. Surely you agree—"

"I agree with nothing you say," the planter lashed out. "You and the rest of your ilk."

Falconer continued his snaking progress across the stone floor. He was three pews from the curtained archway, where the priests entered for the Eucharist, when his danger-honed senses warned him. He rolled forward until his entire body was beneath the next pew, linked his feet and hands around the seat, and hefted himself off the floor.

He heard Felix say loudly, "Did you lose something, sir?"

"Aye, that I did" came the grunting reply.

The curate must have lowered himself so that he was crouched alongside the planter and could cast his voice along the stone flooring. "Are you certain it was here in God's house?" Falconer heard the words with their inherent warning from his precarious position beneath the seat.

"All I know, Curate, is you're talking overloud for a man standing beside me. And I could have sworn you were addressing another man when I entered."

"It is not fitting to swear anything in God's house, sir. Some would say anywhere else, for that matter."

"Aye, so I'm told. Answer me this, Half Priest. Why are you working so far afield from your assigned church?"

"I seek to do God's work wherever I am called, sir."

"As slippery an answer as ever I have heard." The boots scraped again. The planter called to his mates, "Search the house."

"Sir, I must protest."

"Protest all you like, Curate. I'll do as I please, here and else-where. The governor's interested in finding a certain man, same as me."

"Give me his name, sir, and I'll be better able to aid you in your quest."

"Tell me who it was you were speaking with when we entered."

"With God," Falconer's friend said gently. "I seek as always to draw nearer to my Lord and Savior."

Falconer watched from his hanging perch as a pair of boots stepped down the side aisle, pausing now and then to search the pews. Then from behind them came the sound of steel scraping upon steel. Falconer's entire body tensed as he heard the planter say, "I've never shaved a curate. Is that as nasty a sin as filleting a priest?"

The approaching boots turned and took a half step away. Clearly the planter's mates were taken aback by a threat upon a curate. Falconer took this as the best chance he would have and lowered himself to the floor. He crept breathlessly to the end of the pew. Moving at lightning speed, he slipped across the aisle and behind the door-curtain. From this safe perch he peered out at the sanctuary through a slit in the drape.

His old friend and mentor said, "Sir, I remind you where you are."

The planter was dressed in tropical fashion, a loose cotton shirt open at the neck and gaping partway down his hairy chest. People of polite society considered such manner of dress most uncivilized. But the planter was a man utterly at ease upon the estate he ruled as a fiefdom, where the town's morals were a world removed.

The planter held a curved dagger to the curate's throat. He twisted it slightly so that it flickered in the candlelight. Clearly the man was enjoying himself. "If you have any interest in seeing the light of another day, Curate, you'll tell me what I want to know."

Falconer felt his entire body clench with the effort it required not to hurl himself through the curtain and into the church. Never in his entire life had he run from a fight, much less from a friend in need. Yet he knew what the curate would ask of him.

Falconer saw Felix smile and realized he observed a man far stronger than he would ever be. He also sensed the smile was directed at him standing there behind the curtain. He heard his friend say, "The death I fear is one you could never inflict."

"Bah, more priestly nonsense!" The planter swept the knife across the curate's throat, and Falconer almost shouted his terror at the prospect of losing his last friend. But the blade had flashed by without touching the skin. The planter jabbed it angrily back into the sheath at his belt and snarled, "All your kind should be tied to the post and lashed to submission."

"Our kind, sir? You mean the fellowship of believers?"

"You know exactly of whom I speak." The man wheeled about and bellowed, "Did you find him?"

"There's no one about."

"Search harder! He was sitting beside the curate, I tell you!"

Falconer heard footsteps hastening down the stone hall behind him. He slipped into the space between the curtain and a cupboard, crouched down low as he could, and willed himself to meld into the shadows.

The approaching priest was in far too great a hurry to notice Falconer. He swept through the curtains and cried, "Who dares disturb the peace of God's house?"

"I am on the governor's business!" The planter was too far gone to quell his rage. "We seek a traitor!"

Thankfully, the priest did not back down. "You will lower your voice and leave this place, or I shall have the soldiers arrest you!"

The planter snarled in frustration and waved his men back. As they turned toward the doors, the planter said, "I haven't finished with you, Half Priest."

"Go with God, sir," the curate softly replied.

When the nave was empty save for the two men, the priest demanded, "What was that talk about a traitor?"

But Felix simply repeated the words, "Go with God."

Falconer slipped from his hiding space and raced away. He had no question but that the words were meant for him.

Chapter 3

The balcony to Serafina's room was at the far corner of the house away from Saint Mark's Square. Like most of the older villas fronting main canals, the house dropped straight down into the blue waters. The finer homes like theirs were constructed of close-cut stone, making it nearly impossible for a thief to scale the wall from a tethered boat. These façades formed giant mosaics shining brilliantly in the sun. Serafina's balcony railing was made from three shades of limestone and bordered by late-blooming wisteria. From the water it looked like a treasure chest with an open lid. That was what Luca had told her. A treasure box that contained one lovely jewel.

Luca's hand appeared on the ledge. He had a sculptor's hands, broad and flat and very strong. Serafina felt she was more than in love. She lived and breathed to be with this man. He was in her every waking thought and all her most wondrous dreams.

Luca leveraged himself upward until his face came into view. His dark eyes shone with such intensity she thought they were looking to her very soul. "Are you alone?"

Serafina heard the door downstairs close. There was no mistaking the sound. Their front door was more than five centuries old and carved from cypress. The noise echoed through the front hall and up the stairs and through her own closed door. Luca heard the sound as well. His eyes widened in alarm and he began to ease himself back down.

"No, my darling, no! Mother has left. We're alone." She rushed to the balcony's edge and gripped his arm.

"You're certain?"

"Yes, yes!" She urged the young man up and over the stone railing. Now that he was this close, she could not bear to wait another moment. "Hurry!"

"Perhaps I should come another time—"

"No, no, this is fine!" In her frantic haste to hold him there, she wrapped both hands around his upper arm.

"Really, it's better if we wait—"

"I have spent too many days waiting," she implored. Then she saw his smile. "You were teasing me!"

"Only a little."

Serafina stepped away and teased him in return. "You are dreadful. All the other girls were correct about you."

Luca inspected his reflection in the balcony door. His dark hair fell long and loose upon his high starched collar. He tightened the silver catch holding the white scarf at his throat. "Whatever do the young *signorinas* say about me?"

"I shan't tell you now," Serafina returned archly. In truth, the young ladies in her art class spoke endlessly about Luca di Montello. Much of what she had learned about him had come from their gossip. Though Serafina never joined in, she had listened intently to their every word.

She had discovered that Luca had been a military officer in the Milan regiment. Decorated twice for bravery before his twenty-second birthday, he had resigned his commission over a disagreement with his commanding officer. As a result, Luca had been disowned by his family. The di Montellos were minor royalty from Bologna. But Serafina also knew this would be a matter of some contempt in her father's eyes. As he put it, these days the Bologna magistrates would sell a title for a barrel of smoked Venetian perch.

In their first private conversation, Luca had confessed the real reason he had left the military. He hated the army, he told her. Not because of the discipline or the drills or the danger. Because it had kept him from his one true passion.

Luca di Montello was a sculptor. And a very good one indeed. Good enough for some of his concepts to have been acquired by the Murano glass factories. Good enough to gain a place teaching at Venice's foremost art institute. Despite the dark rumors regarding his past, there was no questioning his ability. It was even said that Luca di Montello might soon become one of the youngest artists ever admitted to the Royal Academy.

All the young ladies in Serafina's art class professed to be in love with him. Tall and dashing, he moved with a buccaneer's flash and verve. There were rumors within the academy as well. Of an affair with another professor's wife, or a scandal with a model, or even of a duel avoided when the other man fled Venice. But none of this was substantiated. In class, Luca di Montello was a harsh taskmaster. He criticized forcefully when he felt a student's work was not acceptable. He was demanding and tended to bark when a kind word might have done better. He was also handsome, strong, and twenty-nine years old.

And he had vowed his love to Serafina.

"How long do we have?" Luca asked.

"Not long enough." The words sprang out. Serafina's hand flew to her mouth and her cheeks burned. "What a forward thing to say."

"No. It was beautiful." He opened his arms and gripped her so fiercely she could feel the pounding of his heart. Or perhaps it was her own.

They had met surreptitiously numerous times in the cafés and on promenades. They had spoken in the alley behind the art academy and even stolen a few swift embraces. Each occasion had added to a hunger that now left her breathless.

Luca asked again, "How long?"

"Until the sun no longer touches the rooftops."

"An hour, then." He stroked her fine hair. "That seems like forever, after waiting this long to see you."

"And hold you," she whispered. How could she speak like this? She, who had never before been embraced by a man? Yet the words rose of their own accord.

"And kiss you," he murmured, raising her chin.

She had known it would be like this. Known and yet not known, for how could she have been certain? She had never kissed anyone before Luca and never kissed him for more than a brief fiery second. Until now. His embrace was rough and smooth at the same time. He smelled of the charcoal he used for his sketches and of something distinctly male.

When he lifted his mouth from hers, it was to lead her back into the chamber. "What a delightful room. And look, your paintings are here, and these are your etchings. Have I ever seen the one there?"

"Not now, Luca, please. We have only—"

"No, please, just a moment. Why, Serafina, this is exquisite. Who was your model?"

"My mother."

"The lines are so delicate, the colors delightful. Are her eyes really so blue?"

"Yes. Please—"

"And this one? Who is this drawing of?"

"My half sister."

"Older or younger?"

"Older. I told you. I am the youngest."

"Of course. You did tell me. About the three half sisters, one of which is so cruel to you." He tapped the paper. "What is this one's name?"

"Gabriella. She hates this drawing."

"I can see why. It is full of the most remarkable rage. Never would I have thought a young lady like yourself capable of capturing such passion." He smiled at her. "Remind me never to make you angry."

"You are about to," she replied stoutly. "Making me wait for so long, then coming here and risking everything only to go on about stupid drawings."

"They are not stupid, my love. You have such talent it astonishes me. Nothing about this is stupid."

"Coming here and whispering like this and placing us in such danger only to talk about what we could discuss in the academy is worse than stupid."

"Ah. What a lovely pout. I had no idea you could make even a pout look so beautiful."

His kiss was beyond all she could have imagined. The atmosphere of feverish joy was overwhelming. The excitement of his embrace was intoxicating. But the risk they were taking, and the threat of being discovered, was everywhere. As was the nagging shame she felt over disobeying her parents.

Yet she was in love. Her parents wanted her to remain a child, bound to their will and even to a man she cared nothing for. But true love called to her. And love she would follow. Wherever it took her. Even into the embrace of a man her parents would never accept.

Serafina also felt the pain of having him so near and yet knowing that in less than an hour he would leave. She must go back to being the youngest daughter, the child. This time she was the one who broke off their embrace. She whispered, "Tell me again."

"I love you."

She kissed him. "Tell me once more."

"*Ti amo.*"

"Again."

"My golden-haired delight, come over here with me." Gently he guided her over until they were seated upon the edge of her bed.

Serafina knew a line had been crossed in lowering herself down beside him. Another rule broken, after so many others, all in the space of these frantic heartbeats. She felt she should tell him it was wrong, but then everything was wrong here.

Then he spoke the words that had filled her dreams since their first hurried conversation. "Marry me."

"Yes, oh yes."

"We will run away together," he murmured. His hands drew her over until she was seated in his lap. She wanted to resist, and at the same time she could not be close enough to the man she loved. Luca said, "We will find a priest and be together forever as man and wife."

She clung to him with all her strength. To break away would be sweetest anguish. Oh, how could she release him back to the shadows and the approaching night?

They kissed once more, then she risked a glance out the balcony window. Serafina gave a small cry.

"What is it?"

"It is time." She wept the words.

"It can't be."

"Look. The sun is almost gone."

"But I've just arrived."

"How can you leave me? How can I bear it when you go?" She felt her heart was breaking.

"Then I'll come again."

"But I want you to stay with me *now*."

"My darling one—"

The door behind them creaked open. "My child . . . *No!*"

Serafina landed upon the floor as Luca bolted to his feet. "Signora, I—"

"You *monster!*"

Serafina cried aloud. The shame was scalding, but what frightened her most was the sight of Luca bounding across the room to the balcony doors. "Don't leave me!"

Her mother shrilled, "Guards!"

Luca clambered atop the balcony railing. He cast her one final glance. Then he sprang outward and dove into the canal.

Serafina collapsed on the floor like a broken doll.

Chapter 4

Never had Serafina's bedchamber felt so constricting. In truth it was rather a sizeable room. All the upstairs chambers were similarly proportioned, with hand-painted beams running across their high ceilings. But only Serafina and her parents had balconies. Which had been another reason for friction between Gabriella and herself. When Serafina had been born, all the upstairs chambers had been occupied by the older sisters and her parents. Her crib had first been set at the foot of her parents' bed. When she outgrew the crib, she had then slept briefly in Gabriella's room. But her sister, who was both very private and extremely possessive, had shrilly objected. So Serafina's childhood bedchamber had been downstairs in what was now a small parlor. The room possessed two barred windows and overlooked an alley. Gabriella had teased Serafina that her parents did not want her and the bars were meant to keep her caged. Serafina's mother had overheard her and flown into a rage unlike any Serafina had ever seen.

Until, that is, the day she had discovered Luca in Serafina's bedchamber.

When the oldest sister had married, Serafina had been granted the prize bedchamber. Gabriella had wailed over how she, being older, should have the choice room. Bettina Gavi had replied that the bedchamber was Serafina's in partial compensation for how Gabriella had treated her.

Serafina now sat in a high-backed chair with a scrolled leather seat. She gazed around the chamber and wondered if Gabriella would move in once she left.

Because Serafina knew she was leaving. Oh yes. It was only a matter of time.

Today marked the end of the second week since Serafina had been locked inside her room.

The day that Luca had visited her, Serafina's mother had revealed a scalding rage. How *could* Serafina have *done* this? Did she not realize the *scandal*? The *danger*? On and on her mother had railed, until her father had returned home. He had been summoned from his business chambers by a house servant. The urgency of the servant's message had brought him racing from a meeting with the Austrian prince who served as Venice's first minister. Serafina's father had heard Bettina's tale, then leaned against the doorframe with a fist clenching his chest. His face had gone pale, and he had stared at his daughter in utter horror. Then his cries and accusations had joined with his wife's.

Serafina had been blistered by her mother's ire. But her father had shocked her far more. Her father's title was consiglière. Serafina knew the normal English translation was "counselor." But another word, perhaps the more correct translation, was "conciliator." That defined her father perfectly. He lived to conciliate, to bring peace between fractious groups and people. He soothed. He stroked. He counseled. He was, by nature and by profession, a peacemaker.

But not this day.

After Serafina's parents had grown hoarse, they had left her. But not for long. Serafina's mother soon returned with two servants. They had shut the slatted balcony shutters normally closed only at night and sealed them with a great storeroom lock. Serafina had silently vowed not to show any emotion nor to speak at all. But the sight of that great padlock clicking into place had reduced her to tears.

"This is no one's fault but your own." Her mother's voice shook as she spoke. "You have sought to live without regard to your family. Now you must learn to live without light."

But Serafina was not weeping because of the pall cast over her bedchamber. She wept because it would now be so much harder to escape.

When the bedroom door had shut and she was locked inside her darkened room, she had found the strength not to wail in distress only because of the words that echoed through her heart and mind.

Marry me.

Twice each day the upstairs maid brought Serafina food and water and emptied the vessels by her dressing table. Each evening the maid returned and lit a small candle. Occasionally her mother or father came and stood at the door and spoke to her. Gradually over the days their tone grew less irate and more worried.

Serafina counted the hours by the length of the shadows upon the floor and the ringing of Saint Mark's bell tower. She counted the days by marking a sheet in her sketchpad with drawing charcoal. The shutters had narrow slats, designed to let in air. The room remained mired in gloom, no matter what the hour. There probably was enough light to draw, but her art did not interest Serafina now. She had nothing to read. When the evening candle burned down to nothing, Serafina went to bed. She slept poorly.

The result was not as she would have expected. She did not pine away. Instead, she gradually lost all connection with the life she had known before. Household noises drifted from beyond her locked door. She was mildly pleased to find she did not yearn to join them. But she did listen constantly for any shred of sound upon the balcony. From the boats passing along the canal, she heard the melodious voices of the singing gondoliers and the raucous cries of the floating merchants. Both called to her equally. In her mind, she had already bid the world of her childhood farewell. She dreamed of nothing but Luca.

The fifteenth night since the dreadful scene, Serafina awakened from a fitful sleep. She leaped from her bed before she was fully aware of what she had heard. She ran to the tall glass doors leading to the balcony, closed against the cool night breeze. She flung them open and stood there before the locked shutters, panting so loudly it was impossible to hear anything other than the frantic note of her breath.

When she could manage to whisper, she asked, "Luca?"

The night was utterly still.

"Luca, is that you? My darling, have you come for me?"

There was a slight snicker of sound. Nothing more. A hand might have tentatively tried the balcony shutters. "They have locked me in." She had to struggle not to scream out the words. She wanted to shriek until the voice was torn from her body or the lock broken and the shutters flung back. "Luca, you must bring a tool, a weapon, something."

There was another hushed hint of noise. So soft it might have been a cat. Then nothing. She stood motionless for a long time before returning to bed. She slept soundly for the first time in two weeks.

The next afternoon, just after the churches of Venice struck three, her mother unlocked the door and entered. "May we have a moment together?"

Had it been any other day, Serafina might have remained silent. But today she was filled with the impatience of a prisoner awaiting release. "Do I have any choice?"

The words clearly shocked her mother. She drew back a moment. "You can ask me to leave if you prefer."

Serafina studied her hands. "It does not matter whether you stay or you go."

"How can you speak to me in such a manner?"

She did not raise her eyes. "How can you keep your own daughter imprisoned like this?"

"What else are we to do with you?" Her mother shut and locked the door, then crossed the room. She sat in the empty chair. On the table between them was the morning tray with its half-eaten meal. "You are not eating enough."

"When am I to be released?"

"Nothing has been decided."

"What is it you want from me?"

"Want? What do I *want*?" Her mother collected herself. "No. I promised myself I would not grow angry again. Tell me this, daughter. What is it *you* want?"

"That should be simple enough."

Even in the half light she saw her mother tense. "No."

But today, this time, it was not enough to silence her. "I want to marry Luca."

"No. A thousand times, no!"

"Then do not ask me again."

"You dare use this tone with your mother?"

"You asked the question. I have given you my only answer. I want to marry Luca. You refuse—"

"You will never see him again! Never! Do you hear me! I and your father forbid it!" Bettina's anger turned the simple twisting of her hem into a fiery gesture. "Have you learned *nothing* in this time?"

Serafina chose silence. What good would it do to speak further? Luca would come for her. If not, she would escape. There was nothing else for her but this. No other life except with him.

But for her mother, the silence was the most irritating response she could have made. Bettina's footsteps rang angrily across the floor. "I had hoped, *prayed* for an apology. You think I *like* treating you this way?"

Her mother fumbled the key from her pocket. She found it necessary to use both hands to fit it into the door lock. "All I ask for is respect. Respect for me, your father, your heritage. A sign that you are willing to obey us. Some indication that you have grown up enough to be trusted. . . ."

Her mother slammed the door upon her unfinished thought. The lock clicked back into place. Serafina sat and listened to the footsteps echo off into the distance. She returned her thoughts back to the one core issue.

Escape.

The days stretched on with Serafina remaining locked inside the shadows, mostly alone. Her parents visited her every few days—sometimes separately, other times together. Toward the end of the third week, Serafina realized that her best hope of escape was by convincing her parents that she was over the infatuation. That she could be trusted.

But she was not good at subterfuge. Her mother had always been capable of seeing through her when she lied. Serafina tried it anyway. She claimed that she wanted to become the dutiful daughter once more. But before she had finished speaking, Serafina's mother broke down and sobbed. Her father held Bettina and stared at his daughter. His expression suggested he had no idea who his daughter had become. He did not say another word as he drew his weeping wife from the room. And again locked his daughter inside.

That night Serafina became convinced of the problem. It was her parents' age. If they had ever known what it was like to be in love, they had forgotten. They couldn't help themselves. It happened with the years. She saw that now.

Serafina stared up at the dark ceiling and saw Luca's face smiling at her. Some obstacle must prevent him from coming for her. She was certain of this. But a new worry gnawed at her. How long would he wait for her? How long before he would give up and accept that they could never be together? For herself, she knew she would wait forever. She had discovered love and knew there would never be another for her. But Luca was older. Did this mean he might find another? Serafina knew all too well how the other girls in their art class had yearned for him. Would he give in to their entreaties? Would he forget her? Serafina touched her own forehead, wondering if perhaps she had a fever.

Toward the end of yet another sleepless night, she had an idea. One that held promise of escape. Finally.

She rose from her bed and began making preparations.

Because she had neither quill nor proper paper, Serafina wrote using her finest charcoal drawing pencil. She wrote upon half a sheet of drawing paper, which was coarse and very thick. She finished writing just as the house was coming awake around her. As she folded the letter, Serafina realized that she was signing away her life in Venice. She wondered at how little this seemed to concern her.

She knew she should be filled with remorse over the distress she was causing her beloved parents. And now she was preparing to sever connections to the only city she had ever known. She loved Venice. This water-borne realm was the only place she had ever imagined calling home. And her family was the finest in the whole world. Yet here she was, giving it all up without a backward glance.

Serafina considered this as she used the remnant of the previous evening's candle to seal the letter. Her parents had decided to put themselves and their home and even this city on one side of love's divide. On the other side stood Luca. She had been forced to choose.

In truth, there was no choice at all.

The upstairs maid, Carla, unlocked her door. Serafina had come to know the difference between the sound her mother made inserting the key and that of the maid. Carla was more hesitant, as though she had to resist the urge to knock. Carla was eighteen years old and had been in service to the family since she was thirteen. In a sense, she and Serafina had grown up together.

Over the weeks, Serafina had detected a hint of sympathy from the maid. Serafina also knew Carla loved to gossip. Her mother had once said they should discharge her because of how the family's secrets were spread about the street. But to let go a young woman such as Carla without references meant she could never find another place of service. She would be reduced to working in one of the weaving mills or the silk dying factories.

Serafina's mother was far too good-natured to do this without extreme cause. So Carla had been warned and left in place as the upstairs maid.

"Good morning, mistress." Carla was careful in her movements. Clearly she had been given strict instructions by Serafina's mother. The girl set the tray and the bowls down just inside the room and turned to lock the door behind her. Then she brought over the breakfast tray and set it where Serafina had been writing. "I hope you slept well."

"I never sleep."

Carla sighed. Up until now, that had been the extent of their morning conversations. Carla always sighed. But she never said anything more. Her dark eyes showed a certain wisdom far older than her years. Serafina examined the face before her, wishing she had come to know this young woman better. "I need to ask you to do something for me."

"I can't."

"You could," Serafina said softly, "if you did not tell my parents."

Carla straightened. She openly examined Serafina. "They would dismiss me."

Because she was listening so intently, Serafina detected a number of unspoken hints. Carla had not said no. Which meant she might do this. But there was something more at work here. In that fleeting instant, Serafina realized she was no longer addressing a maid. Carla had become her equal. Even perhaps her superior.

Serafina whispered, "What do you want?"

Carla's eyes flickered about the room, then came to rest upon the corner of the dressing table. "You have such lovely things."

Serafina knew instantly what the maid saw. There upon the table sat Serafina's jewel box. The carved little box with its velvet interior contained only three items of any real value. All of them had been left to her by her grandmother, her father's mother. Serafina loved all three items dearly. Even so, she did not hesitate.

Serafina slipped the tiny golden key from the bracelet on her left wrist. She unlocked the box and opened the inlaid top. She picked up the ruby brooch. She held it between them. "Is he still here?"

Carla's face came alive in a manner that not even the room's murkiness could mask. "He has been dismissed from the art academy. But he is still in Venice."

"Can you find him?"

"I know where he lodges."

The news caused an icy shiver to course through Serafina. She realized with a shock that Carla was quite attractive, although in a dark and somewhat earthy manner. Serafina fought down a sudden urge to grip the woman's shoulders and shout at her, demanding to know how she knew such a thing. But the impulse was instantly dismissed. Luca loved *her*. "Will you take a letter to him and deliver his reply?"

Carla's gaze never left the brooch. "Yes."

Serafina took the letter from her pocket. She kissed the seal. Together with the brooch she placed it in Carla's outstretched hand. "Go. Hurry."

The day loitered in torturous fashion. Never had the slatted light seemed to travel so slowly across the floor of the room. Serafina endured what felt like eons of doubt. Finally, however, the key scraped into the lock, the door opened, and the maid reappeared.

Serafina remained seated in her chair only by gripping the arms and holding herself back. To her mind, Carla's motions were more languid than ever before. She moved across the room, taking precious minutes to settle the tray upon the table between them. Finally, Serafina could stand it no longer. "Well?"

"I saw him."

"You gave him the letter?"

Carla's focus came to rest upon the jewel box. Serafina knew she wanted more payment. But she also knew there were only two more items of any value. And there was a great deal more that needed doing. "Well?" she said again.

Carla seemed to accept that she would receive nothing further at this point. Her gaze hardened. "He says yes."

"That's all? Yes?"

"I was hoping for additional payment. After all, I have risked—"

Serafina leaped up so swiftly Carla gasped and backed away. But not fast enough. Serafina gripped the maid's arm with a hand transformed to steel. She moved forward until her face was inches from the maid's. *"Tell me."*

"H-he is thrilled beyond words," the maid answered in a fearful rush. "H-he yearns for you with every b-breath. He will be where you wish and counts the passing moments as he would the loss of his own life's blood."

All strength drained from her body. Serafina released her hold and stumbled back to the chair. "He loves me," she whispered.

"He adores you." Carla seemed to find no pleasure in the words. She reached into her pocket and drew out a sealed page. "He sends you this. He says the smudges are from his tears."

Serafina resisted the urge to open it immediately. She would not allow this woman to see her weep. And weep she would. Of that she had no doubt. Besides which, they had little time.

She fumbled with the jewel box's tiny catch. Her hands trembled so that when she lifted the pearl necklace, the pearls swung and glimmered between them. "You shall have these if you do what I say."

"Say it then." Carla's expression had taken on a hypnotic intensity. "But be swift."

Serafina had thought it out with great care. She told her exactly what she wanted. "Will you do this?"

"That is two things, not one."

"This for the first, the comb for the other."

"Show me."

Serafina allowed the pearls to drop into her other palm. She clasped her hands together, hiding them from view. "Not until the first task is done."

Carla lifted her eyes from Serafina's hands. She measured the younger woman very carefully, then said, "I will do as you ask."

By the light of the lone evening candle, Serafina unsealed the letter. She knew Luca could not write, or at least not write well. He had confessed as much during one of their earliest private conversations. He had failed at different schools and driven away all but his art tutors, until his parents had thrown up their hands and ordered him into the military. He was good with his fists and with weapons, but he hated taking orders. He could fight, and he could draw, and he could work both stone and clay. His painting was marginal, or so he claimed. But Serafina thought his oils to be absolutely beautiful in their emotional power. He was a very sensual artist. Which made his response to her letter all the more potent.

It was a drawing of her face. Serafina looked down at herself and wept with the knowledge that he really and truly loved her. There was no other way he could have expressed such a vivid emotion unless he himself shared it.

Her image looked out of the page with an expression that was both dreamy and yearning. It was exactly how she had felt when he had entered her bedchamber and kissed her and drawn her close.

Serafina jammed one fist into her mouth to stifle the noise of her sobs. Impatiently she cleared her eyes and examined the drawing. She saw the smudge marks and wept the harder, for she knew he had first drawn her and then leaned over the page, hungering for her as she did for him. She saw three longer smudges where his fingers had traced their way around the border of her face. She traced the marks and felt the fire of his touch upon her anew.

She remained where she was, touching the page and weeping, until the candle expired and cast her into the darkness of another lonely night.

Chapter 5

Falconer awoke from the nightmare, his heart pounding and skin clammy with sweat.

It was the same harrowing dream he had endured for three long years. He could not recall whether he had first had the dream and then given his soul and life to his Creator or the dream had started after his baptism. Falconer had spoken of the dream with only one man, his friend Felix, the curate. After Falconer's acknowledgment of its fearful power, the curate had told him that Falconer had always carried the nightmare in one form or another. The only difference was now, with God's help, Falconer had the strength to face its torment head on.

When Falconer had asked why God did not take the terrible dream from him, the curate had simply said that God's timing was not man's. In the meantime, Felix told him, Falconer must learn patience and study the message of Paul's thorn in the flesh.

Falconer now rolled from his bunk, missing his friend mightily. Many extraordinary results flowed from coming to know the Almighty. One was that he was so afflicted by loneliness. Falconer had spent most of his life in utter solitude, even when he was surrounded by a warship's teeming humanity. Falconer slipped to his knees and said his morning prayers, imploring God to keep his friend safe. He ended his petition as he had every morning and evening since leaving Trinidad, begging for help in this futile and frustrating journey to England.

Three weeks he had traveled, certain he was not only followed but hunted. And while he had journeyed far, the direction had turned out to be consistently wrong.

The only vessel departing Trinidad the day Falconer had met with Felix and narrowly dodged death had been headed to Grenada, his home island. Once there, a friend among the planters had brought Falconer alarming news. Strangers were about in Grenada's capital, dangerous men armed with cutlasses and official documents. The strangers were asking about Falconer and his habits. Did he poke his nose into affairs that had nothing to do with his trade? they asked. Did he seek information about slaving? A mate of the planter ran the tavern where the strangers were staying. This man had heard how they planned to put Falconer in chains and sail away.

Two hours later, Falconer met up with a fisherman, who took him as far as Ronde, a mean little island north of Grenada and home still to Amerindians. Falconer carried nothing save his sword, the secret documents collected under enormous danger, and two pouches of gold. From Ronde he made his way to Saint Vincent, then on to Guadeloupe. Neither island harbored any large vessels, which was not unusual for the time of year. The spring tradewinds were long gone and the summer tempests just beginning. Falconer continued his meandering progress across the Antilles. In Port-au-Prince he boarded a foul-smelling craft packed with smoked eel heading for Saint Augustine in Florida.

On the third day of their voyage, he saw for the first time why the seas were so starkly vacant. When at dawn he arose from his hammock, he faced a cloud wall rising to the highest heavens. The solid barrier chopped away the sea and the sun. Falconer found himself recalling the old seamen's tales of those who sailed off the world's edge. For a moment he almost believed them.

The wind rose with the daylight, blowing strong and steady from the southwest. Which meant the wind was blowing *into* the storm, as though even the breeze was being sucked into the maelstrom. The captain and his two mates talked long and hard over their passage and decided to hold to their course. To turn and flee for the Grand Bahama harbor would have meant beating against the rising wind. And once there, they would have no guarantee of safety, for the Bahama harbors were notoriously exposed.

They made landfall in Saint Augustine the next day, and still the storm remained poised upon the horizon. The next dawn was still stained by the dark menace. The wind blew constant and strong from the land. Falconer snagged a berth on a land-hugging trader making the run northward to Charleston in the Carolinas. Charleston was the largest port south of the nation's capital. The seas were massive, with peaks as tall as the vessel's single mast. But the wind remained steady and the skies utterly clear, and they made good time.

Charleston harbor did indeed hold two European vessels— one British and one French. But the ships were little more than floating hulks. Both had lost their masts and managed to reach port only by jury-rigging a spare boom as a lateen sail. The harbor was filled with news of a storm so massive none had found its eye. Not even the oldest sailor could recall a storm so large this early in the tempest season.

Four days later, the storm had abated somewhat. At least, the dark wall no longer climbed against the horizon. But no ship was willing to attempt an Atlantic crossing. So Falconer took berth on a vessel headed even farther north, to Georgetown and Baltimore. Anything was better than this idleness, he thought.

Three days out, they caught a small taste of the storm they had missed. The sky darkened and a light rain fell. Then out of nowhere they were slapped by a careless hand, a wind so strong it heeled the two-masted vessel over until the gunnels were drenched. The captain feared his vessel would flip and cried aloud to God. It seemed that God heard them, for as swiftly as the wind came, it passed. They arrived to find Georgetown mourning four of their own fishing fleet that had not been so blessed.

The Noble Fugitive

Boots in hand, Falconer slipped down the stairs and entered the main hall. The seaman's mission was located in the George-town harbor and offered simple berths to crewmen and laborers. Falconer seated himself in the farthest corner from the entrance, his back to the wall. He had given the mission hosts only his first name and assumed he was safe. But old habits died hard, and he eyed every new guest who found his way into the hall.

The church bells struck six in the morning, and already the day felt oppressive with heat and summer damp. He sniffed the air wafting through the open window. He smelled sweet river water, distant storms, and the surrounding city. Falconer had never felt comfortable very far from the sea. The air seemed empty and strange without its taste of salt.

By the time the others awoke and the room had filled, Falconer had finished his breakfast of tea and gruel. He returned to the task he had begun the previous day—the repair of a hole in the kitchen wall. He had never shied away from work. Putting his hands to such an undertaking as this had a calming effect upon his mind. He could lose himself for hours, praying from time to time and drawing close to God through honest toil.

A minister from the neighboring church came into the hall, greeted the men, and led them through a hymn and a brief hom-ily and prayer. Afterwards Falconer resumed work. Time and again his mind returned to the quandary that had ended so many of his recent prayers. Why was God allowing circumstances to place so many barriers between him and his quest? Had not his Maker called him into the crusade against slavery wherever it was found?

"Are you well this morning, Brother John?"

Falconer started at how the pastor had managed to approach him unnoticed. "Well enough, Father. Thank you for asking." He had a hunter's trained ability to sense any approach, yet this man had walked over casually as he pleased and settled unnoticed into the seat next to Falconer. His instincts had obviously been dulled by his frustrating lack of progress.

The young man smiled. "I am Methodist, Brother John. Our

57

Lord Jesus referred to the Lord of all as Father. We prefer a more modest title."

"Pastor, then. Yes, thank you. I am well."

"You look fit enough. And the women speak of little else save how you help them. Is there no task you consider beneath you?"

The pastor no doubt referred to how he had spent the early part of the week on his hands and knees, scrubbing the kitchen slate floor as he had holystoned many a deck. "I have never shirked from work or duty, sir."

"I only know you as John. Might I ask your surname?" When Falconer did not reply, the pastor eased back in his seat. "You carry secrets, I see."

"Only so that I bring harm to none, sir."

"Tell me this, if you will. Are you a Christian?"

"I hope and pray the good Lord will recognize me on that day."

"You are not certain?"

Falconer spoke slowly. "I would like to be."

"But . . ."

"I have committed many a misdeed, sir."

"As have we all. Yet the Lord allowed himself to be nailed to a tree for this very reason, that all have sinned and fallen short of grace." The young man was of an age as Falconer, though his face remained pale and unlined, his gaze soft, his demeanor scholarly. "You have lived a hard life?"

"Aye, that I have. Very hard."

"And gone far astray."

"Beyond the limits of your imagination, sir." Falconer felt the sudden urge to confess to this gentleman pastor with the open-hearted face. Not to impress nor to shock. But for a reason that he could not even identify. The words welled up, such that he had to clench his jaw to keep them inside. *I was once a slaver,* he wanted to say . . . *I have sold my own brothers and sisters into bondage. I am no better than Joseph's kin.* But he did not speak, since to do so could mean risking all.

The pastor did not seem the least bit put out, either by Falconer's response or the morose silence that followed. He had a way of seeming comfortable both by this reserved man and the hard parson's bench where he sat. "What brings you to Georgetown, can you tell me that?"

"Aye, I suppose, if the reasons stay between us."

"You have my word."

The pastor's guileless face invited trust. "I have been living these past four years in the Windward Islands," Falconer told him. "You know of them?"

"The name only. They are British possessions, I believe."

"Some are. Others are French, Dutch . . . a few in the Antilles are Portuguese. I ran a chandlery."

"This is not a dangerous profession, at least in these parts."

Falconer shot him a guarded look. "Who spoke of danger?"

"A man comes by ship out of the hardest storm any can recall this early in the season," the young pastor replied. From his tone he might as well have been taking his ease among close friends. "He refuses to give his name. He lives as though he does not have a farthing to his name. He works well and hard at any task given him. And daily he visits the Georgetown port, seeking passage to Britain."

Falconer wondered if he had made a mistake in trusting this man's demeanor. "You know a very great deal for a man who wears the cloth."

"I ask questions, I listen well, and I speak of nothing that might bring harm to another. So what brought you north?"

"To speak of this might, as you say, bring harm."

The pastor smiled, as though he expected nothing else, and changed the subject. "Your ship was caught in the tempest?"

"The tail end, nothing more. Even so, we rocked like a bell ringing out a midnight fire."

"Why Georgetown?"

"I heard of the merchant ship yonder." Falconer pointed out the window to where two of the ship's three masts protruded above the rooftops. Resting at anchor was as fine a ship as any he had seen, a clipper sheathed below the waterline in copper. Falconer was stubbornly set against such new ideas, as were most seamen. Their lives rested upon staying with the tried and true. But a bosun's mate who sailed with her claimed they had made the crossing from England in twenty-one days, slipping under the beam of the approaching storm. "I gather she is aimed for England," Falconer went on. "But none can tell me when they will be off."

"Indeed." The pastor laced his fingers across his vest. "Might I ask what mission takes you across the waters, and in this most perilous of seasons?"

"The season is not of my choosing. As for the purpose . . ." He shook his head. "I cannot speak of it."

"You do not trust me."

"Forgive me for saying it, sir. But I have no reason to do so."

"What if I were to give you my word as a fellow believer that I shall hold your plight in confidence?"

Falconer longed to speak with someone. The burden felt so much greater because he was forced to carry it alone. And concern for his friend the curate added mightily to the weight.

For over thirty years, a determined band of British Christians had fought the might of the slavers and their allies in both Parliament and the royal court. Their aim was the total eradication of slavery throughout the British empire. The planters had successfully resisted them with two essential claims. First, that without the slaves they currently owned, the entire British supply of sugar and coffee and cocoa would fail. Second, the planters did not *add* to the existing slaves. They simply used those they had. In time, or so their claim went, slavery would cease to be an issue.

Falconer knew this to be a vast and despicable lie.

He himself had piloted a slaver long after the trade had supposedly been outlawed. Slave vessels continued to ply their tragic trade under a variety of flags. Throughout the Caribbean, the illicit commerce flourished. Planters bought the slaves they needed at clandestine auctions in out-of-the-way villages. They forged documents claiming that the slave had been owned since birth. Falconer knew this because he was carrying the proof.

What was more, the British governor knew of this. Which suggested the Crown itself profited from the supposedly illegal trade. And if not the Crown, someone within the royal court. This was the conspiracy their friend Jaime had sought to confirm when he was caught and killed. All Falconer could say for certain was that the secret connection between the island slave trade and London was at such a high level that the Crown's representative would do anything to suppress it.

Even chase a suspect over a thousand miles north.

"I have met men who would falsely give their word and swear any oath, so long as it brought them their desired end," Falconer finally replied. He hesitated, then added, "Some even wore the cloth."

"Then let me confide this." The pastor checked about him. The mission hall was emptied now of other boarders. Two ladies used a stave to lift the smoldering porridge pot off the fire. Otherwise they were alone. The pastor leaned forward and said quietly, "Word is being passed around the riverfront. A reward is offered for news of a man tall in stature and stern in demeanor. Handsome in a rakish manner, one going by the name of Falconer. A man wanted throughout the Caribbean."

"Wanted?" Falconer studied the face before him and realized he had underestimated the soft-looking pastor. "Wanted for what?"

"For murder."

"That is a lie."

"You do not deny being this man?"

"I admit to nothing save my utter innocence." The pastor studied him with an intensity to match his own. "A man was slain the day I departed from Trinidad. A friend and a brother. But I had no hand in his killing, save that we shared the same cause."

"And what cause was that?"

"Again, sir. It is a secret that is not mine to share."

"If you refuse to trust, you shall never know the comfort of sharing your burdens."

"There was a third within our band." Falconer paused to wipe the sudden sweat from his brow. "Our curate and the man who led me to salvation. His last words to me were to take great care in whom I entrusted myself. There are turncoats and spies everywhere. Again, sir, those were the words of a believer, a friend, and my leader."

The pastor regarded him in silence for a long moment. Falconer felt a juncture had been reached, one where he could not see a way forward.

Finally, the pastor sighed. "I confess this is beyond me. I feel God's hand upon our meeting. Despite my natural reluctance, I find myself wishing to believe you."

"I can only repeat what I have said before, sir. I mean no one harm. And I had nothing to do with my friend's death, save a sharing of a cause and a passion for our Lord."

"Enough." The pastor thumped his fists upon the table and rose to his feet. "That must be enough for me and for anyone. It is no longer safe for you here. Bounty hunters are offering silver for word of a tall man bearing a scar on his face. Among our guests are those who would sell whatever information they can."

Falconer touched the disfigurement, the scar that ran from his jaw to his cheekbone's peak, where a pike had sought to take out his eye. When Falconer smiled, the scar contorted his mouth. He was not smiling now. "Where can I go?"

"I must call upon a friend. I ask that you accompany me."

"Might I ask who this friend is?"

The pastor walked to the front door and opened it, then waved Falconer forward. "A man who has learned to be as close with his secrets as you."

Chapter 6

To Falconer's surprise, the carriage halted at a bustling Georgetown crossroads. The air was filled with the clattering racket of a city in full cry. Hawkers called their hoarse boasts. Produce wagons trundled past, the drivers shouting for the horses to make greater speed. The raised sidewalks were packed, and the thoroughfares were a solid line of traffic. "What manner of place is this?"

"An emporium." The pastor opened the carriage door. "Come."

"You mean a trading establishment?"

"Just so." The pastor looked carefully about. "We must hurry."

But Falconer remained where he was. "I thought we would be visiting a cloister, someplace where I might be hidden away until—"

"This man we are to see is as trustworthy as any on earth."

"But—"

"The longer we remain here, the greater the risk of someone identifying you. Come!"

Reluctantly Falconer followed him out of the carriage, tipping his hat low over his face. The vast emporium was as large a structure as Falconer had seen. They entered by way of a coffee shop. The smell of roasting beans and brewing chocolate took him back to Grenada. But the pastor did not linger. Instead, he walked to the rear and spoke softly to an older woman by the register. She nodded and pointed at a door shielded by embroidered leather curtains. The pastor motioned Falconer to follow him.

They mounted two flights of stairs, pushed through another door, and navigated a hall filled with clerks and bustling office personnel. The pastor was obviously well known, for he was greeted by many and challenged by none. The succeeding offices grew finer and quieter. Falconer slowed to examine oil paintings adorning walls of the next long room. The most recent resembled the ship at anchor in the Georgetown harbor.

"This way!" the pastor called.

Beyond the offices lay a very fine apartment that smelled of linseed oil and age. "These are the owner's quarters?" Falconer inquired.

"They served as such a long time ago. Nowadays the Langstons reside in a house by the river. These chambers are used by visiting family and friends." The pastor knocked on a walnut door. When a maid opened it, he said, "Good day to you, miss. Mr. Powers is expecting me."

"The doctor is with him."

"I hope he has not taken ill again."

"Only with impatience." The maid held the door open. "Perhaps you can convince him to rest as the doctor wants."

"I would have more luck parting the Potomac." He turned to Falconer. "Wait here. I won't be long."

The paneled room was filled with furnishings from an earlier age. The carpet and the oak-planked flooring looked very old indeed. The drapes were shut, the light muted. The room had managed to trap a bit of the previous night's coolness. Falconer seated himself in a high-backed chair. His neck and shoulders ached from bearing the weight of fatigue and worry and futile travel. Between the nightmares and the necessity of constantly watching the shadows, he was not resting well.

He was in a half doze when a sound brought him jolting to his feet. It took a moment to realize what he had heard. The mewing was so high-pitched as to resemble the squeak of a stubborn hinge. Falconer searched the dim corners for a kitten.

To his astonishment, he found not merely a cat. The kitten was held in the arms of a little girl. Falconer was so shocked by his failure to sense yet another person's presence, he stood speechless in the center of the room.

"I surprised you," the child said.

"Indeed you did."

"If you tell my father he will scold me. Papa says people don't like to be startled." She coughed slightly. "But I enjoy doing it. I feel almost invisible. Are you here to see my father?"

"That depends upon who your father is." Falconer realized the girl sounded far older than she appeared. "What is your name?"

"Hannah. Hannah Powers." Her coughs had a dry, brittle quality. They caused her entire form to tremble. "And you?"

Falconer crossed the room and knelt beside her. Though she watched him with wide-eyed awareness, she gave no sense of fearing his approach. The kitten, however, mewed softly. "If your cat had not cried, I would not have noticed you at all."

She lifted the little creature to her cheek. "My uncle found him. We named him Ferdinand."

"That's a very long name for a very little cat."

"It is my favorite name in the whole wide world. Ferdinand will grow up big and strong, you wait and see. Not like me at all."

"I am certain you will grow with time."

"But I won't, you see. Not like my mother and father. I have heard them worry about me. They say I don't eat enough. They say I am too quiet." She coughed again. "And I've been sick. Papa too. That's why we're still here."

"Where is your home?"

"England. I was born in the house next door to this one. But we have lived in London for almost seven years. I came back with Papa. He and Mama wanted me to see our family here again. But we both caught the croup."

Falconer reached over and stroked the kitten. It was a very little thing, trembling in the way of a creature not yet weaned.

"That must have been quite awful."

"It was. I heard the doctor say he feared he would lose us both."

"You hear a very great deal."

"People don't notice me. I suppose it's because I'm so small and quiet." She spoke in an adult's matter-of-fact manner. "But I listen well and I understand better."

"Of that I have no doubt."

"For instance, I noticed you did not give me your name."

Falconer withdrew his hand from the kitten's head. "How old are you?"

"I shall be eleven in October."

She looked to be about six, but Falconer had no experience whatever with young girls. "Were I to close my eyes, I would think I was addressing a lady twice your age."

"My father says I make up for my smallness with an intelligence that competes with William Wilberforce. But I know that's nonsense. No one is as wise as Mr. Wilberforce."

The name brought Falconer to full alert. It was the one his friend the curate had told him would remain true to their cause. Hopefully. "Your father and Wilberforce are friends?"

"Oh yes. And Mama too. That's why she isn't here with us. One of them had to stay and work on the pamphlets. Mr. Wilberforce claims the pamphlets help ever so much with the cause." She cocked her head. "Why will you not tell me who you are?"

He mentally tested several responses. The silence drew out. The child seemed utterly comfortable with the wait. The words that he finally spoke seemed to choose themselves. "Because I'm afraid."

Hannah Powers found nothing extraordinary about his answer. "Would you like to hold my kitty? It makes me feel so much better when I'm frightened."

"I don't know why I said that." Falconer eased down until he was seated on the floor beside the child. "I've never spoken such a thing in all my days."

"I was very afraid when I was sick. Especially after the doctor said what he did. I'm not looking forward to dying, you see. Not yet." She handed him the kitten, who mewed once, a piercing note, then licked Falconer's thumb.

He felt the little beast tremble in his hand. He lifted the cat up to examine it more closely in the room's dim light. The kitten had a soft gold fur, with faint tiger stripes a half shade darker. Yet its eyes were an astonishing blue, the color of a perfectly clear dawn sky. "What a beautiful little creature."

"Ferdinand is my best friend," she said simply. "I don't have many friends, you see."

"No," Falconer said quietly. "Nor I."

"Mostly I don't mind being alone. But I missed people when I was sick. I think that is why Uncle Reginald brought me the kitty."

Falconer felt a most remarkable sense of closeness to this young girl. "My name is John," he finally said. "And I think your cat is hungry."

"I think so too. But I can't go down to the kitchen. Cook will scold me for being out of bed. But I grow ever so tired of lying down. They thought I was asleep, you see. That's why I can come in here. But only if I'm quiet."

"Then I shall go to the kitchen for you." He handed back the kitten and rose to his feet. "What are you feeding the little beast?"

"Milk with a bit of sweetie biscuit crumbled inside." She examined him. "Are you sure you won't tell me your last name? Papa says I'm only to address an adult by the last name."

He crossed the room, deliberating at this sudden urge to trust a stranger, and a child at that. But in spite of all who relied on him, he could not. "Are you good at keeping secrets?"

"Better than almost anyone."

He couldn't help himself. He believed her. "Then let us make this one exception to your father's rule."

"I am very pleased to make your acquaintance, Master John." She smiled, and the entire room seemed to glow. "Ferdinand will be ever so pleased to dine with you."

The door opened to a narrow landing and a set of winding stairs. Falconer debated whether to return and ask where the kitchen was located. Then from above came the sound of voices.

A man protested hoarsely, "I cannot abide this imprisonment!"

Falconer heard the pastor who had brought him reply, "You must think of your child, Gareth."

"I think of little else. Her and her poor mother. Erica must be frantic with worry by now. Our return to England is three months overdue!"

"You are alive. You have written. She of all people—"

"I have no assurance that my letters have arrived. We've had no word from her in months."

Another said, "You have heard how the storm wreaked havoc with our shipping." The voice carried the authoritative stamp of a church elder or doctor. "I really must insist upon your remaining where you are until your strength has improved."

"And I tell you that nothing would strengthen me better or faster than a few days at sea."

Falconer decided he had heard enough and headed away from the argument. The staircase wound down to a rear hallway that ran like a glass-sided porch behind the emporium. Falconer saw a work yard and warehouse to his left, while to his right rose an imposing brick house. He entered the family residence via the connecting door and followed the scent of baking bread into the rear kitchen.

A sturdy woman wearing an apron and with flour upon her face and arms was pulling loaves from an oven set low upon the flagstone floor. She softly sang a hymn Falconer recognized from his own church.

The woman gripped the wooden spatula with both hands and hefted the loaf. But as she turned to set her load upon the central table, she spied Falconer poised by the door. She gasped with genuine fear and dropped her ladle with a clatter.

Falconer remained caught by the echo of her singing. "The Lord's blessings upon you and your hearth, ma'am."

"Land sakes," she fluttered. "But didn't you give me half a start."

"My abject apologies."

She bent over and used the edges of her apron to lift the steaming bread. She continued to shoot him quick little glances as she brushed off the loaf. "Big hulking brute such as yourself, hardly the sort I'd be expecting to offer me proper greetings."

He touched the scar on his face. "I came by this in darker days."

"Well, you've got a fair way of talking, I'll grant you that." She eyed him as he crossed the kitchen, lifted the utensil from the floor, and swept the remaining three loaves from the oven. "Some would say that's not proper work for a man who looks like a bandit."

"Others might reply that God's servant should set his hand to whatever task is placed before him."

"Well, I never." She arranged the loaves for airing, her eyes never leaving him for long. "What do they call you?"

"Brother John."

"I am Mavis. But most around this house know me as Cook."

"Your servant, ma'am."

"And what brings you to my dusty hearth, Brother John?"

"I seek a bit of milk and sweetie biscuit."

"Is that a fact." The edges of her mouth tugged upward. "Is that imp out of bed again?"

"What imp might that be, ma'am?"

Mavis laughed aloud and waved a finger at him. "You're no good at playing the innocent, not with that great ragged slice running down your face. So you might as well not try."

"I see I am defeated."

"Aye, that you are, sir." The woman drew down a bowl, pulled half a biscuit from a jar, and crumbled that inside. Then she hefted a large white pitcher, removed the cheesecloth from its mouth, and poured the cup half full. "She's captured your heart, has she?"

Falconer did not need to ask whom she meant. "Indeed so, ma'am."

"I've raised five daughters of my own and seen twice that number run through this kitchen in the fourteen years I've worked for the family. And never have I known such a one as Hannah." She took a silver baby spoon from the table drawer and stirred the mixture. "Can't imagine what it'll be like 'round here when she returns home. Empty, my poor old heart will be. Empty and missing a little angel with eyes like the noonday sun."

"And her smile," Falconer murmured. "I am fortunate she is not older, for when she smiled at me I should have fallen and never managed to rise."

The cook eyed him fondly now, her former reserve gone. "Aye, she's captured you sure enough."

She handed him the cup. "Mind that tiny creature doesn't eat too much or too fast. If only it could teach the imp to eat a proper meal, I'd count myself satisfied to let her go."

The kitten might have been both tiny and very young, but it knew enough to recognize food. The effect of Falconer returning with the bowl and spoon spurred it into action. Hannah opened the curtains so they could enjoy the kitten's antics. As Falconer lowered himself, careful not to spill the bowl's contents, the cat danced about him. Had it been a month older and stronger, Falconer was certain it would have climbed him like a tree.

Falconer offered Hannah the bowl. "Do you want the honors?"

"Oh no," she replied, her beaming face brighter than the sunlight streaming through the window beside them. "I want to watch."

The cat certainly did make for good theater. Falconer seated himself and crossed his legs in the space between them. The cat appeared boneless as it slid around his legs and crawled about his boots and cried in a most plaintive manner. When Falconer did not act fast enough, the kitten clambered into his lap, planted two paws on his shirt, and cried mournfully up at his face.

"You little scoundrel," he said. "What a noisy little beast you are."

Hannah clasped both hands over her mouth and giggled.

He gripped the cat firmly with his left hand and set the bowl on the floor to his right. The cat did not like being held this far from its food and squirmed and protested magnificently. "The cook warned me not to let it eat too fast."

"Once I let Ferdinand eat from the bowl, and he almost drowned."

Whether the kitten was of the male persuasion, Falconer had no idea. But he liked the cat's spirit. "You would make a grand ship's cat."

"Oh no," Hannah said. "Ferdinand is to stay with me."

"Of course he will." Falconer filled the silver spoon with milk and biscuit and brought it to the cat. "Anyone can see the pair of you are inseparable."

The cat was intent upon devouring the spoon as well as the food. Moreover it wished to eat with both forepaws as well as its mouth. A good deal of the milk was splashed upon Falconer's knee. But he did not mind, for the girl's laughter filled the room with a rare gemlike quality. He gave her surreptitious glances as he spooned milk and biscuit for the kitten. Hannah's features were so finely drawn as to appear ethereal, too delicate to reside firmly upon this harsh realm. Dark plum-colored smudges encircled her eyes. Her skin was translucent, such that Falconer imagined he could study not merely her face but the flame of life itself.

He was filled with a sudden illogical desire to do all he possibly could to protect this child from any peril.

The girl noticed his gaze then. She did not shy away but instead met his stare full on, as would a woman thrice her age. Her soft laughter died away. Her eyes, the color of smoke upon a winter's sky, seemed to open until he could look straight into her very soul.

So it was that the pair of them were discovered. The door opened and a man's voice said, "What's this, then?"

Falconer rose swiftly to his feet, cradling the cat in his left arm. "Your pardon, sir."

The man bore the same half moons beneath his eyes as his daughter. For father he was, there was no mistaking the resemblance. Despite the day's growing heat, he wore a quilted robe belted about his waist. Beneath were rumpled nightclothes and slippers. He carried himself at a slight crouch, as though fighting against both his evident weakness and some internal pain. Yet even in this weakened state, he held a remarkable sense of power.

"I see you have met my Hannah," the man observed dryly.

Falconer sensed he faced an officer of one sort or another, a leader of men. And he responded in proper fashion. "I meant no disrespect to you or your family, sir."

"Indeed." The man examined his daughter. "Were you not meant to be asleep?"

The child remained seated upon the floor. "Ferdinand was hungry."

"Any excuse will do in an emergency," he said, but he was smiling now.

Falconer hazarded to add softly, "Any port in a storm."

The man's focus returned to him. "You were a ship's officer?"

The kitten did not like being ignored like this and began mewing and impatiently patting Falconer's hand. "At one time, sir."

"A pirate?"

It was a fair question, Falconer knew. The scar on his face was not the only aspect of his demeanor that shouted of such a life. Even so, the query stung. He would have liked to be considered a better man. Not to mention how the child continued to observe him in wide-eyed silence. "I have been many things, sir. Most of them foul. But never a pirate."

"My friend tells me he feels God's hand is upon you." He

glanced down at his daughter. "And clearly my Hannah thinks highly of you. For you are the first outside the family she has let handle her new friend."

Falconer glanced down at the squirming kitten. This news made the young child's calm acceptance even more precious. "I find myself deeply moved by your daughter, sir."

"As are many. But in your case the sentiment seems to be reciprocated."

Hannah coughed once, then said, "I like him, Papa."

"So I gather." Weak as he was, the man's eyes held the force of an iron grip. "The question is, can we trust him?"

"I seek only to serve my Lord, sir."

"You will excuse me for saying that coming from a man such as yourself, the words seem astonishing."

"Nonetheless they are true." Falconer took a breath, wishing anew that he had been a better man. "I stand as living testimony that no matter how dark a life, no matter how far a man has strayed, Christ still can offer both salvation and hope."

"Amen," the young pastor murmured over the shoulder of Hannah's father. "I say, amen."

Gareth Powers's scrutiny bit deep. Falconer felt as though the gentleman examined the very depths of his being. Then, in the space of a mere heartbeat, he faltered. Falconer actually saw his strength fade, like a candle puffed out by a sudden gust of feverish wind. Gareth Powers folded in upon himself.

Had Falconer not been there to catch him, he would have collapsed to the floor. Hannah cried and rose to her feet. The pastor rushed forward to help, but Falconer already had the man's weight in his grip. "Allow me to help you."

"Papa!"

"It's all right, daughter. Nothing save a passing spell," he murmured, then permitted Falconer to hold him about the chest. "The bedroom at the top of the stairs, if you please."

"Of course, sir."

The stairway was a tight fit for two men moving together.

Falconer turned sideways and hefted his charge until the man's feet scarcely touched the steps.

He could hear the man's labored breathing. Falconer brought him into the bedroom and eased him down onto the bed. But when he made to leave, the man said, "Stay, if you would."

"Perhaps you should rest."

"I have rested until this bed has become my prison." But as he spoke, he settled himself beneath the covers. "I find myself sharing my friend's assessment of you, though I cannot say for certain why. And I fear that my fevered state has left me unable to trust my instincts and clarity of vision."

"I can only repeat what I have said before, sir. I seek only to be a worthy servant of our one true Lord."

"Your words are a genuine tonic." The man's eyelids began to sink. "I find we have need of your strength, my daughter and I. Would you be willing to sign on as our traveling companion?" He forced his eyes open.

"I could not promise to remain with you for very long, sir. I am on a mission of some urgency."

"You seek passage to England, is that not so?"

"With all possible haste."

"You have visited the ship at anchor in Georgetown?"

"As fleet a vessel as ever I have laid eyes on."

"The doctor tells me I should permit the vessel to depart without us and seek passage later in the season. But I am impatient to return to my wife and our own shared mission." He rounded his eyes in an attempt to remain fully alert. "I feel certain that were we to have a trusted ally on whose strength we could rely, the journey itself would do us a world of good."

"On the doctor's advice I cannot speak, sir. But for myself, nothing would do me more honor than to assist you and your daughter through the journey."

The former intensity returned to his gaze. "I don't believe I have introduced myself. Gareth Powers is my name."

Falconer bowed slightly. "Your servant, sir."

"And you are?" When Falconer hesitated to respond, Gareth

added, "I am known as one who safeguards many secrets."

Falconer recognized there was no way forward but in honesty. Not with this man. "John Falconer, at your service. Late of Trinidad and Grenada."

"I understand there are men seeking to do you harm."

"For crimes I had no hand in, save sharing the same mission as the brother who met an untimely end."

"Talk of your mission shall have to wait. For the moment, I would ask that we pray together."

The request was utterly unexpected. "Sir?"

"I find there is much to be learned from how a man addresses his Maker."

Slowly Falconer lowered himself, this time to kneel beside the bed. He bowed his head and said, "Father, I know thy mercy has no earthly bounds. The fact that I am here today is all the evidence I require. Thou knowest my mission, and my urgency. If it is thy will that this man and his daughter trust me to serve them, please grant them the clarity of vision to see thy hand at work. I ask forgiveness for all my multitude of failings and weaknesses, so many they are beyond count. I ask for thy wisdom and strength. For without thee, dear Lord, I am nothing. Nothing save dust and mortal loss. Humbly do I pray in the Lord Jesus' name, amen."

Falconer felt not so much ashamed by his words as exposed. Never before had he expressed himself in prayer so openly before a stranger. He was slow in raising his head, fearing what he might find in the man's gaze.

But Gareth Powers was sound asleep.

Chapter 7

Carla was a slender young woman who moved so silently most people did not even notice her passage. Which was perhaps her intent. Serafina had never thought about such things before. Now, however, when so much rested upon Carla being able to do what she said she would, Serafina found such matters of critical importance. Carla seemed able to float through a room, moving from shadow to shadow in utter silence. When some new chore needing doing, her mother usually found another servant for the task. Carla was, Serafina supposed, quite clever in a strange sort of way.

Today her cleverness paid off superbly. For when Carla brought the morning tray, she appeared to have gained a substantial amount of weight overnight. Her middle in particular seemed rather distended. But her wraithlike movements meant she had been able to slip through the house unnoticed.

Even so, the woman was perspiring and breathing heavily. She did not even bother to set the tray down before hissing, "Show me."

Serafina drew the pearls from her pocket. "And now you."

Carla hefted her apron. Wrapped about her middle was a full set of clothing, the kind a manservant would wear. There were dark breeches and a white shirt with sleeves that tied about the wrists. The matching vest had black cloth buttons. "These were the smallest I could find." She untied her apron and released the burden at her back. This proved to be a crushed tricorn servant's hat tied with twine about a pair of buckled shoes. "You can stuff the shoes with your drawing paper."

It was a good idea. Serafina liked the fact that Carla had been giving this careful thought. She handed the maid her pearls as if they were of no consequence, only a means to what was truly important. She quickly lifted her own skirts and stepped into the pants. They were loose but would suffice.

Suddenly the entire affair came into sharp focus. *I am going to do this.* The air seemed to have been sucked from the room, it was so hard to find breath. "Is the housecleaning schedule the same?" Serafina demanded.

Carla's eyes swiveled to the jewel box. "Show me the comb."

Serafina did not hesitate. She unlocked the box and withdrew her final treasure. Her finest. It was a hair comb of jade so pale it looked like translucent glass. It had come all the way from China and was very old. The jade was curved slightly, carved into a series of teeth as long as her fingers. At the crest were two doves kissing.

Serafina held the comb tightly as she lifted it for inspection. Carla's eyes held a hunger that was almost violent in its intensity. Serafina let Carla look for a long moment, then slipped the comb into her pocket. Carla's focus remained upon the unseen comb.

"When do they begin?" Serafina demanded.

"In an hour."

"How will you do this?"

"The signora used to ask me to return the key every time I brought you your meals. But now she lets me keep it. She only asks for it if she or your father are coming for a visit."

This was what Carla had said before. But it was vital to be certain. "You will come for me when they are busiest?"

Carla nodded slowly. "I will come."

The activities of the house grew around her. Serafina knew the rhythm so well she could follow all the actions, confined though she was in her room. The first Wednesday of each month, three footmen from her father's office arrived. Together with the house staff, they moved all the heavy furniture. They rolled back the carpets, carried them downstairs, and beat the dust out of them. They aired out the mattresses and bed linens. They polished the floors. Then they replaced all the carpets and the mattresses and the furniture. It was a long and arduous day. Everyone knew what was required and moved swiftly about his task with little conversation.

Serafina dressed in the men's clothing, using the spare moments to stitch up the shirt and pants so they fit her better. She took her time. There was little chance her mother would visit on such a busy day. Her father never ventured near the house on cleaning days. Serafina shredded several sheets of her drawing paper and wadded it into the toes and heels of her shoes. She was careful not to make the fit too tight. She might have to walk for a very long time.

She knotted her hair and stuffed it down the back of her shirt. She buttoned the vest, fitted the tricorn hat down tightly, then examined her reflection in the mirror. Even in the chamber's half-light she could see strands of her shimmering hair. She took off the hat and pulled her simplest scarf from her top drawer. Sometimes the footmen knotted a bandanna about their foreheads to keep the sweat from their eyes. She tied the scarf about her head and knotted it at the back. She replaced the hat and inspected her reflection once more. It was not perfect, but it would have to do. She would simply have to move quickly.

She found herself caught by the gaze looking back at her from the mirror. They did not appear to be her own eyes, any more than the strange young figure in the dark vest and trousers could be herself. Even in the dim room, the eyes looked feverish, glittering at her with an almost manic light. Serafina's own reflection caused her stomach to churn even worse than before. The frenzied intensity she saw in the mirror shook her to her very core.

She forced herself to turn away.

She paced back and forth. The noise outside her chamber

reached a new crescendo. Or perhaps it was merely the thunder of her pulse.

The key scratched in the door. There was a quick knock. A pause, then a second time. Carla's signal.

Serafina flew across the room. Carla stood blocking the door and facing away from her. She did not speak. Nor did she move. Instead, her hand rose behind her back.

Serafina placed the jade comb into the waiting palm. Carla gave it a lightning inspection and slipped it into her pocket. She scouted the upstairs hall in both directions, then stepped aside.

Serafina heard her mother's voice call, "No!"

She froze, her heart pounding in her chest. She heard her mother say, "Don't drag the settee! See the scar you've made? Raise it clear of the floor!"

Serafina sighed away the freezing fear. To her left Carla's breath hissed out, releasing her own terror.

One of the footmen emerged from Serafina's parents' bedroom, staggering under the weight of a rolled carpet on his shoulder. He saw nothing but the next step ahead of him as he moved carefully for the stairs.

Without thinking, Serafina slipped past Carla and moved in behind the footman. She pretended to hold up the rear of the rug and matched his tread down the central stairs. She heard the man's huffing breath and gasped along with him, her entire body trembling. She glanced through the railing and saw the front hall was empty. The house was filled with sounds of banging and scraping but no alarm.

She was able to take nothing with her. The footmen who helped on cleaning days carried nothing of their own.

When the footman turned the corner at the base of the stairway, Serafina slipped through the front doors.

She stopped there, blinking in the light. She had not been out of her chamber in three weeks and three days. The midday light, at the height of a Venetian summer, was piercing. Serafina knew she could not stay where she was. She stumbled down the front stairs, nearly falling at the bottom.

"Here now, lad." Strong hands kept her aloft. "Pay attention where you lay your feet."

Serafina caught herself just in the moment of opening her mouth to thank the unseen man. She stepped away from his grasp and moved into the shadows. She angled her hat to hide her face further. She moved along the wall, not even certain in which direction she was headed. For the moment, anywhere would do so long as it was away.

Away. What an unearthly strange word to use with such abandon. Away from home and family and Venice. Away from all that she cherished. Away from the only life she knew. Serafina's eyes adjusted to the outside brilliance as she realized she was moving into Saint Mark's Square. She increased her speed. *Luca!*

She was midway across the square when she was jostled by a berobed merchant, and her hat tumbled down. She recognized the man as a friend of her father's. "Watch where you're going there!"

Serafina knelt upon the cobblestones and fitted the hat back down tightly. She made her voice as gruff as possible. "Sorry, sir."

"Sorry won't do it! You young ruffians don't own the square, you know!"

She remained crouched and still until the footsteps moved away. Slowly she rose back to her feet and began walking forward. She held herself to a steady pace and kept her eyes downcast, as footmen running errands often did. At her feet the pigeons strutted and cooed. The sunlight beat upon her shoulders. Around her rose the noise and bustle of Saint Mark's Square at midday. The minstrels sang their way from café to restaurant, and the waiters bustled at their tasks. The chatter was light and constant. Away!

She took the lane that led from the square to the Grand Canal and crossed the Rialto Bridge. Shaped in a series of long stairs, it was a broad footbridge of stone so old it dated back to Venice's earliest days. A gondolier swept under the bridge as she passed over, dipping his long pole into the water in time to his soft melody. That was why they sang, her mother claimed, to time the strokes of their poling and keep them in the proper cadence.

The sudden memory halted her at the crest of the footbridge. What good would such knowledge do her, wherever she was to roam? Venice was unique in all the world. She knew its heart, she knew its alleys, she knew the bridges and the canals and the people. Would she ever find another place that called to her so, that she would call back to as home?

Serafina shook herself back to the present. She realized that her gaze was fastened upon her family's villa along the canal. But this was her home no more. After twenty-four days of captivity, she was free. Her heart tugged fiercely at her, for ahead of her lay Luca and a future that she had already claimed as her own. Away!

She arrived at the closest street to the mainland market square. It was the perfect place for such a rendezvous. The stallholders squalled a constant barrage of sound. The patrons quarreled in the good-natured Venetian way, demanding the best product and then arguing for the lowest price. Servants shoveled refuse to the waiting garbage vessel. Fully laden barges docked and were swiftly unloaded. Chickens and pheasants squawked from their cages while children cried. The air was filled with noise and heat and odors.

She started to enter the square's one fine restaurant. But a passing waiter scowled a warning. Serafina realized that dressed as a footman, she was not welcome. As upon the bridge, the wrenching realization weakened her resolve. What was she doing? Instantly the answer came in the form of the name she dare not shout aloud. *Luca!* She stepped beneath the corner of the restaurant's awning and searched the passing faces. He had to be here!

Then she spied them.

Venice's merchant guild had its own troop of guards. The medieval tradition had passed out of favor in most other Italian cities. Venice stubbornly clung to the old ways, even though true authority was now held by the Austrian Crown. The small cadre of private guards was known by the color of their vests and the shape of their hats. She knew them, many by name, because they accompanied her father during official ceremonies or when he was greeting visiting royalty. But they were not here to fulfill some ceremonial duty. They purposefully entered the square and scouted carefully about.

Serafina ducked around the corner. Could they be searching for her? How was that possible? Even if the alarm had already been raised, how could they have deduced so quickly that she was . . .

Carla, of course! Serafina pressed a fist to her mouth. Luca could not have read the letter himself. He could only manage a few words, and these in a halting fashion. He would have had someone read the letter to him. It had been Carla. What if she had sounded the alarm herself, planned the betrayal from the beginning? Serafina risked another quick glance into the square. The guards were spreading out, moving slowly among the stalls. They inspected each face, male and female, with cautious scrutiny.

She pressed herself tight against the wall. *Where is Luca?* Of all times for him to tarry! Or had that poisonous Carla lied to him about their rendezvous? Frantically Serafina sought a better place to hide. Yet if she hid, how would he ever find her, if indeed he was looking?

But the guards were drawing near, and the closest one was turning into the last line of stalls. Only a dozen or so people stood between them. Heart in her mouth, Serafina risked another glance into the square. Luca was nowhere to be seen.

Then a figure turned her way. A man in robes of office. She knew those robes. And the face beneath them. Serafina slammed herself back onto the wall. But not fast enough. Her father had seen her.

"There!"

She sprang from the wall and leaped down the alley. But her way was blocked by a trundling vegetable cart. It filled the lane from one wall to the next, driving a flock of protesting people ahead of it. Serafina pressed into a doorway with half a dozen others and watched the high muddy wheel pass before her face.

"Don't let her get away!"

The guards berated the drover, urging him to move the cart faster, to turn the donkey aside, to do anything so long as he got out of their way. Her father's voice rose again above the tumult. "She's in the doorway! I see her! A golden ducat for the one who halts the woman dressed as a man!"

The donkey brayed as a guard leaped onto its back and clambered up on top of the cart. Serafina scrambled around the cart's rear corner. But she was not fast enough. A strong grip clutched at her vest. She shrieked and struggled so hard the buttons popped. She wriggled free from the vest, but in so doing she lost her balance. Arms windmilling, she stumbled backward.

And fell headlong into the canal.

She came up gasping and spitting water rank with refuse from the market.

"Luca!"

Serafina attempted to swim away, only to be halted by an iron grip about her neck.

"Luca!" she screamed again.

Hands dragged her bodily from the water. "I have her! The gold is mine!"

"Get this cart out of my way! Hold her fast!"

"Luca!" Her breath was constricted by the man's grip. Still she managed to shriek so loudly the words tore at her throat. *"Save me!"*

But Luca did not appear. Only two more muscular guards, who added their own strength to the hands already imprisoning her. Serafina fought with all her might.

"Luca!"

Chapter 8

Falconer awoke the hour before dawn, plucked from sleep long before he was ready. Perhaps he had always lived with the nightmare for company, as the curate had suggested. Perhaps it was only now that he was strong enough to understand it for what it was. So Falconer began his morning as he did all dawns when the nightmare's aftertaste still lingered. He prayed for strength to shoulder his burdens once more and to do the will of the One he sought desperately to serve.

The dawn was free of humidity and heat. Falconer shivered as he dressed, not so much from being cold as simply from the contrast. He walked into the kitchen and lit the fire, set a kettle on to boil, then stepped into the courtyard behind the emporium. He breathed deeply of the remarkably cool air. He stayed where he was until the kettle began to sing. He made himself a pot of sailor's tea, which required a heaping fistful of leaves. The brew he poured through the sieve and into his mug was as black as tar. To this he added a double spoonful of molasses from a clay jar set beside the stove. He walked to the doorway and stood on the top step, looking out over the courtyard.

As the light strengthened, he noted a pair of perfect magnolias against the building's shadows. Mockingbirds trilled such a variety of melodies it was hard to follow the pattern. The jays were awake now, and the crows. Falconer could see that the coffee shop, through which he had passed the previous day, had a carefully tended garden surrounding its two bowed windows. A tall hedge of some flowering shrub blocked the patrons' view of the outbuildings set in the remainder of the courtyard. There was an open-sided shed for packing freight and building crates. Another with slits for windows served as a miniature drying barn. Falconer could smell the old scent of roasted coffee in the still air. It was an altogether agreeable space, filled with the fragrances of fresh-sawn wood and hard work.

A voice from behind startled Falconer from his reverie. "I would imagine the view must be rather confining after your sea-bound vistas."

Falconer shook his head at this family's ability to approach him unawares. "I have been landlocked for several years now, though rarely this far from the sea."

Gareth Powers eased himself into a seat by the stove. "Doing what, might I ask?"

"Running a ship chandlery."

"Ah." He shifted closer to the flames, clearly finding the dawn's chill not to his liking. "Was this work part of your mission?"

"In a sense. A merchant hears all manner of news, often earlier than others." Falconer drained his mug. "I am in your debt, sir, for granting me berth here."

"You will repay your debt if you would serve me a draught of whatever you are drinking."

"It is but sailor's tea."

"It smells like an elixir, this time of day."

"That would be the sulfur in the molasses. Sailors search out whatever sweet they can find for the day's first mug."

"Well do I know it."

Falconer bent to his task of preparing another mug. "You were navy?"

"Infantry."

"American?"

"British." Gareth nodded his thanks when the mug was handed over, took a great sip, and sighed contentedly. "My daughter is very taken with you, I must say."

"And I with her." Falconer settled into a chair across the table from Gareth. "She has the most remarkable . . ." He stopped, unable to select from the list that sprang to his mind. Smile, heart, gaze, intelligence, spirit.

"Indeed." Gareth started to say something, then turned to look out the open door. He finally settled on, "Do you ever feel as though God is not guiding the vessel of life with a sincere hand?"

For Falconer, the words distilled the moment down to some hidden essence. "Were I not afraid of blasphemy, sir, I would wonder it very much."

"I set off on a journey from England that was meant to last just nine weeks. Reginald Langston, the master of both this house and the emporium, is also owner of four ships. The one at anchor is especially swift. We had problems with our American enterprise. Not the emporium. My wife and I are pamphleteers, working mostly from Britain. But earlier we lived in Georgetown and started a press here in America. The man we had left in charge here passed on, and I needed to find a replacement. I thought I would bring my family, but there was a crisis in Britain."

"Your daughter mentioned as much. She said your wife was required to stay behind." Falconer's chair creaked as he leaned back, affecting a relaxed air that he did not feel. He watched Gareth pause to sip and examine the daylight spreading beyond the doorway. He knew the man was not merely relating his journey. There was a deeper message here. He found Hannah's image there in his mind once more. He recalled the young girl's smile. It was a remarkable sensation, to feel such trust for virtual strangers. Especially now, when his life was filled with the threat of mortal danger to life and mission.

"We arrived in April and I went about my work," Gareth Powers continued. "Then we both became ill. First my daughter, then me. Consumption, the doctor called it. Or the croup. Or any number of other names. As though identifying it might speed the healing process."

"Stronger men than I have been lost to that foul malady."

"I was desperately ill and made sicker still with worry over my beloved Hannah." Gareth set down his mug so as not to slosh the liquid as he coughed. The act doubled him over. He gradually straightened, wiping his mouth with a handkerchief drawn from the pocket of his robe. The words came hoarser now. "Three months and nineteen days we have been here now. Word has no doubt reached England of the storm that passed to the east of us. I am certain my wife believes we were lost at sea. I fear for her well-being, sir. I fear for my family."

"You want to return."

"I *must* return. There is my wife, and there is my work." Gareth stopped then and sat with his face directed at the rising sun.

Falconer rose from his seat, picked up Gareth's mug from the table, and made them both another tea. When he was reseated, he said, "You need someone to be strong for you."

"And my daughter."

"And strong for Hannah. Of course."

Gareth lifted his mug, then looked straight at Falconer and said, "What I need to know, sir, is whether I can trust you to be our rock."

Falconer considered several replies. Finally he said, "May I ask you one thing, sir?"

"Anything you like. Whether or not I can answer is another matter."

Falconer liked that response. There was a great sincerity to this man, a remarkable openness for one who clearly knew the importance of confidences. "Do you know a man by the name of William Wilberforce?"

Gareth's face creased, as though stricken by some deep internal sorrow. "Why do you ask?"

"Your daughter mentioned him." Falconer chose his words carefully. "It has to do with my mission, sir. Of this I am charged to maintain strictest secrecy. Not for myself. For the sake of others."

The pain in Gareth's features only deepened. "Then I fear you must prepare yourself for a great shock."

The sense of defeat that had lingered on the horizon throughout his futile voyage north intensified. Falconer nodded.

"William is desperately ill. He has been ill so often, it is hard to discern whether this is not just one more bad spell. But before I left, he appeared to be going blind. One further reason I am so desperate to return. The longer we remain, the less likelihood I have of seeing my friend alive again." Gareth reached over and gripped Falconer's arm. "I repeat what I said before. What I must know, sir, is can I trust you?"

Falconer studied the man's intensity. Here, he realized, was someone he wished to know better. "Sir, I give you my word as the Lord's servant. I shall serve you and your daughter to the utmost of my ability."

"I must warn you," Gareth said. "There are those who may seek to do me harm."

"As they do me," he responded calmly. "A foul wind blows across the face of our earth, sir. For those who do God's bidding, danger is but a part of the day's burden."

"You are not afraid?"

"Almost constantly, sir. But not of being in harm's way." Falconer had never before spoken of his internal struggles. "I fear failing my Lord. I do not deserve His gift of salvation. I never will. He reached into the world's darkest depths to save me. I am ashamed of so much I have seen and done, sir. Mortally ashamed. All I can do now is seek to do one thing right. Just this one small thing."

Gareth released Falconer's arm and used his handkerchief to wipe his face. "I see my daughter was right."

"Sir?"

He needed both hands to push himself up from his chair. He nodded his thanks when Falconer rose and took his arm. Gareth said, "We shall begin preparing for our departure this very day."

Chapter 9

The day after they brought her home, Serafina awoke to discover the devastating chill had reached from her heart into her bones. ·

A guard was now stationed outside her door. She saw him glance inside every time the door was open. Sometimes it was a footman, sometimes a maid, occasionally someone she did not recognize. Serafina never saw Carla again. It hardly mattered. Her parents visited her several times that day, and the next. They raged with her at first, then simply ordered her to talk. But what was there to say? Every time she spoke Luca's name, they flew into a new fury. And there was nothing else Serafina wished to say.

She stopped eating. Food held no interest. Her body felt disconnected. The hours came and went in slatted patterns of sunlight across her floor. The gloom brightened and then dispelled. The second day of her fever, Serafina heard a musical patter upon the balcony. At first she thought it was Luca's step. But then she realized that it was just a summer storm. The sky could cry for her as she gave in to what she hoped would be her final illness.

The fever ravaged her, and time lost all meaning. Her mother's voice became a litany of worry. Her father came and went, moving about like a shadow. Doctors were vague shapes who probed and then softly spoke a variety of somber observations. Serafina lost the ability to focus, or perhaps simply the will. Occasionally she would weakly call for Luca, a dim echo of the keening cry in her heart. If her father was in the room, he would storm about. Sometimes her mother wept.

But Luca never answered.

One afternoon she awoke to discover a stranger in her room. Serafina knew it was not her mother because the hair spilling down the back of the stranger's dress was dark. The stranger turned around. Serafina realized it was her half sister. Gabriella moved about the room on silent feet, studying everything with an intent and satisfied air.

Serafina must have made a small sound, because Gabriella turned toward the bed. "You're awake. I'm so pleased."

Serafina had been very young when she had first realized that Gabriella genuinely detested her. The other sisters had certainly been cold to her. But Gabriella's taunts had held a different air even then. Now she wore the expression Serafina had come to fear as a little girl.

"I thought you should know," Gabriella said. "Father is going away. And he is taking your mother with him when he goes."

Serafina was so weak she could not move, nor did she care to. But her thoughts were clear for the first time in days, and she realized the fever had left her. But she had no interest in speaking.

"Away, yes. Far away," Gabriella taunted. "To America. Father has some secret mission he must perform for the merchant council. They were supposed to have already departed. But they couldn't, you see. Not with you causing this terrible stir. But now the merchant council has said Father cannot wait any longer. The work has become very urgent. Everyone would be so proud of him, were it not for you."

Gabriella sat down on the side of the bed. Now that she was close, Serafina realized with a start that she wore a new comb in her hair. One of palest jade, carved into the form of two doves kissing.

"Oh, do you like my comb? I was so surprised to find Carla with it in her pocket. I had been watching her, you see. I was worried she might try something." Gabriella smiled as she touched the comb. "Since you were careless enough to lose it,

Father said I should have it. Your mother objected, of course. But Father said you did not deserve it anymore. Now it's mine." She touched the pearls around her neck, held in place by a ruby red brooch. "Just like these. All mine."

As Gabriella leaned over the bed, Serafina noticed that no amount of corn-silk powder could mask the roughness of her skin nor any amount of jewelry soften the hard edge to her dark gaze.

Yet Gabriella's voice remained as gentle as a silken noose. "Eugenia and her husband are moving back into the house." Eugenia was the oldest half sister. Gabriella reached out as though to touch Serafina's face but did not actually make contact. Her tone was almost musical. "Her husband is taking Father's place as head of our trading business. It was deemed only right that they should live here and act as guardians of the estate."

Gabriella smiled dreamily, her pleasure exquisite. "Eugenia has already said I could have this room until my wedding. After all, since you cannot be trusted to go out on the balcony, why should you remain here?"

Gabriella obviously savored each word. "You will be moved back into the downstairs parlor. Surely you remember your former bedroom. The one with bars on the narrow window. Eugenia and I have talked everything through. You will be placed in my charge. And I will make you behave. Of that you can be very certain, my beautiful sister. Once Mother and Father are away, I will make certain that you are the height of respectability."

Gabriella rose to her feet with a very satisfied sigh. "And now you know everything."

Slowly she walked to stand by Serafina's desk. She paused there, examining something upon the wall. "Well, almost everything. There are two more items. Small matters. But you might find them of interest."

Slowly, with her gaze steady upon her half sister, Gabriella plucked the sketch Serafina had done of her from the wall. "Father has discovered something about your precious Luca." The name held such venom in Gabriella's mouth that Serafina could not quite suppress a shudder. But the murky light must have masked it, for Gabriella continued blithely, "I don't know what it is. But your mother cried and cried for hours when she heard the news. They both have been so very upset. Don't you worry, though. As soon as I learn what it is, you can be sure I shall tell you."

Gabriella gripped the drawing with both hands and slowly tore it in half. "Also you might want to know that Roberto's family has broken off his engagement to you." She then tore the half into quarters, and the quarters into eighths. All the while her focus was steady upon the figure lying in the bed. "Hardly a surprise. After all, why would anyone want to marry you? Especially now that the world has seen what I have always known."

The door to the hall flung open. Serafina's mother demanded sharply, "What are you doing in here?"

"Just having a little visit with my dear sister." Gabriella smiled down at the bed. "Look. She's finally awake."

Serafina's mother moved to the bed and peered down. Her eyes were haunted, as though she had somehow managed to seize hold of Serafina's fever. "My child," she murmured. "Are you better?"

"She will be soon," Gabriella said, moving toward the door. "I am very certain of that."

Their mother observed Gabriella's departure with a worried frown. She saw the bits of paper dangling from Gabriella's hand and turned to study the wall. When the door closed, she returned her attention to Serafina. "My baby, my heart, won't you eat a little something? For me?"

Serafina studied her mother's face. She saw the fatigue and the stress and the pain, and she knew it was her fault. A tear burned its way from the corner of her eye. She nodded. Of course she could do this much, for her mother.

Everything else could wait until her parents were gone.

But Serafina's fever did not give up that easily. The next morning it was back again, renewed in strength. To Serafina's scattered mind it was as if she were being ravaged by a creature only she could see.

Several nights later, although Serafina was never certain how many, she woke to find herself being lifted by very strong hands. Whoever was carrying her smelled vaguely of tobacco and something acrid, perhaps tar. She was being carried inside her own blankets and bed linen, bundled up like an infant. She started to call out, but then she heard her mother's voice beside her and felt her cool touch. Serafina wanted to speak with her, to apologize for all the trouble she had caused. But the words were too much of an effort, and she drifted off again.

Her dreams that night were scattered fragments of smells and sounds. She dreamed that she was lowered into a gondola and it was poled down a canal. Serafina knew this was impossible. After all, hadn't her parents done their utmost to keep her imprisoned? She smelled the sweet fragrance of Venice's watery lanes and drifted away once more.

She awoke again, but only partly, when she was lifted a second time. Or perhaps again it was a dream. This time she found herself unable even to open her eyes.

She next awoke to daylight. But not the illumination through her wooden blinds. Instead, there was a single round hole in a wooden wall.

Serafina rubbed her eyes. She studied her surroundings. The room was indeed wooden, as was the narrow bed in which she lay. The walls were curved and heavily beamed. Sunlight poured through the round window to her right. The room was filled with the smell of salt and the sound of rushing water.

She was on a ship. She could feel the faint motion now, a gentle rocking in time to the sound of splashing waves.

The door bolt slid back, and her mother entered the cabin. "Good morning, my precious daughter." She bore a tray, which she set down gingerly upon the little table beneath the porthole. "I feel as though I must learn to walk all over again. Your father is dreadfully ill from the ship's motions. Now I have two to care for."

Serafina realized her mother thought she was still in the throes of the fever and spoke to her in the manner of one who did not expect to be heard. She licked dry lips and whispered, "Where am I?"

Her mother stiffened in amazement. She rushed to the bedside. "You truly are awake! My dearest one, how do you feel?"

Serafina again licked her lips. Her mother responded by pouring water from a pitcher into a pewter mug, then lifting Serafina's head to hold it to her lips. Some of the liquid dribbled down the side of her face, and she coughed.

"Slowly, my dearest one. Slowly. The water is not going anywhere."

She lay back, her chest heaving from the effort. "Where am I?"

"On a ship. Will you eat something?"

Serafina nodded, meaning she knew this was a vessel. But her mother took it as a signal that she would eat. Serafina accepted the food because she had no strength for an argument. But the food was tasteless. She swallowed and again asked, "Where am I?"

"I will only answer your questions if you finish your entire bowl. There. You see? I can be difficult as well. No, don't bother asking anything more, my daughter. I shall not answer you until the spoon clanks upon the porcelain."

So she allowed her mother to spoon in the gruel as if she were a little child, unable to feed herself. She found comfort in the simple act of lying there and being fed. But a sorrow as well. For with the meal came a growing clarity. Serafina knew the fever still lurked about. But for the moment her mind was clear enough to see once more the pain and suffering etched upon her mother's face. Serafina wept in her heart for the distress caused to the one person she loved most in all the world. Except, of course, for Luca.

She heard the rushing water more clearly now and knew with

dreadful certainty that every second took her farther away from her beloved.

She could remain silent no longer. "Why wouldn't you let me go to him?"

The spoonful of gruel hesitated midway between the bowl and her mouth. This time her mother answered, in a voice turned deep with gravity. "Because he was not right for you."

"He was, though. If only you would see that, none of this would have happened."

The spoon remained poised in midair. "My dearest, I have something to tell . . . Are you strong enough to hear what I have to say?"

Serafina knew there were all sorts of arguments her mother could frame. Logical statements about how Luca was not this or not that. None of which mattered. "Why couldn't you make them see? Couldn't you let me have what they kept from you, Mother?"

"Make them . . ." She looked askance at her daughter. "My dearest child, I would have done anything to have protected you from this."

"But you couldn't. Don't you see? I do love him. But you treated me just like your parents did you. And you let them." She struggled to keep her voice from breaking. "They took your true love from you. Just like you took Luca from me."

Her mother dropped both spoon and bowl with a clatter. "You still remember what I told you that day? You were only a tiny child—"

"I remember everything."

"For years I regretted saying anything to you. I prayed you had forgotten. When you said nothing more, I thought my prayers had been answered."

"I said nothing because you told me not to. Never." The gruel filled her with a languid tiredness, such that the words poured out in a gentle stream. It was the most she had spoken since being recaptured. "You asked me to promise and I did. But I remember."

"It was a terrible, terrible mistake to say what I did." Her mother raised a fist to her forehead. "Why am I tormented like this? What did I do wrong?"

"You did nothing wrong, don't you see? Nothing except keep Luca from me."

"Luca was wrong for you!"

"I love him." The tears had come without her realizing it. Both mother and daughter were weeping and yet fighting to keep the sobs from tearing their words apart. "Why can't you see that?"

"Not see it? Not *see* it? Daughter, the entire *world* sees you have been poisoned by this man! I have news for you, my darling. But your father has spoken and I agree. You are not well enough to hear what we have learned!"

"You are the one making me ill!"

"Enough! This has gone far enough!" Her mother leaped up from the bed, stumbling over the bowl. She picked it up and flung it onto the tray. "You will *not* speak with me that way."

"Why won't you see—"

"I see *perfectly*. I see a *child* who will not accept that her parents know what is best for her! I see a *child* who must be protected!"

"I am not a child!" Serafina said the words as if there were a breath between each one.

"Are you not?" Her mother could not pace. The room was too small. "Then rise from this bed!"

"I love—"

"Do not speak to me of love. Would an *adult* love her parents and cause them such grief? Would an *adult* lie abed all these weeks, refusing to eat until she grew ill and close to death?" The room seemed to vibrate with the force of her mother's words. "You say you are an adult? Then stand up and show me!"

But the fever was creeping up again. Serafina could feel its power overtaking her once more.

"There, you see? A child I said, because a child you are." Her mother quivered with rage. "A child who is not strong enough to hear the truth about this man she claims she loves!"

Her mother opened the cabin door, picked up the tray, and

slammed the door shut. Serafina lay still as death. The center of her chest was a hollow cavity, filled with a pain she knew would never go away.

Yet Serafina's health did improve. The fever finally abated. One day for an hour or so. Then for three, then an entire morning, and eventually for a full day. She woke sometimes in the darkness of her little cabin and could sense it in the distance. Just waiting for a chance to return.

But she could not allow it to consume her any longer. For every day that passed took her farther from her love.

Serafina would never have thought herself capable of such determination. She had always been called willful. But this was something else entirely. She saw the world through a single lens. She needed strength and cunning to return to Luca. She had to make herself both well and strong.

She ate everything that was presented to her. As soon as she was able, she began exercising upon the deck. Because her father remained ill from the ship's motion, Serafina was spared the necessity to dine with the ship's officers and the other cabin passengers. Instead, she ate in her room. Often her mother joined her. But their conversations remained strained after the argument. Even her mother's pleasure over Serafina's recovery was muted by all that was left unsaid.

Serafina wished for some way to broach the distance and share her heart. But something in her mother's dark-rimmed eyes said there was nothing to be gained from even trying.

They sailed the length of the Mediterranean. But once they passed the Gibraltar Straits, instead of aiming for America they turned north and east. Like most ships destined for a North Atlantic crossing, the ship was owned by British merchants. Serafina's mother spoke of these matters to make conversation over a meal. The American ports charged higher tariffs to all European vessels not flying the British flag. Half of this vessel's cargo was bound for England. They would stop briefly in Portsmouth, only long enough to unload Italian goods and take on a shipment of English wool. Serafina made a tight mask of her face when her mother divulged this information. But that night and several after she lay awake and planned.

Her mother had an aunt who now lived west of London, she recalled. Agatha had also been her mother's closest childhood companion—more like an older sister. Agatha's family were skilled craftsmen and woodworkers. Agatha was also Serafina's godmother, but Serafina had not seen her in more than ten years. Agatha's husband had journeyed from Italy to England and taken over a furniture business in a place called Bath. But Agatha sent her a letter and a gift every birthday. The letter was always warm and cheerful and signed "With love from your aunt Agatha." The gift was normally a beautifully bound volume of English literature. Serafina always wrote her thanks in English, taking pride in her ability with this difficult language. And she had made her way slowly through several of the books, improving her English skills.

Now Serafina clung to the vague image of a woman she had last seen as a child. Agatha was Serafina's final hope.

Serafina began taking her turns on the deck when she was certain her mother would not be around. She came to know several of the seamen by name. They would doff their caps or touch a knuckle to their forelocks as she passed, observing her movements in furtive glances. One of the midshipmen tried several times to strike up a conversation. Danny was a cheerful lad who became utterly tongue-tied whenever she approached. But Serafina had years of experience dealing with stammering young men. She pretended not to notice as he struggled to shape the simplest comment. She smiled prettily and ignored how his face blushed crimson at whatever remark she made.

From time to time she entered her parents' cabin and sat with her father. The gentleman scarcely noticed her presence. He lay supine upon his bunk and groaned softly at each motion of the ship. The ship's doctor came once while she was there, explaining that most people recovered in a week or so. As was her custom, Serafina's mother had gone topside for a breath of air while her daughter sat with her ailing husband. The doctor was pleased with his ability to administer a tincture of laudanum. This was a new remedy for seasickness, the doctor explained, the first discovered to have a positive effect. The patient was able to hold down small meals if the first bite was taken with a spoonful of the potion. Sleep came before the meal was finished.

When the doctor left, Serafina rose and cast about the cabin. She moved almost without conscious thought. She knew what she needed, had known it for some time. But it was only now, as the doctor's tincture offered her this chance, that her plan took full form.

Her father's clothes hung from two pegs on the side wall. Serafina found his coin purse in the inner pocket of his long coat. The clasp made a loud noise when she opened it. She glanced over at the bed, but her father remained motionless with his back to the room. Carefully, so as not to permit the coins to clink, she took out four of the gold ducats. There was a slight difference to the weight of the purse, but not so much as to be noticed. Or so she hoped. Serafina rolled the coins up tightly into her handkerchief, knotted the ends together, and pocketed the money. She slipped the purse back into the coat and resumed her seat. She forced her hands to remain still in her lap. She took several unsteady breaths. Only now that she had done it was she nervous. Only now did she feel a gnawing sense of guilt over her deed.

The following Sunday, Serafina accompanied her mother to the shipboard service. Her mother spoke what she called an adequate English. But today she insisted that Serafina translate. It was a subtle means of drawing her out of her internal world, and Serafina tried to object. But her mother merely chose seats on the rearmost bench and pointed her face determinedly forward.

The shipboard vicar was a young English priest returning from a sojourn in Rome. He was bright-eyed and jocular as he spoke first a few words of welcome in halting Italian. But when he started his sermon, it was in English.

The vessel was four days beyond Gibraltar and three from Portsmouth. The North Atlantic was a far cry from the gentle Mediterranean. The ship cleaved through great waves of froth and slate-gray water. The air was biting. But that was not why Serafina shivered.

"Why have you stopped translating?" her mother inquired softly.

"I—I . . ."

"Hurry, now. I want to understand what the Englishman is saying about our Lord."

But Serafina's tongue seemed unable to shape the words. In fact, the vicar's words left her speechless.

"I came to Rome a stranger in a strange land," the young man was saying. If he noticed the cold reserve with which most of the Italians received his presence, he made no sign. Instead, he seemed filled with a brisk good cheer that matched the wind-swept day. "I came seeking to learn and understand. I feared I would find only hostility, for I am an apostate in many of your eyes, an Anglican in a Catholic world, a breakaway. But I found only a Roman welcome, only offerings of peace, only a desire for harmony. And that is what I wish to speak with you about today. Harmony amidst life's impossible conflicts."

The vicar was able to balance himself against the ship's swinging motions with an ease that suggested he had lived shipboard for years, rather than spending his time in a Roman seminary. His eyes were as bright as the sky overhead, his voice bell-like in the clear air. "Our churches have spent years and years quarreling over so many issues. Take absolution, for instance. I could add my own voice to the centuries of argument. But for just this one moment, let us try and search out areas where we are in harmony.

"The Scriptures tell us that the Lord offers forgiveness to all sinners. As far from the east is to the west, so the Bible tells us. So absolution, or the forgiveness of sins, is something we all can agree upon, yes? Good! Excellent!" He beamed over the silent gathering as though they had all joined with him in joyful accord. "So what must we do in order to be forgiven, or as you say, absolved? Here again the Scriptures are clear. We must address the Lord with a contrite heart, yes? Is that not true?"

Serafina's mother turned and began to say something. But whatever her mother saw in Serafina's face caused Bettina to remain silent. She simply stared at her daughter for a moment, then turned back to face the speaker.

"A contrite heart," the vicar repeated. By now the whispered translations were being greeted with nodding heads among the Italians. Many remained stone-faced, with crossed arms and an attitude of resistance. But all were now carefully listening. And the vicar's smile grew larger. "And what else? Well, we are told that we must turn from our sins. That we must repent in our hearts. Only then, when we are contrite in our confession and earnestly seek to sin no more does our confession have meaning.

"And to whom must we confess? Why, to Jesus, of course. So what happens when we kneel in the confessional? Do we speak to the priest or do we speak with God? Jesus says clearly that we must place no man, no human authority between ourselves and our Lord. But sometimes we are weak, yes? Sometimes we need another who will aid us in seeing clearly the truth within our own heart. Sometimes we need a human friend who will help guide us first to confession and then to true repentance."

There was nothing new in what the vicar was saying. Serafina had heard similar sermons any number of times before. But this was the first time she had heard a message since Luca's visit. And it was the very first time she had heard such in English. The lesson was clear in a way that spoke directly to her aching heart. Serafina tried to argue that her love made everything all right. After all, did not the same Scriptures say God was love? And was her struggle not all about her one true love? A gust of wind blew her hair free from its braid and cast it across her face. As Serafina fitted her hair back into its comb, still it seemed as though the veil remained before her eyes.

"So my friends, I urge you to remember these points when you next enter the confessional. Fall upon your knees before God, not man. Speak with a contrite heart, addressing the Most High God. Ask for our Savior's forgiveness. Then turn away from your wrongdoing." The vicar raised his hands high over his head. "Go and sin no more."

Chapter 10

Again the nightmare awoke Falconer in the gray mist before dawn. But this day he did not mind. Not even its lingering dread could compete with the thought that greeted him upon awakening. This was the day! They would depart for England with the tide.

The gathering and stowing of cargo had taken far more time than expected. Or so Reginald Langston, Gareth's brother-in-law, had claimed. In truth Falconer suspected the doctor's pleas had convinced the merchant to be cautious and slow with his work, granting Gareth more time to recuperate. Though the patient had chafed with impatience, he could not complain. After all, the trading vessel's departure had already long been delayed on his account.

During his eleven days within the household, Falconer had entered into a pattern of sorts. He clambered downstairs to the empty kitchen, where he used flint and steel to light the cooking stove. After breakfast he retrieved a pail and implements he had claimed as his own. The aged handyman was unwell, so without being asked Falconer had taken on the old man's early day duties. He filled the pail from the well and began mopping down the coffeehouse floor. He then proceeded to clean the emporium's floors, starting at one end of the long building. In the process, he admired the fine wares gathered from right the world around, displayed upon tables and in the shop-front windows.

By the time Falconer completed the stairs leading to the second-floor offices, the house was awake and bustling. Falconer greeted the earliest clerks and shopkeepers, then slipped through the empty café into the courtyard. There he began cleaning and polishing the bay windows of the café's rear alcove.

"Ah, I thought I'd find you here."

Falconer recognized the voice. "Good morning, Mr. Langston. I trust you're well."

"Well enough, what with my friend and brother-in-law off for England today." Reginald Langston was a tall gentleman with ruddy features. His easy manner matched his strong vein of common sense. Falconer liked the man immensely. "Don't tell me you've been cleaning the floors again," Langston said.

"I am most uncomfortable with idle hands, sir."

"You and I share that trait. I have always felt happiest when I am busy, no matter how lowly the task." His face creased in worry. "I hope you have not been out on the street. Those wretched fellows hunting you only need a few seconds to do their worst."

"I have remained indoors as promised. But I deem an assault most unlikely this time of day, Mr. Langston. The street is empty. Any attack would be easily spotted."

The proprietor of Langston's Emporium had a keen gaze. "I gather you've been attacked before."

Falconer studied the glass and used the dry towel at his belt to polish off a fleck of dirt. "More often than I care to count."

A woman's voice said, "Reginald, the merchant is ready for you to count the coffee sacks."

"Have one of the clerks see to it, would you, my dear?"

"If you wish." Lillian Langston was well into middle age yet retained an astonishing beauty. "Mr. Falconer, I know our old groundsman is most grateful for your assistance."

"Thank you, and a very good morning, ma'am."

"Have you spoken with him yet?" she asked her husband.

"I was about to, when you arrived."

"Please do continue then."

"Very well. Mr. Falconer, I'm a plainspoken man, sir. My wife and I share Gareth's impression of you."

"And Hannah's," Lillian Langston added.

"And the child's. Of course." A shadow crossed his features. "How I shall bear seeing her sail away this very day is beyond me."

Lillian Langston slipped her hand through her husband's arm. "Let us remain upon the subject at hand, my dearest."

"You are right, of course. Mr. Falconer, I have desperate need of good men. It would be an honor to have you join us when your duties are completed."

Falconer looked from one shining face to the other. "Sir . . . I hardly know what to say."

"Say nothing, or say yes." Lillian Langston was an active member of the emporium's management and could draw a smile from the grouchiest clerk or customer. "We know you must complete your mission. We are speaking of afterwards."

Falconer found it necessary to clear his throat. "You have opened your home to me, a complete stranger. And now this . . . I am at a loss."

Reginald turned formal in the face of Falconer's gratitude. "I shall supply you with a letter of introduction. Show it to any of our agents or ship's officers. Whatever you need, it will be granted."

Lillian Langston reached over and patted Falconer's arm. "And when you are ready, return and join us."

The farewells were difficult for Gareth Powers, Falconer could tell. Not because of any sorrow he might have felt over separation from family and friends. Rather because his illness continued to leave him drained. Falconer knew the man was suffering. But he had also seen in the man's eyes a silent appeal for Falconer to say nothing. So Falconer quietly added his strength to his new employer and friend.

Gareth tended to speak very little these days. He measured out every word as though wondering whether it was worth the energy required to form it. Falconer had no idea whether it was right for the man to journey across the Atlantic. He also knew any advice he might offer would be tainted by his own fierce desire to further his quest. So he remained silent and helped Gareth with whatever the man sought to do. Their communication sharpened to where Falconer could often gauge the man's need before he even lifted a hand, much less spoke.

And Falconer remained utterly enchanted by tiny Hannah.

Falconer dressed carefully in his new traveling clothes. The Langstons had insisted he take a pair of fine coats and matching dark trousers from the Emporium's best stock. He packed his new valise with his remaining articles and carried it down to the courtyard. After stowing the final packets into the carriage, he returned to the floor above his own bedroom and knocked on the young girl's open door. "I see that you are ready."

"I have been ready since yesterday. I was awake before you this morning." She lay on the bed as ordered, dressed in a pearl-gray traveling frock. The kitten was asleep on her hip, a tiny bundle of golden fur. "Can I get up now?"

In reply, Falconer sat upon the bed. "I want to ask a favor."

"Of me?"

"None other. I have never had experience with young ladies, you see. I do not know how to speak with them. So I would like to address you as I would an adult."

Hannah's eyes went round with surprise.

"In return," he continued, "I ask that you be utterly honest with me. A very long voyage awaits us. And I am concerned about your father's health. There, you see, I am trusting you with something that I should only share with an adult."

"He's very sick. But he misses Mama terribly."

"I agree with you on both counts. What I need to know from you is, how are *you* feeling? We have a busy and trying day ahead, with many new experiences. If you come downstairs on your own, will you be strong for all we face? Or should I carry you?"

She studied his face very intently. "I suppose I should be carried."

"I think that is wise."

"But I shall be so ashamed."

"I can understand that. If I were in your position I would feel exactly the same."

Her face had the translucent quality of fragile porcelain. "Most people would tell me there's no reason to be embarrassed."

"I imagine they would."

"I think I shall like talking with you like an adult. Can I ask you questions in return?"

"If you wish."

"Will you answer me the same way?"

He hesitated. "To be truthful, I rarely speak of myself to anyone."

"Will you speak to me?"

He took his time responding. "I shall try."

She pointed at the scar on his face. "How did you get that?"

Falconer found himself unable to meet her gaze any longer. He slipped his hand into his pocket and extracted a length of pink ribbon he had purchased in the emporium. He prodded the kitten with one finger. "Wake up, little beast."

"Does that mean you won't answer me?"

Falconer watched the kitten yawn and stretch luxuriously. It greeted him with a rusty little meow and tried to nestle against his hand. "It was a pike."

"What is that?"

"A pike is a weapon. Like a spear, but with a shorter handle. It has both a pointed end and a hook. So an attacker can gouge and then rip." With practiced skill he tied the ribbon into a little noose. "I shouldn't be speaking of this to you."

"Did it hurt?"

"At the time I was rather too busy to notice. But afterwards it burned like someone had doused my face with fire." He slipped the ribbon over the kitten's head, fitted it behind its ears, and tightened it slightly. Then he tied an additional knot so the noose could not constrict any further.

"Who did it to you?"

He continued to avoid her gaze as he tied the ribbon's other end to her wrist. "One of my own men. It happened during a dreadful storm. There was . . . trouble."

"Is that why you have bad dreams?"

He lifted his eyes to look at her. "How did you know about those?"

"I hear you." She pointed with the hand now attached to the kitten at the floor by her bed. "At night."

He started to deny it. But could not. "The days before I came to ask God for help and forgiveness were very bad. I dream about them sometimes."

Falconer sat and waited, dreading the next question. How this tiny wisp of a child could leave him stripped bare and defenseless was a mystery. But he knew that whatever she asked, he would answer.

Yet Hannah's response was merely to raise her arms up and say, "I'm ready for you to carry me now."

A thunderhead loomed on the eastern horizon by the time the farewells were done. Falconer sniffed the air and detected the faint tendrils of a rising wind. Cat's-paws, the sailors called such faint gusts. Landlubbers tended to fear storms. But a good sailor knew the real question was the wind's thrust. And these cat's-paws were drawn from the proper quarter. They could clear land by nightfall if the captain was ready to bear sail.

But the farewells lingered still. Falconer called a warning, "We must be off."

The cook was the last to release little Hannah and back herself from the carriage. "You be well, my heart. And remember your old Mavis from time to time."

"I miss you already," the child replied, wiping at tears.

"Oh my darling lass, don't you go weeping on me. My heart is already fit to burst." The cook turned from the child and used the apron's corner to dry her eyes. Then she gripped Falconer's hand with both of hers. "If ever I was wrong about a man, it was you, good sir."

The lady smelled of dough and vanilla and had arms as strong as old iron. "I shall miss your laughter and your wisdom, ma'am."

"Take good care of these two, promise me that."

"With my life."

"Then they go in safety." She patted his face, though it was doubtful she managed to see him clearly. "Of that I have no doubt."

The last to bid him farewell was Mrs. Lillian Langston, who offered her hand and the words, "I shall look forward with great anticipation to your return, sir."

"Ma'am, you must understand, I cannot promise anything. But if it is in my power, I could think of nothing finer than to accept your husband's offer."

"My husband is as excellent a judge of men as ever I have known. He eagerly awaits the day you shall work alongside him." She stepped closer. "A word of advice. At the first sign of trouble, seek out his agents. The list in your pocket may prove a great shield against danger of any kind. I know from first-hand experience that his reach is great and his allies loyal."

Falconer bowed formally over the hand. "I feel far stronger now than even a few moments before, ma'am."

"Go with God, John Falconer."

The kitten did not much appreciate its new leash, silken or not. In fact, it cried loud enough to be heard over the rattling clamor of a carriage making its way through crowded streets. But no one paid it much mind. Hannah watched idly from her corner of the carriage as the little animal struggled to push the noose back over its ears. But clearly the farewells had wearied the child, for soon enough she appeared to drift away.

Gareth Powers slumped beside her in the other corner and winced over the worst of the bumps. Reginald Langston accompanied them, observing his brother-in-law with silent alarm. Several times he started to speak, yet restrained himself until they passed through the scarred stone gates marking the harbor entrance. The carriage slowed there, joining a long line of coaches and supply wagons moving toward the quays.

Gareth opened his eyes then and glanced out the side window. "Finally," he murmured. "Thank the dear Lord above. Finally."

Reginald could hold himself back no longer. "Brother, are you certain—"

Gareth stayed him with an upraised hand. "Don't. I beg you. I can't spare the energy for further argument."

Reginald sighed and shook his head.

Gareth turned from his inspection of the schooner. "If staying in bed was the answer, don't you think I would be healed by now?"

"I do worry about you, Gareth, you know."

"And I am forever grateful for your kind support." Gareth turned back to the three masts thrust into an overcast sky. He said to himself and the approaching storm, "I long for my dear wife with a hunger that clenches my very soul."

"I miss Mama too," Hannah said softly. "Awfully much."

"I did not realize you were awake, my sweet child."

"I'm so very tired of sleeping." She smiled. "Does that sound silly?"

"Quite the opposite. I could not have said it better myself."

Reginald turned to Falconer and asked, "What say you to this voyage and their state of health?"

"I would rather not speak to it, sir."

"And why not, pray tell? Come, my man. I value your opinion."

"I try to have none," Falconer replied simply. "I am too constrained by my own desires and needs. Any outlook I offer would be marked. If they say go, I am ready. But I do not wish to say more, for the words could well be an untruth fueled by my own strong need."

Reginald nodded slowly. "The more you speak, sir, the more I urge you to return and accept my offer."

Gareth turned his head from the window to ask, "What offer is that, pray tell?"

"I shall let Falconer tell you when he is ready."

The carriage moved farther into the harbor's tumult and halted. The driver leaped down, approached the side window, and said to Reginald, "Looks like this is as close as we can come, sir. The wagons at quayside are packed up tight as eels in jelly."

"Can you walk from here?" Reginald asked his brother-in-law.

"If I must."

But Falconer said, "Stay as you are."

Both Reginald and Gareth noted the change in his tone. "What is it?"

Falconer did not reply. Instead, he opened the carriage door and stepped lightly onto the high carriage wheel. Carefully he surveyed the crowd.

"Falconer?"

"A moment." There was nothing to be seen. Nothing, that is, that he could identify. But he smelled trouble. It was a knack born upon long experience, a hunter's ability to read signs and follow his intuition. There were moments like now when he could not say what troubled him. But danger's foul odor drifted in the rising wind.

There. To his right, where the crowds were thickest, a man with a battered tricorn hat. He was using a wagon wheel as a ladder and was scouting the perimeter—as Falconer himself was doing. Watching for them. Falconer was sure of it.

There again. Another man, similarly dressed in dusty hat and road-worn cloak, though the day was stifling hot. This one stood upon a lamppost's base and craned over the throngs. As he did so, his cloak blew back, revealing a musket.

Falconer slipped back inside the carriage. "Go shipboard," he told Reginald. "Walk with the driver. Find two strong and trusted seamen. No officers. Men who know their way around a fight."

"What is it?" Gareth demanded.

Falconer stayed him with an upraised hand. To Reginald he continued, "I want you to remain shipboard. Let the driver lead them here. Do you travel armed?"

Reginald's eyes had widened. "Don't be absurd! We're in the harbor of our nation's capital!"

The driver was obviously of a different view. He said through the carriage door, "I always carry a pistol, sir."

Falconer reached under his seat and came up with his sheathed sword. "Keep it at the ready."

Reginald started to object. "But—"

Falconer shifted slightly to look directly into his face. It was a habit he had learned when commanding a vessel. All he needed was to reveal a trace of the intensity, a hint of the experience behind his words. Whatever Reginald saw there in his face was enough to silence the man, as swift as a hand to his mouth. "Hurry," Falconer said.

Reginald clambered down from the coach. He cast a final glance back at Falconer.

"Best we do as the man says, Mr. Reginald, sir," the driver urged.

Reginald hastened with the driver toward the quayside. Falconer watched until they were lost in the press of men and wagons and animals. He checked carefully from both windows, then turned back to the two remaining passengers. Gareth was observing him with full alertness now, showing the steady calm of one who had been under fire before.

Hannah, however, had scrunched up tight against the seat's

opposite end. Falconer sat next to her, checked carefully out the window, then took one of her little hands in his. "Do you recall our conversation this morning?"

Slowly she nodded.

"I want you to do exactly as I say, and without either hesitation or fear." He spoke with a calm cadence, gently pressing his words through the child's evident alarm. "I will protect you. You must remember that at all times."

"Can I be a little bit afraid?"

"Of course. Everyone feels some fear."

"Do you?"

"Yes, I . . ." Falconer checked himself at the sound of shrill piping. He knew the sound very well. The bosun's roar was loud enough to dim the harbor's racket. "Master coming aboard!"

Not long now. Falconer returned his attention to the young girl. "Everyone is afraid at times, of something. The key is to use the fear."

"H-how?"

He glanced across the carriage. "Your father knows."

Gareth met Falconer's eye before replying, "What does not destroy you makes you stronger."

"Like this ailment?" Her voice was tiny but clear.

"Just so." He coughed softly. "When you are afraid, let honesty help you identify the true reason. Use the energy to heighten your senses. Use the peak of your abilities to forge ahead. Don't freeze, don't panic. That's the key."

"I see I am right," Falconer told Gareth, "to address the child as I would an adult."

"In many respects she is an adult already," Gareth confirmed. "Her body has merely not caught up with her mind and her spirit."

The girl's next question was cut off by the arrival of two sailors. One was a muscled brute with the eyes of a heartless fighter. The other was smaller and more cautious, standing a half pace back and scouting constantly. The muscled man knuckled his forehead and said to Falconer, "Captain ordered us to help you board, sir."

"Your name, sailor?"

"Connor, sir. This here's MacAughley."

"I'm Falconer." He opened the door but did not step down. Instead, he fished in his pocket and drew out two gold half sovereigns. "I believe in paying well. There's half a crown for the each of you when we arrive on board. Good Georgie gold. Now then. You've both seen some close-quarters work?"

"Aye, sir." The muscled sailor seemed to find grim humor in such a conversation with a man dressed in landlubber's clothes. "That we have."

"Here's how I want to play this. Connor, you're to give the gentleman here a hand. His name is Powers. He's been tested by the croup. Don't let him tell you he's strong enough to make it on his own. I aim for us to move at boarding speed. Is that clear?"

"Aye, sir. Clear enough."

"What about me, sir?" MacAughley asked.

"I want you to drift away. See who might be after doing us harm. If you can, capture them. But above all don't let them injure either of these here." He turned to the two passengers. "Ready?"

"Yes." Gareth replied for them both while Hannah gave a careful nod.

Falconer motioned Gareth forward. As Gareth descended to the cobblestones, Falconer unsheathed his sword. He despised how the sight of steel drew blanched fright from the child. "Remember what I said," he told Hannah. "I will not let anyone harm you or your father. Do you trust me?"

She responded with a shiver of a nod. Her eyes did not leave the naked blade.

Falconer stuffed the scabbard into his belt. He gripped the sword's hilt with his right hand, then scooped up the child with his left. "One hand tight to my neck, now. Hold your knees high as you can when I run. And keep a firm grip on the kitten."

As he slipped through the doorway, a splinter of wood was

blasted from the doorframe above his head. He heard gunfire and smelled the sudden cloud of sulfur. The attacker was very close indeed.

Screams arose from the surrounding crowd. People milled and shoved in every direction, uncertain from which quarter the danger arose. Falconer tumbled to the ground, his body crouched over the child. Hannah did exactly as ordered, gripping him tightly with one arm and both legs. He rose swiftly, the child clinging to him like a well-trained whelp.

"Together now! Boarding speed!"

Two more shots rang through the sudden stillness. They sounded like the cough of a great hoarse beast, one against whom Falconer had fought far too often.

The market erupted into panic-stricken bedlam. Connor scooped up Gareth Powers with one arm and with his other swept out a long, curved blade.

"Give them a shout and let them know we're on the attack!" Falconer ordered.

With Gareth between them, Falconer and Connor gave a furious roar and surged forward. They waved the blades over their heads as they ran. Animals and people shied away in startled panic, shrieking in unison and parting before them. All but one man, who shoved his way forward against the surge and tried to take aim with a long-barreled musket.

But Falconer did not seek to evade, as expected. Instead he ducked and raced straight at the shooter, roaring all the louder. Before the attacker could adjust his aim, Falconer drove his blade up sharp against the barrel. It slid the length of metal with a shrill screech. Falconer used the handguard to punch the rifle straight upward. The man's shot hit nothing but cloud. Falconer's charge was relentless. He used the pommel to sweep the musket out of the man's grasp, then clouted the man's forehead. The attacker blinked once and went down. All the while Hannah clung to him, making nary a sound.

Falconer stumbled over the man's legs and might have fallen had Gareth not reached over and kept him upright. Together the four of them pounded along the quayside and up the gangplank and into the safety of the ship.

As Falconer deposited the child into the arms of a wide-eyed officer, he said, "Please tell me you are all right."

"I'm fine." She held to a breathless calm. "You told me I would be, and I am."

"What a fine, brave girl you are."

"I'm not. I'm sick and I'm scared and I'm little." She hugged her kitten under her chin.

"You are brave and more. You make me proud to call you friend." In a sudden impulse he reached forward and kissed her forehead.

Falconer turned to Gareth. "All right, sir?"

"Thanks to you."

Falconer started to tell him it was not that way at all. That in truth he had brought danger upon all their heads. But Reginald chose that moment to thrust his way forward, followed by a burly man wearing a captain's pips upon his shoulders.

"What on earth was that all about?" the captain demanded.

"I aim to determine just that," Falconer told him. "In the meantime, I'd be grateful if you could please send men for our cases." He turned to Connor. "Let's go find your mate."

"Aye, sir."

Together they hurried back down the ramp. All their ship-mates were crowded along the foredeck and ship's railings. They pushed their way through the throng, back to where MacAughley stood over a man seated upon the cobblestones. "There was two others that I saw," MacAughley reported, "but soon as they spotted me, they scarpered."

"This one will do." Falconer crouched down.

The attacker was holding his forehead where Falconer had clouted him. Falconer scraped the steel of his blade across the cobblestones between them. It was enough to bring the attacker to full alert. "Listen carefully. You just heard the man. Your mates have disappeared. You're all alone. You have two choices. I hope you're hearing me, because we don't have time for lies or repetition. How many choices do you have?"

The man glanced about, seeking refuge.

Falconer raised his sword, as though making to clout him once more. "Answer me!"

"Two!" The man shied away, or tried to, but Connor was holding him on one side now and MacAughley on the other. "Two choices!"

"That's better. The first choice is to have these two seamen hustle you on board. We're headed east on the tide, but I suppose you know that."

"You can't! I got rights, I do!"

"Rights." Falconer scraped the sword's blade a second time, scarring the stones. "Of course you have rights. You have the right to a trial at sea, before a captain's tribunal. You have the right to be found guilty of attacking innocent passengers. You have the right to hang from the yardarms until dead."

"No! I didn't—"

"Then your body will be sewed into a sailcloth sack with a cannon shot for company. And you'll be dropped overboard, to sink and sink and finally rest upon the black ocean floor."

The man was sweating mightily. He started to protest, but suddenly a flicker of recognition sparked in his eyes. "You-you're him!"

"What's that?"

"Him! The man they's hunting. The murderer from Trinidad!"

Falconer rocked back on his heels, dumbfounded.

Connor noted Falconer's concern. "All right, sir?"

Falconer forced his mind to work. The man's response was genuine enough, he was certain of that. Which could only mean one thing. Falconer had not been the target. If he had been, they would have known whom to go for.

Which meant they were after Gareth.

Falconer moved in close. The man tried to flinch away. "You knew to go after the man with me. That much is clear. Did you even know his name?" When the man hesitated, Falconer thumped him with his open hand, but not hard. "Speak!"

"Powers, they said. A pamphleteer."

"Here's your second choice, then. Answer my questions, and swiftly now. Give me what I need and we'll set you free."

Connor protested, "Sir!"

The attacker glanced at the muscled sailor holding him by his shoulders, then turned back to Falconer. "Straight up, you'll let me go?"

"Give me what I seek," Falconer repeated. "Who sent you?"

"Don't have a clue. Honest, they didn't tell me nothing but go after the pamphleteer Powers."

"How did you know who that was?"

"Been sitting outside the Emporium for weeks, I have." The man's eyes gleamed now with frantic hope. His words tumbled out. "The man's been seen walkin' a time or two. But he's always been in a crowd. And he's never been out for very long. So we heard 'bout the ship's sailing and we knew it was time. Now or never, that's what they told me."

"Who told you that?"

"Them who hired me. The two that got away."

"Describe them."

"Mates, in a matter of speaking. Know them from the taverns around these parts. Done a bit of this and that."

"They must have told you who it was that hired you."

"A banker. That's all I know."

Falconer was rocked back a second time. "What did you say?"

"A banker, I know that for a fact." The words pressed out faster still. "Somebody who wants Powers dead and gone. Wants it bad enough to pay us good silver for the job well done."

"I'll give you well done," Connor roared, cuffing the man.

"Hold there," Falconer ordered. He said to the attacker, "Describe the banker."

"Couldn't do that. Never seen him, have I."

"They must have told you something."

"A narrow man, they said that much. A British gent. Older." The man turned to whining. "I done what you said. That's all I know, I swear. I was just hired to do a proper job on the man."

Falconer rose to his feet, ignoring the multitude clustered about him. Half answers and mysteries pressed in from every side. "Let him go."

"But sir, the captain . . ."

"Release him. I'll speak with your captain."

As soon as Connor's hands unclenched, the man wasted no time. He leaped through the throng and disappeared.

In the distance the bosun's whistle piped the men aloft. "Let's be off," Falconer said, "else our ship won't make the tide."

Chapter 11

Serafina's vessel slowly entered Portsmouth harbor. The wind was strong against them, and the port's entryway was lined with ships from every corner of the globe. There was no clearance for the harbormaster to safely maneuver them under sail. So the ship's two longboats were lowered and joined by another from the port. The oarsmen heaved so hard their groans could be heard from the foredeck. Serafina was there, accompanied by Danny, the young midshipman. The wind whistled through the rigging and clutched at Serafina's hair, tearing locks free from her head scarf.

"A cold, hard day for late July," Danny said, stumbling only slightly as he spoke. "Wouldn't you agree, Miss Gavi?"

"It feels like winter."

"Aye, that's Portsmouth for you." The crimson rose from his collar. "Perhaps as you've been ill, you'd care for my cloak?"

"No thank you, signore."

He fumbled slightly over her refusal, then went on, "As I was saying, the weather—"

"Please to excuse me, sir." Serafina turned away from the young officer. "My father is coming."

"Of course, of course." He cast a nervous bow and backed away, his face a bright scarlet. Two seamen snickered from the rigging.

Serafina's father made it up the foredeck stairs by leaning heavily upon his wife's arm. "Ah, you are better as well, I see."

"Hello, Father." Strange how merely saying those two words left her choking down a vast sob.

"It is good to leave that prison of a cabin behind, wouldn't you agree?"

"Oh yes."

"The prospect of leaving harbor tomorrow for the open sea fills me with dread, I don't mind telling you."

Her mother offered, "The doctor assures us the ailment will soon pass."

"As he has said every day since we left Venice. How a merchant of our water-borne city could be laid so low by the open seas is a mystery." He grimaced and clutched the side railing as the ship swayed slightly. "Perhaps you should lead me back downstairs, my dear."

"Of course. Serafina, would you please aid us?"

She moved up close to her father's other side. She had gained much strength over the past several days. Her legs trembled slightly as she took some of her father's weight, but it was not from physical weakness. This was the first time she had been this close to her beloved father since Luca's visit. She wrapped one arm around his back, touching her mother's arm in the process. Her father let one arm rest upon her shoulder. As they maneuvered slowly down the foredeck stairs, he said quietly, "I have missed you, Serafina."

"And I you." This time the tears escaped, one from each eye.

"You are genuinely better now, I trust."

Her mind cast upon what the morrow held, and she found herself unable to respond. She released her father as they entered the narrow passage leading to the cabins. She trailed along behind her parents as they reentered their room. Her father groaned mightily as the ship rocked back and forth, buffeted by the squall. He lowered himself into the bunk. "Perhaps you should ask the doctor to bring a bit more of his remedy."

"No, my dear, we can use it only when truly needed. We shall be resting at anchor in but a few minutes."

"You have no idea how long the minutes stretch," her father

said. "Or how endless are the hours."

But I do. The thought was so clear Serafina feared for a moment that she had spoken them aloud. But her mother remained intent upon settling the blankets upon her father in his bunk. Serafina quietly slipped from the room.

She went back on deck and chose the railing that looked out over the gray waters to where a rain line swept steadily toward them. The only other person on that side of the deck was the English vicar, who nodded affably in her direction but did not speak. Serafina gave a quick curtsy and turned her face away. She had spent the past three nights arguing with herself over his sermon. Seeing him here only brought up the conflict anew.

Go and sin no more, the pastor had said. Serafina resisted a sudden urge to turn back and snap at him that his words meant less than nothing. She had sinned. Yes. But she did not feel contrite. How could she? She had been *forced* to sin. Serafina leaned upon the railing and raised her face to the first drops of rain. It would do no good to argue with the vicar. What could such a man as that possibly know about love?

Her father came to Serafina's cabin the next morning. The ship had lain quietly at anchor since the previous afternoon, but Serafina had slept little. Last night the ship's timbers had creaked and the wind had continued to whistle through the cracks and the riggings. Twice the bosun's whistle had signaled the change of watches. But mostly she had listened to her own heartbeat and to her father's snores. The cabin walls were not very thick. That morning she had heard the ship come awake around her. She had also heard her parents talking and knew what her father was going to say to her long before he arrived at her door.

"Good morning, daughter." There was color to his features and a clearer light to his gaze. "I hope you slept well."

"Thank you, Father. You are looking better."

"Your mother was right not to let me have more of the potion. Last night was the first time since Venice that I was not troubled by the most dreadful dreams." He wore a suit of somber gray, with a starched collar held in place by a simple gold stickpin. "Did you have a nice breakfast?"

"Tea and porridge. The same as every morning." Cabin passengers were served on deck in decent weather and at anchor. Many had taken their morning meal at the railings, where they had studied the city and planned their one-day excursion into Portsmouth. The ship was scheduled to sail with the predawn tide, and everyone had to return before sunset.

"I would not know, as this is the first morning I managed to eat more than dried biscuit. I finished three bowls and am still ravenous." He pulled his vest tight across his somewhat smaller waist and announced, "Your mother wishes me to ask you if things are settled now."

Serafina knew all about this, for she had heard every word of their discussion. She knew the reason she had not been invited to join them for breakfast was because their debate had continued right through the meal. Her parents were going ashore. Her father wanted Serafina to join them. Her mother did not. Her mother had tried to explain that things were not better, as her father wanted to believe. But her father, ever the conciliator, hoped for peace and harmony once more within their little family.

"You are looking much better than . . . before," her father continued.

"I am stronger now, thank you."

"But that is not what I asked."

Serafina examined her father carefully. He was a very good man. Gentle in demeanor, strong in character. "You have always been so very good to me," she said and felt the lump grow once more in her throat.

"My dear sweet child." He came over and settled onto the cabin's tiny stool. "This whole wretched ordeal has been such a trial."

She nodded, loving him deeply. "It has."

"I hope you realize that everything we did was out of love and concern." He patted her knee. "I knew your mother was wrong in her thinking this morning. It is so heartening to know the miserable affair is behind us now."

Slowly Serafina shook her head. "I fear you misunderstand me, Father."

"But you said—"

"I do love you. And I wish things were different. Truly I do. But my heart has been given to Luca. I am his betrothed."

Her father rose to his feet so swiftly the stool clattered upon the planking. "I forbid it!"

"That changes nothing."

"But . . . but I am your father!"

"And Luca is my beloved." Serafina repeated silently, over and over, the words she had clung to as she had waited for his return. *I will remain calm.* "If only you could accept—"

"Outrage!" Her father's weakened state was revealed in the mottled complexion that spread up from his collar. "Scandal!"

"Only because you and mother make it so."

"You will remain in your cabin until we return, do you hear me?" His hand fumbled for the door lock. "You are forbidden to leave this chamber! And tomorrow you and I shall have words. Oh yes. There is news which I deem you are now well enough to hear!"

Serafina bowed her head and held herself against the slamming of the door. She listened to the strident tones with which he reported to her mother. She waited as their angry footsteps retreated down the passageway and out on deck. She sighed at the pressure of her swollen and aching heart. Then she stepped onto the floor. She balanced her inkstand and quill and sheets of parchment upon her small travel chest. And she began to write. The letter was quite brief, but it required a long time to complete. Over and over she had to stop and wait for her composure to return so that she could see the words take shape and write them with a steady hand.

Chapter 12

Serafina marveled at her own ability to cope. As she began her journey before dawn, swirling emotions rocked her being with fearful force. But her voice remained clear, and she saw her way calmly through each step of the journey.

From the Portsmouth dock where the longboat had deposited her, Serafina made her way to the inn. There she changed one of her remaining ducats for a handful of silver. She was certain the innkeeper cheated her and demanded that he rethink the first offer he made, though the number of crowns and shillings meant nothing to her. But she found she had been correct, for the innkeeper flushed and added a half-dozen more coins to the pile, then threw in a breakfast of cold stew and sweet tea.

Over her meal she allowed the cowl of her cloak to fall back, but then she noticed several of the men examining her in a speculative fashion. She replaced her hood and kept it close around her face throughout the remainder of the day.

She took the post coach to London because all the swift public carriages were headed that direction. The journey was good and bad, depending upon the stretch of road. Some segments were so smooth the carriage might as well have been traveling upon calm seas. And indeed that was what Serafina dreamed when she fell asleep. She was very tired after the previous few nights. She had thought she might just doze off for a moment, but she fell into such a deep sleep she could not awaken herself, or so it felt. She dreamed she was aboard a ship. Only this was not the vessel that had carried them from Venice. This one rocked back and forth as it sped away from the other ship, the one that carried her mother and father out to where it melted into the distance. As she watched the ship disappear, she was struck by a certainty that she had made a terrible mistake.

Serafina woke to a hollow feeling in the center of her being. She stared out the open window and whispered the name of her beloved. Over and over, like a litany, to remind herself why she had taken this course. *Luca*.

In order to keep from falling asleep again, she joined in conversation with the woman seated across from her. She learned that there was a new train service running from London to Bristol, and one of the stops was Bath. Serafina had heard of trains but never seen one. Traders in her father's circle spoke of steam eventually being used to power ships, though few believed it was possible. She did not know how she felt about riding upon a train. But she knew she wanted this journey to end as swiftly as possible. She needed to arrive in Bath and find Aunt Agatha and obtain the necessary funds to travel back to Venice. Perhaps Agatha would travel with her. Serafina brightened at the prospect of a companion.

But her heart ached so. Added to the burden of loneliness was the image of what her parents would endure when they discovered she was no longer aboard the ship. And what if the vessel turned around? What if it returned to Portsmouth? No, her conversations with the young midshipman had confirmed this was impossible. Modern trading vessels held to a tight time schedule. No, the ship would not turn back, no matter how her parents pleaded. Serafina wiped away a tear at the thought of all the distress she was causing.

The coach journey to London took six hours. All the other passengers seemed pleased with the time, but Serafina arrived feeling hot and miserable. The ship's motions had never bothered her, but the jerky carriage ride and the dust through the open windows left her queasy. Besides which, two of the men insisted upon lighting long clay pipes, adding a thick tobacco stench to the air.

The coach made two stops in London before halting at a tall stone edifice. Over the front portals was inscribed "The Royal London to Bristol Rail Offices and Coach Lines." Serafina was very glad to step down.

The crowds here were unlike anything she had ever seen. Every inch of road and walkway was packed. The men, all bearded, wore long dark coats and rounded hats. Their skin was very pale, as though they never saw the sun. The women dressed exactly the opposite of the men, their clothing reflecting every color of the rainbow and shimmering in the July afternoon. Her own dark cloak was very drab and hot, but she decided not to cast it aside. She was, after all, alone in a strange and faraway land.

Serafina dodged around carriages and peddlers' wagons and street urchins. She made her way up the central stairs. At the top, to one side of the main portals, was a small office marked "Sailings." She changed course and went inside.

The three men behind the counter were all busy with other customers. Serafina waited until one became free. The chamber was cramped and airless and full of tobacco smoke. She could feel her queasiness returning, but she desperately wanted to learn about transport back to Italy.

The gentleman behind the counter wore a striped vest and had ink stains encircling his shirt cuffs. He gave her a narrow-eyed inspection, trying to peer into her hood's shadows. "Yes?"

"P-please, I am seeking passage to Venice."

He tilted his head this way and that, clearly displeased with the mysterious way she hid herself. "Venice, as in Italy?"

"Yes."

"Out of our territory, that is." He sniffed his disapproval. "Have to take that up across town. Next."

But she did not want to make her way across London, spending more of her swiftly vanishing coins, and risk getting very lost in the process. Reluctantly, she raised her hands and slipped the hood back.

The clerk's eyes rounded. A murmur rose from other men within the room's confines. Serafina kept her gaze intent upon the man on the counter's opposite side. "I must go to Bath on the next train, sir. I do not have time to go anywhere else. Please, you can help me?"

The man fumbled for something beneath the counter top without taking his eyes from her. He came up with a leather-bound ledger, which he flipped open. He scanned page after page, lifting his eyes now and then. "You're Italian, are you?"

"Yes, sir. From Venice." Serafina knew everyone was watching her now. She endured the stares and the murmurs because she had to. "I just want to go home."

For some reason, saying that one word left her choking down tears. *Home.* Her throat constricted so tightly she could scarcely draw breath.

The clerk was neither young nor old. His beard was dark with a few strands of gray around the ears. Yet he patted her hand like a favorite uncle. "There, there," he said.

The gift of sympathy was too much to bear. She could feel the tears coursing down her cheek. "Forgive me, sir. I am so tired."

The clerk motioned at someone behind her. "You there, stand up, why don't you, and offer the lady a stool. Now sit yourself down, miss. Would you care for something? A cup of tea, perhaps?"

"Thank you, no. I just want—"

"Venice. Yes, well, Venice is not as easy as one might wish." His ink-stained finger traced its way down the page. "There's two lines plying the Amalfi Coast, don't you know. And another makes regular stops down Genoa way. But Venice, now, that means sailing right 'round the boot and up. . . . Here we are. Venice, Italy. There's a sailing set for the third of October."

"But—but that is months away!"

"Aye, well, you could sail to Genoa, like I said, and coach across. That's possible, I suppose?"

"Yes, of course." One coach to Bologna and another to

Venice. She shuddered at the thought of such travel alone and unaccompanied. "Please, how much is a ticket?"

"Well, now. That depends. You'd want a cabin, I suppose. And it's for you and . . ."

"My . . . aunt."

"The two of you, a private cabin . . ." He turned his page, then dipped his quill and made rapid calculations on a bit of scratch paper. "Thirty-two pounds and sixpence."

"Please, sir, you will write down this sum? And where I must go for the passage?"

"Aye, that I will, miss. With pleasure." He wrote in a practiced hand, then dusted the paper and handed it over. "But it's Bath you're after today, is it?"

"Yes, my aunt, you see, she lives near there."

He pulled out a steel vest watch and flipped open the case. "Then you'll need to make haste, miss. There's a train outbound in less than an hour, and not another until this time tomorrow."

She leaped to her feet. "Where do I go?"

"Wait, now. I can write you up a ticket—you'll be needing that. Just you, is it?"

"Yes, sir. Oh, thank you." She fished out her handful of remaining coins. "Please, you will tell me what it costs?"

He cocked his head to one side and smiled. "New to these shores, are you?"

"Yes, I just arrived this morning at Portsmouth."

"Portsmouth? Today?"

"Yes, sir. And took the coach up. P-postal, I think they said."

"Isn't that an astonishment." He took far too long selecting the coins from her hand. "Inbound by sailing ship this morning, up by coach, now the train to Bath. No wonder you're tired. Have you eaten?"

"No, but sir, the train—"

"We'll be certain you make the train." He turned to a youth lingering in the back of the office area. He flipped the lad a coin and said, "Have Maggie do up a bit of roast and buttered bread and a traveling pot of tea. And right smart too."

The lad scampered.

"Oh, sir, I can't thank you—"

"None of that, now." The man flushed slightly. As he scribbled into a form book, he asked, "Where'd you learn your English?"

"Venice, sir. At school."

"Never could get my mouth around the sounds of other tongues myself." He eyed her speculatively. "Your folks don't have a worry over letting you wander about on your own?"

"Oh yes." The thought renewed the burning to her eyes. "They are so very worried."

"There, now. Shouldn't have said a thing. None of my affair." He tore the page from his book and handed it over. "Here you are. London to Bath."

"Thank you," she said, choking slightly on the sorrow and gratitude both. "You are most kind."

"Pleasure, miss. Harry!"

"Here, sir." The youth arrived back, breathless and bearing a small hamper.

"Good lad." He nodded at Serafina. "See her ladyship makes the proper car, will you?"

"Yes, sir. This way, miss."

Serafina reached across the counter and took hold of the man's hand with both of hers. "You are a very, very good man."

"We mustn't give your young man a reason to be jealous." He smiled through his embarrassment. "Pretty lass like you must have a suitor."

"Yes, sir. It is why I rush as I do."

"What's the gentleman's name, then?"

"Luca, sir. His name is Luca."

"And don't you have a nice glow about you when you say his name. I hope he realizes how lucky he is." He leaned back. "Have a pleasant journey home, miss."

Only when she turned from the counter did Serafina realize the entire office was still watching her in silence. The men all doffed their hats as she passed. She held herself very erect and kept her eyes fastened upon the door. There she turned back and ignored all the gazes save one. "Again, sir. From the bottom of my heart. Thank you."

Then she pulled the hood back over her hair and face. And she followed the young man along the next step of her journey.

Toward Luca.

The train was even less comfortable than the coach. The car jerked and rattled horribly. The rough passages were so treacherous she spilled more of the tea than she drank. But Serafina ate and drank her way through every smooth stretch, for the meal seemed to quiet her stomach, or perhaps it was just the image of a friendly face helping her onward.

The late afternoon sun angled through the windows, making the car stiflingly hot. The windows had to remain tightly shut, however, as the engine emitted a constant stream of soot and smoke. Even with the windows closed, every surface was covered with gray dust. Yet their speed was so astonishing Serafina could scarcely mark her own discomfort. Indeed, every person on board could speak of little else.

The other passengers said the train reached thirty-five miles per hour on the open stretches. Serafina had no idea what the numbers meant. But the speed was both exhilarating and terrifying. The countryside outside the window was only a blur.

They arrived in Bath station just as the westering sun joined with the golden hills. Serafina made her way to the front of the station, through yet more throngs of people and hawkers. She found herself moving behind a couple whose porter cleared a way forward. She observed how they stepped to a line of waiting carriages. She watched others and saw how they gave the driver an address and then entered. There was none of the bartering she would have expected between a traveler in Venice and a gondolier. Everything seemed very straightforward.

She approached the next carriage in line and said, "I wish to go to Harrow."

But as she started to enter the vehicle, the driver demanded, "'Ere, now, 'ang on a tic. Will you be after the manor or the village?"

The words meant nothing and the man's accent was mystifying. "Please excuse me, sir. I wish to go to Harrow."

"And I was 'earing you the first time, wasn't I. Is you wanting the manor or the village?"

"I don't . . . My aunt . . ." She stopped. "What is a manor, please?"

"The big house. Harrow Hall."

"Oh, yes, now I understand. My aunt, she worked there before. But not now."

"So it's the village you're wanting. That's quite a way to be going this time of evening. Hard going, that road, after dark." He was a coarse-featured man, his face blistered from riding through all manner of weather. "Cost you the better part of 'alf a crown."

Now she was back on familiar territory. She had no idea how much it was he had said. But she was a merchant's daughter and knew never to accept the first price for anything. "Too much."

"Eight shillings, then. Can't do you better than that."

"All right," she said, fingering what remained in her pocket. "But hurry."

"Got no need to 'ang about, now, do I." He cracked his whip. "Gerrup, there!"

Serafina imagined her aunt would be scandalized by a variety of things. Arriving alone after dark, for one. Running from the ship and her parents. Traveling across southern England unescorted. As the carriage jounced and rattled over the rutted road, Serafina knew she should have been formulating a fair response to all her criticisms. But she was awfully tired. Her bones ached from fatigue and the rough journey. Her mind felt so jostled, she could hold on to no thought for very long.

Serafina forced the stubborn window open and breathed deeply of the English evening air. The one thought that came back to her over and over was that she dared not tell her aunt how she obtained the money for this journey. Of all the things she had done to arrive at this point, this most left her twisted inside. It was a wrong as deep as her fatigue. She had stolen from the people who loved her and wished for her only the best. Though they disagreed with her and did not accept her need for Luca, still they were her family. And she had stolen from them.

She tried to see the stars overhead, but the carriage was passing through a forest so thick the boughs formed a living tunnel. She tried to pray but found the words leaden and thick in her mind. She felt as though she passed through a spiritual burrow as dark as the night. *Go and sin no more,* the vicar had said. Serafina rubbed the moisture from her cheeks and turned away from the sky she could not find. Why did it seem as though the entire world stood between her and the man she loved?

They traveled long through the dark. The farther they went, the worse grew the road's condition. Finally the carriage pulled past a pair of impressive gates, closed up tight against the night. They continued for a mile and more, a tall stone wall now running alongside the road. The wall drifted back a ways, and she smelled woodsmoke. The carriage entered a hamlet consisting of several dozen stone cottages lining both sides of the lane. The driver called softly to his horse and halted before a house with windows aglow and a tavern's sign hanging above the entrance. Without a word to Serafina he leaped down, straightened his back, and asked through the window, "Who is it we're after, miss?"

"E-excuse me?"

"The name of them what's expecting you."

"Oh. Donatella. Signora. That is, Mrs. Agatha Donatella."

"Uppity sort of name for a body livin' out here in the Wiltshire countryside." The driver turned and walked to the door.

An aproned innkeeper answered the driver's knock. As he pointed the way, Serafina caught the fragrances drifting through the night air. Of a fire burning cedar chips and a roast and tobacco and companions sheltered against the night. She wished she could simply lie down right here and go to sleep.

The driver drove her down to the last house in the village. It was larger than the others, with a full second story. But as Serafina alighted from the transom, she found herself sharing the driver's sentiment. This place was so far removed from Italy. Why had her aunt remained here?

She fished out some coins and handed them up to the driver. "Thank you, sir."

The driver inspected the coins in the light of the lantern that hung by his right shoulder. " 'Ere now, you've given me too much."

She accepted her change. He tipped his hat to her, then clicked to his horse. As Serafina watched him depart, the moon slipped out from behind a cloud. She realized she could see her breath. She turned and looked again at the house. In the moonlight, the stone walls and slate roof gleamed with a hard light. She had never thought she could ever feel so far away from Venice. From home.

The perfume of roses and flowers she could not identify wafted along the walkway. Somewhere deep inside the house, a candle glowed. Otherwise, the night was dark and very silent.

Her knock sounded loud in her ears. She waited and was about to knock again when she heard a slow scraping footstep from within.

"Who's out there this time of night?"

Serafina found herself trembling such that she could not find the strength to reply.

The voice was sharp and querulous. "I know you're standing there, I can see your shape. Speak up!"

"A-aunt Agatha?" she asked in Italian.

"Chi è?"

"It's me, Auntie. Serafina."

The lock rattled open. Then a second. The door swiveled back. "Saints in heaven above."

Her chattering teeth made hard go of the words. "H-hello, Aunt A-agatha."

"Ah, child, let me look at you" came the faltering response. "For a moment there I thought the hands of time had been drawn back. You're the mirror image of your dear sweet mother." The woman leaned on her cane and peered out into the dark night. "Where are your parents?"

Only then did Serafina let her resolve melt away in a flood of weary and sorrowful tears.

Chapter 13

The room where Serafina awoke was very strange indeed. A waist-high wall joined to a steeply slanted roof. Beams thicker than her waist jutted out at odd angles. The room smelled of dust and disuse, and the wood was pitted and scarred by a time beyond her imagination. A low table hugged the wall opposite her bed, and beside that stood an armoire and a narrow sofa. Or so Serafina imagined, for all the furniture except the bed remained covered in white sheets. No one had been upstairs in quite some time. In the morning light, she could see where her footsteps had left marks along the dusty floor.

Voices drifting up from downstairs drew Serafina from her bed. She crossed to a window alcove set deep in the roofline. The morning was cold and tasted faintly metallic, as though even in July there remained a hint of winter. Somewhere in the distance a dog barked. A blacksmith began a steady banging upon his anvil. A horse whinnied and doves cooed. Serafina took one more strengthening breath and turned away.

She dressed quickly. As she walked down the stairs, the voices grew silent. She followed the morning scents into the kitchen. Her aunt was seated in a high-backed wing chair pulled up close to the fire. Another woman stood stirring a pot on the stove. The two ladies turned to eye Serafina's appearance with identical expressions—neither welcoming nor hostile. Serafina found enough of her voice to say, *"Buon giorno, Zìa."*

"You said last night that you speak English, yes? You will use only that in my home." She indicated the woman. "You may greet my friend Beryl Marcham."

"Good morning, madam."

The woman eyed her distantly. "She's even prettier than you said."

"Well, I did warn you."

"She could be trouble, you know. Very serious trouble."

"I'm not insisting, Beryl."

"No, you never would." The woman stepped away from the stove and smiled down at Serafina's aunt. "Because you know I would never refuse you anything."

"You owe me nothing."

"On the contrary, I owe you everything." The woman's smile slipped away as her gaze returned to Serafina. "You should address me as Mrs. Marcham. The only 'madam' in this village is the lady of Harrow Hall. And should you meet her, you will address her as 'my lady.' But it will be unlikely that you shall see her at all. These days she rarely rises from her bed. Do you understand?"

"I–I'm not certain, mad—Mrs. Marcham."

"I will explain things in due course," Agatha said.

"Very well." Without the smile, Beryl Marcham held to an expression of stern authority. "You must be on time, young lady. Punctuality is critical."

Something in the way Mrs. Marcham looked at her left Serafina quaking more than the previous night. "Y–yes, Mrs. Marcham."

"She has an agreeable way about her," Aunt Agatha offered.

"Won't do her much good, not with those looks." Mrs. Marcham started for the door. "You'll show her how to hide that hair of hers in a kerchief, I suppose."

"You know I will."

"And speak to her about the manner of dress."

"Don't I always?"

The two women exchanged a look. "I'm off to the village market for a few items," Mrs. Marcham said. She gathered up her basket and left without another word or glance in Serafina's direction.

Agatha studied the closed door, kneading the head of her cane.

"Is–is everything all right?" Serafina couldn't control the tremble in her voice.

"You must be hungry." The woman spoke the words while still eyeing the closed door. "There's some fruit in the bowl by the window and husks warming beside the stove. The water's just off the boil. You know how to make tea?"

"Yes, Aunt Agatha."

"I'm not at all well, you see." She spoke the news in such a blunt manner she might as well have been discussing the price of bread. "I have put off writing your mother about my state for too long. I hated sharing my distress with anyone, most especially with my dear Bettina. Which makes this business all the harder." She rose slowly from her chair and made her way to the table.

"I'm sorry, Aunt Agatha, I don't—"

"Please come over here and sit down."

Serafina put an apple on a plate and pulled a cane-backed chair up closer to the kitchen table. Her aunt Agatha was stern by nature, Serafina saw that now. Though the morning was overcast, there was enough light through the broad rear window for her to see her aunt clearly. Serafina had been so tired the previous evening that little had registered. She had sat here in the kitchen and eaten a cold meal, then climbed the stairs alone to bed. Her aunt had asked her a few questions and then stopped, realizing that Serafina had been too tired to even think clearly, much less deal with such complex issues as why she was alone and where her parents were.

"You still look exhausted," her aunt said.

"I'm fine. Thank you for your hospitality." She tried to bite into the apple, but her stomach rejected the thought of food. Her limbs felt wooden. She could see the answer in her aunt's expression, the answer to the only question that mattered.

Her aunt was not going to help her return to Luca.

"You must eat, child."

"Perhaps later." She pushed the plate aside. Just looking at the food made her feel weak and nauseous. What was she to do?

"Very well. If you won't eat we must talk. Look at me, please."

She had struggled so hard and done so much, and where had it brought her? To the cold stone kitchen of a cold house, in a cold land on the other side of Europe from her beloved. She had one gold ducat and some strange silver coins to her name.

Her aunt thumped her cane upon the flagstone floor. "Look at me!"

Serafina did as she was told.

"Take the sugar there in the pewter pot. Spoon a heaping portion into your tea. Another. No, don't argue. You are depleted and you need the strength. And we must talk. All right. Drink it down. Yes, I know it's too sweet. But it will make you alert and there is much to cover. I don't want you growing faint on me. Drink it like medicine. That's it."

Agatha had the manner of one used to giving orders and being instantly obeyed. The woman was not cold nor uncaring. But she was stern to the point of harshness. She wore a long dress of charcoal gray, utterly unadorned save for a small ivory pin at her collar. There were neither rings on her fingers nor ribbons in her steel-gray hair. Her eyes were as direct and forceful as her tone.

"Now I want you to start from the beginning and tell me exactly how it is that I am sitting in my kitchen facing the daughter without the mother."

Serafina did as she was instructed, though she could scarcely identify the voice as her own. She released the words in a dull monotone, barely above a whisper. On and on she spoke. She held nothing back. Why should she? Her only purpose was to return to Luca. Either her aunt would help her or she wouldn't. Serafina described the fever and the boat and the journey and the final argument with her father. Only the theft of her father's ducats did she hold back. Nothing else. Then she stopped. The kitchen felt crammed tight with her futile words. She could not bring herself to ask this stern woman for help. It was hard enough even to meet her gaze.

Her aunt did not look at all well. Her hands continued to knead the cane, as though seeking to mask the tremors that came and went through her body. Every now and then she winced and then resumed her severe expression, leading Serafina to believe she was fighting a constant battle with herself.

Finally she heaved herself to her feet. When Serafina rose to aid her, she said, "No, I can rise on my own. But can you cook?"

"A-a little."

"I assume that means almost not at all. Look there, see that clay pot with the cork stopper? Measure out two handfuls of the milled oats into the smallest copper pan and set it on the fire. Add enough water to cover the oats and then a bit. Take a pinch of salt from the little urn here on the table. Then use the long wooden ladle there and stir constantly. I won't be long."

"I'm not hungry, Aunt Agatha."

"I did not inquire as to your internal state. I gave you instructions. You must grow accustomed to doing as you are told without question."

"Yes, ma'am." Serafina hastened to obey.

Her aunt moved with tiny steps, at most a foot's length at a time. Serafina had the pot filled and set on to boil before her aunt exited through the kitchen's side entrance. Agatha was not a tall woman to begin with, and she was made shorter by the way she bowed over the cane. Even so, she made no reference to her own discomfort.

By the time she returned, the porridge was done. "Take two of the flowered bowls there from the shelf. Give me half a portion only. I want you to eat the rest."

"I couldn't possibly, Aunt Agatha. Please, I have no appetite."

"You are clearly starving, and your body needs nourishment. I can see your needs better than you. There's some barley sugar up there, and cream in the larder. Put a good spoonful of each into your bowl. Now sit yourself down and let's pray."

Agatha maneuvered herself slowly down into the chair at the

head of the table. She leaned her cane against the neighboring chair, then reached over and took her niece's hand with both of hers. "Oh dear Lord, oh heavenly Father, my friend through all the blows that life has cast my way, I beseech thee now, be with us."

Serafina's head slowly rose. This seemed quite unlike her aunt. Someone so authoritative and stern, she would have expected her prayers to be as dry as old bones. A swift repetition of some formal prayer, perhaps a sign of the cross, and finish. Instead, her aunt's entire face was one huge earnest crease, her pain evident now. And something more. Her fervor was an emotional plea that cracked both her resolve and her voice.

"Oh dear Lord, thou hast seen me through very much," the woman continued. "In the midst of my harshest days, my worst tragedies, my greatest fears, I have known thy peace. Surround us now, I pray. Grant us both the strength we do not have. Make me a better person, one able to aid this dear girl through her own harsh discoveries—"

"No!" Serafina jerked her hand away and leaped to her feet, the chair clattering to the flagstones behind her.

Agatha lifted her head with the same slow motion of every action. Her features calmed. But the light did not leave her eyes. Nor the quiet fervor from her voice. "Amen, and amen. Sit down, my child."

"I won't . . . You can't—"

"First we shall eat this lovely bowl of porridge. Then we shall talk about what is and can't be changed."

"Luca," she whimpered.

"The gentleman can wait. This meal cannot."

Serafina stared at her aunt, then looked down at the bowl and grimaced.

"I will not be sharp with you. Not now." Her aunt spoke in the manner of one reminding herself. "But we shall discuss nothing until your bowl is empty."

"You-you know something about Luca?"

"It matters not whether we wait all day," Agatha replied,

folding her hands in her lap. She showed strength in her resolve, yet the sternness was not there. "But first you *will* eat."

Her entire being was so filled with dread that the porridge congealed into lead lumps she could hardly swallow. She lifted her eyes for quick glimpses of her aunt's face, but the woman held to her word, remaining silent until Serafina had spooned up the last appalling bite.

"Excellent. Set the bowls and pot to soak, would you?" Serafina could feel Agatha's eyes upon her as she rose unsteadily and moved to the basin by the window. "My dear child, others may judge you, but I shall not. I want you to know that."

"W-what have you heard?"

"Come over here and sit down." Serafina's trembling approach was met with a compassion that cracked the woman's severe façade wide open. She reached over and once again took hold of Serafina's hand. "I will tell you the news. But first I want to share something of myself. Will you hear me out?"

Serafina could not find the strength to speak, nor even truly nod. Her aunt continued anyway. "I married a skilled craftsman from our village, a woodworker by trade. Jacob was one of four men brought over to redo a salon in Harrow Hall in the Florentine style. The lord of the manor liked his work so much he offered to become Jacob's patron. I went to work as a lady in waiting, and eventually rose to manage the entire household staff. Our God never saw fit to grant us children, but still we were both happy with our lot and fulfilled in our marriage. Then last year Jacob was taken. . . ."

Her entire body seized in a fierce tremor. She waited it out, as she clearly had many times before. She drew a ragged breath and continued. "The doctors have a variety of words for my ailment. But the truth is, my sorrow and my loss have congealed in my bones. I am not long for this earth, and I do not care. But I can no longer see to my own needs. The lord of the manor has assigned me a bedroom and parlor in the old house, where I shall remain for the rest of my days."

Agatha straightened herself with great effort. "In the midst of my worst despair and sorrow, I learned one valuable lesson. I can sit here this day, with my own end drawing close, and tell you this with utter certainty. The Lord is near. He will see you through. No matter what. Tell me that you hear my words."

Serafina tried to draw a breath. But she could only stare at her aunt in desperate appeal.

Agatha released one hand and reached into her pocket. She paused with the page partly revealed, her face creased in indecision. Slowly she returned the paper to her pocket. She resumed her hold upon Serafina's hand. "I received a letter from your mother. You may read it later. I had heard from her once before, after she discovered you with the man. . . ."

Luca, she wanted to say. No, she wanted to scream the name. Shout it to the heavens. *He is dead.* Serafina could see it in her aunt's eyes. Luca was gone. No. It was too terrible to bear. She wanted to cram her fists to her ears. But she could not move.

"In this second letter, my dear Bettina wrote to say you had become so ill that she and your father feared you would be taken from them. They put off the journey to America as long as they could, which granted your father the time to hear back from his allies. He had sent word out, asking both within the military and elsewhere for information about your young man's background." Agatha's grip tightened. "Luca was not as he seemed, my dear. He deceived you in the most horrible of manners."

He is alive. Luca lives. Yet there was no relief to be found in the realization. Instead Serafina shivered with a sudden chill.

"Luca . . ." Agatha had to struggle with herself once more. "Luca is married."

No! She thought she had screamed it. For the wail inside her chest rose like a great shrieking wind. But her face was so frozen she could scarcely form a whisper. "No."

"It was confirmed by three trusted sources. Luca is married. He has two children."

"No."

"He was in the military at the time. He had gained some reputation as an artist, such that he was withdrawn from regimental duties. He painted portraits of many senior officers and even some of the royal court. He completed several ornamental scenes for palace halls. He was rumored to be involved in several scandals."

"It . . . it can't be," Serafina whimpered.

"He seduced a general's wife." Agatha spoke with compassion, as though seeking to cushion the blows she was forcing herself to deliver. "Or so it was widely believed. Though again nothing was proven, this time the evidence was quite strong. But because his fellow officers wished to protect the general's reputation, Luca was permitted to resign his commission. That is why there is no official scandal attached to his name, do you see? Luca's wife returned to her family. Luca traveled around the country for two years, working on other commissions and leaving behind him a trail of smoldering gossip. There have been other women, my dear. He preys upon young women. That much is certain. Eventually he moved to Venice, which as you know has been largely cut off from Italy since becoming part of the Austro-Hungarian Empire. There his reputation was unknown, and there he . . ."

When Serafina rose to her feet, Agatha did not object. But she said, "I spent all of last night worrying over how best to tell you. In truth, there is no good way to impart such news. But I decided it was better for you to hear it from one who has loved you since before you were born."

Serafina stumbled across the room, not headed in any particular direction, only seeking to flee the words that struck her so brutally. Her hand found a latch. She fumbled and managed to open the rear door. She flung it back and nearly fell down the steps and outside.

The market was quite large for such a small village. The square was framed by a church, a priory, a coaching inn, a smithy, and a village green. There were perhaps thirty stalls in the market. They sold every manner of ware and produce, clearly serving a larger population than the village alone. A pair of pipers strolled back and forth in front of the inn, dancing in time to their melody while a girl of perhaps seven walked from table to table asking for alms. The inn's patrons ate from a lamb shank that was turning slowly over a bed of coals set by the inn's far side. Smoke from the cooking fire filled the square with fragrance.

Serafina found an empty bench just beyond the village market. It was an odd place for a grieving woman to sit. But the noise sheltered her somewhat from the barrage of her thoughts, though the cooking odors made her feel nauseated.

Luca was married. The words might as well have been drawn from an alien language. Her Luca. The man for whom she had sacrificed so much. Married.

A pair of young men approached her. They jostled one another with rude courage as they spoke to her. Serafina heard the voices but could not make out the words. They laughed and tried to flirt with her.

She lifted her gaze. Whatever it was they saw in her eyes was enough to silence them and turn them away.

Luca. A father.

Serafina buried her face in her hands. She had abandoned everything. She had lied. She had stolen. She had run away time and again. She had given up everything she owned, everything that held her to her place in the world. For a man who had lied to her from the start. For a man who did not love her. For a man who had . . .

The horror of it all left her breathless.

"All right. Enough of that."

Serafina lifted her head, not due to the words but the tone.

"I won't have a young lady in my charge sitting about in public like this. It won't do at all." Beryl Marcham set the heavy wicker basket down at Serafina's feet. "Sit up straight. No, not like that. Look at me, girl. There should be a bolt of steel running from your hips straight up to your ears. Your spine is always straight as an arrow. That's better. Good. Don't ever let me see you bowed over. You are never to display such a manner in the great house, do you hear me? Never."

Mrs. Marcham settled herself upon the stone bench alongside Serafina. "Regard how I sit. This was the first lesson your aunt taught me, and one that has served me well. See how my chin is always at this angle, slightly elevated yet not lofty? This is proper for a woman in service to a grand manor. You must stand erect and yet remain subservient to all the masters and mistresses. Keep your eyes downcast when being addressed, but don't cringe. Never cringe. The younger men of the household will see that as a weakness, as an opportunity." She examined Serafina's face. "Do you have any idea what I am speaking of?"

In truth, Serafina had not made sense of the words at all. She gave her head a small shake.

"You're not mute." The words were like cold water dashed in her face. "I shan't tell you this again. You will address me aloud and end your sentence with *ma'am* or *Mrs. Marcham.*"

"Yes, ma'am. I-I mean, no, I didn't—"

"That's better. There is never a shame in admitting you don't know something. Just as long as you listen carefully when instructed." Her words had a practiced manner, as though spoken a hundred times before. "You strike me as an intelligent young woman."

"Thank you, Mrs. Marcham." Serafina could not believe this was happening. Her entire world was shattered and lying broken at her feet. *Luca is married.*

"The duke's only son is twenty-six and a wastrel. I would not speak so to my other staff, but you are Agatha's niece, and you are also quite beautiful. So I must warn you that if you give him half a chance, he will make trouble for you."

She waited a moment, granting Serafina an opportunity to speak. When Serafina did not reply, she went on. "If there is trouble, no matter who is to blame, the staff will always be at fault. That is the way it is within a great house. So you must guard yourself well. Dress severely and plainly. Hide your hair and as much of your face as is practical. I will do my best to hold you to duties which keep you out of the public rooms."

"F-forgive me, ma'am. But I still don't . . . You said duties?"

She looked askance at Serafina. "Did your aunt tell you nothing?"

"No, ma'am. That is . . ."

"Agatha is gravely ill. It hurts me to say this, but I fear she is not long for this earth. She cannot take care of herself, particularly in that drafty old house of hers. So she is moving into rooms at the back of Harrow Hall. It's the master's wishes, and I agree. Agatha has any number of friends among the staff. She will be well cared for."

Serafina's mind simply could not make sense of what she was hearing. The woman was kind enough, in the manner of one trained to be severe and standoffish. But to Serafina's mind the words would simply not come together.

The woman evidently saw Serafina's confusion, for she grew exasperated. "Well, you can't simply be allowed to remain on your own! Do you have funds?"

"Money? N-no, not—"

"There, you see? Arrangements must be made. Agatha trained me and raised me to where I am today, managing the staff of a great house. She has asked a favor. A great favor, I must tell you, for it is rare that a woman with no proper background or training would be taken on like this. I shall expect you promptly at four Monday afternoon to show you around the manor and explain your duties."

Mrs. Marcham rose to her feet, gathered up her basket, and started to leave. Then she turned back. "I don't know what your difficulty is, young lady, and I don't need to know. I will give you some advice that you would be wise to take to heart. There are any number of tragedies among the staff of a great house. I have my own. Agatha . . . well, you see how your aunt is."

She stopped once more, clearly wishing for some sort of response from Serafina. When the girl remained silent, Mrs. Marcham's tone became more strident. "I hope you are listening carefully because I shan't repeat myself. Life is often not how we would like it. Your duty is to get on with your work and not dwell upon whatever misery you might carry. And above all else, you are not to burden others with your woes. Nor are you to give any heed when someone else seeks to bend your ear. There are gossipers among the staff who would love nothing more than to tell you tales, and spread yours about for others to hear. Pay them no mind, do you understand? Work hard and work well. Time and work will cure you."

"No." The one word was all she could manage.

Beryl Marcham started to correct her, then stopped and changed course. "One final word. You mustn't enter service thinking you shall be receiving special attention because of your aunt. And if you want to get along with the others, you will not seek out Agatha every time something does not go your way. The other staff will be watching, as shall I. They can make your life miserable, if they have a mind." The woman hefted her basket. "You'd be well advised to work hard and learn the value of silence."

Serafina watched her march away. A number of the stall-holders doffed their caps at Mrs. Marcham's passage. She responded with brisk nods and occasionally a word or two. She did not glance back to where Serafina sat.

Serafina found herself envying the woman and her unfeeling nature. If only she could cast aside her problems and live as though they did not matter.

She sighed her way to her feet and started back toward her aunt's house, moving unsteadily. No matter what Mrs. Marcham might have said, time would do nothing for her wounds.

She felt a thousand years old.

Chapter 14

Shipboard life was as close to a home as Falconer ever expected to find upon this earth. Bound by water and froth and wind, enclosed by clouds and rain and sun, and surrounded by the close company of others who knew the sea's moods. Yet not even this could ease Falconer's predawn wakings. Instead, the nightly terrors seemed to grow worse. That dawn he awakened with the cries of his friend Felix calling to him for help.

He came aloft and released his worry and the nightmare's last tendrils to the early morning air. His prayers came in the sweeping steadiness of the waves. He leaned upon the railing and watched the morning strengthen, and he prayed for Felix and his own mission, feeling the helplessness that only a strong man can truly know. Then he greeted the mate at the wheel and took a mug of sailor's tea with the others coming on watch. Sheltering himself by the lee rail, he opened the Bible the curate had given to him soon after his first prayer of repentance.

Falconer knew why his nightmare had cut more deeply than usual. The previous evening Gareth Powers had finally felt strong enough to speak with Falconer about his own quest. The two men had been astounded to find they shared a loathing of the slave trade and a determination to see it ended. Gareth had spoken of his writings, of the frustration they had known on both sides of the Atlantic in working against a tide of evil that seemed at times unstoppable. Falconer had listened and felt less alone than he had since departing Trinidad. Too soon, Gareth's strength had waned, and Falconer had taken to his own bunk, thrilled by the knowledge that he had gained not just a new ally but another friend in Christ.

The ship's captain found him there by the lee rail. A storm-hardened man of graying years, his sea-borne coat was salt encrusted, his cap mildewed from countless seasons. "A good morning to you, John Falconer."

"Sir." Falconer used his finger to mark his place and rose to his feet. Passengers were not expected to rise in the presence of officers, but a lifetime's habit died hard.

"Join me on the quarterdeck, if you have a mind."

"Honored, Captain." The captain's quarter was restricted to the senior officer on deck and those whom he specifically invited. Falconer slipped the Bible into his jacket pocket and took the steps three at a time.

"Reading the Good Book, I see."

"It anchors my day, sir."

"As fine a habit as any I could name." Captain Micah had a seaman's gaze, clear and far-reaching. "You have on-board experience, I take it."

"I entered the service at age twelve."

"What is your age now, if I might be so bold?"

"I shall be thirty this coming winter."

"I would have taken you for much older." He studied the younger man. "Command of a vessel ages a man swiftly."

"That it does, Captain. That it most certainly does."

"How old were you when you walked your first quarterdeck?"

"I was twenty-five, sir. A truly foul day."

"A battle?"

"With nature and with man."

"A storm." Captain Micah nodded somberly. "You lost your skipper?"

"Washed overboard by a wave so large it snapped his lifeline like it was made of spider webbing." Falconer could still hear the man's shrill cry. "Took our mizzenmast and six good mates as well."

The captain had the sense to turn from the raw emotion on Falconer's features. He pointed south and east, the quarter from which a squall approached. "What say you about the gauge of this wind?"

Falconer studied the approaching squall line. The sea was a legion of waves, marching in massive unison. The troughs were as deep as the ship was high, but there was no danger to their size. The distance between each was a constant valley, broad enough for the ship to rise and fall in steady rhythm. "The squall will pass by noon, is my guess. The afternoon will blow clear and steady."

"And farther out?"

"A storm far to the south. A big one." Falconer took a deep breath. "I can smell it."

"Aye, I agree with you, sir. I warrant there are sailors praying their last, down below the horizon." He wiped his eyes clear of the salty mist. "Were this your command, sir, what orders would you give?"

"North by east," Falconer replied instantly. "Put more miles between us and whatever the nights may hold."

The captain wheeled about and used a shipboard bellow to reach the lieutenant standing duty by the steersman. "Barnes!"

"Sir!"

"Set a new course ten points north! Send the men aloft!"

"Ten points it is, sir! Bosun!"

"Sir!"

"Pipe the men aloft!"

Falconer assumed the captain would dismiss him then, and made ready to depart. Instead, Captain Micah observed, "I find it uncommon strange that a former shipboard commander would find himself as a landlubber's manservant. No offense intended."

"None taken, sir." Falconer tested several responses before saying, "God's directions are difficult to fathom at times, Captain."

"Indeed. Indeed." Micah fumbled with a loose button on his

greatcoat. "Langston's has a policy that all who command their vessels must be Christians. Most are elders within their home church."

"I did not know that. But having met Reginald Langston, I am not surprised."

"I count it an honor to serve the man and the house," the captain went on. "He told me to pass along to other skippers I meet that we are to aid you if the need arises."

"I am deeply grateful, both for the man's offer and your acknowledgment, Captain."

"Don't mention it." He continued to worry the button. "You may have noted that we have no priest nor pastor on board this voyage."

"I found your Sabbath message last week most inspiring, sir."

"I was wondering, that is . . ." Micah managed to pluck the button free. He made a business of stowing it into his pocket. "Would you offer us the Sabbath message on the morrow?"

"Sir." A blow from an unseen foe could not have shocked Falconer more. "I am not good with words."

"You are a Christian and a sailor. You have known command, and now you serve. All aboard have observed your manner of Scripture reading and prayer." The captain hesitated, then added, "I would not ask this, sir, except that it came to me as a strong impression in my own morning reflections."

Falconer felt stricken by the news. "You think God spoke of this?"

"I am certain of it."

"Then I can hardly refuse." His entire body felt weighted down. "You will excuse me if I take my leave?"

The rain stopped as predicted just after midday. Falconer carried Hannah upstairs and settled her into a sheltered alcove rimmed by water barrels. The kitten thrived on shipboard life, as did its young mistress. Ferdinand had learned to endure its ribbon leash, save for the occasional bursts of protests when it sought to claw the thing off its neck. The ribbon had to be replaced every few days. Sailors were notoriously fond of cats and had taken to competing with one another to offer the next bit of leash. But it was not merely the cat that had charmed them. Within minutes of Hannah being settled into her blanket-covered corner, she was visited by two midshipmen, the bosun, the second mate, six seamen, and an off-duty lieutenant. Falconer tolerated their chatty ways and held himself removed from the discourse.

Hannah waited until the last seaman had been sent aloft. "Something is troubling you, I can tell. Is it Papa?"

"No, he seems to be making solid progress."

"I don't see how you can say that. All he does is sleep."

"He is resting well, which is far more than could be said while ashore. His color is good, he eats everything put in front of him."

"Shouldn't he be up here taking in the air?"

"Rest," Falconer repeated. "I heard it any number of times from the doctor. Rest and more rest. If your father can sleep, that is the best thing he can do for himself."

Hannah nuzzled the kitten to her cheek. "Do you see how Ferdinand is growing?"

"He is becoming a truly fine little beast."

She dangled and twirled her slender gold necklace for the kitten to bat about. "Will you tell me what it is that bothers you?"

Falconer took a two-handed grip upon the railing. "The captain has asked me to speak at tomorrow's Sabbath gathering."

Hannah did not even need to think about it. "You will do wonderfully."

He stared at the waif. "How can you say such a thing?"

In the wind and the sunlight, Hannah's smile provided its own warmth. "Because it's true."

"I am not good with words."

"Then you will ask God to speak for you."

Falconer squatted down beside her. "Lass, I am a sinner and a wastrel. God's mercy keeps me alive. Nothing more."

"Then that is what you will tell them." She settled her hands into her lap. Falconer had the sudden image of Hannah having learned the tone and the mannerism from her mother. "I know what Papa would say."

"What is that?"

"He is always talking about the book of Acts. He loves how the disciples simply explained who they were. Before, without God. Now, with God. They spoke of how God changed them."

Falconer found no strangeness in confessing to this little child, "I'm afraid."

She smiled. "What did you tell me in the carriage about fear?"

"You have an answer for everything."

"No I don't. Not really." She brushed the hair from her face. "I'm little and I'm weak and I'm . . ."

"You're what?"

"Nothing."

But the bond between them was growing enough for Falconer to suggest, "You're not alone, lass. Not anymore."

Her gaze had the radiant quality of daybreak. "And neither are you."

Falconer did not sleep that night. The next morning he arose with the sense of facing a battle he could not win. The day broke clear, a steady wind blowing from their fairest quarter. The waves were enormous but steady, their progress constant. Over a mug of sailor's tea, Falconer tried to tell himself this was a good sign. But his pounding heart could not be convinced.

By the time the sailors had rigged the benches and stretched a sail over the foredeck as a canopy, Falconer's blood thundered in his ears. He doubted he had strength to rise. The captain came over and spoke words Falconer could scarcely make out. The captain patted him on the shoulder and departed.

Falconer wrestled through the jumble his mind had made of the man's communication. The captain would offer a Bible reading. Falconer would then speak. Two minutes or an hour, it did not matter. Falconer would do fine, so the captain had said. Falconer looked over and realized the crew and passengers were gathering. He needed three attempts to rise from the water keg he was using as a stool.

He seated himself on the front bench and bowed over the Book in his hands. Falconer remained as he was when the others rose and sang. He tried to beg for guidance, for inspiration, for wisdom. But his mind was so blocked with anxiety he could not even shape a proper prayer.

The first words that made any sense whatsoever were from the captain's reading. Falconer knew the Bible passage well. Captain Micah had a bark of a voice, even when standing at the front of a Sabbath gathering. He had spent too many days shouting his words against wind and storm and hail to soften them now. The passage battered its way through Falconer's dread, from the second chapter of Jonah: "They that observe lying vanities forsake their own mercy. But I will sacrifice unto thee with the voice of thanksgiving; I will pay that that I have vowed. Salvation is of the Lord."

The captain stepped aside and looked down to where Falconer sat. This time Falconer's legs obeyed when he tried to stand, yet there was no strength to his walk. Instead he let the ship's swaying motion carry him forward. He gripped the forecastle railing with one hand, and with the other he clenched the Bible to his chest.

He looked up and out. But not at the gathering. Instead he studied the storm-tossed sea. And he uttered the first word that came to his mind.

"Murderer!" He did not mean to bellow. But the strength it took to speak at all left him using the same storm-laden voice as the captain. "Slaver! A cruel and hard man! A man you'd best never allow on your lee quarter! A man you can never trust! A man whose only friends are the dagger and the blade!

"That is how I was known. And that is who I am!"

The vessel shot down the face of the next wave. It plowed through the watery gorge and bucked like a steed of wood and canvas. Sea spray blasted Falconer's face. He did not bother to wipe his eyes. "The accusations were true then, they are true now. I stand before you convicted of all the wrongs one man can commit. True! Guilty! I am that man!"

He balanced himself against the ship's rise and opened the Book. His hands trembled so hard he could scarcely turn the pages. Finally he gave up, for the words were far more clearly visible inside his mind. "Now let me say to you the words that go before what the captain read: 'I went down to the bottoms of the mountains; the earth with her bars was about me for ever: yet hast thou brought up my life from corruption, O Lord my God. When my soul fainted within me I remembered the Lord: and my prayer came in unto thee, into thine holy temple.'"

A pair of seamen slipped down the rope ladder connecting the mizzenmast to the main deck. They padded across the deck upon hardened bare feet and stood at the back of the last bench. Falconer felt for them. He too had once come crawling forward, seeking what he could not even name. If only he could speak with the same force as Felix. If only he had that blessed man's ability to make God's invitation live.

But he would try. For those two seamen and for the third who poised upon the mainmast's yardarm, some fifteen feet above Falconer's head. He spoke not to the gathering. He spoke to these three. His brothers. He knew them well. Them, and their needs.

"God has brought me from corruption. Me, the least worthy of all. He has drawn me from the pit of my own making. And what he has done for me, he can do for you! All you need do is fall to your knees! See your claim to live without God for what it is, a lie! The worst lie of all. A lie that leads to the grave!"

This time he managed to find his place in the Scriptures. "It was a seaman who spoke the words you heard the captain read. A sailor tossed upon the great open waters, swallowed by the beast of darkness and doom. Hear now what happened after Jonah spoke to the Lord his God: "'And the Lord spake unto the fish, and it vomited out Jonah upon the dry land.'"

He held the Book aloft. The hand that had become molded to a sword's hilt. The hand that had done so much wrong. But Falconer saw not the Book, only the hand. And the shame of it clenched his throat up so he could hardly speak his final words. "Salvation comes from the Lord."

He stumbled back to his place.

Chapter 15

On Monday the English country sky was the shade of old pewter. But the colors of the surrounding trees and blossoms shone defiantly joyful at summer's presence, regardless of the cool day and the overcast sky. In the daylight Agatha's stone cottage held a solid serenity. One corner of the roof sagged somewhat, as though time's hand had weighed too heavily upon it. The chimney at the other end was crumbling. The gate was rusted and stuck halfway open. But the front garden was a brilliant and tangled profusion of summer blooms.

After a breakfast she was forced to eat, Serafina moved about her aunt's house with no recollection of time's passage. She had barely slept but was not so much exhausted as numb. Later two young men arrived from the manor and helped prepare boxes and bundles for Agatha's coming move. Agatha sent Serafina out on several errands. Serafina completed her tasks and returned to the house, scarcely aware of where she had just been.

She carried her basket up the flagstone walkway into the cottage and found the table in the front parlor piled with dark dresses. Her aunt asked in greeting, "Do you wish to eat a bite before leaving for the manor house?"

Serafina stared down at the dresses. Ever since she had been told the terrible news about Luca, information would not come together for her in any logical manner.

"Look at me, child."

Serafina forced her focus around to where her aunt sat in a high-backed chair. "I can't go on."

"You must." Agatha pointed with her cane at the dark pile. "These are old but usable. You and I were once of a size. I held to a bit more weight before the illness. The lads are off fetching a wagon. Let's see if any of these clothes fit you."

Slowly, reluctantly, Serafina did as she was told. Her aunt selected two from the pile that fitted her well enough. They were a simple charcoal gray, long sleeved, with high white collars that could be removed and exchanged for washing. The buttons up the front were covered in the same gray material.

Her aunt indicated several folded white scarves upon the table beside her chair. "Take one of these and do up your hair. No, don't knot the scarf under your chin. You're not going to market. You're entering service at a great house. Bend over and let me show you." Fingers no longer deft but skilled from years of practice placed the scarf low on Serafina's forehead, then reached around behind and knotted the kerchief tight against the back of her neck. "That's it. Excellent," Agatha said. "There's a mirror above the sideboard. Go have a look at yourself."

The dress material felt coarse against her skin and made a swishing sound as she crossed the room. She stared at a stranger's reflection, a young woman in a servant's garments, with eyes that stared back at her without any expression at all.

Her aunt moved in her slow, careful manner until she stood behind Serafina. She did not reach out to hold her, but the sympathy was clear in her voice. "Sometimes the only way to survive is by taking the first day, then the next, one step at a time. Just get through this hour, this day, the night, and then the day after. And almost without your realizing, you will find that things have changed."

"They haven't for you," Serafina replied. She did not recognize her own voice. The words sounded empty of everything, almost shapeless. "You're still sick and alone."

"Some matters do not change," Agatha agreed, her tone holding none of its usual sternness. "Inwardly though, where it counts most, things have altered remarkably. My faith has become a rock. I can say these words with certainty for the first time in my entire life. God Almighty reigns on high, above all the traumas and sorrows this world has cast my way. That is one great truth, is it not?"

Serafina found herself recalling the young vicar on board the ship and the way she had dismissed his words. The space where her heart beat burned even more painfully. The image in the mirror blurred somewhat.

If Agatha noticed Serafina's reaction, she gave no sign. "The master of Harrow Hall has granted me a place where I can live out my days, surrounded by people who care for me. That is a great blessing. And soon enough I shall join my beloved Jacob in heaven. There to dwell with our Lord for all eternity."

Agatha turned and began her slow retreat to the chair. "Now, let us speak of more practical matters. Jacob and I had a bit of money saved up. We used most of it to buy this house. The rest was lost to his illness. Now there is nothing. Do you understand what I am saying?"

"Yes." Her aunt had spoken the same words to her yesterday, though their implication was clearer in this repetition.

But Agatha pressed on, no doubt wanting to be absolutely certain she was being both heard and understood. "I cannot offer you what I don't have. So I have made the only arrangements for you that I can. You shall enter service at Harrow Hall. The letter I wrote to your parents yesterday will go off to Bath this afternoon, and from there to America. No doubt in time they will send funds and instructions. But that could take months. Either you will join them there or return to Venice. That is for them to say. Come help me into the chair, please."

Serafina crossed the room and took hold of her aunt's arm. The woman weighed almost nothing. Slowly Agatha lowered herself, sighing as she came to rest. "That's better. Thank you."

"We could stay here and I could look after you," Serafina said tremulously.

"A month ago, I might have agreed. But matters have gone too far. My illness has worsened. The house is sold and I am moving. And that, my dear, is final." She kneaded the top of her cane as she inspected her niece through eyes still bright and wise. "Besides which, I have the feeling that this time in service is precisely what you need. Activity, and thinking of others besides yourself."

"I don't want—"

"What you want or don't want is not what we are discussing." Her severe manner returned. "None of this is as we would have it. But matters have been taken from our hands. You will await word from your parents. In the meantime, you will enter into service."

"But—"

The cane thumped down once. "You will attend Mrs. Marcham, do you hear me? You will see to whatever duties she assigns you. You will work hard. And you will grow as a result."

Serafina felt the will to argue drain from her. What did it matter? Her life was ended. There was nothing for her now. No family, no future, no hope.

"There is something else, something I would ask that you take and hold close to your heart in the coming days." Agatha waited until Serafina had lifted her gaze to continue. "Even in the midst of life's winter, when death and desolation is all around you, *God is*. Grant Him time and space, and He will work in you. He will open doors. He will create new life from the ice of old bones. He will show you hope where you are sure none exists."

Agatha was held by something so intense her entire face became illuminated with joy. "He will show you the way ahead."

Under Agatha's instruction, Serafina prepared a cold midday meal. She could not have described the food, and each morsel went down with a struggle. But she ate because her aunt brooked no dissent. Soon after the few dishes had been washed up, a drover's cart pulled before the gate. Agatha stood in the doorway and leaned upon her cane as the middle-aged man doffed his cap and stepped forward. "All right, Mrs. Donatella?"

"Better than I deserve, Peter. How is your dear young Harry?"

"Terrible, he is. Like to be the death of me." But he was smiling. "Word is you'll be moving up to the great house shortly."

"That's right. Tomorrow will be my turn."

"Be grand to have you around again."

"I can't imagine why, what with all the work you have. Why anyone would want to bother with me is a mystery."

"It's Mrs. Marcham. She just don't know how to handle the place. Too soft, she is."

They were both smiling now. "I don't believe that for a minute," Agatha retorted. "Especially since I trained her myself." She turned from the door slightly, granting space for Serafina. When the younger woman held back, Agatha pulled her firmly forward. "This is my niece Serafina. I want you to meet Peter, the head groundskeeper. His wife, Emily, is the pastry cook."

"Your niece, is it. I warrant she'll prove a good worker. Hop aboard, lass. Don't want you to be late on your first day." He took hold of the old case supplied by Agatha for Serafina's few things and dropped it behind the seat. Then he offered her his free hand, which felt like tree bark. He doffed his hat once more, then clicked to the horses. "The two lads will be back around to help you shift your own things tomorrow, Mrs. Donatella."

"I'll be waiting." Agatha watched Serafina gravely, not offering a wave of any kind, her entire demeanor a warning and a charge.

The groundskeeper did not take them back through the village, as Serafina would have guessed. Instead, he headed out in the opposite direction. Once beyond the last house, a tall drystone wall crept back in closer to the lane. There was only enough room between lane and wall for a line of sheltering elms. "So you're niece to our Agatha."

"Yes, sir."

"No need for sirs, lass. Not between the likes of us. Peter's the name my dear old dad gave me, and it's fine by all who know me."

"But Mrs. Marcham—"

"Aye, well, the head of staff is a different kettle of fish. They're in between, if you catch my meaning." He glanced her way. "You're fresh from the old country, are you?"

"F-from Venice."

"So you don't have a clue what I'm on about." They came to a break in the wall. This particular entryway was marked not by stone columns as in the front, but rather by houses built close to either side of open iron gates. He clucked to the horse and guided it around the corner onto the unpaved rutted lane. To either side stretched more small stone houses. Fenced garden plots separated them from the estate's open fields. Serafina spied goats and a pond with geese and ducks. Somewhere a rooster crowed. "Mrs. Marcham and Cuthbert the butler are them what deal with the manor folk. We see his lordship from time to time. And the young master, of course. But Mrs. Marcham and Cuthbert speak to them regular. The pair of 'em runs the house. You catch my meaning?"

"I . . . I think so."

"You mind what they say to you and you do as you're told. You'll get on well enough." He eyed her shrewdly. "Long as you keep out of the way of the young master. I reckon your aunt's warned you about him."

"Just a little."

"He's a scamp, is young Stewart. A scamp and a scallywag." He entered into a tunnel formed by trees so ancient three men could not have grasped hands around their trunks. "The young master is a good shot, mind. And a fair hand with a horse. Loves the countryside, I'll grant him that. But you'd best steer well clear. Keep yourself belowstairs and out of sight, that's my advice."

The trees fell away and the tunnel opened. Serafina gasped at the sight.

"Aye, the old place is a stunner, I'll give you that." The groundsman spoke with genuine pride.

Despite the overcast sky, the house shone golden in the afternoon light. The three-story main portion was stone and very square. Windows higher than a man were flanked by pillars carved from the stonework. A much older house stretched from the manor's opposite side, a structure of narrow windows and heavy beams embracing plastered walls. The two edifices taken together seemed the size of a small village.

He pulled the carriage up to a low building of brick, perhaps four times as large as her aunt's home. "Step down, lass. I'll hand down your case."

"W-where are we?"

"This? Oh, the duke had a mind to separate the kitchen from the main house. It's all the rage, or so I'm told. Keeps the smells and such away from the living quarters."

"That will do, Peter. I'll take over from here." Mrs. Marcham appeared in the kitchen doorway. "Come along, young lady. There's no time for gawking."

"I'll be seeing you around, lass." The groundskeeper dropped the small case to the ground and flicked the horse's reins. "Hyah, get up there."

Mrs. Marcham gestured impatiently. "You must learn to move more swiftly when you are called."

Serafina had just picked up her satchel and started after the housekeeper when a young man appeared at the main house's rear entrance. Serafina saw how Mrs. Marcham stiffened at his arrival.

"Here now, what's this?" the young man asked in a languid drawl.

Mrs. Marcham's tone grew coldly polite. "Good afternoon, sir."

"Why, Mrs. Marcham, do we have some new household help? I haven't seen this young lass around before."

"She will be helping Cook in the kitchen."

"The meals will be far more tasty, I'm sure." Though Serafina kept her eyes lowered, her one glance revealed fawn-colored slacks tucked into riding boots that gleamed with a mirror shine. "Where ever did you find her?"

"She is Mrs. Donatella's niece."

"Is she now. How fortunate for the old lady. You there. What do they call you?"

Mrs. Marcham touched Serafina on the shoulder. "Come along."

Serafina followed the housekeeper toward the doorway.

"Here now. Don't I deserve a civil reply?"

Mrs. Marcham halted in the kitchen doorway. When she turned back to the young man, her expression was flinty. "I do hope I shan't have cause to speak to your father, sir."

Serafina kept her face angled toward the kitchen. But she heard the young man's casual good humor vanish. "My father won't be around forever to protect you, Mrs. Marcham. You would be well advised to remember that."

"Sir." The woman remained as she was for a long moment, and then she sighed and asked, "Are those all your belongings?"

"Yes, Mrs. Marcham."

"Inside with you." As she directed Serafina forward, she murmured beneath her breath, "Just as I said. Trouble."

Beryl Marcham maintained her distracted air as she ushered Serafina through the kitchen. At the side of the building closest to the main house, Mrs. Marcham descended a set of stone stairs. Her footsteps and words echoed loudly as she led Serafina along a stone tunnel. "This leads from the kitchen to the manor's dining hall." The echoes made it hard for Serafina to understand her words. "If you help with serving food, you will carry everything back and forth along here. And you will hurry, do you hear me, young lady? Everything must arrive at the dining table while still piping hot."

At the tunnel's end they climbed a circular stone stairs. They came up into a flagstone antechamber, one lined with tall windows. "The maids' rooms are along this way," she said and started down a narrow corridor. The wood floor was scuffed a brownish gray. The walls were painted but unadorned. Mrs. Marcham knocked on a door, then opened it. "You should be comfortable here."

A grimy window overlooked the swept yard between the kitchen and the main house. The floor was the same raw planking as in the corridor. There were two very narrow beds, both with mattresses rolled up on wooden slats. The only private space was a pair of drawers beneath each bed. A wash table and basin stood in one corner. Hooks lined the walls.

"We're a bit understaffed at the moment. But you mustn't think you will enjoy this room by yourself for very long." She pointed to the bed on the left. "Take that one. It will have the morning light. Now leave your things, and let's review your duties."

Serafina followed her back down the hall and into the small foyer. Mrs. Marcham pointed to a tall set of polished doors that stood opposite the stairs. "These lead to the principal rooms. You must only enter these when you are specifically sent there on your duties. We must be absolutely clear on this point."

"Yes, Mrs. Marcham."

The doors creaked open. A man of regal bearing with white muttonchop sideburns stepped through. He gripped the lapel of his black long coat with one hand and eyed Serafina down the length of his bony nose. "A new charge, is it?"

"Yes, Mr. Cuthbert. Serafina, you may curtsy to the chief butler."

She did as she was ordered. "Good day, sir."

"Serafina, did you say? What sort of name is that?"

"Italian," Mrs. Marcham replied. "She is Agatha's niece."

"Is she, now. I hope she won't be putting on airs and expecting unfair advantages as a result."

"Not for long, I assure you of that."

The butler eyed Serafina a moment longer but addressed the housekeeper. "I noticed the encounter with the young lordship."

"Very little escapes your attention," Mrs. Marcham noted archly.

"Could be trouble, that."

"Not if I have anything to say about it."

"No. Of course not. Where do you intend for her to begin?"

"Scullery maid," she replied. "I'll instruct Cook to add duties as she sees fit."

"That should keep her out of harm's way." He lifted his chin a notch. "Work hard, young lady. Mrs. Marcham is a fair mistress. You'll learn that soon enough. Earn her respect, and mine." He nodded to the housekeeper and disappeared.

"Come along." Mrs. Marcham swept through a battered swinging door. She pointed up a narrow spiral staircase. "Up here lodge the male servants and footmen. All but the groundskeepers; they reside above the stables. You are *not* to go upstairs under any circumstances. Do I make myself clear? Any maid found either up here or above the stables will be instantly dismissed."

"Yes, Mrs. Marcham."

"This way." She pushed through an outer door and entered the late afternoon light. A wet chill was already gathering. The housekeeper's skirt swished over the grass as she hastened around the kitchen outbuilding. Serafina had to hurry to keep up.

Set far back from the kitchen were the stables. Between them was a mound of logs rising higher than the kitchen roof. A young man of Serafina's age worked with an ax, breaking the logs into kindling.

"This is Harry, the groundskeeper's son. His duties . . . well, you can see them for yourself."

With one easy gesture the young man swiped his brow and pulled off his sweat-stained cap. A broad smile creased his tanned features. He offered a cheery "A grand afternoon, I'm sure, Mrs. Marcham."

"This is Serafina. Mrs. Donatella's niece. She will be serving as scullery maid for the time being."

"And it's wonderful to have the company, I'm sure."

"You are to show her the proper duties and refrain from all else, is that clear?"

Not even her frosty retort could dim his exuberance. "Clear as the day itself, Mrs. Marcham."

The housekeeper continued to Serafina, "The main rooms contain thirty-four fireplaces. You are to clean them out each morning and lay new kindling. But do not light them. The butler will do this himself, if required. You are to complete this first duty before the house awakens. You do not tend to the fires in the private rooms. Those will be seen to by the servants of each lord and lady. Each evening you will return through the rooms and fill the wood baskets and light any fires which require it."

When the housekeeper paused, Serafina knew enough to respond, "Yes, Mrs. Marcham."

"Between these duties you will serve at whatever task is assigned you by Cook." She pulled out a miniature pocket watch pinned to her vest. "Now if you will excuse me, I must see to dinner preparations."

As the housekeeper's purposeful stride carried her away, Serafina turned back to the footman and said, "Thirty-four fireplaces?"

"And a heap of grand old stairs to climb between them." This too did not dim his smile. "Never you mind. Tell me again what I should call you?"

At his ruddy complexion and stout good cheer, a tiny ray of hope found its way into Serafina's leaden heart. "S-Serafina."

"And what a lovely name that is. At this time of year, you won't need but one basket of wood per fire. Come winter, now, we'll all be puffing a good deal more from the work. But winter's eons away and we've got a splendid roast pudding for our supper." He clunked his ax down into the earth and picked up a pair of woven baskets—massive affairs as broad as Serafina's outstretched arms. "Let's fill these with kindling and I'll show you about the old place."

Chapter 16

A sailor would have called the morning very thin. Falconer stepped down from the carriage and sniffed the still air. He was in London, a city he did not know. A damp mist encased the world. He stood upon a square flanked by grand houses with a park across the way. Rows of trees lined the cobblestone lanes, they in turn showcasing stout Georgian townhouses.

Falconer rubbed his back and shoulders against the carriage frame, seeking to ease away the knots. He could not recall the last time he had felt this tired. He watched as a man he had roused from his bed not an hour earlier mounted the stairs three at a time and knocked on the front door. The man was named Daniel and claimed to be Gareth Powers's former sergeant major. Falconer found no reason to doubt the man. Although Daniel's long hair was now more gray than black, he still carried an impressive bulk about his massive frame. When the door did not open swiftly enough to suit him, Daniel pounded with a force that made Falconer wince.

The front door was flung back by a large, very cross woman in nightdress and matron's cap. "What on earth do you . . . ?" her tirade began. Then she recognized the man looming over her. "Daniel!"

"Aye, Mattie. Is the missus here?"

"Where else would she be, the hour before dawn?" She glanced around the big man, taking in the carriage and horsemen. "Is there news?"

"What about the Aldridges, are they in?"

"Everyone's fast asleep."

"Go rouse them, Mattie, that's a good girl."

She returned her gaze to the former soldier. "You have news, don't you. Is it the bairn? Tell me little Hannah is well."

"I'll tell you that and more. But only after you awaken the house. The missus deserves hearing my news first of all." Daniel waved at where Falconer stood by the carriage. "The man's traveled day and night and day again, Mattie. Is there food?"

"Not yet, but there will be soon. Take him back to the kitchen." Then she was gone.

"You can come up now, sir," Daniel said to Falconer, then continued to the two men on the carriage, "You lads can hop down and stretch your legs."

One of the horsemen objected, "We were ordered to never let Mr. Falconer out of our sight."

"And I'm telling you he couldn't be safer here if we locked him in the cellars of Westminster," Daniel retorted.

"Make ready for a swift departure," Falconer instructed the men. "I warrant they will supply us with fresh steeds so we can start back soon enough."

Inside, the house was filled with a rising clamor. Doors banged and voices shouted. Feet ran to and fro. Falconer rubbed the weariness from his eyes and followed Daniel through the foyer and down the hall. A maid curtsied and offered Daniel a nervous smile. "Mattie says I'm to serve you coffee."

"Grub," he corrected. "The gentleman's hollowed out."

Falconer dusted the road off his coat and trousers. "Coffee will do."

"Nonsense, if you don't mind me saying it, sir. When was the last time you had a hot meal?"

"I don't remember."

"There, you see?" Daniel said. "A soldier always eats when it's on offer, and Mattie keeps as fine a kitchen as any you'll find in London town." He turned back to the maid. "Kippers and ham and fresh-baked bread, that's the ticket."

"I'll see to that." The maid rushed back to the kitchen with her message, and the two men heard Mattie say, "Go find me a robe so I can look halfway decent for the guests. I was just up to light the kitchen fire when this great hulking gent here comes and disturbs my morning."

Daniel led Falconer into the kitchen. The maid swiftly returned with a quilted robe, handed it to the cook, and asked fearfully, "Is there news?"

"Aye, and it must wait for the missus," Mattie complained, banging her pots. "Though how a body is expected to survive such dread, I haven't a clue."

"What I've heard of the news is good," Daniel assured them. "But the rest must wait for Mrs. Powers."

"Praise be all the saints in heaven," Mattie said. "You men sit yourselves down. The two of you standing here crowds the very air, you're so big."

But before they could settle in, there came a rush of feet down the stairs. Two women came in—very different in appearance, yet both cut from the same cloth, or so it seemed to Falconer. They wore robes over nightclothes, hair tumbling down in nighttime disarray. Yet there was nothing sleepy about their expressions. Both looked alarmed and clung to one another with frantic hope. One demanded breathlessly, "You have news?"

"Are you Mrs. Powers?"

"I am," said the taller of the two.

He bowed. "John Falconer at your service, ma'am. I bring warm greetings from your husband, who instructed me to say he longs to see you again."

The two women were joined by a man of severe bearing. He rested one hand upon the shoulder of each woman and held them close. Erica Powers asked in an imploring voice, "And my baby?"

"Hannah is quite well, ma'am, and also sends her love."

"Finally," the smaller woman murmured, "our prayers have been answered."

The cook clasped her hands to her ample middle and whispered, "Thank you, Lord Jesus. Thank you."

"Then why are they not here?" Erica Powers demanded.

"The same reason it has taken them so long to return from America, Mrs. Powers. Croup."

"But they *are* in England?"

"Arrived at Portsmouth docks . . ." Falconer frowned and sought to calculate the time. But he could not make sense of the miles and hours and endless road. "What day is it?"

"Never mind that!" She moved quickly toward him. "Tell me where they are!"

"Harrow Hall, ma'am. In Wiltshire. They—"

"I must go to them." She would have fled the room immediately except for the man once more putting a firm hand upon her shoulder.

"I sense Falconer here has not completed his report," he said.

"But—"

"A moment, Erica. Please." The man asked, "You have more?"

"Yes, sir. But I was instructed to be discreet."

"My name is Samuel Aldridge. This is my wife, Lavinia."

"I have heard of you, sir." Falconer glanced at the cook and her assistant.

"They are family," Samuel Aldridge stated flatly. "As is Daniel here."

"Sir." Falconer returned his attention to Erica Powers. "Your husband and daughter were attacked at Georgetown harbor. Mr. Powers said I must warn you that there are spies about."

"Spies and worse than spies," Aldridge sternly agreed. "Is that why they went to Harrow?"

"Partly, sir. Gareth, that is, Mr. Powers, did not feel up to traveling into London first, though he sorely wanted to see you, Mrs. Powers. He also did not want to risk a single night in this home. Not for himself alone, but for the child and your own sakes as well. Even then he debated coming here first, but I urged him not to, and I am glad he heeded my word."

Aldridge declared, "It is not like Gareth to send another man into danger. What are you not telling us?"

"In truth, sir, he has not been at all well. He slept almost the entire first nine days we were at sea. He appeared better for a time. Then his fever returned, and the past few days have been a close-run thing."

"I must fly!" Erica wheeled about. Samuel Aldridge did not hold her back. Lavinia Aldridge rushed to follow her upstairs.

"A fever, did you say?" Aldridge asked.

Falconer wished for all his faculties, for clearly these people were anxious for details. "I feared we would lose him, sir. He has been most unwell."

Aldridge gripped the nearest chair back. "But he lives, you say."

"His strength of will is remarkable to behold." Falconer felt a wave of weariness sweep over him as he tried to maintain his wits during his report.

"Sit, man, sit. Mattie, bring the gentleman something to eat."

"I'm on it, sir." Swiftly the place before him on the table became crowded with plates and utensils. "Here you are, Mr. Falconer. Yesterday's bread is all we have, I'm afraid. But it's still fine, I warrant, and nothing spices up the food like a good appetite. A Wesleyan cheese, and butter I churned myself, and some honey. And coffee, now, and cream, and you just wait, I'll fry you up—"

"Mattie," Aldridge said mildly.

"Sorry, sir. I'm going on a bit, aren't I? I'll be quiet as the tomb now. Not a word more."

Aldridge drew out the chair next to Falconer's and seated himself. "You came into Portsmouth, you say."

"Aye. Yesterday. Just before dawn. Mr. Powers and I talked this through at length. He tells me Harrow Hall is owned by a strong ally of yours. It being a walled estate and somewhat isolated, he and the child could hopefully rest safely and gain strength. I volunteered to come straight away for his wife. It was the only reason he agreed to go on to Harrow, if I would travel here without delay."

"A wise course. How is Hannah?"

"I'm no doctor, sir."

"Tell me what you know."

"She is weak and has her spells. But she seems to be making more steady progress than her father."

"She is young."

"Aye, sir."

"And an angel," the cook added, busy over the fire.

"That she is, ma'am."

"How did they get to Harrow Hall?"

"I hired a coach at Portsmouth. We bundled Gareth, that is, Mr. Powers . . ."

"Call him as you will. I take it you are not a manservant but a traveling companion."

"I agreed to do what I could for father and child, sir. But I am on a mission of my own."

"What is it? Is there something I can do to help?"

Falconer hesitated. The man's strength and bearing resembled Gareth's on his few good days.

"Speak up, man. Gareth and Erica Powers are as close to me as my own kin. We moved Erica into my son's bedroom so as to help her during the uncertainty and fear. She was wasting away with worry over Gareth and the child." Aldridge nodded his thanks when the cook set a plate and cup of coffee in front of him. "Gareth should never have made that journey to America."

"Begging your pardon, sir," Daniel put in, "but he had to go."

"His place was here."

"Mr. Wilberforce himself urged him to make the journey."

To that Aldridge made no response save to sip noisily from his cup.

Falconer ventured, "I hear Mr. Wilberforce has been unwell."

"He has spent years making ill health a profession." Yet Aldridge's tone held no criticism, only deep concern. "But this time I fear for the worst. Why, do you know him?"

"I was told to seek him out."

"Well, that will have to wait, I'm afraid. The man is seeing no one. I am as close to him as any, and I've not laid eyes on him in almost two months."

Falconer leaned back in his chair, defeated. "Then I fear my cause is lost."

"Nonsense!" Aldridge's tone boded no argument. "William Wilberforce may be a great and even singular man. But he is far from alone. He is mighty because he has allies!"

"I was told to trust only him," Falconer replied.

"Then you were told wrong. You must trust God above all else and those whom you find thrust into your path by God's good hand!"

Falconer studied the man. Though he had no hint of military bearing, still he held power as natural as any Falconer had ever seen. "I shall think on your words, sir."

The two ladies burst back into the room, dressed in traveling clothes and each with a small bag. "We are ready!"

Falconer struggled back to his feet. "I am to deliver you personally, ma'am. Mr. Powers's orders."

"You are all done in," Aldridge protested.

"Daniel can see me to Harrow," Erica Powers said. "How are we to travel?"

"His lordship has sent his coach, but I must go with you."

"But you've not eaten a morsel," the cook protested.

"Pack it up, Mattie. I warrant this is a man not given to shirking his duties." Samuel Aldridge offered Falconer his hand. "You will think upon what I have said."

Falconer recognized the command for what it was. "I shall ponder long and hard, sir."

"A man is only as strong as his allies. God's right hand must sometimes be aided by his servants here on earth." Aldridge followed them down the long hall to the front entrance. As he passed the foyer table, he leafed through the papers and letters awaiting him. He selected two pamphlets and slipped them into Falconer's coat pocket. "It will do you good to read these in your spare time, sir. Now go, and God speed to all of you."

Falconer ate his breakfast as the carriage wound its way through mist-clad London. Mattie had thrust a second basket of food into the hands of the two ladies, but they were too distracted to eat yet. They talked endlessly, but Falconer remained silent. He ate his meal and inspected the man seated across from him. Daniel had the look of someone who knew his way around a fight. Falconer found enough comfort in Daniel's presence to allow himself to fall into a deep and dreamless sleep.

He awoke to their jouncing passage through a little stone village. He plucked out his vest watch and had difficulty focusing upon the numbers. He held the watch to his ear.

"You have slept eight hours, Captain Falconer."

Falconer wiped his face with his hands and peered from the window. "Captain no longer, ma'am. I am merely acting as your husband's manservant, Lady Powers."

"I bear no titles. And I doubt very much that a man of your bearing is anyone's servant."

Falconer started to deny it, then recalled whose wife this was. "There is much truth to your words."

She lifted the basket lid. "I see there are still some victuals, if you are hungry."

"Indeed, ma'am. Thank you."

"Tell me of your crossing, please."

"Nineteen days from the Potomac River's mouth to Portsmouth." The biscuit crumbled in his lap as well as his mouth. "Had I not been aboard myself, I would not have dreamed it possible."

"And Gareth? What can you tell me of him?"

He took in the way she twisted her kerchief in her lap. The edges of her mouth were crimped with strain, and her eyes were clouded with fatigue on a journey filled with unanswered questions. "He is a most remarkable gentleman, ma'am."

"I meant in regards to his health."

"He has been sorely tried. But I trust he shall recover."

"And Hannah?"

Falconer smiled. "I fear I am held captive by your daughter."

"She—" Then something beyond the window caught her eye. "Are those the Harrow gates?"

Falconer had no idea, as his previous visit had been in utter darkness. But the carriage knew its way and made the wide turning. The graveled lane ran straight and true beneath a double parade of elms. "A place of wealth and power," he murmured.

"And history," Erica Powers added. "There are so many tales about this place and the people who have made their home here. The current lord of Harrow Hall is a fine man, a wool merchant and weaver from Gloucester. He is a good friend of ours, a believer and an ally in our struggle. And a supporter of Wilberforce. I understand you know Wilberforce."

The driveway stretched ahead, seemingly without end. Falconer craned and spotted a deer in the distance. "Only by name, ma'am. I have never laid eyes on the man."

Erica was so intently focused upon the empty lane ahead she may well have not heard Falconer's answer. "The last earl of Harrow lost his titles and his land when he backed the American colonies in the war for independence," she murmured. "Charles was his name, and we were distant relatives." The way she twisted her handkerchief, the manner in which she craned her neck to see ahead, it was doubtful the woman heard even her own words. "The current lord acquired the house from the Crown some twelve years back . . . There!" She leaned forward. "Finally! The house! Oh hurry, driver! Please hurry!"

Before the carriage had swung around the forecourt and halted, Erica Powers had opened the carriage door and stumbled down its steps. She ran across the gravel, calling, "Gareth! Hannah! Where are they? Where is my family?"

Daniel leaped down from the carriage and watched the two women disappear into the great house. "I reckon they're safe enough here," he said to Falconer.

"I should agree."

"You look better rested." Daniel studied Falconer. "My gut tells me the major has found himself a battle-hardened ally."

It was rare that Falconer had to look up into the face of any man. "The major, you say?"

"We still call him such, those who served with him in the regiment. The major doesn't take to it, so we speak differently when we address him."

Falconer nodded slowly. "Gareth Powers is an uncommon man by any measure."

Further discussion was halted by the appearance of an older gentleman at the top of the stairs. "Here now, what's this?" The older man wore an impeccable dark suit, the long tails of his coat dangling below his knees. In the front it fitted around his ample girth with a double row of polished silver buttons. His mutton-chops were a hand's breadth in width and added severity to the scowl. "I run a proper household here. Proper, do you hear me? Menservants are not permitted to loiter about the forecourt discussing the weather!"

He halted on the last step but one, so that he was able to stare down his nose at the two taller men. "Your names, if you please!"

"Daniel and Falconer, sir." The big man answered for them both.

"Which of you is assigned to the ailing gentleman and his daughter who arrived last night?"

When Falconer chose to remain silent, Daniel offered, "He is, sir."

"And you, I gather, are the only escort the newly arrived ladies elected to bring along?"

"That is correct, sir."

"A sorry state of affairs. What with my staff already stretched to the limit."

"We left in a bit of a rush, sir." Daniel had retreated to parade-ground formality.

The older man sniffed loudly. "I am Cuthbert. The lord's chief butler. I am not someone you wish to get on the wrong side of. Is that clear enough?"

"Aye, sir."

"Then you will unload those bags and carry them to the

guests' rooms. Their apartments are located in the Jacobean Wing." He swung himself about. "His lordship likes to dine early. They are expected to table at the stroke of six of the clock."

Daniel waited until the ponderous old man had slammed the front door to ask, "Where were we?"

Falconer smiled. "Allies."

"Right." Daniel did a slow turn, studying the ground with a soldier's eye. "Looks quiet enough hereabouts."

"We were attacked in Georgetown Harbor. Three men. Armed with smooth bore rifles. It was a close-run thing."

"You think you were tracked here?"

"My guess is, word would not have reached these parts yet. Our crossing was uncommon swift. But I'd say it's only a matter of a week. Perhaps less." Even so, Falconer felt a hint of trouble. There was no reason for it. He had just said it himself. But the feeling gnawed at his innards.

"I'd best go off-load these wares and see to the family," Daniel said. "You coming?"

"In a minute." Falconer felt drawn by what he could not name. "I want to have a look around."

"Take in the field of fire," Daniel agreed. "Meet here in an hour?"

"By the stables," Falconer replied. "No need to draw the butler's ire."

Chapter 17

Serafina's days remained a blur of work and weariness. She rose before the dawn, awakened by the clamor of the household staff coming to life. The youngest cook rose earlier still, lit the main stoves, and set a great iron vat of tea to simmer. There was always a basket of bread husks set on the table, made by slicing the previous day's bread and leaving it on cooking pans overnight by the dimming fire, the last duty of the last cook each evening. The various maids and houseboys and gardeners came stumbling in each morning and wordlessly took a cup and a husk of toasted bread. They stood about and slurped their tea and ate the piece of bread without speaking or hardly even glancing about them. Mrs. Marcham arrived and issued terse instructions for the day. Soon enough they scattered to the morning's first duties.

Harrow Hall held eleven great rooms plus a large front foyer with marble fireplaces at either end. Each morning Serafina swept all the fireplaces. She then carried the ashes out to the compost heap behind the farthest barn. The fireplaces were scattered about the manor's first and second floors, and emptying all thirty-four and bringing in fresh wood required more than two dozen trips to and from the barn. She climbed upwards of forty flights in the morning and the same number again each evening.

As the household gradually came to life and the fires were set, Serafina's duties shifted from the manor to the kitchen stoop. She and two of the youngest footmen cleaned and polished the women's shoes and gentlemen's boots, as many as fifty pairs if there were guests. When these were finished, she polished cutlery and silverware. The two boys, both aged thirteen, would snigger and whisper as they worked alongside her. Serafina suspected they talked about her, but she did not bother to find out.

At four o'clock each afternoon, the staff was summoned by the ringing of a large bell. They gathered at two kitchen tables opposite the main stove. The larder was behind one locked door by the men's table, the sugar storeroom by the women's table. When Mrs. Marcham had discovered that some of the younger lads were being jostled and kept from eating their fill at the men's table, she made room for them at the women's table.

There was a general rush for places, as the tables were not large enough to seat all fifty-one of the household staff. Those who came late, including the men summoned from the farthest fields, either sat on benches lining the wall or squatted in the doorways. But there was always enough food for everyone. Mrs. Marcham saw to that. Several times Serafina heard the servants talk of how the lord kept a good table, all watching Mrs. Marcham as they said it. This was as close as any came to praising their mistress.

Their afternoon dinner consisted of a large dish of stew or a big joint of cold beef or lamb or pork, served with bread and cheese. On Saturdays the pastry cook brought out steaming trays of fruit cobbler and clay jugs of fresh cream to pour over each portion. After dinner the senior staff returned to their chambers and dressed for the dinner service. When he was well enough, the lord often entertained guests from nearby estates or up from London for a visit to the English countryside. Serafina did duty as a dishwasher. She was rarely in bed before midnight. The hour before dawn, it started all over again.

If she started to enter a great room and heard talk, she quietly backed out unseen. She had never even met the lord of the manor. The wife she had seen occasionally and once been introduced to her by the cook. But it was unlikely the frail woman even noticed Serafina. She had been preoccupied with that evening's meal, as one of their guests was to be a Cabinet minister. Serafina worked through her days with her eyes downcast.

Her duties were so overwhelming she rushed about in a haze of constant fatigue. Her body ached horribly the first week, but gradually she grew accustomed to the chores and the strain. Serafina's greatest difficulty was her hands. Carrying the heavy baskets rubbed them horribly. Harry showed her how to wrap her hands with rags to cushion them against the basket's chafing, and this helped some. Yet washing dishes softened the hands and opened the blisters. In truth, she did not mind either the pain or the chores. They kept her mind occupied and away from the ache at the core of her being.

She had Wednesday afternoons and Sunday mornings free. She spent most of these hours in bed, sleeping with the same desperate insistence of a starving woman being offered extra food. Her exhaustion became almost a friend, for it held back the nightmares. But she often woke with her face streaked by tears and her heart's wound reopened by dreams she could not remember.

Serafina spoke hardly at all. She had no friends among the staff. The other servants accepted her silence as simply her most obvious trait. That and her beauty. She could feel the men watching her sometimes. But as she was Mrs. Donatella's niece, they left her alone.

She occasionally caught a glimpse of the young lord of the manor. Whenever Serafina spotted him, she slipped away as quickly and unobtrusively as she could. Occasionally she had the feeling he was stalking her—taking his time, moving with the calm patience of a predator who had marked his prey. She was frightened of him but did not know what else to do besides flee.

On her free afternoons and mornings, Serafina awoke from her comatose slumber and went to the kitchen. Staff were permitted to stop by for bread and cheese and tea on their half days, so long as they stayed out of the cooks' way. Serafina took her chipped mug and her slice of fresh-baked bread and wedge of good Cheshire cheese into the corner between the front entrance and the tunnel stairs. She stood and watched the red-faced kitchen staff move in easy concert, their heads wreathed by smoke from the fire or steam from the great stew vats. They worked as hard as any of the staff, yet seemed to always have time for a nice word. When she had made her tea last as long as she could, Serafina went for a visit with her aunt.

Twice each week she visited Aunt Agatha, who had been given a pair of rooms on the ground floor of the old manor. Several times Serafina had intended to speak with Agatha about her concern over the young lord. But the older woman was never alone. She had many friends among the staff, and they were constantly dropping by for a chat. Agatha showed a stern visage toward her niece, a silent warning for Serafina to remember her place at all times, particularly in front of the other servants. Serafina's worries remained unspoken.

She wondered whether she should mention her fears to Beryl Marcham. But what was Serafina to say? That the young lord often appeared around unexpected corners, or she found him leaning against the wall with his arms crossed, leering at her? That he drawled out words that might have been lewd invitations but were spoken so softly she could flee and pretend not to hear them? That some evenings she turned from bending over the ballroom fireplaces and was certain she had been observed, even when she saw nothing but an empty room? She knew how the implacable housekeeper would respond. That unless Serafina had something specific, something definite, there was nothing Beryl Marcham could do. And if there was indeed trouble, it all would be viewed as Serafina's fault.

Thursday afternoons were young Harry's time off. The groundskeeper's son used this time and all day Sunday to hunt on the grounds. Mrs. Marcham gave him an extra half day at the groundskeeper's request because Harry was the best shot among the staff and kept down the number of vermin. Those afternoons were particularly difficult for Serafina, as she was left to fill all the kindling bins alone. By the end of her duties, her legs could scarcely hold her upright.

On this particular Thursday, by the time she had finished all but four fireplaces, Serafina was so weary she paid no attention to where she placed her feet. She had made the journey from the house's back entrance to the woodpile so often she did not need to look where she was going. There were new guests occupying several of the apartments. Houseguests meant more fires, and more fires meant more trips to refill the kindling bins. The bell for dinner had rung long ago, and hunger gnawed at her middle. But Mrs. Marcham had made it abundantly clear that she could not eat until the last fireplace had been seen to.

She was so tired she staggered as she rounded the outside wall of the kitchen. Two more journeys and she would be done. The shadows and her half-closed eyes made her stumble. Only this time there were strong arms waiting to catch her. "Have a care there, lass."

She responded to the voice as she would to the burning of an open flame. But when she tried to jerk herself loose from his grasp, the young lord held her fast. He pulled her back behind the huge woodpile before she could shape a response.

"You dare not scream." Though she kicked and struggled, the young lord maintained his languid tone. Stewart Drescott's grip was painfully strong, no doubt from handling horses. "It'd merely be my word against yours, don't you see."

"No. Please. You mustn't—"

"Ah, but I must. You've kept me waiting long enough, don't you think?" He released one hand long enough to strip the kerchief from her head. "Let's have a look at you, now."

"No! You—"

"You're as lovely a ripe peach as ever I've seen." Though the voice retained its languor, his features pulled back into a feral mask. "Smile for me now."

She found herself looking into the face of the fever beast in her worst nightmare. "I'll scream."

"We've been through all that. You won't, you know. Now smile. I do love a pretty girl's smile."

Suddenly she was weeping and so tired she could not think.

She hated the sense of weakness, the fear, the helpless defeat.

"Oh well, if you won't smile, then you won't." His hands wrapped themselves about her neck. "But you will kiss me, won't you. Oh yes."

He bent toward her. She ducked her head as much as his grip allowed. She felt the fingers tightening their hold. She screamed then, but softly. For truly she felt as trapped as she had ever been.

As suddenly as he had appeared, he was gone.

Her sudden release left Serafina crumpled upon the earth. Her arms felt branded where he had gripped her. She shielded her face with both of her arms and wept a plea of denial.

"Are you hurt?"

It was a stranger's voice. The fact that someone else had joined them gradually sank through her terror.

The young lord's voice was reduced to a hoarse groan. "Unhand me!"

The toe of a boot nudged Serafina. "You're safe now, lass. Look up here."

Reluctantly she uncovered her face enough to see above her, silhouetted against the sunset's trailing edge, a giant of a man. "Did the man hurt you?" he asked.

"N-no."

"Can you rise?"

Slowly Serafina forced herself back to her feet. The stranger was broad of shoulder and possessed an astonishing strength. He held the young lord suspended by one hand, gripping his jacket and shirt. Feebly, Drescott struck at the stranger's hand and forearm, but he might as well have been striking a tree trunk.

"This man attacked you?" the stranger asked.

"Yes."

"That's a lie." Stewart's air was constricted by the huge man's grip upon his collar. His voice was a coarse growl. "I'll have you horsewhipped."

"Will you now." The man seemed utterly unfazed by the words. "I suppose that means you're something like a highborn gentleman then."

Serafina shakily confirmed, "H-he is the son of the duke."

"Which duke would that be?"

"This is his manor. Harrow Hall."

"So. I come upon a defenseless maidservant being attacked by a man of wealth and power. Someone who believes he can do with others as he pleases. Is that right?"

Stewart Drescott sought to bend the fingers back but failed. The toes of his boots scrabbled across the ground. "L-let me go!"

The stranger turned so as to face Serafina, giving no notice to the young lord's feeble attempts to free himself. He asked gently, "Has he done this before?"

"H-he has only spoken to me."

"And you haven't been leading him on."

"No, sir. N-nothing."

Drescott protested, "That's a lie!"

"If I see him, I run away," Serafina went on. "But he—"

"She's a harlot, I tell you!"

The stranger tightened his grip. "Go on, lass."

"He follows me. He says things."

"Me? A lord? Follow a belowstairs strumpet about?" The words were scarcely more than a rattle now. The man's face was swollen and red. "What utter rot!"

The stranger inspected her for a moment longer, then turned back to the young man. "Be still."

Though the words were quietly spoken, the threat was clear. The young man choked, "I'll have you driven from the estate."

"Aye, you might at that. But here's something for you to think about." He raised his free hand and formed a fist the size of a mallet. "Take a very good look at this. I have broken a man's neck with one blow."

Stewart beat upon the stranger's forearm. "You don't frighten me!"

"Ah, but I should." He lifted the young man a few inches higher, until his boots were clear of the earth. The arms and legs windmilled and his eyes bugged out with the effort of drawing breath. The giant continued, "You should be very scared indeed."

"You're choking me!"

"Just as I suspect you were about to do to this young maiden." But he lowered the young man until his boots touched ground once more. The leather toes kicked up dust as Drescott sought to relieve the pressure upon his neck. Both hands struggled to release his collar.

"Now, the next time you see this young lady, tell me what are you going to do."

"I'll have the dogs put on your—"

The stranger tapped the young man's cheek with the side of his open palm. The hand traveled less than a foot in distance. Even so, the power was enough to rattle the young man's vision. His eyes traced about, his hands went limp.

"Pay attention." He shook the young man, waiting until the eyes came back into focus. "What you are going to do is this. You're going to run."

The lord started to protest once more. But the hand came back up in preparation for another open-palmed blow. Stewart flinched and remained silent.

"Now tell me what you're going to do the next time you see her."

He muttered something.

"Louder, now. I can't hear you."

He croaked the word. "Run."

"Good lad. And here's one other thought to carry away with you." The stranger re-formed his fist and tapped the young man gently upon the temple. "If you speak rudely of this young woman, if you sully her name in any way, if you make any trouble for her, you'll feel this. Now tell me that you understand."

"I understand."

The stranger abruptly released his grip. Stewart crumpled to his knees. He coughed once, twice, rubbing his neck where the starched collar had bitten deep.

"Now get out of my sight."

The young lord rose unsteadily. He started to lift his gaze toward Serafina. But the stranger anticipated it and stepped between them. He made the fist once more and swung it to within an inch of Stewart's face. "And you best remember what I've said. Because I meant it, every word."

The young man stumbled away.

The stranger turned back to Serafina. Now that the danger was passed, she felt ready to collapse once more.

Her weakness must have been evident in her features, for the man reached for her. His grasp was strong, yet he held her in the most gentle of manners. Suddenly she was sobbing. She could hardly breathe for the strength of her crying.

"Shah, now. It's passed you by, the danger. The storm came close, but you were saved. By the grace of all that's right in heaven above, it's safe you'll stay as well."

The relief mingled with the terror, and the closeness of her peril left her nauseous. She clung to his arm. He drew her closer still, but there was no threat to his manner. He smelled of dust and manly strength. "What were you doing back here alone, lass?"

"M-my d-duties . . ."

"You're done with your duties for the night."

"No, sir. Th-there are still four f-fireplaces—"

"They won't be seen to tonight, and that's final. Have you eaten?"

The simple concern left her unable to speak. She shook her head.

"Best clean up first, else there will be talk." He steadied her with the same arm that had held the young lord and walked her to the horse trough by the side of the nearest stable. "I don't know this house, but I know people, and a pretty lass like you will have tongues wagging if you give them half a reason. So this will stay just between us, right?"

He gave her his kerchief, which she dipped in the water and used to cleanse her face. He left her leaning against the stone trough as he went back to the woodpile and returned with her head scarf. He watched her fumbling efforts to retie the scarf. He motioned for her to lean forward, and he did it up himself, tying it up snug against the nape of her neck. "Never done this for a lass," he murmured. "But many seamen wear the same manner of headdress."

It was strange how one man's touch could scald her with fear and loathing and another's be so comforting. "Wh-who are you?"

"My name is John Falconer."

He had a most astonishing scar. She only saw it now, running across his cheekbone. He could easily be mistaken for a man of deadly peril. "I owe you my life, John Falconer."

"You owe me nothing, and that's God's truth." The evening light was dimming fast, but he might have flushed at her gratitude. "I am but God's servant, called to do what little I can for the bruised reeds in this world."

She did not understand all that he said, but the underlying comfort was clear enough. "I am Serafina."

"A name as lovely as the lady herself." He motioned toward the kitchen. "Let's go see if we can't find us both a morsel of supper."

Chapter 18

Falconer rose at his customary hour and for the usual reason. He washed and dressed and left the male servants' corridor, taking the rear staircase. Outside he walked the house's perimeter in the predawn gloom. Falconer assumed there was no risk of danger yet. Even if the attackers from Georgetown had managed to find another vessel immediately, taking a similar northern route with the same following sea, Gareth and his family had a few days' respite. A week at most, Falconer reckoned. He followed the gardener's route around the home, not so much to check for danger as to get a lay of the land. And to make some sense of the confusion in his head.

The customary lingering nightmare was this morning matched by another image. One of a lovely face surrounded by hair so fine it captured the light of dusk.

Falconer had journeyed far on several continents and found that most young lovelies were able to spark certain hungers, attracting young men like a siren's song. They were strongest in innocence when their power was unfiltered and magnetic. Any young man would dance his courtship ritual, displaying whatever was best and finest about himself.

One brief encounter, however, was enough to assure Falconer that Serafina was a much rarer breed. To Falconer's mind, Serafina held a quality so refined as to place herself ever beyond reach. She belonged to some princely realm. A place where mere mortals like himself might never enter.

Falconer paused at the home's southern quarter. Here the square Georgian manor was connected to a far older dwelling of wattle and beams as thick as a ship's timbers. A candle glowed through one of the diamond-shaped lead-paned windows. Falconer knew the Powers family resided in that wing. From the surrounding forests an owl called to its hunting mate. As he observed the old house, he recalled eyes like shattered gemstones. How was it possible for such a beautiful young woman to carry such pain she wept with every breath?

He swung about at a hint of sound. Falconer reached to his belt, but he carried neither sword nor dagger. Then he recognized Daniel's huge form. "What are you doing up?"

"I saw someone prowling about. Thought it might be you." Daniel spoke with a voice pitched between a whisper and a growl. "I figured you'd be inspecting the perimeter like any good officer."

Falconer resumed his pacing. "All's quiet. Go back to bed."

Instead, Daniel fell into pace beside him. "How long do you reckon the calm will hold?"

Falconer hesitated, then decided if Gareth and Erica Powers trusted this man, so should he. "A few days, perhaps a bit longer."

"Unless the danger was already here and waiting for the major's return."

This of course was Falconer's greatest concern. "What do you know?"

"Nothing I can name. But Mrs. Powers remained in England to continue the major's work. There've been spies and worse lurking about our printshop. Twice they tried to burn us out. Mrs. Powers moved in with the Aldridges for her own safety."

"Which means they may indeed have followed us here." Falconer thought of the pamphlets Samuel Aldridge had stuffed into his pocket. They were upstairs in his room, unread. Falconer had never been a great one for reading. "They're pamphleteers, I'm told."

"That and more. You have heard of the calls for social reform?"

"I have not set foot in England in years," Falconer replied. "And never ventured inland before."

"William Wilberforce is their leader. As fine a man as it has ever been my honor to meet. They seek any number of changes. Most of them are above my simple head. The central cause is the obliteration of slavery."

"Mr. Powers mentioned as much to me. But his illness kept us from discussing it very deeply."

"Nothing is closer to their hearts, besides God and family." Daniel stopped and turned, staring into Falconer's face. "Their cause strikes home, does it?"

Falconer had a sudden sailor's image of a ship making slow progress as it entered a river mouth. There was a certain moment, twice each day, when the river's flow joined with the tide's change to create an ebb so strong it could halt the swiftest vessel. The water would rush by, the sails could all hold fistfuls of wind, and still no forward progress was made. Even the wisest of sailors could miss the moment, for the river's tidal change was far removed from the sea's. In some river mouths, the difference was thirty minutes, in others a full two hours. Knowledge was everything.

It was precisely how Falconer felt just then. He had fought to make way. His quest was simple. Deliver his evidence to a trustworthy ally, then return to the West Indies and rescue his friend. Yet every step forward had left him no closer to either goal. "Samuel Aldridge told me I needed to find allies I could trust."

"If you're an anti-slaver as I suspect, you couldn't find better mates for guarding your back than these. The Powers and the Aldridges have been at the struggle for years. They're not in Parliament, and their names don't appear on any masthead save the pamphlets that bear their name. But they are major forces working behind the scene in the cause."

"You don't know," Falconer said softly, "what your words mean to me."

"The time of combat in Parliament is coming." Daniel spoke with the steady assurance of one who had read the battle lines with experienced care. "That's why Mrs. Powers remained behind. We're winning. At long last, and with God's help. And further change is on the wind."

"The reformists swept into Parliament six months back." Daniel paused and took a noisy drink from his mug. "Whigs, they're called. Never could get my mind around the labels these politicians choose for themselves. Sounds to me like a nasty breed of dog." He sipped again. "Where was I?"

"Reform." In truth, Falconer paid the former soldier only half a mind. He had returned to his room to retrieve the two pamphlets and now studied them with care. Reading had never come easy to him, and many of the words were long. But the message here was unmistakable.

"There's a powerful new middle class rising in the cities and countryside both. They've no patience with the old ways. A vast number of these folks are strong believers. They want change on every level. They want better care of the poor. They want schools. Hospitals. A government that provides for its people. A country where taxes are fair, and the roads are safe, and folk are free to move about. A decent wage for a decent day's work. The list is endless."

The kitchen was gradually filling with sleepy servants. But today was different. They did not seat themselves at the table with the two strangers. Instead, as they slipped in for their mug and husk, most lingered nearby and listened avidly to Daniel's words.

"Top of the list is slavery. Trade in new slaves was outlawed a while back. But there's rumors that the trafficking has continued. Hard to know, of course, because it's all gone secret. And it's so far away, down in the Spice Islands and the West Indies." Daniel eyed him. "Where did you say you were from?"

"For the past few years," Falconer replied, "I've run a chandlery on Grenada."

"Well, now." Daniel leaned back in his chair, signaling it was time for Falconer to do the talking.

But Falconer had no interest in divulging secrets in the company of so many strangers. He was about to say as much when a sound drew him from the chair.

Daniel spotted the sudden shift and moved impossibly swiftly for such a big man. "Trouble?"

Falconer headed for the door. "Stay where you are."

He recognized the sound for what it was as soon as he passed through the kitchen door. He walked around the kitchen and followed the noise back to the side of the stables. A cheerful young man was stripped to the waist and humming a tune under his breath as he wielded an ax. Falconer immediately knew that the lad was no trouble. He whistled sharply.

The lad looked over and lost his rhythm. "Who are you?"

"A friend. The lass, is she about?"

Though he was wary of Falconer's demeanor, the young man took a firmer grip on the ax handle. "She's not to be played with by the likes of you."

Falconer held up an open palm. "I mean no harm. She was attacked yesterday."

The ax lowered. "By the young lord?"

"Foppish, slender, thinks all the world is his plaything."

"Aye, that's the one. Stewart Drescott." The young man's face flushed with anger. "Did he hurt her?"

"I found them in time. Where were you?"

"Hunting. My half day off. The lass didn't say a thing to me about it this morning. But then again, she wouldn't. Hardly speaks a word, our Serafina. Quiet as a little blond ghost."

"Where is she now?"

"Seeing to the fireplaces in the great rooms. But—"

Falconer headed back, treading on silent feet. He did not run, for he could feel eyes upon him over by the kitchen. But he walked at a pace that few could match for long. He bounded up the rear stairs, slipped through the portal, and halted. A scraping sound led him down a servants' corridor and through a pair of painted double doors. He stepped into a room of vast proportions. Six tall windows marched down one side, matched by gilded mirrors upon the opposite wall. Two marble fireplaces adorned either end. A figure knelt before the one closest to where Falconer stood. He stepped back and stood in silence.

Serafina gripped the basket with one hand and plied a small shovel with the other. A brush and pan were tucked into pockets of her apron. Rags tied around her hands were turned gray by the soot. She worked steadily but slowly. Falconer could hear the sighs of her breath, small gasps that could almost have been sobs.

She brushed the remnants of ash into her pan and flicked that into the basket. She rose slowly. Only then did he realize she was trembling. Whether from fear or fatigue, he could not tell. She gripped the basket with both hands, and the strain of lifting it shown upon her features. He had not noticed her bandaged hands the previous day, or perhaps he had but discounted them. Many scullery servants wore protective cover on their hands. But the way she winced as she hefted the basket suggested more at work than just tender flesh.

Her face was more heart shaped than oval, he noticed. Two strands of hair had emerged from her scarf and fell like wisps of cloud over one eye. Ash was streaked across her forehead where she brushed at the lock of hair with a hand stained black. Her eyes were clear of tears, but Falconer suspected it was merely because she had shed them all. Never had he seen such a tragic face upon one so young.

And young she was. A woman, yet hardly so. He had no ability at judging a woman's age, but he doubted Serafina was more than twenty. He watched her take shaky steps toward the opposite fireplace, and suddenly he felt ancient beyond his years.

The servants' entrance to the room was nicely adorned. The formal entrance, however, was palatial. The broad double doors were formed from rare woods inlaid with a golden crest. One caught the sunlight as it swung open and banged against the wall. A man's voice called out, "There she is!"

The words drew a terrified gasp from Serafina. She dropped the basket, which tumbled upon its side and spilled a cloud of ash over the parquet floor. She groaned at the sight. Then again at the advancing man.

"Shame, girl. I shall have to punish you for that carelessness." The young lord stepped lightly upon polished calfskin boots, the silver buttons glinting on his velvet day coat. "And for the manner of my dismissal yesterday."

"No," she whimpered.

"Come, come. What harm is there in a bit of fun? You can't be content with this dreary existence. Not a lovely lass such as yourself."

"I'll—I'll scream."

"You won't, you know. The house will awaken, a storm will ensue, and it would be my word against yours." He opened his arms. "And now there is no hulking great brute to interrupt us."

Falconer stepped through the doorway. "Wrong again."

The man leaped into the air and spun about. "You!"

"None other." Falconer started a measured tread across the floor. "I warned you what would happen if—"

"Keep away from me!" The young lord fled the room.

Serafina watched Falconer's approach above hands clenched to her face. Her chest heaved and her entire body trembled.

"It's all right, lass." He bent over and righted the basket. "Hand me your brush."

She did not respond. He reached over and slipped the brush and pan from her apron.

She kept her hands before her face. "A-are you a guardian angel?"

Falconer laughed out loud. "I have been called many things. But that is a first."

"Then who . . . ?"

"The name is Falconer. John Falconer. As I told you last

night." Up close she was even more lovely, a perfect figurine dressed in ashes and servant's weave. "Is Serafina your first name or last?"

"First. My name is Serafina Gavi." A lilting accent added tragic melody to her words.

"There, you see. We are suitably introduced." He reached over once more. "Now let me see your hands."

Reluctantly she offered one hand. He took hold of fingers tapered and fine. And soft. These were no worker's hands. Gently he peeled back the rag, but not far, because he could see the blisters were suppurated and clinging wetly to the cloth.

He looked up at her. "Why did you not tell someone?"

"About what?"

"About . . ." He let her pull her hand free. "Lass, those wounds must be seen to, else you could be scarred for life."

Her gaze opened further. Falconer crouched beside the pile of ashes and watched as her eyes revealed a depth of pain that drew him up sharp. She started to speak but was halted by the sound of rapid footsteps in the hallway.

"What's this?" a woman gasped. "What on earth is going on here? Serafina, how could you?"

Falconer rose to his feet, saddened that their moment's solitude was over. "It was not her, ma'am."

A severe woman in a dark high-necked dress marched forward. "And just who, pray tell, are you?"

"Manservant to Mr. Powers, ma'am." He gestured to the young woman cowering behind him. "She was attacked. Again."

To his surprise, the woman did not disbelieve him. Instead, she turned to Serafina and asked, "The young lord?"

"You knew?" Falconer heard the grating anger in his voice. "You knew and did nothing to protect her?"

Whatever the woman saw in his face, it was enough to back her off a pace. "Stewart Drescott is the only son and heir."

"Which matters not a whit to me." He turned to Serafina. "Have you eaten this morning?"

"N–no, sir."

"Go and have your breakfast. No, leave the basket. I'll see to this mess."

The woman tilted her chin. "I give the orders in this house."

"Then tell her to go!"

The woman distanced herself another step. "Leave us, Serafina."

When they were alone, Falconer demanded, "Is this the way you protect those in your charge?"

"I had no idea this had happened." She studied the man before her. "You're sure about this? She was actually attacked?"

"Last night. Out by the woodpile." He pointed at the dirtied floor. "And again just now."

The woman suddenly looked very worried. "Serafina is niece to my predecessor but is utterly untrained for proper household duties. I don't know what to do with her."

Falconer made short shrift of the remaining ashes. He hefted the basket, rose to his full height, and said, "I do."

Chapter 19

The manor's older wing was in itself one of the largest houses Falconer had ever entered, far grander than any of the island plantations he had visited. And it was itself dwarfed by the newer Georgian structure. He walked the passage connecting the old house to the new. Lead-paned windows flanked him on both sides, overlooking carefully tended rose gardens. At the end was a winding staircase of darkened beams and pickled oak flooring, hard as stone. Falconer climbed to the middle floor, knocked on the ancient peaked door, and was invited to enter.

The apartment was designed as four interconnecting chambers. There were two such guest apartments on the second floor. The Powers family occupied one apartment, the other was currently empty. On the top floor, a narrow corridor ran directly under the roof's eaves, opening into five servants' rooms. The ground floor held three larger chambers that had been renovated into single-room apartments.

The Powerses' front room was full to the brim when Falconer entered. Gareth Powers rested upon a daybed, a leather settee with a long tongue that could be used either for sitting or reclining. His wife was in a high-backed wing chair drawn up close enough for her to keep one hand upon his shoulder. Hannah was seated upon the floor by her mother's chair, teasing the kitten with a ribbon. Daniel stood in the corner behind the door, as unobtrusive as any man his size could be. A second wing chair was occupied by a gentleman in a quilted robe, a silver cane in his hands, a benign smile upon his features. The chief butler stood by the window, one hand gripping his lapel. He frowned mightily at Falconer's ash-stained knees but said nothing.

"Ah, Falconer. We were just speaking about you." Gareth's voice was weak yet clear. "Do join us."

"It is good to see you awake, sir."

"Nothing could do more for my health than to be reunited with my dear wife," he replied, gripping her hand.

Erica Powers added, "Gareth was just relating how you saved his life."

"And mine," Hannah added from the floor.

Erica smiled at her daughter, then blinked fiercely and struggled to say, "I owe you everything."

Falconer found it hard to shape a response. The Powers family was bound together by far more than glances or caring gestures. Despite their illnesses and all the months apart, Falconer felt the power of their connectedness. Theirs was a gift denied to him by all that he had been, all he had done. "I count it an honor to know and serve your family, ma'am."

Gareth said, "I don't believe you have met our host, Lord Drescott."

"Sir."

"An honor, my man," the elderly gentleman responded. "A delight and an honor. I am given to understand that you were once a sea captain."

"That is correct, sir."

"Which holds the corresponding rank of colonel in the land forces." The old gentleman had the ability to smile without moving his features. "Which means he outranks you, Gareth. Strange for a manservant to outrank the master, wouldn't you say?" He chuckled in merriment at his own joke. The butler harrumphed his indignation.

"With respect, sir," Falconer said, "Mr. Powers served in the king's forces."

"And you did not?"

"No, sir."

"Whom did you serve, then?"

Falconer swiveled his gaze to Mrs. Powers. "I regret to say that I once commanded a slaver."

But the news did not draw out the shock and dismay Falconer expected. He had the distinct impression that Gareth had already shared this information with his wife. The old man twisted his cane so that the silver head captured the sunlight. "Did you, now. Did you. How utterly fascinating. Perhaps you know the story of John Newton."

"I fear not, your lordship."

"Pity, that. He was a shipmate of yours, in a manner of speaking. A slaver who converted to the faith and went on to become a vicar. A wonderful gentleman. Had a remarkable way with verse, as it were. Penned quite a number of lines. 'Amazing Grace' was one of his hymns, a personal favorite of mine. He died some time back, I don't recall exactly when."

"Thirty years ago," Gareth supplied.

"Was it that long? Was it? My, but I can see him more clearly than people I met last week. A stalwart man, he was, strong in both faith and action. I miss him."

"As does William," Erica Powers said. "He spoke to me of Newton just last month."

"Did he. How fascinating. How is dear Wilberforce?"

Erica drew in upon herself. "Not well, I'm afraid."

"What a pity. He will be sorely missed." The gentleman tilted his head sharply to one side. Only then did Falconer realize he was blind in one eye. "You are quite a sizeable fellow, aren't you."

"Yes, sir."

"You and that other fellow standing there in the corner, you compress the air, you do. Wouldn't want to come up against the either of you in a fight." He seemed cheered by the thought. "You are a believer, I take it."

"I am, sir."

"Good. Jolly good." He thumped his cane upon the flooring. "We need men such as yourself in the struggle ahead. Strong and stalwart and leaders in battle. Like Newton. Pity he's gone ahead of us to Glory. Thirty years. My, but it seems like we were talking just the other day."

The butler addressed the old gentleman in an entirely different tone. "Perhaps you'd care to come down for breakfast, sir."

"Have I not eaten yet?" He fumbled for his vest watch. "My, look at the time. No wonder my belly's given in to grousing. Gareth, will you join me?"

"If you will permit me, sir, I think I should remain at rest awhile longer."

"Of course. Silly of me to ask." Before the old man could lean upon his cane, the chief butler was there at his side and helped lift the man to his feet. "Kind of you, Cuthbert. Don't know what I'd do without you."

"Sir." The butler said more softly, "You wished to inform your guests of the two men arriving later today."

"Did I, now. And who might they be?"

"The two members of Parliament, my lord."

"Indeed so. You are a prize, Cuthbert. A veritable prize among men." He turned back. "Allies to our cause are stopping by. This day, is it, Cuthbert?"

"Either this evening or tomorrow morning, sir."

"Quite so. They are here to ask me for help, no doubt. Which is a pity. I would so like to aid them, but you see my state. A shuffling old man, hardly able to help myself."

"You are a prince among men," Erica Powers said softly.

"Kind of you, my dear. Very kind. I was hoping I might ask them to meet with you instead. If any can help them, I warrant it would be you two." At their nods, he turned to the door, Cuthbert at his side.

Falconer watched the old man's shuffling departure and understood why no one wished to speak with him about his only son.

When the door closed behind them, Falconer dropped to the floor beside Hannah. "I need to ask a favor."

The girl's eyes widened. "Of me?"

He nodded. "There's something that needs doing, and only you can manage this."

She looked from one parent to the other. Clearly no adult had ever spoken to her in such a manner before.

The kitten mewed loudly at being ignored. Falconer scooped up the animal, which promptly began purring. "There is a young servant lass here at the manor. Her name is Serafina. She is in some sort of trouble. I can't say precisely what it is. But I do know for certain that she needs a friend."

"You want me to be her friend?"

"It's a lot to ask, I know. But I think you would do her a world of good." Falconer looked to the parents. "Serafina has run afoul of the young lord."

"A scoundrel if ever there was one," Erica agreed darkly.

"It would be good," Falconer added, "if Serafina could find quarters outside the main house."

"There is an extra room here," Hannah said. "One next to mine."

"She is a likely enough lass," Falconer went on to Erica. "More than that I cannot say."

Hannah's parents exchanged a look, then Erica replied for them both, "Perhaps then we should have a word with the young lady."

Serafina sat alone in the kitchen, though surrounded by noise and people. She had positioned her chair away from the central table, pushed back into an alcove between the central fireplace and the spice cabinet. The stone wall felt cool to her back. Three kitchen helpers peeled vegetables and chattered away. The cook and the pastry chef were busy by the ovens, casting the occasional comment to their mates as they worked. The steam was heavy and rich. Serafina dipped her husk into her tea and huddled down into her chair. She ate because she knew she needed the nourishment, though the sensation of hunger seemed to belong to another person. She sipped her tea and tasted the sugar, yet she could not claim anything as belonging to herself—not the flavors nor the moment's ease. She felt as though her spirit had been wrenched free of her body, that she was seeing everything from a very great distance.

She could see how the past days had been spent running away. Not from this place, nor from the work, nor even from her attacker. No, it mattered little where her physical form was. So long as she could escape from the agony of looking inward.

But the morning's shocks had left her unable to flee any longer.

Luca had lied to her from the beginning. He was married. He had been involved with at least one other woman, also married. He had promised her what he needed to promise in order to have what he wanted. And what he had wanted was not marriage. Nor love.

She in turn had taken his lies and twisted them into lies of her own. She had claimed her actions were motivated by love. Whether there had ever been any truth to this, she could not say. But she now realized that much of what she did had been aimed at avoiding anything, any *truth* that might deny her what she wanted.

Only now there was no escaping the fact that what she had wanted had never existed except within her own imagination. And all the people she had hurt along the way, her parents especially, had only sought to protect her.

Serafina started slightly as the cook leaned forward and refilled her cup with steaming tea. She tried to form a thanks, but her mind did not seem capable of words just then. Even so, the kitchen drew slightly back into focus. She realized that others had come in, and one of them was the headmistress. Without actually understanding the words, she sensed that people were whispering about her.

A waking nightmare gradually took form in the steam spiraling up from her cup. She saw anew the young lord, felt his hand upon her throat, and saw the fierce hunger in his eyes. She shuddered at the thought that this was perhaps her punishment. And shuddered again at how she deserved that and more.

Then another shadow fell over her. She smelled the man before she saw him, a mixture of soap and smoke and male strength. She did not look up, nor did she move to draw away as he pulled up a chair and seated himself next to her. He settled a clay bowl into his lap. The smell from the steaming water was pungent but not unpleasant. He then reached over and took her cup and the remaining husk. She turned just enough to see the white cloth laying over his shoulders, the way his strong hands knew precisely what to do.

Falconer took hold of her left hand. He turned the palm upward and prodded gently at the places around the edge of the filthy rag. He then dipped her hand into the bowl. It stung mightily. She winced but did not try to draw away.

"Steady now," he murmured. "That's a good lass."

Serafina lifted her gaze a fraction more. It was safe to examine him now, because he was intent upon her hand. He kneaded the rag, releasing the ash and clouding the water. "Hot water, the hotter the better," he said. "Mixed with brine and vinegar. You know the word *brine*?"

"Salt."

"Sea salt," he corrected. "But I reckon whatever Cook uses is good enough in a pinch. Hold still now, this may sting a bit."

She bit her lip as he began unraveling the rag. When he had to tug to release it from her flesh, he did so with remarkable gentleness. Swiftly enough the rag was lifted from the water. He withdrew her hand, wiped it with his clean cloth, and carefully inspected the palm. He grunted over what he saw. "Let's have the other one now."

Serafina continued her oblique inspection of him. He was a warrior. Of that she had no doubt. His face held an angular strength that was fierce even in repose. His dark hair was oiled and drawn back into a tightly knotted pigtail, like Venetian sailors she had seen along the city's harbor. His eyes were almost as dark as his hair and held an alert intensity. His hands and wrists were very strong. She saw with an artist's accuracy a remarkable resemblance between this man and Luca. Yet the similarities were all superficial. How she could say this with any certainty, Serafina did not know. Yet there was a calm force about this man, one so potent it reassured even her.

He dried her right hand and gave it a careful inspection. Then he rose and carried the clay basin over to the doorway and poured out the dirty water. Everyone in the kitchen was casting glances her way. Serafina dropped her eyes to her hands. The blisters looked raw and angry.

"No, don't touch." The man walked over and reseated himself. The bowl was refilled with clean water. "All right, put them both in. Aye, the water's hot. But it'll do you good."

She forced her hands into the almost scalding liquid. The blisters felt like they were being stabbed with tiny needles.

"Nothing better than brine and vinegar. It's what we used for the young middies when the hemp burned their hands. I don't suppose you know what a middy is, though, do you."

Serafina shook her head. Then she realized he could not see her, for his attention remained upon her hands. "No, sir."

"I'm not a sir, lass. Do you remember my name?" He kept his voice low.

"John Falconer."

"That's it. Most folks call me by my second name alone. Falconer." He kneaded the palms with gentle stroking motions. "There's ash in the skin, which troubles me. But you're young enough, maybe you won't scar overmuch. A middy, lass, is a young midshipman. They join the crew as young boys and get their learning before the mast. That's how I learned the sea. I stood my first watch at twelve years of age, high on the mizzen, in every weather the sea could throw at me."

His voice was as soothing as his touch. He kneaded one hand after the other, halting just as the flaking scabs drew such pain she almost cried out. He seemed to know how much she could take, which was when he released one hand and started on the other.

He directed his voice to her hands as he asked, "How did you let them get this bad?"

What was she supposed to say? That the pain, like her fatigue, had helped her escape from looking inside? She felt a hot tear course down her cheek. "You are too kind."

Falconer looked into her face for the first time since seating himself. His eyes tracked the tear. She could see him clearly now. The scar coursing up his cheekbone only accented the gentle light to his eyes. She blinked and released another tear.

"Who hurt you, lass?" he murmured.

"Nobody. I did it all to myself. And to others." Serafina had to stop then, for to say more would have meant releasing the sobs that clenched her up tight.

But her remark only deepened the gaze. As though he understood what she meant. Which of course was impossible.

Falconer kept his voice so low the kitchen clatter rendered his words only for her. "Do you trust me, lass?"

"Oh, yes." She did not need to think that one through.

He turned to the cook and called, "I don't suppose you have any goose fat I could use."

"That I do, sir. That I do." The cook passed over a covered bowl, glanced at Serafina's hands, tut-tuted once, and retreated to the stove.

He withdrew Serafina's hands from the pinkish water. Falconer dried them carefully, then coated the palms with the fat. He tore a clean cloth into strips and bound her hands. "You can't leave Harrow Hall, is that right?"

"I have nowhere else to go."

"What about family?"

Her answer was very broken. "They are lost to me."

He cast her another glance, full of meaning. There and gone in a dark flash of comprehension. "Then we must find you a place where you'll be protected from the young lord. I have friends here. People I think you should trust. I do."

He looked up once more and saw she did not understand.

"There is a young girl. Hannah. She has been very ill. She needs a companion." He waited. When Serafina did not respond, he went on, "Will you meet with her parents?"

Again she did not need to think this through. "I will do whatever you say."

Chapter 20

Falconer tossed and turned on the narrow creaking bed. This early morning had not been marred by his habitual nightmare. He had been awake for hours. He lay on his back and stared at the ceiling. The predawn light was a pale wash upon the world, a perfect canvas for the mind's images. He could study her as though she were there before him now.

Serafina was a singular beauty. But there was far more than loveliness at work here. He sensed a kindred spirit, one who had been torched by her own mistakes. It left him hoping for the impossible. Yet his years of facing deadly risks had taught him to measure the odds. And the odds here were all against him. She was young, she was lovely, she was highborn. He still felt the soft flesh of her hands in his. He saw the way she held herself, heard the manner of her speech, and knew this was no servant maid. Which meant that whatever her transgressions, her beauty would draw her back into the front parlors of some man far richer than himself. Someone who knew the proper ways of highborn life. Someone other than John Falconer.

He finally rolled from his bed and dressed and lit a candle. His glance fell upon the two pamphlets. They too had given him much to feed upon. Falconer found his place in the Bible and began his readings. But this day, divine communion did not arrive. Her face was there upon the page, the shattered gaze staring up at him.

Falconer rose, wrenched open the door, and made his way down the passage. The previous afternoon he had shifted his berth from the servants' corridor to a chamber set in the rafters above Gareth and Erica's apartment. Daniel snored away in the next room. Softly he started down the stairs, boots in hand.

But on the next level he was greeted by a small voice saying, "Serafina has nightmares too."

"Lass, you should be resting abed."

"I slept almost all yesterday afternoon. Where are you going? Can I come?"

"Not out into the dawn chill." Before Hannah could protest further, he added, "I was just going for tea. I'll bring you back a cup."

When Falconer arrived in the kitchen, the cook was already bustling about. "You're up early," he greeted her.

"His lordship likes his early matins, he does." She was busy setting out a breakfast upon a silver tray.

Falconer realized it was Sunday. The week's onward rush had stolen away his sense of time. "Is there a church nearby?"

"You're a churchgoing man, are you?"

"I am."

"Wouldn't have thought that myself, you with the manner of a battler and a bruiser about you."

He decided there was nothing to be said to that. He turned at the sound of footsteps and found himself facing the chief butler. Cuthbert was dressed as always in long coat and starched white shirt. "Good morning, sir."

"How's the young lady?" Cuthbert asked.

Falconer supposed he was speaking of Serafina but could not be certain. "I hope she's resting, sir."

The butler nodded acceptance and said to the cook, "His lordship is asking after his breakfast."

"Which is ready and piping hot." When the butler had departed, she asked Falconer, "You're after tea, I suppose."

"For myself and the Powers lass."

"She's a pretty one for such a little waif."

"Careful," Falconer said. "She'll steal your heart clean away."

"I believe I noticed another lass doing that to you yesterday." She clattered about, giving him no chance to object. "I'll make up a breakfast tray for the family, shall I?"

Falconer felt the warmth in his face as he accepted the tray. The cook gave him a knowing smile and said, "The church in Harrow village is attended by all the servants who have a mind. It makes for a nice walk through the forest, there and back. A mile down to the side gates. You'll see the steeple from there. Makes for as fine a courting spot as any I've seen."

He trod back across the rear walk, arguing with himself more than with the smiling cook. He climbed the stairs to discover Serafina standing in the hallway. For a moment he let himself believe she awaited him. She wore the dark servants' garb, her hair bound and hidden beneath the head scarf. She curtsied and said, "Good morning, sir."

"I asked you not to address me so. How are you today, lass?"

"My hands are better, thank you." She kept her eyes downcast. "Hannah decided to go back to bed."

"Probably for the best," he acknowledged, though Falconer wondered if she had done so to let them be alone. "Will you take tea?"

Serafina followed him into the apartment's front room. "I am instructed to go to the kitchen for my breakfast."

Her voice and accent made a song of the simplest of words. "From now on, you shall eat with the Powers family."

She fumbled with her apron. "And the fireplaces?"

"Those are someone else's responsibility now. Sit yourself down there."

Falconer made rather a mess of pouring the tea, but she did not seem to notice. Serafina avoided his gaze as she whispered thanks and accepted the cup. "You say your hands are healing?" he asked.

"They don't hurt as much."

"A good sign. I'll have a look at them later." The thought of holding those soft palms once more gave him pause. He drank his tea, then said, "There's a church service this morning. I thought I might perhaps go. Would you—"

"No. I can't. I mustn't." The words were a tumbling rush.

"Do you not believe in God?"

"Oh yes. But . . ."

Falconer inspected her carefully over the rim of his mug. "Drink your tea, lass." When she had taken a tentative sip, he asked, "You are a Christian?"

"I was. Before . . ."

Her voice had returned to the shaky whisper of the previous day. It reminded him of distant birdsong. "Before what?"

She set down her cup. And shook her head.

Falconer sighed. His gut churned, but his mind felt crystal clear. Which was a remarkable feat. On the one hand, this young maiden ignited a hunger in him as fierce as any blaze. Yet there was something else at work here. He knew this with a visceral certainty. He sighed again, trying with all his might to push away his own selfish longings. "Look at me, Serafina."

Meeting her gaze made it even harder to think beyond what he wanted. He felt awash in human desire. His voice grated in his own ears. "You said you trusted me."

"I do."

"Then tell me what it is that keeps you from church."

"I have sinned." The words ended in a soft moan.

"Go on."

"I loved a man who was very, very bad. All knew it but me. I have lied and stolen and deceived. I ran away. I . . ." She dropped her chin once more. Back and forth she shook her head.

Falconer shut his eyes. His prayer was a desperate plea. *I am so weak, I am so frail, I am so human. Help me to do right here, Lord. Because without thy direction and strength, I will only wreak havoc on this gift of trust.*

He opened his eyes and rose to his feet to go and stand by the window. "How old are you?"

"Seventeen," she told her bandaged hands. "Eighteen in three months."

"There are worse things," he said quietly, "than being seventeen and having loved the wrong man."

Her head still bent, she confessed, "I have betrayed every person who ever loved me."

Falconer responded with a voice coppery hard, as beaten and hot as tempered metal. "When I was seventeen I *killed* my first man."

Serafina looked up, obviously struggling to make sense of his words.

"You think you carry guilt? You think you are too far removed from salvation for the Savior to care over your soul?" He struck his own chest with a fist shaped as though it held a dagger. "I am living testimony to how wrong a life can go. And how far the Savior's reach extends."

The shame of confessing left him hunched over. But he forced himself to continue. "God has found a way to reach me. What good I am to Him, I cannot say. I feel as though my tread shames the stones of every church I enter. But Christ died for me. Of that I am utterly certain. Whatever you have done, He holds out his arms for you as well."

He could not stay with her longer. Falconer crossed the room and opened the door. "I shall leave for church in one hour."

Falconer dressed with as much care as he could manage, given that everything he possessed was travel weary and salt stained. He wiped his boots with a hunk of the breakfast bread in an attempt to bring out what shine was left. He chose the cleanest of his shirts and the only pair of trousers still holding a crease. He went out to the stables and borrowed a wire brush from the stable lad and did what he could for the state of his coat.

Harry, the young man who worked the woodpile, was seated by the stables greasing down a pair of shotguns. "I've curried horses who looked better after a day's ride over open country," he commented wryly.

Falconer tossed the coat over a nearby rail. "I don't know why I bother."

"It's a bonny enough day," Harry agreed, misunderstanding. "You won't be needing such cover."

"That coat was given to me by a fine American gent. But a month's travel on the open seas has near about done it in."

"There's a slop chest we can all draw from." Harry propped his gun against the stable wall. "That's what the sailors call it, right?"

"How are you knowing I'm a sailor?"

"What you said to Serafina."

Hearing her name upon the lips of another brought a flush to his features. He scowled. "You were listening?"

"Not me. But word carries fast around here."

The young man walked into the stables and returned bearing a long coat with bone buttons and a velvet collar. It was a fashionable item, with a long split tail similar to the butler's coat. "I can't wear that," Falconer objected.

"Don't see why not. The young lord won't be seen in anything for more than a single season." Harry held it up to the light. "This was cut big so he could wear it as a top coat. It should fit you fine."

"This belongs to the lordship's son?"

"That or one of his guests. Try it on." Harry took a step back. "Bit snug about the shoulders, but you look ready for the high street, you do."

Falconer liked the lad and his merry grin. "I'm much obliged."

"There's those among us who've taken a liking to our blond ghost. You've got friends among the staff now. Especially Miss Agatha. You met her yet?" At the shake of Falconer's head, Harry said, "She was Mrs. Marcham's predecessor. Beloved by all. Serafina's her niece."

"Why is Serafina here?"

"A proper mystery, that is. Lot of speculation, but Miss Agatha is the only one who knows, and she isn't saying." Harry grinned. "You find out something, you let me know, will you? Fair exchange for the coat on your back."

When Falconer returned upstairs it was to find Serafina waiting on the landing. She was accompanied by Hannah, who said plaintively, "It's true, then. You're going to church."

Falconer noticed how the young girl wore a fresh long dress and had brushed her hair and tucked it into a hat tied in a bow under her chin. She clutched a coat to her chest.

The door behind them opened, and Erica Powers came into view. Falconer nodded a greeting. "Good morning, ma'am." He then turned his attention to the child and said, "You look right lovely this morning, lass."

"I can't go, can I?"

"It's a mile walk to the gates, and no telling how far beyond that to the church."

Hannah gave her mother a pleading look. "I feel so much better, Mama."

"A mile, darling," Erica said gently. "In each direction."

Falconer had an idea, one that brought a smile to his face. He reached out. "Let's be having you, then."

Hannah slipped on her coat, yet said doubtfully, "You can't carry me all that way."

"Let's just go see what we can find, what do you say." Falconer lifted the girl and carried her out. Serafina and Mrs. Powers trailed along behind.

When they arrived at the stables, Falconer said, "Hannah, say hello to Harry."

"Good morning, Master Harry."

"Hello, lass." The lad wiped his hands with an oily cloth and turned his attention to Falconer's other companions. "Good morning, I'm sure, Mrs. Powers. How is your husband?"

"He rested well."

"That's good, ma'am. I'm glad to hear it."

"I was wondering," Falconer said, "if there might be a steed gentle enough to carry the young lass to church."

"A horse?" Hannah's voice rose to nearly a squeal. "For me?"

"I've got just the one," Harry exclaimed. "You just stay right where you are."

Harry disappeared into the stables and returned leading a dappled gray mare. "We keep this old lady around for the odd guest who doesn't know one end of the horse from another."

"She's so big" was Hannah's comment.

"Aye, but she's a sweetheart."

The horse nuzzled Harry's shoulder as he flipped a blanket over its broad back and strapped on a sidesaddle. Hannah observed the world with round eyes as Falconer lifted her into place.

"What do you think?" Falconer asked Erica.

She responded by saying to her daughter, "You will mind your manners and do exactly what Mr. Falconer tells you."

"Yes, Mama."

Harry handed Falconer the reins. "Follow the trail leading away from the kitchen. Through the forest, the gates will be right there in front of you. Look there, see the others making their way?"

Serafina and Falconer walked in silence, with Hannah perched atop the horse. Hannah was as happy as if she had just been handed the world. Falconer draped the reins over his shoulder, but the horse needed no control. It fell behind the pair of them and matched their pace without a tug upon the leather.

As they entered the forest, a breeze caught the edge of Serafina's bonnet. It fell back on her shoulders, revealing hair that glowed like gold in the sunlight. To Falconer's mind it transformed her face to yet another level of loveliness. Serafina must have sensed that he was watching her, for she gave him a shy smile as she returned her hat to its place and retied the bow.

The tiny smile was cast in such sorrowful lines it wrenched Falconer's heart. "I have been where you are, lass."

He expected her to deny it. Instead, she looked at him a long moment, then said very softly, "Are we friends?"

"I would like that," he replied, his voice so gruff he scarcely recognized it as his own. "Very much."

She returned her gaze to the lane ahead. "It was very nice what you did, finding a way for Miss Hannah to come."

The child spoke then. "I am ever so high up."

"You look so very nice up there."

Hannah tucked her dress about her legs. "Isn't she lovely?" she asked, stroking what she could reach of the horse's mane. "What do you think her name might be?"

"We must ask Harry when we return." Serafina glanced at Falconer. The sorrow was softer now, but still evident. "You do not know of what you speak."

"I know enough."

She shook her head but did not turn away.

"Destroyed by your own hand. Lost to the world and yourself both. No punishment is fitting. No pain too bitter. A great gaping wound where your heart should be. Every act a terrible crime. Every thought—"

"No more, please."

"Lass, Serafina, I do not speak to condemn you. I speak because I know. I know . . ." He stopped. Everything he said was doubly tainted. He could not release this longing for her. And he felt his own inadequacy to explain. He shook his head.

To his surprise, Serafina asked, "What do I do?"

"When there is no hope, no future, no life ahead," Falconer said to the path by his feet. "When all is lost, seek God. Take His future as your own."

"What does that mean?"

"I am no good with words," he sighed.

"No. Tell me, please."

"Ask Him not just for healing but for a purpose. Those were the words given to me in my own dark night."

"And does He? Heal, I mean."

He looked over and saw the strain of sleepless nights, of terrible guilt there upon her young features. "I can't lie to you. I still carry the thorn. But I have found hope. And I go forward because of Him."

The message was so inadequate Falconer wanted to apologize. But before he could, Serafina nodded slowly. She turned back toward the path ahead, but not before Falconer spotted something new in her features. Not healing. Certainly not that. But a sliver of calm, of hope.

Chapter 21

Like the surrounding cottages, the Harrow village church was built of ancient stone and possessed a squat Norman bell tower. The church was also very full. Their appearance garnered quite a number of turns of the head from other household staff. The only remaining spaces were well at the back. Hannah remained between Falconer and Serafina as they slipped into the pew.

It was the first time Falconer had sat in a proper church since Georgetown, yet he found little of the longed-for peace. Instead, the service was constantly disturbed by his own internal musings. The longer he remained in the church, the more audible became his thoughts.

He was a fighter, not a thinker. He was best when aimed at a purpose. He could move with a focused passion that carried him over almost any obstacle.

But not this.

Falconer sensed a divine purpose behind his being here with the lass. He could not name the last time he had felt such certainty. God had brought them together. God wished to use Falconer for His purpose. The girl needed not Falconer, but God.

The sermon ended without Falconer having heard more than a few words. As the others rose to pronounce the Creed, Falconer gripped the pew back in front of him and rested his forehead upon his hands. His was a terse warrior's prayer.

He remained as he was, hoping against hope for some divine

response. Around him voices droned. Within, however, stirred nothing save weakness and improper longings.

I can't do this. I am not strong enough. Thy desire is for someone to speak to her for thyself. I want her for myself. The more I am with her, the less real my words seem. I speak of thee and think only of me. Find another to do thy bidding. Take this temptation away from me.

He lifted his head and was surprised to find that he was sweating. And more surprised still to see that the others were filing from the church. The service had ended, and he had not noticed.

What was worse still was how Serafina observed him. He saw trust there, and he felt it was unfounded. She should not be trusting him at all. But knowing the truth was not enough to release him. He sat and knew as long as she gazed at him, he could not rise.

She gave him another small smile, a gift of open trust. Then Hannah stood, and Serafina rose to accompany her from the church. Numbly Falconer followed them outside. He hefted Hannah onto the horse's back and led the mare through the gates and back toward Harrow Hall.

Only when they were a ways down the forest lane did he notice it.

When he stopped in his tracks, Serafina asked, "What is it?"

Falconer shook his head, not in response to her query but rather to clear his mind. The wind had stopped. There was a storm on the horizon. Was that what alerted his sense of caution? He could not be certain. Perhaps it was nothing more than his own internal disquiet.

But Falconer sensed more, an external danger. He sniffed the air, willing himself to push aside the internal quandary and do what he did best.

He smelled sulfur.

"What's the matter?" Serafina asked again.

In reply, Falconer wheeled about. "Can you ride?" he asked her.

"I have a few times."

"Hannah, slide up so Serafina can sit in the saddle. That's a good girl."

Serafina allowed Falconer to help her into the saddle. "Lass, you must keep tight hold of both Hannah and the reins," he instructed. "Ride as fast as you safely can." He pointed to where the stragglers were disappearing into the woods. "Join up with the others. Put yourselves in the midst of them."

"What about you?"

Falconer slapped the horse's flank. "Go!"

Serafina and Hannah both cast worried glances behind as the horse galloped away. Falconer remained where he was long enough to be certain the pair would not fall off. Then he sniffed the air once more to confirm the direction. He stepped off the path and entered the forest cover. And he ran.

He found a game trail that paralleled the lane back to the house. Now and then he spied the horse pulling ahead. He ran harder, his mouth open wide to keep himself from gasping aloud. He placed each step as carefully as he could, ducking under branches and disturbing the air no more than necessary.

Then he spotted them.

There were two of them. The men were dressed in hunting green and almost melded into the trees. From the forest lane they would be invisible. But the hunters had not expected to be observed from this angle. Their attention was upon the lane.

At the sound of the horse's thundering hooves, they raised their weapons, aiming long rifles at the two helpless riders. The trigger was sparked by a slow fuse. Falconer knew many hunters who preferred these ancient pieces, for they were legendary in their accuracy. They needed to be. Such guns took forever to reload.

Falconer's mind raced faster than his legs as he shot forward. He had time to notice the pockmarks on the closer man's face. Time even to notice the second man's scarred hands as he swiveled his musket around and took aim at Falconer. But Falconer shifted his run such that the first man stood between them. The second attacker tried to shift his aim, but the surrounding trees blocked him from traversing the long barrel.

Falconer crashed into the nearest man, smashing him into the second. Both attackers tumbled back, and one of the guns went off in a coughing bellow of smoke. But the bullet flew high, frightening a flock of pigeons and causing someone on the trail to cry out in alarm.

"Flee!" Falconer shouted to Serafina and Hannah. He ducked as the attacker whose gun had fired plucked a long-bladed knife from his belt and swung it in an arc of flashing steel. "Run!"

The second man was up now and trying to bring his gun to bear. Falconer ducked another knife blow and reached for the spent rifle now lying on the forest floor. He tripped and fell over an unseen root and kept rolling. Which was a very good thing, for he heard the second gun cough and felt the wind of a passing bullet somewhere near his head.

Falconer came up with the rifle at his chest. He caught the attacker's knife on the gun barrel as it took aim for his eyes. Metal screeched upon metal as he parried the blow.

Falconer clipped the knife wielder's hand with the flint, parried a swipe from the other attacker, and then swung the barrel in a short sharp arc that caught the knife wielder between the eyes. The man blinked in the blurry manner of one striving not to go down. Falconer ducked a swing from the other rifle and applied the barrel a second time. The man went down hard.

The second attacker turned and fled. Falconer started to follow, but the attacker probably knew these woods far better than he did and could well have prepared an ambush. Plus, there was the risk of others laying in wait, but Falconer doubted that. These were not soldiers. They had clustered together for companionship. Falconer's gut told him the pair acted alone.

He searched the man's pockets and found little of worth. Wadding, a powder horn, six spare round shot, a flint box, more slow fuse, and a plug of foul-looking tobacco. Then he spied a paper in the man's vest pocket. He unfolded it and started in genuine alarm.

He was looking at a poster for one John Falconer. The drawing was of a snarling wolf of a man, one with evil eyes and a scar from mouth to ear. The warrant named him as highwayman, murderer, and enemy of the Crown.

In his shock, Falconer did not hear the horse until it was almost upon him.

The second attacker had not in fact fled. He charged at Falconer with a fierce snarl and drawn blade. But the trees were too closely set for the horse to move easily. Falconer crouched and leaped to one side. Then, when the horse had to swerve about a pair of saplings, he sprang away, taking cover behind a thick oak.

The rider jerked hard on the reins. He was breathing as hard as his steed, and his feverish eyes swept the area as he took aim for another strike. The horse snorted and pawed the leaf-strewn earth.

The man Falconer had knocked to the earth chose that moment to rise unsteadily to his feet, his back to Falconer. He spied the horse and reached out to the rider. The horseman could not charge as he wished, for now his mate stood between them.

Falconer searched the forest floor until he saw a likely looking branch. He hefted it and took aim as he would with a spear.

The rider snarled and rammed his sword back into its sheath. He gripped his unsteady mate and pulled him up onto the horse behind him. They wheeled about and sped into the forest.

Falconer raced for the great house.

Chapter 22

Falconer emerged from the forest at a dead run. The light was dim and the air much colder, as though the season had changed in the few minutes it had taken him to return to Harrow Hall. Servants were clustered by the kitchen's rear door, watching him with anxious expressions.

"Was that gunfire?" Mrs. Marcham called.

Falconer gasped out, "Where are the girls?"

"In the Powers' apartment. But what—"

Falconer sprinted up the stairs to be greeted on the landing by a stern-looking Daniel. No sight could have given Falconer more comfort. He managed to ask once more, "The girls?"

"Both safe. You?"

Falconer bent over, hands on his knees. "Winded."

Behind Daniel stood Gareth Powers, now dressed and wearing boots. "Who were these assailants?"

Falconer held up his hand, puffing both from the exertion and the strain of battle. He had walked away from many confrontations. Sometimes the worst fears were caused by what *might* have happened. This time, however, his greatest worry lay in the hours ahead.

He straightened. "I must speak with you and your wife."

"Come in." Gareth looked drawn, but he held himself with a soldier's stiff resolve as he entered the apartment's front room and announced to the little group, "He's all right."

Hannah tore herself from her mother's embrace and ran over. "I was so frightened!"

"The important thing is you're safe now." Falconer knelt and accepted the young girl's embrace. "I'm sorry you were endangered, lass."

"I wasn't scared for me. I knew you would protect us. I worried for you."

"I am fine as well." Gently Falconer released himself. He rose to his feet and walked over to where Serafina stood beside Erica Powers. "You were not hurt?"

"No, only frightened."

"You did well, lass. Very well indeed. Not all would have kept their wits about them as you did."

"I only did what you told me to."

He stared into those wide gray eyes. Conscious of those watching, Falconer finally asked in a low voice, "Would you take the young one in back while I have a word with her parents?"

"Of course." Serafina reached out her hand to Hannah. "Come with me now."

"But I want to hear!"

"If you come, I will make something for you." Serafina looked Falconer's way as she added, "A secret thing."

This drew Hannah forward. "I love secrets."

"Come, then."

A freshening wind moaned around the house's corner. Falconer glanced out the window, gauging the change as he would at sea. The new week appeared to be minted upon storms from all quarters.

He drew a paper from his pocket, the one taken from the attacker's vest coat. But he did not reveal the contents. Not yet. "I must ask you something. I would ask for your oath as well, but I am given to trust your word alone."

"We have always been truthful with you," Gareth Powers replied.

"Well I know it. When I arrived in London to escort Mrs. Powers, Samuel Aldridge handed me two pamphlets and urged

me to read them. His intent was to demonstrate you were people
of strength and purpose. But what I discovered . . ."

When he paused, Gareth urged, "Go on, man."

But Falconer found himself captured by two memories. "The
priest who brought me to your home in Georgetown—"

"He was a Methodist pastor," Gareth corrected. "What of
him?"

"He felt that God's hand was upon the meeting. I found it
hard to believe then, after all the trials and delays I had faced. But
now that I am here . . ."

Gareth prodded, more gently this time, "Yes?"

"Do you remember asking me if I ever felt confused by how
God lets the world stand in our way? How it seemed impossible
that He guided our steps when life went so terribly wrong?"

"I do remember that." Gareth nodded slowly. "It was a low
point for me. I should not have questioned the Almighty."

Falconer looked into Gareth's face a moment. "I feel we
should start this moment with prayer," he said.

The three of them, Daniel and Gareth and Erica Powers,
moved to make a circle, and Erica said, "Please lead us."

"Ma'am, I have no way with proper words."

"God is after your heart, not your speech." She cut off further
argument by bowing her head. The two men followed suit.

Falconer took a breath and cleared his throat, then began
slowly, "Heavenly Father, at times you chart a course that we cannot fathom. But I sense a greater meaning to all this. A deeper
bond than any we here on earth could forge. Show us what is to
be done and provide strength to stay the course. Amen."

He raised his head. Falconer's sense of rightness had solidified.
Wilberforce was ill, and these people were here. If God's hand was
indeed upon them, would it not be wrong to delay further?
"Felix, the curate who brought me to our Lord, is battling the
slave trade throughout the Caribbean. We have gathered evidence
revealing that despite what the law says, the trade in slaves continues."

"As we have long suspected," Erica said.

"I'm afraid we have indeed known this," Gareth quietly said. "We knew in our bones in spite of Parliament's edict."

"But we had no proof. And without proof . . ."

Falconer went on, "We have put together a list of islands and towns where the slave markets thrive. We have numbers, still incomplete, and mostly guesswork. Enough, though, to show that an illegal trade continues on a substantial scale. They have moved this evil commerce to outlying villages, places far removed from prying eyes. But it happens. On almost every island where there are significant plantations within the British empire, the slave trade still persists."

"You have these records with you?"

"In my room." When Gareth started to ask for them, Falconer hastily added, "There's more."

The keenness with which they listened was all the confirmation Falconer required. Now was time to reveal the appalling truth. "The trade continues with the Crown's knowledge."

Gareth breathed, "What do you say?"

"Not the king, though he may have knowledge of this traffic in human lives. But people within the court, officials close to the Crown, are involved."

"How can you be certain of this?" Erica asked, eyes wide in disbelief.

"I have proof. I have the governor of Trinidad's own seal upon a license to hold a monthly market."

"And this means . . . ?"

"The market is held in a town so small and so removed no one in their right mind would even *think* to travel there. It requires traversing the entire island. There is no decent harbor, just an anchorage when the waters are absolutely calm. Otherwise the vessels risk being dashed upon sheer cliffs. No, there is only one reason why such a market exists."

"Slaves," Daniel said.

"Precisely."

Erica Powers shook her head. "No. I am sorry, but this is not proof. The governor could be an unwilling party."

"Not so," Falconer replied. He had also required solid evidence before risking his life and that of his best mate. "The license was for *renewing* the market. And the payment was enormous."

"How much?"

"Two thousand gold sovereigns."

The sum rocked them back a step. Two thousand in gold would purchase the estate where they now resided. "How did you come upon these documents?" Gareth asked.

"My best mate was the governor's driver. He heard them discussing many things."

"Names," Gareth demanded. "Was anyone at court mentioned specifically?"

"Just one. My mate was after confirmation when they captured him. He is gone from us now."

"And they discovered you were working with him?"

"Jaime would never have confessed. But we were known as close mates. So those behind the trade assume that I too stand against them."

"How can you be certain?" Erica asked.

"Because the attack in the woods just now was directed at me, not you." He handed them the poster. "Here is proof."

As the page with his likeness passed from hand to hand, Falconer added, "And they knew the curate was a friend of mine. It is for his sake that I must hasten back to Trinidad."

"But you mentioned a name, someone at court."

"A banker. We heard his name several times. We were seeking proof when Jaime was captured."

Husband and wife exchanged dark looks. Gareth asked, "A banker, did you say? One in London?"

"You can't possibly mean Simon Bartholomew," Erica exclaimed.

Falconer looked at the woman in shock, then was surprised again when Gareth Powers began laughing.

Erica frowned. "You find this humorous?"

"I find this astonishing," Gareth replied, smiling broadly. "I find this utterly miraculous."

"I fail to understand you," his wife said. "Our nemesis is now shown to—"

"To be the criminal we always knew he was." Gareth explained to Falconer, "We have known and fought Simon Bartholomew for almost twenty years. A sign, you sought, was that not what you said to me in America? A means to be certain that you could trust us with the fate of your comrades?"

"I do trust you," Falconer said.

"But a sign you shall have. The man behind this illicit trade is the same man who sought to destroy my wife's family. Not once, but several times over."

"A truly evil man," Erica said softly, "without fear of man or God."

Gareth stepped forward, smiling once more. "I think we should begin writing a pamphlet based upon the news Falconer has just supplied. Then I believe we should make haste to introduce our friend Falconer to the men fighting in the front line."

"I agree about the pamphlet," Erica said, "but I worry that you may not yet be fit for such a journey into the political fray."

"I cannot permit you to travel back to London without me," he said firmly. "No, my dear, please do not argue. On this point I am quite adamant. I will remain in the background; I will let you hold the pen. But our attackers have found us. And earlier than expected. I must know that you are safe. Which means we must all travel together."

"Promise me you will not tax yourself."

"That I do." He pointed to the Wanted poster in his wife's hands and asked Falconer, "What does that tell you?"

"First, they are powerful enough to recruit a vessel as swift as our own," Falconer replied. "They lost no time in making the journey to England. They then searched until they discovered our whereabouts."

"They are powerful and determined both," Gareth agreed. "Anything more?"

"They consider us such a threat that they will spare neither expense nor energy to attack us."

"Do you hear that, my dearest? Attack *us*. Falconer is one of us now."

They were interrupted by a knock on the door. At a call from Gareth, the door opened to reveal Cuthbert, the chief butler. He gripped the lapel of his dark coat and announced, "Lord Drescott's compliments, sir. His guests have arrived."

"Who are they, may I ask?"

"Two members of Parliament, Mr. Powers. Lord Sedgwick and Henry Carlyle."

"Most astonishing," Erica breathed.

"Miraculous, I would say," Gareth said. "These are two of our allies in the battle," he explained to Falconer. "Your news could not have come at a more opportune time."

"May I ask where we are to go?" Falconer asked.

"For the family, somewhere safe." Gareth's smile broadened. "But you, my friend and ally, you must make straight for the battleground."

Serafina knocked on the door and entered without waiting. Her aunt was cozy in quilts, her legs stretched upon a stool. A generous fire kept the rising storm at bay. As usual, Aunt Agatha was not alone. This day, Mrs. Marcham was visiting.

Mrs. Marcham lifted her chin at Serafina's appearance. "Why are you not properly dressed in the clothes your aunt gave you?"

"I am told that I shall be traveling soon, Mrs. Marcham. Tuesday at dawn." Serafina wore a dress loaned to her by Erica Powers. The high-necked frock was of light blue serge lined at the neckline and cuffs in ivory lace.

"Is that so? Why was I not informed?"

"It has only just been decided, ma'am."

"By whom?"

"Mr. and Mrs. Powers, ma'am. Mrs. Powers asked me to dress thusly."

"So you think you can depart the manor without a by-your-leave?"

Serafina realized this conversation was going to take time she did not have. She took a quick breath and asked as humbly as she could, "Might I please have a moment alone with my aunt, Mrs. Marcham?"

The housekeeper showed genuine surprise. "I beg your pardon?"

"Be a dear, Beryl," Aunt Agatha said mildly. "Clearly the young lady is under some considerable pressure."

"Yes, very well. If you're quite sure."

"It appears Serafina's time with us is coming to a close," Aunt Agatha said and patted her old friend's hand. "Thank you for the lovely tea. I shall look forward to speaking with you later in the week."

"Of course." Mrs. Marcham rose, inspected Serafina one more time, then left without a word.

"Come sit down beside me, dear." Agatha watched her approach. "What has happened to your hands?"

"I damaged them with the work, the firewood. But they are getting better." She picked at the edge of one bandage. "I wished to apologize for all the trouble I have caused."

Her aunt slowly nodded. "I see that progress is indeed being made. Very well, child. Your apology is accepted. Now tell me. You intend to travel with the Powers family?"

"They have asked me to do so. And I cannot stay here."

"No," Agatha agreed. She stared out the window at the cloud-swept horizon. "I dread the thought of this great home coming under the sway of young Drescott."

But Serafina had not come to discuss the manor's future. "Aunt, could you please tell me, what does it mean to repent?"

Agatha moved her head to inspect her niece more closely. "Repentance means to turn away. This much you know, yes? Our Savior, when he spoke to the woman who had sinned, said to her, 'Go and sin no more.' That is repentance in its purest and simplest form."

"It does not seem enough," Serafina murmured.

Agatha seemed to understand her perfectly. "Jesus did not come to punish, child. He came to save. You should ask each of those you have harmed for their forgiveness, the same as you do with the Father. When it is granted, you accept it. You move into the future. You seek to never repeat the sin." She paused a moment, then added, "Daily you seek the strength you need through Scriptures and prayer."

Serafina kept her attention focused upon her hands. The good captain had again treated them with brine and goose fat. "I have been such a fool."

"Indeed. And now you must turn away from the mistakes, seek forgiveness from God and man, and face your future."

"Would you pray with me?"

Her aunt smiled so warmly the lines of pain and loss rearranged themselves. "I should think of nothing finer."

Chapter 23

Falconer strode the path from the old manor to the stables. He studied the afternoon sky and wished for open seas. But it was an idle thought, for his heart was not in it. He should have felt great relief. His secret, guarded for months and many miles, was now entrusted with stalwart friends. He had no doubt but that he had done the right thing. Felix would approve. He would accomplish whatever it was Gareth and Erica had in mind, then return to Trinidad and see to his friend's safety.

Yet Falconer's emotions boiled like the clouds and the wind, like the furious squall that beat the trees and fields with fists of rainfall to the north. He wanted to go, *needed* to leave, just as soon as his mission here was complete. Yet any departure would sever the fragile tie he had to Serafina.

Serafina. The sound of her name on his lips was a hopeless groan to an uncaring wind.

It was the wrong time to have fallen in love, and with a lass far beyond his reach. He had been entrusted with her safety, and perhaps with a divine motive as well. But all he could think of was how the days ahead would be diminished by her absence.

"There you are!"

Falconer started at the sound of that young voice. "What are you doing out in this storm, my little one?"

"I like it!" Hannah danced a little circle. "And I'm better, see?"

"I think you're excited over the coming journey to London." He swept her up, reveling in the feel of those two slender arms wrapping about his neck. "You mustn't get overtired, lass."

Falconer entered the old manor's rear entrance and climbed the stairs. He set her down on the landing. "Now I want you to rest easy. Will you do that for me?"

"Yes." She smiled mischievously. "I have a secret."

"Your father often says he's never met someone who likes secrets more."

"This one is about you." She whirled about and raced into the apartment. "Wait right there!"

He heard soft footfalls and turned to face Serafina. Only she looked quite different. The surprise pushed him back a step. "You look proper lovely, ma'am."

She smiled nervously. "Please, I would prefer that you call me by my name."

He fumbled with his hat. The design of her dress was unlike anything he had ever seen. Not that he had much experience with women's finery. But Serafina's manner had changed as well. She held herself erect. Her hair was pulled back and hung like a golden veil down her back. "Your gown is most fetching."

"It's not mine. But thank you."

Her voice was the same and yet different. She spoke softly, yet the quality of defeat was missing. "You are better?"

"Thanks to you and . . ." Her eyes rounded at something behind Falconer's back. "Oh no, you mustn't!"

Before he could ask what she meant, Hannah said, "Why not? It's him, isn't it?"

Falconer wheeled about. "How do you manage to sneak up on a body like that?"

Hannah smiled proudly. "Mama says I can surprise the sparrows when I have a mind." She held out a rolled sheet of paper. "Look!"

"What do you have there?"

"Nothing," Serafina hurried to reply, reaching to intercept Hannah's surprise. "It's nothing. Hannah, you mustn't—"

"Serafina is an artist! Mama says she's not seen anything finer in any gallery!"

Serafina looked horrified. "You showed this to Mrs. Powers?"

"You didn't tell me not to."

"But . . . you . . . you . . ." Serafina's face was scarlet.

Falconer took the rolled-up sheet and offered it to Serafina. "I won't look if it distresses you."

She hesitated a moment, then whispered, "You may look."

Slowly he unrolled the sheet. What he saw left him turned to stone.

Hannah danced in place. "There! Did I not say it? She's an artist!"

Falconer was looking at a man who was both himself and someone far finer. The drawing showed him bowed over his hands, clenching the back of the pew. He was praying with a calm fervor and singular intensity. The drawing was shaded in a manner that gave the impression of one removed from the earth.

"There is no scar," he said numbly.

"I did not see it," Serafina replied simply. "Not then."

Gareth Powers appeared in the doorway and cleared his throat. "Falconer, excellent. I hoped that was your voice I heard."

Swiftly he rolled up the parchment. "Sir."

"Lord Drescott's guests are upstairs. Could you join us, please?"

"Certainly."

Erica Powers stepped into the doorway beside her husband. "Would you two please join me in the back room?" she said to her daughter and Serafina.

When the trio had departed, Gareth said, "This way, Falconer."

Gareth was as somber as Falconer had ever seen him as they made their way into the apartment's parlor. "Might I have the honor of introducing Lord Sedgwick and Henry Carlyle," Gareth started. "This is the gentleman we have been telling you about. John Falconer, late of Trinidad and Grenada."

Sedgwick was a bulky man, big-boned and carrying more

weight than he probably should. But his features held a cheery glow, and his eyes were burnished with a resolute intelligence. "I must rise and shake your hand, sir. Well done, I say. Saving the young girl Hannah has made you my friend for life."

"Saved her twice," Gareth added.

"Yet once it was from a danger I brought upon her myself," Falconer noted.

Sedgwick moved with motions as great as his form. The gold watch chain that crossed his ample middle shimmered in the light as he disagreed. "Stuff and nonsense. You saved her. That's the issue here, not who's at fault. For we are all partly to blame, if you want to come right down to it. Anyone who dares stand in defiance of these scallywags. Is that not the truth?"

"That's all very well and good, but it doesn't bring us any closer to a workable solution," said the second man, Carlyle, who was the exact opposite of Sedgwick. Carlyle was a dry man, little more than skin over bones. He was dressed in a brown serge suit that hung upon his frame. Even his voice was a dry rasping murmur. "We are in danger of losing everything."

"A mere setback," Sedgwick objected, steering Falconer across the room. "Seat yourself here by my side, my good sir."

"It is *not* a setback, and you know it. Gareth, tell your man what we face."

"John Falconer is his own man, as I have repeatedly said."

Carlyle drifted a hand through the air before him. "Tell him, if you please."

"Very well." Gareth turned to Falconer. "A vote has been set on Parliament's calendar."

"About the slave issue?"

"Just so. We expected to have a major battle on our hands, with the Crown and allies throwing up procedural barriers and delaying this vote for months."

"Years," Carlyle said. "A generation and more."

"But they have permitted this vote to come forward with a minimum of fuss. We were surprised."

"Astonished," Carlyle said. "Alarmed. Extremely concerned."

"Do hold your comments to yourself," Sedgwick complained. "You asked Gareth to tell him, did you not?"

Gareth continued. "Our two allies are here because they have polled the members. We stand to lose the vote."

"But they can vote again, can they not?" Falconer asked.

Sedgwick blew out his cheeks, all bonhomie gone now. "Once a vote has gone against us, it would be dreadfully difficult to bring it forward again. Certainly not until after the next election."

"Longer," Carlyle corrected. "Allies within our own party will see this as a difficult and dangerous course. Because those who vote with us this time will be attacked by the Crown's supporters."

Falconer looked from one face to the next. "What of the information I have brought? Is this not enough?"

Erica Powers had quietly entered the room and now spoke for the first time, in a tone as bitter as Falconer had heard. "Those who waver look for a reason not to help us."

"What we must have is hard evidence," Gareth said. "Something that demonstrates a clear and indisputable link between the Crown and this trade."

"A finger upon the trigger," Sedgwick agreed, studying Falconer intently.

"I have given you all I have," Falconer said.

Gareth leaned forward, his elbows on his legs. "Will you testify before our allies?"

"In Parliament?" Under other circumstances, Falconer would have fled the room. "I must warn you, I am not good with words."

"But hearing the news from a man who carries the mark upon his face." Sedgwick looked hopefully at his mate by the window. "Will that not carry the day?"

Carlyle examined Falconer thoughtfully. "It may. Now that I have seen him, perhaps. But I fear those who are undecided will seek the safe course. They will say we exaggerate. They will say there is nothing hard and fast that shows slavery is indeed a recognized component of Crown commerce."

"If this ongoing traffic is merely a local affair," Gareth explained to Falconer, "some will claim it is a matter for the navy. They will order sweeps. The fleet will be sent."

"And then the fleet will come back," Erica said to her hands. "And the matter will be forgotten. And another generation of innocent people will suffer."

"That cannot happen," Falconer declared. Fear's clammy fist squeezed his insides, but he said, "I will do as you ask."

The rear bedroom was the apartment's smallest chamber. There was scarcely room for the two of them, much less Erica when she returned. Erica stood before Serafina with the rolled paper in her hands. "I want you to give careful thought to what I have to say."

Serafina had never seen the woman look so grave. "Yes, ma'am."

Carefully she unrolled the sketch Serafina had done of Falconer. When Serafina started to protest, Erica held up one hand. "Wait, please. Hear me out. That is all I ask."

"I had not meant for anyone to see this."

"My daughter did not know. And I must tell you, I feel God's hand was upon her action."

Hannah piped up, "Me?"

"Shah, my dearest, listen well and remain silent. I will answer all your questions later." To Serafina she went on, "I know artists. I know how difficult it is to release one's hold on a work. I know this same reluctance when I must give my writings over to the printers, and I write mere pamphlets."

"Falconer has already seen my sketch."

"It is not Falconer I wish to show this to." Erica reached into her pocket and came up with a folded paper. "Look at this, if you will."

Serafina gasped aloud over the picture on the Wanted poster. "This is not him!"

"Indeed not."

"It looks as he does, but this—this man is evil!"

"He is most certainly that." Erica set the two pictures side by side. She pointed to the poster. "A man without God." She then pointed at Serafina's portrait. "A man who knows the Savior's grace. A hundred thousand words could not say what is demonstrated by these two pictures laid side-by-side."

Serafina looked up. "I-I do not understand."

"We will be returning to London. As I have already told you, we want you to travel with us. I want you to do two things. First, let me publish this portrait of yours, right alongside the Wanted poster. The two together."

"No, please."

"Pray about this. I can ask for nothing more." When Serafina did not protest further, she continued, "Then, if you feel it is the right thing to do, speak with Falconer. Ask him to describe for you scenes from his past. Images that will speak as clearly as this portrait here of the life he knew." Erica studied Serafina's face, as though seeking to determine whether she was strong enough. Then she added, "The life he knew as a slaver."

"No." Falconer expelled the word like breath punched from his body. Serafina's request struck him like a blow. "I cannot do what you ask."

"It is not I who ask, John Falconer. It is Mrs. Powers."

"If she knew what it was she requested, she would never have uttered the words." A bead of sweat worked its way down his spine. The thought of describing his vile experiences to this young woman left him nauseated. "Most certainly not."

Serafina searched his face, her gaze filled with both sadness and a remarkable calm. "Mrs. Powers would like to use my drawing of you as well."

"Of me? In their pamphlet? Lass, I can't . . ."

"I said the very same thing. But she asked me to pray. Which I will. Yet even now I know the answer. How am I to refuse these people? She thinks this may help."

"I can't imagine how that would be possible." Falconer wiped his forehead.

"Nor I. But I trust her. And Mr. Powers. And you."

He struggled to find some way to tell her of the shame the request drew forth, but the air remained caught in his throat.

She touched his arm. A gentle contact, as soft as her voice. "I have caused you distress, John Falconer. I am sorry."

"It is not you, lass."

"I have made you remember pain. I know . . ." She dropped her hand along with her eyes. "Will you do as Mrs. Powers asked, and pray?"

"Aye." Falconer knew he would give this young woman anything she asked. "Aye."

Chapter 24

Toward dawn Falconer finally gave up on sleep. Though he was exhausted, thoughts of the coming days and what was being asked of him blasted apart his fitful dreams. He lit a candle and tried to read the Scriptures, but the words passed before his eyes in a meaningless blur. He knelt at the side of his bed and began to pray. Yet even here he felt trapped and unable to force through what he wished to ask for. His new allies needed him to speak to the wavering members of Parliament. He could see how critical this need was every time he glanced at their faces. He had heard the earnest appeal and knew they were counting on him. How could he ask for this cup to pass from him? Who else could take his place? So he could not pray as he wanted. He prayed instead for strength, enough in fact to resist the gnawing terror.

And fell asleep there upon his knees.

When he awoke, sunlight fell full upon his face. Falconer groaned as he pushed himself to his feet. His knees ached abominably. And yet he had a sense of a miraculous freedom. He could not recall the last time he had awakened without the choking noose of night terrors still wrapped about him.

He bent and stretched until the pain lessened and feeling returned to his feet. Then he prayed again, only this time standing upright. Fear over the coming days was still with him. Yet now it was tempered by the certainty that he did not go forward alone.

Once more there was a sense of being unable to frame proper

words. Falconer was not particularly troubled by this. Instead, he merely took pleasure in seeing a new day without the night shadows darkening his vision. He prayed his thanksgiving for this different sort of awakening.

It was then that the idea came to him. Full blown and utterly clear.

Falconer dressed and stumbled his way down the stairway. Daniel's high-backed chair leaned upon the door. A bedroll was stored in the corner of the landing, for Daniel had opted to sleep that night with his bulk guarding the only entrance to the apartment.

Daniel frowned. "Why are you limping?"

"I fell asleep at my prayers," Falconer confessed. "I was on my knees for hours."

"That would certainly do it." Daniel did not seem surprised. "There's tea still, but it's cold by now," he said, motioning at his breakfast tray.

"Cold tea will suit me fine."

Daniel plunked his chair legs to the floor. He cleaned his own mug with the towel covering the tray, then poured it full. "Here you go."

"I am obliged." Falconer finished the mug in a few gulps, then asked, "Where are the two guests from Parliament?"

"Sedgwick has been here since first light. They're hard at work on the pamphlet. Haven't seen the narrow gent this morning." Daniel cocked his head to one side. "Something is up with you."

"I have an idea. A risky one."

"Most good ideas are." He sat up straighter. "I'm your man."

Falconer blinked in surprise. "Don't you want to know what I'm about?"

"What you see before you is a foot soldier in God's battle. Always have been, always will be. I've learned it's more important to trust the man than to know all the steps ahead." He rose to his feet. "The major says he trusts you with his life. That's good enough for me. Now tell me what needs doing."

Falconer breathed deeply. His growing sense of rightness was as strong as the risk ahead. "Ask Serafina to join us. Then go and find the narrow-faced man."

Serafina sat upon the floor next to Hannah. They used a low table as a drawing board, with two pieces of parchment set side-by-side. "I always find the best way to begin sketching a person is with the eyes. Here, I will make a nose for you in the middle of the page—that will give you a point of reference."

Hannah bent over her paper when Serafina was done. "Mama says when a person loves you, you can see right down into their soul."

"Your mother is very wise."

"Daddy says she's the smartest person he has ever met. Smarter even than William Wilberforce." Hannah leaned back and studied her work. "These are dreadful eyes."

"Well, perhaps it would be better if you placed both of them on the same level."

"One of them is down where the mouth goes." Hannah giggled. "I won't ever show this to Falconer."

"Is that whom you wanted to draw?"

"Yes." She bent back over the page. "He's ever so handsome. And when he looks at you, his whole face glows."

"Here, let's start over with another nose up here." Serafina's hair was pulled back in a bow, but she hoped the tendrils around her face hid her blush.

"When he prayed in church yesterday, I could feel it. Inside me. That sounds silly, doesn't it?"

"No. I don't think that sounds silly at all. There. Your nose is finished. And I'll make little curves here, see? These will form the lower lids for the eyes."

"You draw him."

"No, this is your page." Though in truth Falconer's gaze was already staring up at her.

Serafina moved back from the table. Not because of Falconer's unfinished face. Instead, she recalled seeing Luca's drawing of her for the very first time. Whatever had happened to that drawing? Lost now. Like so much else.

Serafina had found herself praying much of the night. Events had come back to her in the form of segmented memories. She prayed and she slept, only to dream of yet another mistake and awaken to pray again. Several times when the anguish had become too great, she had thought of Falconer there in the night. The strength of the man, the force of his gaze, the solidity of his faith. Knowing he was nearby, that he protected her, that he *prayed* for her, left her able to pray for herself.

The knock on the door startled both girls. Serafina rose to her feet. "Yes?"

The other big man, Daniel, opened the door. "Excuse the interruption, ladies."

"Serafina is teaching me to be an artist like her!" Hannah exclaimed.

"Isn't that a grand and good thing." Daniel kept his focus upon Serafina. "Falconer would like a word, miss."

Hannah jumped up. "I'll come too."

"Best you stay and work on the drawing, little one." He stepped into the room to examine her artwork. "What a lovely thing there. Is that a horse?"

Serafina spoke before the young girl could complain. "You know very well that is John Falconer. And you also know it is not nice to jest."

"Aye, you're right. Excuse me, lass. I was talking out of turn." He peered at the sheet a second time. "What an astounding rendition of the good man."

"I'll be back soon." Serafina shut the door behind her and followed Daniel down the corridor. They passed through the front room, where Gareth Powers sat with the portly Lord Sedgwick. Erica Powers worked at the desk by the side windows.

Sheets of writing paper were strewn about the surface. They were so deep in conversation that Daniel had to clear his throat twice to get their attention. "Your pardon, sirs, Mrs. Powers. I was wondering where I might be finding the other gent."

"Carlyle? Still at the desk in the library, I wager," answered the one known as Lord Sedgwick. "He was working his way through a massive pile of correspondence. Said he could trust us to write what was needed here, and his own letters could not wait."

"Thank you. Sorry for the interruption." Daniel ushered Serafina out to the landing. He shut the apartment door, then said quietly, "I'm off to nab the gent for you."

Falconer's voice came from the stairway below. "First listen to what I have to say to the lady." Falconer made his way up the stairs and then turned to Serafina, his visage serious. "We have a terrible problem, lass."

For some reason, she found herself shivering slightly at the word *we*. To be included among these people and their focused intensity was such a gift. "You think I can help you?"

"Perhaps. The slavery issue is coming up before Parliament again. I know this is not your battle, but—"

"If I can help you, I will."

"Wait and hear me out." Falconer briefly sketched out the vote coming before Parliament and the lack of hard evidence. "I'm not explaining it well, partly because I don't understand all the ins and outs of it myself."

"I understand enough. How can I help you?"

Falconer cocked his head to one side. "You don't owe me a thing, lass."

"Yes I do. You, Mr. and Mrs. Powers, Hannah, Daniel, all of you. What do you want of me?"

Falconer glanced at Daniel, who was grinning slightly. He took a breath and explained his plan.

Serafina could not entirely mask her shiver of fear as she replied, "I'll do it."

"It could be dangerous," Falconer warned. "The only reason

I ask this at all is because we may well not succeed otherwise."

"You will protect me." She clung to that as her defense against rising fears.

Falconer glanced once more at Daniel, who was no longer smiling.

"You'd take a word of advice?" Daniel asked him.

"From you? Always."

"Have a word with the major before you set off. Private like."

"Can you arrange that?"

"Can and will." Daniel slipped around the pair of them and knocked before entering the apartment.

Falconer returned his attention to Serafina. "Lass, I wish there was some other way than this."

"But there isn't, is there? You wouldn't do this unless it was absolutely necessary." She worked hard to keep her voice steady. "Just promise me one more time that you will keep me safe."

"With my life."

The way he said that, with an intensity rising from the uttermost depths of his being, caused her to shiver anew. This time for a reason she could not fathom. "Have you thought more of what we spoke yesterday?"

"Much of the night."

"Did you pray?"

"I fell asleep on my knees."

"I . . ." She stopped, not from hesitation over what she wished to say. Instead, she simply wanted to study this good man. The light she found within those dark eyes touched her at the very core of her being.

"Speak your peace, lass."

"I prayed as well. Mostly I prayed over my sins and faults. But I asked God for guidance."

"Did He answer you?"

"Not in words, no. But I feel that the answer is there just the same. Do you understand me?"

He nodded. "So very well indeed."

"I do not know much of this cause. But I know I want to

help these good people. And if they think my poor drawings can make a difference, then I should not question them. I should give them all that I can."

Falconer took his time in responding. "Your drawings are not poor."

"Will you help me in this, John Falconer?"

He sighed long and sad. "When you are so brave, how can I be otherwise?"

She was not feeling the least bit brave, she wanted to tell him. The plan he had suggested filled her with fear. But she could look into his face and trust the strength she saw. He would be strong for her.

Falconer stood in the lee of the stables, Serafina's closeness more than a mere physical presence. "You don't have to do this, lass," he said again.

Once more Serafina wore the drab dress of a house servant. Yet not even the rough gray weave could dim her beauty. "I have asked you to call me by my name."

"Serafina," he said, his heart lurching at the sound. "You've been through so much. This is—"

"Important," she finished the sentence differently than he had intended. "I understand."

He shook his head at the risk they were taking, but he had not been able to think of an alternative. "I will protect you."

Her smiles were growing somewhat more assured and lasting a trace longer. "Of that I am certain, John Falconer."

Daniel appeared around the far corner and hissed, "He's coming."

"And the others?"

"In position."

"Off with the scarf," Falconer said. "But only if you're certain this is what . . ."

Serafina released the scarf and shook her hair free to blow in the wind. She gave him a final look, then hefted her basket and stepped into view.

Daniel slipped up beside Falconer. "If a lass that pretty were to look at me the way she just looked at you, I'd be crowing."

Falconer was too worried to respond. Though they were fifty leagues and more from the sea, the wind and darkening sky indicated a deepwater storm, a tempest that would have them pushing hard away from shore. The whitecaps would tear from the waves and blow as hard as falling rain. When the sky and the sea melded into one gray and ominous sheet, a sailor sought safety by turning away from the shore's teeth. Yet here he was, casting this fragile creature into the maws of danger.

Daniel carried a coil of rope slung over one shoulder. "The lass is a brave one, I'll give you that," he said.

Falconer shuddered. He had borne many tragedies, but were harm to come to this one on his watch, he would be ready for the grave.

Daniel risked a quick glance around the corner. "Here he comes."

"Get back." Falconer lowered himself until he was flat on the muddy earth. He handed Daniel his hat and extended himself inch by inch.

Serafina had walked in the rain across the open ground from the stables to the kitchen and now emerged bearing a basket with dinner for the Powers family. The yard had been emptied of any others by the storm. Serafina's scarf dangled from her neck. Her damp hair lay close to her head now, making her seem even more vulnerable. Carefully she picked her way along the muddy path, her focus intent upon the next step. She was playing her part well.

The two observers could see the young lord loitering in the rear doorway of the great house, watching Serafina as he would a helpless prey.

Falconer's heart was in his throat as he saw Serafina squinting against the blowing rain and now searching in every direction. The kitchen door was shut against the storm. The wind whistled and howled so it was doubtful she would be heard if she screamed.

She attempted to hurry toward the older wing, but her skirt was heavy with mud and rain, and she tripped and nearly went down. She gave a little cry, and the sound cut through Falconer like a dagger. He started to rise. But Daniel nudged him with his boot and hissed, "Not yet."

Drescott descended the rear steps, his wet riding boots gleaming. Serafina stopped, obviously trembling. The young lord started forward, circling around so that he stood directly in her path, blocking her from safety.

Serafina dropped the basket, snatched up her skirts, and ran.

Drescott laughed. In the lashing rain it sounded to Falconer's ear like a beast of prey. The young lord started after her. Serafina risked one glance behind and ran the harder.

Daniel's hand gripped Falconer's arm as he moved into a crouch, keeping him from leaping forward as Drescott raced by. The two of them were locked in shadows and remained unseen as Drescott pelted after the servant girl.

As the distance grew between the pair and the house, they heard Drescott call, "Wait, little one. I have something for you."

"Now," Daniel said, and released Falconer's arm.

They ran low to the ground, keeping to what cover there was. But there was no need for caution. Drescott ran like a hound on the scent, his attention focused on the fleeing prey.

The storm-whipped rain felt like wet hands gripping Falconer and holding him back. The path was so slippery Falconer endured a nightmare's run, struggling hard and making little progress.

He stripped off his coat and threw it to the sodden earth. Ahead, the pair of them disappeared into the forest. "Faster!"

Daniel slipped and almost went down. Falconer grabbed the larger man and kept him upright. But when he turned his attention back to the way ahead, the forest showed him a blank and forbidding face.

Falconer pulled ahead of Daniel as he raced through the first fringe of undergrowth. Once inside the woods he could move more easily, racing with a hunter's ease. He leaped over the low tangle of roots and bushes, keeping one or both arms outstretched ahead to shield his face.

Then he stopped. Daniel crashed up behind him and halted as well. Falconer cast about in a growing panic. He could see nothing. No sign anyone had passed this way.

Daniel opened his mouth as though in a silent roar, breathing as silently as Falconer. They held themselves utterly still.

Nothing.

Falconer wrested the pistol from his belt. He took a deep breath, ready to shout with all his might and release a volley. Which would have made their plans all for naught. Yet anything was better than bringing harm to the lass.

Then they heard her. Not a scream. More a high-pitched protest. Falconer squinted and searched. She seemed both close and far away. The sound seemed to have come from a dozen different directions.

But Daniel was more accustomed to forest hunting. He pointed to their right. "There!"

Falconer soon left his companion well behind. He scarcely seemed to touch the earth.

Then he saw her.

Drescott had her pinned to a tree. He held one hand over her mouth. He spoke to her, his lips up close to her ear while he smiled.

Falconer was running so hard he plucked the man away from Serafina as though Drescott were utterly weightless. Falconer's drive carried the two of them back a dozen paces. Falconer did not so much take aim for the oak as allow them to be halted by it.

He hammered the younger man against the trunk with such force all the air left Drescott's body in one long whoosh. Falconer did not allow himself to strike him. If he did, he would have killed him with the first blow. And he had vowed never to take another's life ever again. So he simply held Drescott there, ramming him bodily into the trunk. Drescott's eyes bulged with the strain of trying to refill his lungs with air.

Daniel raced up behind them and the three became locked in a fierce parody of a dance. Repeatedly Daniel murmured, "Ease up, Falconer. Ease up there."

Falconer released the man and stepped back. Drescott dropped to his knees and wheezed in desperation.

Falconer turned to where Serafina stood, supporting herself with one hand upon her throat and another on the tree. "Are you all right?" he asked.

She nodded without looking up. Falconer understood. She did not want to reveal the fear. He felt drenched by more rage, but not at Drescott. At himself. No matter how good his reasons might have been, he stood convicted by the fear that bowed Serafina over.

Falconer turned around. "Stand him up."

Roughly Daniel lifted the young man and planted his back upon the tree.

Falconer took a step forward. But just one. He could not safely come any closer. "I told you what would happen if you didn't leave the lass alone."

Drescott raised his hands to his face and whimpered with very real fear. "She enticed me."

Daniel growled somewhere deep in his throat.

"Daniel. The rope."

Daniel slipped the coil off his shoulder. He looked up, selected a branch, and tossed over the rope. He handed one end to Falconer.

Falconer made sure he fashioned the noose where Drescott could observe him.

The young man's eyes widened with the shock of understanding. "B–but that's murder!"

"I'd wager you would not be missed." Falconer tested the knots. "But then I'm not a betting man."

"You–you can't—"

"Tie his hands," Falconer ordered.

Daniel drew a short cord from his pocket and made swift work of tying Drescott's hands.

"I am Lord Drescott!"

Falconer handed the noose to Daniel. "That means utterly nothing to anyone here."

"No! You mustn't!"

"Why not?" Falconer watched as Daniel fitted the noose into place, sliced the knot down tight, and tugged the rope upward once. That testing pull was enough for the young man to shriek and for his legs to almost collapse. There was no pain, just the reality of what lay ahead. "Whatever could you offer me that would make me want to spare your wretched life?" Falconer demanded.

Frantically Drescott searched the forest. "Help! Someone! Save me!"

"We're out of range," Falconer said. "Which was what you had in mind all along, wasn't it? Letting the lass run ahead until you knew the storm would mask any noise she made."

"Help!"

"Hoist the man aloft, Daniel."

"No! Wait!" As Daniel began pulling on the rope, the man's voice rose a full two octaves. "I have information!"

"Do you now. That's very interesting." Falconer stayed Daniel with an upraised hand. "Because I have questions."

"If I t-tell you what I know, will y-you spare me?"

"That depends very much on the quality of your information." Falconer stepped forward. At this close range he knew Drescott could see what Falconer's past had done to him. And just how close he was to that final door. "All right. Here's my first question. Who sent the two attackers after us on Sunday?"

Drescott frantically scouted the forest. "Hold up there," Falconer warned. "Before you even think about telling me anything other than the truth, I want you to have a good look at the man holding both the rope and your life in his hands."

Drescott glanced over at Daniel's stone-hard face and shuddered a second time. "I let the attackers onto the estate."

"That's better." Falconer took a step back. "Now then. Here's the next question. And pay careful attention. I wasn't on the path. The two girls were on a horse. I was in the forest. But the attackers still took aim. I saw them draw back their triggers. Which means they weren't after just me. No, don't look around. Keep your eyes on me. This is where your only hope lies. Who were they after?"

"The girl," he whimpered.

Serafina gasped and started forward. Falconer halted her with an upraised hand. "You don't mean the lass here, do you?" When Drescott did not respond, Falconer's voice rapped out like a rifle shot. "Do you!"

"No."

"That can't be!" Serafina cried.

"But it is," Falconer said. "I've spent a long night mulling this over, and it's the only answer that makes sense." He continued to Drescott, "Let me make it easy for you. They wanted to eliminate Gareth and Erica Powers. Keep them from their campaign against slavery. But they've stayed safe in the manor beyond the attackers' reach. So they shifted targets. They reckoned doing harm to the child would most likely cripple the parents."

Falconer stopped then. The storm tossed the boughs high overhead, roaring through the forest like a hungry beast. Rain hit the forest floor with constant drumbeats. The earth smelled sweet, the air held a gentle chill. There was no other sound but the frantic breaths of the man by the tree.

"Tell me what I need to know," Falconer rasped out.

"I didn't want them to harm the child," Drescott pleaded.

Serafina cried a protest but cut it short at Falconer's signal.

"Of course not," Falconer said. "They came to you, didn't they? They already knew where we were staying. They came to you and explained what they were going to do."

Drescott looked at him for the first time. "How do you know this?"

Falconer aimed his response at Daniel. "They hired a swift clipper from America. They knew we traveled together now.

Their quarry was both the Powers and myself. They searched the Portsmouth area and found the coach house where I hired the carriage. They learned our destination from the coach driver." Falconer turned back to the quivering young man. "They must have been delighted to discover we were headed for Harrow Hall. Because they have a hold on you, don't they. What is it?"

Drescott blew out his cheeks and moaned, "I'm seriously in debt. Gambling."

"Who holds the reins?" Falconer lifted his voice a notch. "Who was it that sent you word?"

"He'll kill me if I say."

"But he's not near to you now, is he. And which danger is closer? That's what you need to think about."

Drescott licked his lips. He murmured, "Simon Bartholomew."

"The banker."

Drescott nodded.

"He holds your promissory notes."

Drescott replied to the earth at his feet. "He threatened to ruin me if I didn't help him with this."

Falconer turned to Daniel and said, "Bind him."

Panic rose fresh to his eyes. "B-but you said—"

"That we wouldn't hang you. And we won't." Falconer untied the noose as Daniel pulled the rope from the tree. Together they wound the rope around the trunk, lashing the young man tightly.

"You can't possibly intend to leave me here!"

When they finished, Drescott was fastened from his knees to his chin. Falconer watched as Daniel tested the knots, then said, "I hate to think how many young women you've attacked like the lass here."

"B-but she's a mere servant wench!"

"Which makes your actions even more vile. I urge you to think long and hard upon your way of life. While there's still time." Falconer turned away. "We're done here."

"Wait! You can't!"

They threaded their way back through the forest. Drescott's

voice faded in the distance. *"Wait!"*

As they walked farther from the inglorious sight, two other men slipped from behind sheltering trees. Lord Sedgwick's stout form was made even larger by a voluminous greatcoat. "The cad. The utter cad."

"You heard?" Falconer asked.

"Every word." Carlyle gave Falconer a long and measuring look. "I can see now why Gareth prizes your friendship so highly, sir."

"It is the lass you should be thanking." Falconer could not look over at her. Now that the deed was done, he felt only remorse. They had come far too close.

"Indeed so." Carlyle bowed in Serafina's direction. "You have done us all a great service, ma'am."

Sedgwick added, "I trust the scoundrel did not harm you?"

Serafina's voice still trembled. "John Falconer kept me safe."

Five very subdued people exited the forest and returned to the field, where Falconer retrieved his coat. The rain had stopped for the moment. "You go dry off," he told the others. "I must see to one more matter."

He watched as Daniel led the young woman into the old wing while the two men headed into the main house for dry clothes. Then he turned toward the stables. He found Harry currying down a chestnut mare. "A word, if you please, young Harry."

"Look at the state of your trousers. And your coat." Harry inspected him in amazement. "Been traipsing about the woodlands? In this weather?"

Falconer's shame deepened. The others might call it a good day's work. But he felt Serafina's fear grind inside his own belly. It was wrong. He could not say precisely why. But he would not do it again. "He's done it again," Falconer said. "Attacked Serafina."

Harry dropped the brush. "Who, young Drescott?"

"In the forest."

"That man should be strung up!"

Falconer liked the lad for his simple outrage. "In a few hours he might be wishing that had been his fate."

"What? What do you mean?"

Falconer explained what had happened and how they had left Drescott.

"He's lashed to an oak back there in the forest?" Harry's smile threatened to split his face. "That should teach him right and proper."

"I was hoping you might free him."

"Aye, I'll have a word with my dad. He can happen upon Drescott by chance, if you catch my meaning. The groundskeeper out giving the hounds a walk and what do you know, he comes upon the man."

"We hope to leave with the dawn. It would be good if Drescott is not able to divulge what he knows until after we're well quit of the place."

Harry's grin widened further. "A night in this storm will render any man silent, wouldn't you say?"

Chapter 25

Falconer swung his legs to the floor and sat on the edge of his bed. He waited for his breathing to come back under control. The bedchamber's walls seemed to tremble with the noise he feared he had made.

But all was quiet when he went downstairs. He slipped on his boots and crossed the empty yard. The kitchen was calm as well. A lone scullery maid was busy with the oven fire, the first kettle of tea brewing on the big iron stove. Falconer greeted the young woman and poured himself a mug. He stood by the kitchen doorway and welcomed the next to arrive, chewing his husk of bread and pretending that all was right with his predawn world. Behind him he heard the servants speak of a curious event, how the groundskeeper had come trundling in at first light pulling a dog-cart carrying Stewart Drescott. The young lord had been wrapped in a blanket and was shivering and groaning fiercely.

Daylight gradually revealed a checkerboard sky. Occasional clouds raced by, pausing only long enough to throw fistfuls of stinging rain. Then they raced off north, leaving behind glistening light and a sweet-smelling earth. Falconer recharged his cup and wished for a way to remake the previous day.

He spied Erica Powers crossing the path leading from the old wing to the kitchen. Serafina walked a pace behind, dressed in a high-necked dress of slate blue. Her hair was held back by a ribbon as pale as her eyes. Falconer addressed the older woman from the doorway, but his eyes remained upon the other. "Good morning, Mrs. Powers. You look proper lovely, Serafina."

"The dress belongs to Mrs. Powers," she said, giving him her tiny smile.

"It suits you most well."

Erica Powers remained well away from the kitchen door. "I would have a word with you, Mr. Falconer."

He leaned into the kitchen and set his cup down upon a window ledge. Then he joined Mrs. Powers by the side of the building, allowing her to draw him farther from the doorway. He had no interest in a public dressing down.

"I cannot tell you how distressed I was to learn you had endangered Serafina."

"It was wrong," Falconer said, eyes on the ground.

"The entire affair was . . ." She stopped. "Pardon? What did you say?"

"We should not have done it. You are right. I do apologize."

She paused, clearly caught off guard by his admission. "Why did you not realize this beforehand?"

Serafina spoke up then, as soft as the dawn. "Falconer did not do wrong."

They both turned to her in surprise. "But he endangered your life! He put you directly in harm's way!" Erica said.

"I agreed because I knew he would protect me."

"I almost failed," Falconer confessed.

"But you did not." Serafina looked at him with a clarity, a directness he had not seen before. "You came in time. And we learned who was behind the attack. That was important, yes?"

When he did not reply, Erica Powers said, "Please go see to our breakfast, Serafina."

"Yes, ma'am."

When she was gone, the two of them continued to study the place where she had stood. Finally Erica asked, more quietly this time, "Why did you do it?"

"You heard Sedgwick and Carlyle the same as I did. We needed hard evidence." Falconer stared at the next approaching squall. "But I know now that was only half the truth."

"You wanted—"

"Vengeance." He felt both a burning rage and an overwhelming guilt. If only he could put such feelings away once and for all. "He had attacked Serafina. I wanted to punish him."

"Vengeance is not yours to apply," she reminded him, but gently.

"Aye, that I know." He sighed. "I know."

She studied him. "Might I speak with you about another matter? Something highly personal?"

"You may address me on any matter you wish, ma'am."

"About Serafina."

A bloom of exquisite agony opened at his heart. "The lass, aye."

"She trusts you."

"That I know."

"She is also deeply wounded."

"I am aware of that as well."

"I have refrained from asking about her past and her upbringing because it distresses her so. But I have the impression that she was not raised a servant girl."

"The lass is highborn. No question."

Erica tested her words very carefully. "Do you have much experience with women, Mr. Falconer? I do hope you won't take my question the wrong way."

"Mrs. Powers, I have the highest regard for you and your husband. I understand the question, and the answer is a very simple no."

"She has revealed that a man has hurt her very deeply. Such wounds do not close swiftly. No matter how it may appear, she will need time for her heart, her emotions, to heal. Do you understand what I am saying?"

"I do indeed." Falconer's words were a breath almost lost to the wind. "She needs a trusted friend. And nothing more."

———— ❧ ————

The manor's chief groundskeeper, Harry's father, was as gnarled as old roots. He doffed his cap to the Powers family and Serafina as they approached the waiting carriage. He then motioned for Falconer to step aside. He said quietly, "I brought young Drescott in before dawn."

"I heard."

"Needed to fetch a dogcart. Fellow couldn't take a single step on his own steam." The groundskeeper did not sound the least bit sorry. "He's upstairs shivering in a bath, he is. Doused in salts and steam and trembling like a whipped pup."

Falconer studied the ground at his feet. The old man's evident satisfaction did nothing but convict him further.

"I know of one other lass he's savaged. Maybe more." The groundskeeper's face was as seamed as a winter's field and just as dark. "The old duke's as fine a man as I've ever known. Deserves better, the old duke does. Don't know if I want my boy Harry hanging about the place once young Drescott takes over. Just hope I live out my own time before that happens."

When Falconer still did not respond, the man went on, "There's a number of us here who are in your debt. We're mostly a God-fearing lot. We've watched and been helpless to change things. Now we're praying the young lord will think twice about his ways."

Falconer's confusion was only compounded. He started back to the carriage and mounted up beside the driver. "We must be off."

The groundskeeper pointed east and said, "Take the side road there, the one leading straight into the sunrise. It'll bring you out by way of a side entrance that's only used at harvest time. Least likely entrance to be watched."

Gareth Powers leaned through the carriage window. "We are most obliged to you and all the staff, sir."

"A privilege to meet your honors. Many's the night my young

Harry's read what you've had to say in your pamphlets, what about rights and charity and such." He doffed his cap. "May God speed your journey, sir, and watch over you all your days."

Daniel sat to one side of the driver, Falconer to the other. Both men held cocked pistols. A pair of haying hooks rose between them, as close to pikes as Falconer could find about the manor. The driver was made nervous both by the men and the suggestion of danger. But he handled the horses well, and they made good time. They held to small lanes and saw no one until they reached the outskirts of Bath. After that they were simply one more in a long line of coaches and wagons. Daniel stowed the pikes and they rode safely to Bath's city center.

The station from which the train departed was enough to frighten both beast and man. The horses jerked nervously as they approached, made skittish by the steam rising from the building's other side. The wind picked at the manmade clouds and sent them billowing out over the station and the carriages. Horses whinnied in real fear at the smell of smoke.

The train itself was hardly better. The group had a compartment to themselves, with Daniel stationed in the hall outside. The window was shut against the fumes and the glowing cinders that drifted in the wind. The train started off twenty minutes late, with a grinding squeal and chuffing noises from far in front. The town was soon left behind, and the train accelerated into a long series of curves. Speed and more speed as they swept through one green-sided valley after another. Falconer watched with alarm as the rattling contraption carried them ever faster, until he was certain they were close to flying off the earth itself.

The Powers family, however, had ridden on the train any number of times. Neither the clattering din nor the speed seemed to affect them in the slightest. Even Hannah enjoyed watching the world whoosh by. She delighted in pointing out items that were gone before Falconer could properly see them.

Once clear of the Wiltshire hills, they entered verdant fields. The train's rude vibrations calmed somewhat, and Gareth settled into his corner seat and fell asleep. Mrs. Powers opened the window a fraction, for the wind now blew the smoke away from them. She sat next to Serafina, with Hannah to their other side. Falconer sat beside the compartment door, both to block any entry and to leave the middle seat free for Gareth to stretch out in slumber. The man looked wan but not unwell. Clearly, the days at Harrow Hall had done him good. Pity there had not been more of them.

Mrs. Powers cleared her throat and adopted a formal manner. "Serafina, I hope you will forgive me for prying. But I feel a rather urgent need to know more about you than I do."

Serafina's gaze widened in the manner of a startled fawn. But she said, "I understand."

"I believe you told me you are from Venice, is that correct?"

"Yes. My father's family is old Venetian." She pronounced it in the Italian manner. *Veneziàna*. Yet the lilting manner belied a growing sorrow. "My mother is from the hills."

"Hills?"

"To the north. The mountains."

"Ah. You mean the Alps."

"Yes. Her family are *Dolomiti*. You understand?"

As Falconer observed the two women, he saw in them a great similarity of manner, one that overcame the difference in age and nationality. A former captain he had served under, a hard-bitten merchant seaman who had clawed his way up the ranks in the same manner as Falconer, had scorned such traits. The old captain had called them parlor antics and claimed that they could be taught to any intelligent monkey. The old captain had loathed such people and the class they represented, and the way he had forever been shut out of their ranks by the mistake of birth. But Falconer observed the two ladies and saw something different. He saw the ability to express breeding and custom before even opening their mouths. He saw a different world. One in which

Falconer knew he would never belong.

"You said your family's name was Gavi, is that correct?"

"Gavi, yes." Just saying the word caused Serafina to wince, as though pierced by some unseen weapon.

Mrs. Powers clearly noticed the young woman's distress. Her manner was gentle but insistent. "Your father, is he alive?"

"Yes ma'am."

"What does he do, may I ask?"

"He is a merchant. And a doge."

"Excuse me, I am unfamiliar with that term. What was it again?"

"Doge. It means prince in the Venetian dialect."

Falconer noticed that Gareth opened his eyes to that, then swiftly shut them again. And pretended to sleep.

"Y-your f-father is royalty?" Erica stammered.

"Once. A long time ago. Now the title is a, how do you say it, *formalità.*"

"A formality."

"Yes. Venice is now part of the Austro-Hungarian Empire. The merchant princes still have their council, but all power is held by the king's commissioner."

Neither Erica nor Hannah seemed aware that Serafina's accent had thickened. From Hannah's lap, the kitten complained over how Hannah ignored it. Hannah silenced the animal without taking her eyes from Serafina.

"And where is your father now?" Erica asked.

"America." Serafina turned her face to the window. "My father and my mother, they are in Washington."

"America," Erica repeated.

"The council sent him. They are on some secret mission for the council. I do not think the governor knows. My father, he serves as consiglière."

This time Erica did not ask for a translation. Instead, she glanced at her husband, whose eyes were once more open. "And they sent your father."

"Yes."

The question settled heavily upon the compartment's atmosphere even before Erica spoke the words. "Why are you not with them?"

Tears began to course down Serafina's face. Before the question had been framed, she had started to weep. "I thought . . . I thought I had fallen in love."

Falconer drew a clean handkerchief from his pocket, reached forward, and pressed it into her hand. Serafina looked down uncomprehendingly. She blinked, dropping tears onto the cloth.

"I'm afraid I don't understand," Erica said very softly.

"I fell in love," Serafina repeated, talking now to the hands in her lap. "Luca was my instructor at the academy. For art. He was military. He said . . ."

This time no one spoke. The train rattled and drummed. Sunlight dashed upon the rail car and the weeping young lady. Finally Serafina was able to continue. "He said he wanted to marry me. I ran away. My parents brought me back. I became ill. They carried me onto the ship. It was an English vessel. We stopped in Portsmouth. I ran away again. I came to Harrow, where my aunt lives. She is ill. She had received a letter from my mother. Luca lied about everything. . . ." Serafina could go no further.

Gareth was no longer pretending to sleep. Erica gave her husband a long look. This one saying that she was both confused and very concerned. But she could not bring herself to ask anything more of poor Serafina. Instead, she reached her arm around the shaking shoulders and drew the girl close.

They traveled on for a time, until the silence grew strained. For all eyes remained upon Serafina as she struggled to regain her composure. Falconer found himself filling in all that remained unsaid. He did not know everything, but he knew enough to see her future. Serafina was at heart a very good woman. She would eventually be reconciled with her family. Her parents, however angry and hurt they might be now, would reunite with their daughter. Serafina would be drawn back into the fold of a rich and powerful clan. A clan within which he had no place. Falconer would be seen as merely another usurper. A man scarcely better than this Luca. And in truth Falconer understood the thief. That was how he thought of Luca now. A thief who had ripped the heart out of this beautiful young woman. Falconer felt drawn by the same hunger the thief had no doubt felt. That he restrained himself was of little worth. Falconer felt gouged by the fact that Serafina deserved a man far better than him. One who was not dogged by such a dark and desperate past.

Gareth shifted, as though coming awake. He spoke to Falconer, clearly wishing to divert the attention away from Serafina. "I don't believe you have ever told me where you hail from."

"I come from nowhere and nothing." Falconer heard the acid of disappointment etched into his every word. But he spoke just the same, talking of what had not been revealed for years. He spoke not to Gareth but Serafina. Now was as good a time as any to remind them both that he understood he was not for her. "My beginnings form a wretched story that does not deserve the telling."

"Nonetheless I would like to know."

"My mother was a serving wench in a roadside tavern. My father left when I was four. I am told he was a blacksmith. I remember him not. When I was seven, I was apprenticed to a wandering chimney sweep and ratter. He paid my mother five silver pennies for eight years of my service. When he beat me he always claimed he had overpaid."

It was Falconer's turn to seek solace out the window. "When I was twelve or thereabouts I ran away to sea. The merchant navy isn't so particular about where they recruit their midshipmen. They took me for a likely lad, lied about my age on the signing-up papers, and sent me aloft. What education I received was at the hands of my skippers. I served under ten of them. Six were good men. Four were not. Two of these I hope and pray never to set eyes upon again, for to be in their company would strain the fabric of my oath to God."

He stopped then and realized the entire cabin was watching him. "Have you prayed on this?" Gareth asked.

"Aye. And asked for a healing of wounds that pain me still."

Hannah surprised them all by asking, "Is that why you have nightmares? What those two men did to you?"

Falconer leaned across the compartment. "No, lass, it is not. And I apologize for speaking of them at all. It was a mistake."

She tilted her head slightly and inspected him for a time before saying, "You are very hard on yourself."

He found himself rocked back into his seat. "Another friend once told me the very same thing."

It was Hannah's mother who asked, "Why is that, do you think?"

Falconer retreated to another inspection of the vista that rattled along outside their window. Only now Serafina's face was within sight, and he felt captured anew by his helplessness. "I can only suppose it is because of all the wrong I have done." He could not help himself. He met the loveliest gaze in all the world. He felt her pain as his own. Falconer stared at her so intently he felt able to reach across the distance and touch her cheek with his eyes alone. "And all the mistakes I continue to make."

"It wasn't wrong asking me to help you." Serafina's voice remained hoarse with her tears and confession.

Falconer could only respond with a sigh.

"They were intent upon attacking our daughter," Gareth quietly pointed out.

"We have been through all that." Erica's internal distress was revealed in her voice and the way she drew Hannah close. "Even Falconer recognizes he was in error."

Gareth coughed. "I personally have always seen our own efforts as a battle against evil."

"But with the pen, Gareth. Not with violence."

"Just so. Just so." And yet it was to Falconer that he looked before closing his eyes and resting his head upon the side wall.

Chapter 26

Within the first hour of their arrival, Falconer understood why Gareth Powers had initially refrained from coming to Wilberforce's home. Though the great man himself lay isolated in his chambers, the manor pulsed with energy. Even before they had finished unloading the carriage, word had spread far and wide that Gareth and Erica Powers had returned. People began drawing near, offering a report, seeking a word, a bit of advice, a request for them to help with one matter or another.

Erica saw the large group developing around her husband and took charge. "Daniel."

"Yes, ma'am."

"You are to escort my husband to our assigned chamber." She pitched her voice loud enough for all to hear. "Please see that he is not disturbed."

"That I will, Mrs. Powers."

By the time Falconer had dropped his meager belongings into his upstairs room and had a walk around the home's interior, the staff was being called to dinner. The manor was a far cry from Harrow Hall in every imaginable way. All the folk, whether staff or guest or notable, gathered together in no particular order. The dining hall opened into the front parlor to accommodate the one long table. Everyone helped serve the meal, and then they all took their seats together. The prayer was long and ardent. Fervent murmurs of agreement arose as the prayer moved on to a request for healing for Gareth and for Hannah and for Wilberforce himself.

The meal itself was a lively din of animated chatter. Falconer retreated into his customary shell, observing Hannah, who sat across from him, her cheeks flushed with the pleasure of being included among the adults.

As they were cleaning up, Hannah said to him, "Serafina is in the room directly above yours. Isn't that romantic?"

"Lass . . ." Falconer felt the heat in his face. He couldn't help but glance over to Serafina, surrounded by six other young ladies, in hopes she had not heard the comment. He also noticed the young men who gaped in her direction. Serafina chose that moment to look his way and offer her sorrow-filled smile. Falconer's flush deepened. He said to Hannah, "Shouldn't you be in bed like your father?"

"I rested upon our arrival. And I feel fine. See?" She twirled about, all shining eyes and flowing tresses. "I do think Serafina likes you immensely."

Falconer ducked his red face and lowered himself down to her level. "What I see is a young imp who talks when she should perhaps remain silent."

This only made Hannah's smile grow more brilliant. "Do you suppose that you are falling in love?"

"I—"

"Excuse me, Mr. Falconer?"

"Eh, yes?" He rose to his full height.

"Mr. Powers is wishing to have a word, sir," a young man said.

Falconer made his way to the room at the rear of the house overlooking an untended garden. A small fountain was almost lost to the weeds. Yet the vista held an air of contented welcome, as though part of its very charm lay in how little care it was given. Gareth sat in a velvet robe, obviously borrowed from someone else in the house, upon a horsehair settee drawn up close to the tall windows. The drapes were drawn back to reveal the slowly waning light. The clouds overhead were colored a riot of golds.

"Draw up a chair, please," Gareth invited.

"You look stronger."

"It is exhilarating to be here once more. If only my friend were better."

"You have seen Mr. Wilberforce?"

"Briefly. We had a few words only, Erica and I." Gareth clenched his jaw tightly. "He is not well."

Falconer understood both the meaning and the pain it caused. "I am very sorry, sir."

Gareth nodded. The two men sat and watched the sunset. As darkness took hold, Falconer used a flint to light candles. When he returned to his chair by the window, Gareth said, "I am a soldier at heart. Neither faith nor my work with the pen have changed my perspective upon our struggle."

"Sir, I am grateful for your words. But nothing you can say will change my opinion that your wife is correct."

"Perhaps so." Gareth smiled. "That is the problem we men face. Being confronted with our secret intentions by the women in our lives."

"Aye," Falconer sighed.

"Be that as it may, it is about something else that I wish to speak. There is another battle awaiting you."

"Sir?"

"One fought with words. Yet one that will carry the fate of a multitude of voiceless and despairing souls in the bargain." Gareth straightened in his chair. "There are two responsibilities that only you can fulfill. Parliament we have already discussed. I believe Serafina has already mentioned the other matter. My wife hopes you will describe to them both your experiences within the slavery business so that these may be captured in drawings for our pamphlet."

Falconer felt the hand of bitter memories grip his chest and squeeze very hard. "I have spent years begging God to help me to forget."

"Falconer, I speak to you now as an old soldier. One who carries his own burdens of dread recollections. We do not seek to know about your own personal sins. We wish to have you describe your eyewitness accounts of the current slave trade. But it is *precisely* because of your own previous actions that your account will carry force. You know the evil first hand, agreed?"

"Aye," he said, the word drawn from a well of memories. "I know it."

"And so you shall speak as one who has seen the core of this wicked trade. Your words will carry the weight of one who has been confronted with the magnitude of this horror." Gareth's features showed that he understood Falconer's distress. "You must remember the Lord's promise to turn the dross of our past into gold. He does not promise that it will be easy. But He promises to use us for His glory. Is that not enough?"

"I would like to think so," Falconer said to his hands.

Gareth let the silence linger a moment longer, then asked, "Are you ready to go and serve our Lord?"

Falconer's nightly enemy attacked with a ferocity that surprised even him. He awoke to the utter dark, far earlier than normal. He sat up in bed, chest heaving, and stared out the narrow window to his right. Moonlight cast the front drive into a river of silver. But despite the dream's vivid intensity, he did not feel the normal sense of woe. Instead, he felt strangely calm. He slipped into his clothes, wondering at the welcome sensation. Normally a man of action, he was not given to introspection. Yet here was a quandary worth considering. How could he have just arisen from his worst nightmare in years and yet feel at peace?

Fully dressed, he pulled a stool out from beneath the narrow window table. He seated himself and placed his elbows upon the table's smooth wood. He did not pray so much as wait.

It came to him then. The words Gareth had spoken the day before, of battle and of responsibility and of a charge being placed upon him alone.

With shocking awareness, Falconer now saw his nightmares from an entirely different perspective. He clenched his hands the tighter, willing himself to hold to the course, to understand.

He saw how the nightmares revealed all the forces he struggled against. It was not merely the past that hounded him. It was the present. It was the future. A *new* future. One where he stood in defiance of the evil that had once dominated his every day.

The recurring dreams took on a different meaning then. For now Falconer saw it from the perspective of a willing servant. That was how he viewed himself. A flawed and failing man, a being for whom a myriad of daily thoughts and actions were tainted by all he wished he was not. Yet a servant just the same.

A servant who sought to do his duty. A servant who was attacked every night by all that was evil and demonic, all that wished him to fail.

A servant armed by his Master. A servant who would follow the Master's call.

Falconer lowered his head to the cool wood. He stumbled over his words, as was often the case with him. Yet he knew God heard not only the words but the humble and thankful heart behind them as well.

Then he heard the scream.

Chapter 27

Serafina finally managed to break free. She flung herself upward and away from the terrifying darkness. When she opened her eyes, it was to see alarmed faces in the open door of her little chamber. She sighed and slid down farther into the bed, her heart racing such that it caused her every breath to tremble. But she did not mind. She was awake and safe.

An older woman held a candle in one hand and asked with deep concern, "Are you all right, child?"

"Yes. Truly. I'm fine." And she was. Remarkably, all she felt was the compassion filling this creaky old house. "It was a dream."

A thundering of steps up the stairway resounded through the wall opposite her bed. Before she heard the voice, she knew. Oh yes. He would be there, of course. To shelter and protect.

"Is the lass safe?" Falconer called.

"A dream," the older woman replied as she met him at the door. "Only a dream. And you, sir, are in the women's hall." Others in nightgowns and sleep bonnets melted away to their rooms.

"I beg your pardon, ma'am." He raised his voice. "Serafina, would you care to join me in the kitchen for a cup of sailor's tea?"

She slid her feet to the floor. Outside her door the woman protested, "As you can see, sir, it is still dark outside, far too early for anything save rest."

"I shall be in the kitchen in case she feels otherwise," Falconer said and thumped his way back down the stairs.

The stairway was narrow at that level, for the high floor now used by the women had originally been intended for servants. Serafina's legs trembled as she pulled on a robe and prepared to go to the kitchen. She steadied herself with one hand upon each wall as she descended.

The middle floor held what had been family rooms, just as in her own house in Venice. The thought brought an aching lump to her throat, causing her to grip the handrail tightly to keep from stumbling. When she arrived at the ground level, Serafina paused to wipe her eyes, then followed the hall back to the kitchen.

The kitchen in Wilberforce's manor extended like a brick appendage. There were windows on three sides, and two sets of double doors separated it from the main house, keeping smoke and odors and noise away from the formal rooms. Serafina entered and found Falconer seated at the central worktable with a hot mug and a candle and a Bible set before him.

"Sit yourself down, lass."

She did as she was told. Falconer rose and prepared a mug with sparse motions and set it before her. He did not ask about her welfare, as she expected. Instead, he recharged his own tea, seated himself once more, and sat quietly with the mug between both hands.

In the candlelight she could see characteristics she had not noticed before, such as an aquiline nose and silver traces woven into his hair. Yet he did not appear old. His features were weather beaten and sun darkened in the manner of one who would never again be pale. There were scars about one wrist, as though a rope had burned into his skin, and criss-crossed white scars about his other palm. She sipped her tea and determined that she would like to draw those hands.

"For three years and nine months I have suffered from a dream," Falconer said, speaking to the candle and not to her. "It is always the same. I am chained in a long line of slaves, locked inside the hold of the ship I used to command. There is a great storm. I can hear the sailors arguing. I cannot hear their words, but I know what they are saying. In order to survive, they must lighten the ship. They must throw their cargo overboard. That is all I am to them. I and all the other slaves chained within the central hold. We are cargo. Ballast."

Serafina was surprised by her own reaction. She was not frightened by the image, nor repulsed. Instead, she found herself studying not just the physical man seated across from her. She felt she was inspecting the interior man as well. A man who sought both to share his secret weakness and reveal the depths of his being.

"The hold opens," he continued in a low, soft tone. "The sailors use a pike to grip the chain. I am pulled up and into the storm. In the light I see the other slaves."

Falconer stopped and lifted his mug, using both hands. His breath shook slightly. As though in sympathy, the candle's light shivered.

He set down his mug and went on, "Every slave wears my face. I look at the sailors. They all have my face as well. I cannot halt it as I am pulled over and dropped into the sea." He lowered his head until he was facing the scarred wood between his hands. "I am undone, for I am unclean. . . ."

Serafina's glimpse into the heart of the man seated before her drew forth a realization that caused a soft gasp. *He loves me.*

Falconer misunderstood her intake of breath. "Those words are spoken by an ancient prophet, one who had come before the throne of the Almighty."

He loves me. The realization whirled through her mind. She also understood he was doing his best to hide it. This was why he had avoided speaking her name. How she knew these things did not matter, but she was sure Falconer was reluctant to speak her name because it drew his feelings too close to the surface.

A tear dislodged itself and coursed in heat and sorrow down one cheek.

Falconer noticed that, though he did not appear to be looking her way at all. "I did not tell you this to upset you, lass."

She shook her head but found herself unable to speak. Her

tears were coming more freely now. She wiped her face but could not stop the flow.

"I told you because I want you to know that I understand what your nights are like."

She heard Falconer's words and she also heard the unspoken message behind them. It was as though her own heart could ask questions and hear Falconer's heart give a silent response. And she heard her own heart speak silently in reply. *I have nothing to give you. My heart is shattered and empty. I cannot love. Perhaps I never shall again.*

She lowered her face to her hands and wept with the abandon of one without future or hope.

Falconer reached over and touched her, his hand merely resting upon her shoulder. Serafina felt the gentleness, and more. She could see a man who asked for nothing. She knew that he understood her wounded state. She recalled his talk upon the train and realized he had spoken as he did because he thought himself beneath her station. He loved her and knew it was futile, so he did his best to hide it away. He sought not to pressure, not to demand. Instead, he sought only to give. To protect, to shield, to comfort, to strengthen, to honor. He fought his own desires and wished only to give. Which only caused her to weep the harder.

"I should not have spoken as I did. I am very sorry."

Serafina buried her face in her hands. She wanted to tell him that this was not why she wept, but her sobs would not allow her to draw sufficient breath. She did not even weep because of Luca. She wept because of how wrong she had been. She had known nothing of love. She had lied to herself . . . why? She had believed the lie because she had wanted to make her fantasy real. But love was not built upon fantasy. She saw that now, for the very first time. Love was built upon giving. And Luca had given nothing. He had sought only to take. But she had been enchanted by his lies and she had wanted to believe that her time for loving had come. And as a result she had given her love to a man who deserved nothing.

Finally her weeping calmed. When she sat up again, Falconer

rose and walked to the stove. He took a clean dishtowel and poured a bit of hot water from the kettle. He walked back to the table and handed it to her.

Serafina wiped her face, then dried it with the towel's edge. "May I ask how old you are?"

"Twenty-nine."

"When will you be thirty?"

His dark eyes did not reflect the candle so much as hold a golden light all their own. "I can't say for certain. I don't know in which month I was born. Only that it was winter."

She managed to stifle new tears before they formed. Her breath was ragged and her throat felt raw. But still she spoke. "I have had a dream since childhood of running through the streets of my city. Only they are streets I have never seen before. I am trying to go home. But I cannot find my way. I cry out but no one hears me. And now . . ."

When she began to tremble, Falconer said softly, "You don't need to tell me this."

But she did. "Now there is an animal that is after me. I am a little child in the dream. Always a child, and I cannot run fast enough to escape this beast. I know the beast will devour me. Every street I turn into, it seems that the animal is just ahead of me. Ahead, behind, and to every side. Then I turn a corner, and I hear a growl. Just as it attacks, I wake up."

A wet dawn was spreading beyond rain-streaked windows. Falconer wet his fingertips and stifled the candle. "Would you like more tea?"

"Yes, thank you."

He crossed to the stove and spoke with his back to her. "Perhaps some people in this world are more vulnerable to the beast of the night. I can only speak for myself. I have done things that do not bear thinking about. If this is my fate, there is little I can do to argue otherwise."

Serafina did not so much nod in understanding as tremble with the weight of his words. *I am not as strong as you,* she wanted to say. But what she said was, "When I became ill, after . . ."

Falconer returned to the table with her mug. "After your parents kept you from seeing your man."

"Yes." Oh, how it seared to have him speak of Luca. How shamed she was to think of Luca's supposed strength when faced with the reality of this good man. She forced herself to continue. "I entered a fever. It was with me for quite some time. Toward the end, it seemed to me as though the fever was alive. It was an animal, like the beast of my dream. And if I let myself stay weak, the beast would eat me, just as I feared would happen in my dream."

"None of us are strong enough to stay the course alone, lass."

"How strange those words sound," she replied, "in the face of your own strength."

"All of us are weak in our own way. All of us need the power of God to help us through. So long as we steer our own course, we are blind. We create great wrongs and justify all we do in the name of selfish ambition."

Serafina nodded as she felt his words strip away the lies and lay her wounded spirit bare. She reached across then, as natural an action as any she had ever made, and rested her hand upon his. "You are such a good man, John Falconer."

He stared down at the hand upon his own. A look of abject sorrow took hold of his features.

She understood. The dawn was nothing compared to the illumination that filled the kitchen. "You know that my heart has been broken. I have nothing to give you."

He nodded slowly. He did know.

"It is a poor gift to offer," she said. "But I could think of no greater honor, no finer gift, than to be able to call you my dearest friend."

Dim morning light gradually strengthened. The house was stirring. She knew their time was coming to a close. But one thing remained undone. "Would you please pray for me?" she asked softly.

Falconer's voice was softer now. "I pray for you daily."

"You heap one gift upon the other until they are beyond both measure and count." She compressed herself in an effort to stop the tears. "What I meant was, would you pray for me now?"

"With you, lass," he corrected gently. "What you wish is for us to pray together, yes?"

"Just so. Pray *with* me." She smiled and knew her lips trembled slightly, and did not care. "Is that not a lovely thing to say?"

They bowed their heads and Falconer spoke in his strong yet gentle manner. Yet in truth Serafina heard little beyond the sound of her own heart. And knew the gift of a calm that settled into her, an ability to look ahead with something more than sorrow and shame.

When she lifted her head, she discovered that Erica Powers stood in the kitchen doorway, watching them with an expression that mirrored exactly the sentiment that filled Serafina's heart.

"Forgive me for disturbing," Mrs. Powers said, addressing Falconer. "But I was wondering if you are ready."

He rose instantly to his feet. "I am."

"Ready?" Serafina looked from one to the other. "Ready for what?"

Falconer's features had resumed their sternness. "For the fulfillment of my quest."

"Just so." Yet the gentle light did not depart from Erica's features. She said to Serafina, "You are welcome to join us, if Falconer agrees."

Falconer's solemnity only deepened. "Do you wish this?" he asked Serafina.

"I want to help," she replied, as certain of this as anything since the day she had run away. Perhaps long before. "If I am able, I want to help you all."

They worked through the morning, completing the pamphlet Erica had begun at Harrow Hall. Falconer sat in what had once been the great man's study. He felt Wilberforce's presence everywhere. Gareth lay upon the daybed where no doubt Wilberforce had once rested. Erica Powers led the questioning. There were several others who gathered with them around an oval table of polished cherry. Falconer sat with his papers and his maps spread out around him. Serafina was at the table's far end, where she listened and watched in silence. An hour or so after they began, she opened a large sketchpad supplied by one of the others in the house and began to draw. She showed her work to no one.

Toward the noon hour Lord Sedgwick arrived, moving with remarkable quietness for such a big man. Falconer led them through all the information he had and all the questions he could not answer. Erica was gentle in her inquiries but very probing. By lunchtime Falconer felt drained of strength.

Erica, however, was only beginning. She asked that all the others save Gareth and Serafina leave the room. Even Sedgwick did not remain. A pile of fresh pages were brought, and quill and ink. Several times over the course of the afternoon, she sent for Falconer. Always the task was the same. Erica's pen scratched busily along the page as she asked him about one point or another of his story. Often she sought what she called color, details that would bring the story alive for the reader.

Serafina moved to the chamber's opposite corner. For Falconer, Erica's questions were made more difficult and painful still by Serafina's silent watchfulness. The questions not only brought Falconer back to the world he had sought to leave behind forever. They exposed the very depths of his immoral past. Yet he held nothing back. Falconer spoke to Gareth at these times, using his military voice, stern and emotionless. It was the only way he could mask the internal tumult, the pain of confession. Each time Erica thanked him, then returned to her writing. Falconer understood that she was not being cold in her dismissals. She was simply caught up in her task. Each time he left the room without glancing Serafina's way yet knowing she watched him.

Toward late afternoon the rains ended and the slate-gray heavens rolled back. The manor's gardens shone as though painted with a translucent silver. Every window sparkled. Birdsong echoed through the house. Smiles beamed from almost every face. Falconer kept his sense of impending storm to himself and held himself ready for whatever else Erica needed.

As the others began preparations for dinner, Serafina found him seated on a bench sheltered beneath a rose trellis that had not been trimmed in years. "May I speak with you?" she asked.

"Of course." He shifted over, making room for her on the bench.

Serafina did not sit down. "I have something I wish for you to see. I want you to understand me very well, John Falconer. I have not shown this to anyone. I think it may be what Erica is after. But if you do not wish for this to be seen by others, I will tear it up and never speak of it again."

"Whatever are you speaking about, lass?"

But she was not done. "Erica and Gareth showed me portraits of important people. They are from journals and newspapers and a few books. That is where the other faces come from. I want you to know that. I want you to understand—" She stopped abruptly, and from behind her back revealed a rolled sheet of paper. Serafina thrust her hand forward. "Here."

Slowly Falconer reached over and took the sheet. He unrolled it. And groaned.

"Oh, I knew I should have done something else," she said desperately. "I will do it now. There is still time if I hurry."

"No." He did not realize he had moved at all, except that he could feel the wet earth against his knees.

She had taken his dream, his nightmare, his burden of more than three years. And she had drawn it so well the image shrieked at him. The tremors running through his body and his hands caused the image to become even more lifelike.

He was there upon the foredeck. But not as the captain. As the witness. Part of a crowd of people that included Sedgwick and Gareth and Erica and even Serafina herself. Others pulled the slaves out on the deck. The seamen performing this vile act were people he did not recognize, yet their faces were vividly drawn. A vast and dreadful storm raged all about the ship. Only there was one hint of light, a single tiny ray, that reached down and touched those who prayed upon the foredeck.

Falconer held the drawing to his chest and wept.

"Oh, forgive me, it was wrong, wrong!" Serafina was weeping also. "Please do not cry," she begged. "Let me have it, I shall destroy it and no one will ever know. . . ."

Falconer bent over so that her hands could not take the drawing from him. He could not recall ever having wept before. Certainly not as a man. Nor could he draw enough breath to speak to her now and explain. The image was not tragic. Rather, it provided release.

He felt her hand touch his shoulder, and he wanted to explain. That he saw the truth in her drawing. That no longer was he among those who did the terrible deed. No longer was he counted as slaver and murderer and fiend. Instead, he stood upon the foredeck with those anointed by God. He, the least of men, was among the redeemed. He prayed. He struggled. He *served*.

When he could draw a decent breath, he said, "You must give it to Erica."

"No. I couldn't. You—"

"Lass." He stumbled in his effort to rise. He felt her hands steady him and made it to his feet. He wiped his face with his free hand. "Thank you."

"I don't understand. . . . You believe this is good?"

A robin settled upon the trellis overhead and filled the evening with song. "It is more than beautiful. It is a gift."

Serafina took a long breath.

He unfurled the paper once more. "There is a goodness to feeling such a pain as this. I've said that poorly, but it's all I know at this moment."

She watched him carefully. "I have seen the power your cause holds for you. The goodness that you have brought from the pain and the shadows. That is what I tried to draw."

"You saw it and used it both." Falconer's breath caught in his throat as he studied the drawing anew.

"It does me such good to hear you say that." She glanced

toward the house. "Erica is waiting for me. Perhaps I should show her. That is, if you are certain."

"Aye, lass. She will know how to use it for the most good." The sun rested upon the western treetops now, burnishing the tall grass and the empty fountain and the lichen-covered stones. Her face was illuminated by the soft glow, her eyes given depth and the promise of new life ahead. Falconer stared at her and knew he would never see anything quite so beautiful. "Serafina . . ."

From within the house a bell sounded, the one that was traditionally used to summon a servant. In Wilberforce's manor, however, it was used only to draw everyone to the dinner table.

Falconer turned with her, not certain whether he was relieved or sorry that he had been interrupted.

As they entered through the rear doors, she looked at him and said, "I do so like to hear you speak my name."

Chapter 28

The next morning Falconer dressed with care. He took command of the bath while the rest of the Wilberforce household still slumbered, scrubbing his skin nearly raw. The previous day, Erica and two other women had selected the best of the clothing given to him by Reginald Langston. The items were now laid out upon his bed, cleaned and starched and folded. He combed his hair, oiled it in the seaman's manner, and tied it back with a ribbon. He had neither stickpin nor cuff links. His dress was as severe as a uniform. As was his expression.

He gave himself over to morning prayers, spending a long time on three things in particular. First, he asked for God to be at his right hand through the coming ordeal, and for words and for wisdom that were not his own.

Second, he thanked God for a morning free of his nightmare. He did not take this as hope for the future. Falconer was unable to look further than the next few hours. But he did take the respite as a sign. God had cleared his mind for the coming affray. He was not alone. Of this he was certain.

Third, he thanked God for the previous day's conversation with Serafina. He took great heart from the woman and her words. He could not say precisely what had changed, nor did he wish to linger over such reflections. He was simply grateful for this new friend.

For the moment, it was enough.

He was not the first to enter the kitchen. People greeted him nervously and let him be. Falconer was aware of what they saw. He had seen his own reflection upon the eve of battle. He knew his eyes were as hard as agate, his face tightened into an expression boding danger.

Serafina was seated in a cramped little alcove formed between the food pantry and the dish cupboard. She had pulled over a chair, isolating her within the bustling kitchen. She was hunched slightly over her tea, her face ashen.

Falconer walked over and lowered himself into her field of vision. She looked at him with troubled eyes. He asked so softly the words carried only to her. "The nightmare?"

She responded with a small nod.

He set her mug at her feet and took hold of her hands. "Two things. Are you listening?"

She nodded a second time.

"The first thing. It will pass. With time and patience and prayer. It will pass. Do you believe me?"

"I want to."

"The second thing." Falconer released her hands and rose to his full height, his full strength, his full resolve. Not caring about the eyes he felt upon them. Wanting only to will this fragile lady his strength. "You are not alone."

He felt a hand upon his shoulder but remained as he was until the color returned to Serafina's face. Falconer then looked up at Erica Powers.

She smiled tenderly at Serafina before saying to Falconer, "Come with me."

William Wilberforce's private chamber stood opposite the kitchen and overlooked the rear garden, or would have if the drapes had not been drawn. Dawn cast a faint glimmer only, a trace of light framing the heavy velvet curtains. A pair of candles offered an island of soft light by the bed. With the door shut behind him, Falconer could hear nothing from the house. The room felt like a sanctuary, a haven built midway between earth and heaven.

The figure in the bed was diminutive, his face made smaller by the bandages upon his eyes. One hand rested unmoving upon the cover. Gareth sat in a high-backed chair pulled up close to the bed. Spread upon the coverlet were half a score of pages. Erica's words were set in type now, and the headlines shouted at Falconer as he crossed the carpeted floor. He saw his own name there in bold script. Directly beneath the headline were the two drawings of his face—one from the Wanted poster, the other from Serafina. Her drawing from the previous day illustrated another entire page.

A voice as small as the body asked, "Is that my dear Erica?"

"It is. I have brought John Falconer with me."

"Excellent. Do please make yourselves comfortable."

Falconer lifted a chair and drew it close to the bed for Erica. But he chose to remain standing. He could not see himself seated in such a place as this. Gareth looked up but said nothing.

"Gareth has read to me your words, Erica," continued the man on the bed. "They are excellent, my dear. I only wish you had remained to hear them."

"I could scarcely read them once they were written. They pained me so I broke down and wept," she answered softly.

"They are indeed powerful. Let us pray they offer the final impetus." Wilberforce seemed able to see Gareth through the veil of his bandage. "And the young lady's drawings, are they as powerful as Erica has made them sound?"

"An artillery barrage would not carry more force," Gareth replied.

"Let us hope they carry the day. Now then. What are your plans?"

"We leave for Parliament in an hour."

"The members will have seen the pamphlet?"

"Our presses ran all night. Copies were delivered at dawn."

Wilberforce's breathing was the softest rasp, like winter chaff rattling in the wind. He was quiet for so long Falconer thought perhaps he had fallen back asleep. Then the little man said, "John Falconer."

"Your servant, sir."

"Gareth has told me something of your journey. It has been arduous."

Falconer knew without being told that the man did not speak of his voyage across the Atlantic. "Were it to help rid this world of one such evil, sir, I would count it as naught."

"Well said. Gareth, a bit of water, if you please."

The man had to be lifted slightly from the pillow in order to sip from the cup. Gareth held him with the tenderness he might offer his own child.

When William Wilberforce had resettled upon the pillow, he said, "For myself, hardship has carried both burden and opportunity. I do not seek it, I do not like it. But I have found myself learning in spite of myself. Against my will at times. Groaning and crying aloud all the while. At such times I find myself thinking of Moses. He endured a forty-year trek in the wilderness and at its end died in worldly defeat. But he vanquished all, did he not? He started the history that is now our own."

Erica reached into the pocket of her dress and drew out a handkerchief. Falconer had not realized until then that she was crying.

Wilberforce swallowed with great difficulty. He said softly, "Who will stand in the place of law and judgment? Who will speak the truth?"

Falconer came to ramrod attention. "I will, sir. Send me."

Serafina took her second cup of tea back to her room, entering the small chamber half fearful that she might discover lingering traces of her nightmare. Yet all she saw was sunlight and all she heard was birdsong to accompany the memory of Falconer's strength. She set her tea upon the little desk, made her bed and straightened her few belongings, then pulled out the stool and seated herself. Every room held a Bible. She turned to the book of John and began to read. But in truth her mind returned time and again to the way Falconer had stood over her, a warrior so strong he could battle even her secret beast.

There was a knock upon her open door. "Ah, good. I hoped to find you here."

Serafina rose to her feet as Erica entered her little room. "Good morning. I'm sorry, I don't have a proper chair. . . ."

Erica shut the door, then turned to Serafina with a smile. "The house will be gathering soon to pray over Falconer and what lies ahead. But I wanted us first to have a private word."

"Of course." Serafina seated herself upon the bed so that Erica might take the little stool. "I cannot thank you and your husband enough for all you have done."

"You are most welcome. But that is not why I have come. My husband and I have spoken, and he agrees that I should share something with you. A secret of my own." She gathered her hands into her lap. "The day I met my husband, one of his men murdered my father."

"Oh no." Serafina clutched one hand to her chest.

"I loved my father very much, and to see him slain, lying in the Georgetown street while British soldiers marched by . . ." Erica shook away the memory. "I spent years loathing Gareth Powers. I hated him even though I did not yet know his name. He was my enemy."

"I-I do not understand."

"No. Of course not." She reached over and took one of Serafina's hands. "What I mean to say, my dear, is that sometimes what humanly seems impossible is merely unfinished business in God's eyes."

"You speak of . . ." For once, the name came with difficulty to her lips. "Falconer?"

"I speak of your future. You think your capacity to love has been extinguished. But you must never underestimate the power of prayer. Or the strength of God's healing grace." Erica's fondness showed itself in a smile of promise. "When I was in the midst of my own fury and pain and distress, I thought the future held nothing but more of the same. How wrong I was. Eventually I came to discover my own emotions were holding back God's work in my life."

Serafina could not speak, nor could she turn from the compassion in Erica's gaze. When she remained silent, Erica gave her hand a gentle squeeze and rose to her feet. "I simply wanted to suggest that you pray upon this thought. That you become open to whatever God has in store. No matter how impossible such a future might seem."

She waited at the door for Serafina to rise and join her. "Let God guide your steps in all things. Even love." She took Serafina's hand. "Now, let us go and pray for Falconer."

Chapter 29

After they completed their preparations for Westminster, the house gathered and prayed together. Afterwards, Erica Powers embraced her husband upon the doorstep. She then turned to Falconer and took both of his hands in hers. Eyes filled with a luminosity not of this earth drew him from his panic. Falconer took great heart in knowing she intended to pray through the hours until their return.

She said simply, "Go with God."

Serafina stood beside Erica. She made as if to touch his hand, then withdrew and said, "I shall be with Mrs. Powers. Offering what I can."

Falconer's voice failed him. He nodded thanks to both women, then climbed into the carriage.

Gareth Powers accompanied him. Daniel went as well, as did two more of the former soldiers now employed in the printing house. Falconer felt completely secure. No matter what might happen this day, he felt protected within the power of his allies, both seen and unseen.

As they approached the gleaming bastion, Gareth said, "Do you recall the old lord Drescott speaking of John Newton?"

"The slaver turned vicar. Indeed so."

"He was a particular friend of Wilberforce. I remember William once recounting something Newton had said in describing himself. Let me see if I can recall it. 'John Newton. Liar, thief, cheat, murderer, enemy of Christ and His kingdom, sailing round and round the endless liquid void.'" Gareth turned to Falconer and offered the final word. "'Saved.'"

Falconer breathed long and hard, wishing for all he lacked. Proper words, wisdom, a better way with people.

Their carriage pulled up in front of Parliament and halted before a pair of vaulted gates. Guards in august uniforms and bearskin hats flanked the entrance. A tide of dark-suited men came and went. Falconer asked both man and God, "What would you have me do?"

"Speak whatever our Lord puts on your heart," Gareth replied. "We can ask no more of anyone."

Lord Sedgwick and Henry Carlyle were both there to greet them, bedecked in robes of power and importance. Sedgwick inquired over Gareth's health and offered Falconer his hand. Falconer tried to respond, but he was too overwhelmed by the place and his role.

The gentlemen led them across an interior courtyard. The great of this land were gathered in tight clusters, talking of weighty matters and flinging their berobed arms about. But most paused in their discussions to watch Falconer's passage. Many, he saw, held copies of Gareth and Erica's pamphlet. He tried to keep his gaze steady upon the way ahead, to remain steadfast upon his objective.

They entered a chamber of colored stone, one that rose up in the manner of a chapel to a peaked roof very far overhead. Three great chandeliers, shaped like wheels of gleaming copper, burned with countless candles. Narrow windows of stained glass cast colorful glows upon the floor stones. The noisy hall was full of people.

A man approached, stunted and twisted such that his erminedraped robes brushed along the floor. "What's this? You dare bring such filth into these chambers?"

Gareth replied quietly, "Despite your best efforts to the contrary, we are here and safe and ready to confront the enemy."

"Lies!" the man barked with a high-pitched fury. "Lies and accusations! Where is your proof? Where is your evidence? I'll tell you the answer to that. You have none!"

The chamber gradually had grown still. Falconer saw all eyes upon them now. Some were sympathetic, others defiant, many simply guarded.

"If that is so," Gareth replied, "why are you so terrified to have him speak?"

"Aye," a voice called out. "Let them have their say!"

"Why should I, eh? Tell me that!" The dark little man shot his words out to the chamber at large. "Why should I, a member of the lords' chamber, permit this vermin to attack my good name?"

"Because we discussed it and agreed, Lord Bartholomew!"

Falconer could not halt the hiss that escaped him. "You."

Simon Bartholomew blanched at the menace in Falconer's face. "Stay away from me!"

"You are an attacker of children, a destroyer of souls," Falconer said.

He was not even aware that he had moved, save for the fact that Bartholomew was now scrambling backwards across the floor. "Guards! Call the guards and have this vile liar removed!"

Falconer was not armed, which was good. He used the only weapons he had at his disposal, which were his voice and his right arm. He pointed at the man and used the roar trained to reach the highest mizzen in the fiercest storm. "In the name of Jesus, I rebuke you! For the lies you have perpetrated, for the suffering you have caused, for all the evil you seek to do, I rebuke you in Christ's name!"

The man struggled as though choked by the hand that did not quite reach him. He managed to gasp, "The man is clearly insane."

"If you will not accept his word, then take mine!" Lord

Sedgwick lumbered forward. "I stand today as living witness to this man's accusations! Just as is described in the pamphlet you hold, I heard young lord Drescott confess to Bartholomew's complicity in the attempted murder of innocents!"

"And I as well," Carlyle added. "Every word you hear is true. Every word."

"Lies," the banker protested, but more feebly now.

"Let them have their say," another said, and this time his words were met with a chorus of assents.

"Insane." The banker continued to back away until his twisted form was lost behind a cluster of other robed figures.

"Speak, then," another said, more quietly this time.

Gareth took a single step forward. "I had the honor of meeting with our dear friend William Wilberforce this morning. He sends all of you his blessings and these words." He unfolded a paper drawn from his pocket, and read, "'This is not about accusation. This is about shame. My shame. I take Parliament's shame upon myself for the terrible trafficking in human tragedy. These are the desperate facts. We are all guilty.'"

He lowered the page. "He said something more. 'Here I am, packed and sealed and ready for the eternal post. There are but two things I know. That I am a great sinner. And Christ is the great Savior.'"

Gareth stepped back and signaled to Falconer.

"My name is John Falconer," he said, stepping forward. "When I was twenty-five, I inherited my first command from a dead man's hands. The ship was called Sweetwater, after the merchant prince's family, but the crew had a different name for her. We ferried slaves to the West Indies. The ship sailed under the American flag, but the merchant family is British, and our buyers were all within the British islands."

"Impossible!" a voice cried from the rear of the crowded hall. "Trafficking in slaves has been outlawed for more than twenty years!"

"And yet the law is powerless against such transgressions!" This from Gareth Powers. "Until the industry itself is abolished, such secret crimes will continue! We have but one choice! One!"

Falconer waited for silence. When the assembly was listening once more, he continued. "The night I became master of my first vessel, there was a ferocious squall. A nighttime gale that came out of nowhere, as happens sometimes in the trade wind latitudes. A wave came out of nowhere as well, one so high I could not see its crest. It swept the skipper and six seamen overboard so fast we heard but a single scream. The rest of us clung to whatever was nearest and fought to clear the wreckage. We had lost a mast to the wave as well. The fouled rigging tied us to this sea anchor and threatened to send us all to the ocean floor. When the rigging was cleared and mast gone, the crew wanted to drop our cargo overboard as well. Our human cargo. The poor wretched men and women and children chained within our holds.

"When I refused to let the crew dump the human cargo into the sea and lighten the ship, some of the crew rebelled. I received this scar you see that night, fighting for my life." Falconer touched the jagged line on the side of his face. "Thankfully, the storm abated before the crew could take over the ship. We rigged the spare mast and sailed on."

He could hear his voice echoing off the high ceiling, as though other men now joined with him. A deep rumbling chorus of guilt. "Do not think that I fought for these slaves because I was concerned for their welfare. I fought because it was my duty as skipper to save the merchant's cargo. That was my only goal.

"I can still remember the day I realized just how cold and callous my poor soul had become. I sat in a harbor tavern, surrounded by men I classed as mates. I cared for nothing and no one. That day I watched a former shipmate walk down the line of my newly delivered cargo, giving them water. Another man carried the barrel for him, a man I knew as a thief and a murderer. The two of them stopped by each of these slaves, gave them water, and prayed for them.

"I sat and listened as my so-called mates jeered these two men and their act of kindness. And I knew that I was dead. No matter what strength my limbs might have held or that I was called skipper and captain and wore braid on my sleeves. I was dead. My soul was forfeited. Dead and buried in eternal ashes and shame.

"I went in search of that former shipmate. To this day I cannot tell you why. But I did. His name was Felix, and he serves now as curate of a church in Trinidad. Or he does if Simon Bartholomew and his minions have not murdered him as they did the man who carried the water barrel." He waited for the murmuring to die down, then continued, "I remain as I was, a sinner in need of salvation. I am nothing more than a fighter, with no idea of great matters such as this. But Felix needed help to gather information against the slavers. And I did as he asked. How could I not, after what he had done for me?"

John Falconer pointed at the pamphlets dangling from many hands. "I confess to you these things so that you will know the manner of sinner who stands before you today. But I tell you this. What you see written upon those pages are facts. And I add my voice to Mr. Wilberforce's. To pretend that the slave trade is ended is a lie. You tell yourself this lie so you can sleep well at night. But know this. In truth, so long as you hold the power to change things and do nothing, we are all shipmates, you and I. We have all worked together to inflict further suffering upon innocent souls."

The Parliamentary debate over the abolition of slavery throughout the British empire stretched on and on. Sedgwick and Carlyle came repeatedly to the Wilberforce home. Sedgwick was most eager to spend time with Falconer and endeavored to explain the nation's politics.

They were seated in the front parlor, where Serafina had served them tea before settling down in a high-backed chair by the glowing fire. The English seasons were a mystery to Falconer. Here it was scarcely an inch into autumn and already the day could be called wintry. Falconer could tell Sedgwick was enamored with Serafina. The man was not unattractive, in a very large and ponderous sort of way. He was probably only a year or so older than Falconer, and the power of his position, and his obvious wealth, gave him a stately air.

Falconer assumed that in time he might become impervious to the way other men looked at Serafina. That is, if he was granted more time in her company. He observed the passage of days with an odd mixture of impatience and dread. Whatever Parliament decided, his work here was almost done. He did not know how much longer he would remain in England. But it was a matter of days. And the thought of leaving Serafina behind felt as heavy as an illness.

Sedgwick set down his cup. "Might I say, sir, your testimony before the members of Parliament carried astonishing force. I truly believe it may well have tipped the balance."

"I can hardly see that it mattered at all, what with this constant delay."

"This is not delay, sir. Not at all. A proper Parliamentary delay is a matter of years, not days. No, the august body is nearly galloping ahead. Strange as it may seem to you, this is breakneck pace for Parliament."

"*Strange* is the word I certainly would have chosen."

"We have waited forty years for this chance, my good man. Forty years! The Tories have controlled Parliament since the wars with America. But the Whigs hold the majority now. Change is what the people want—change and reform. And change is what we shall bring!"

Falconer glanced to where Serafina observed the gentleman with alert and intelligent eyes. He was struck by the painful realization that they would make a fine couple. Serafina was just the sort of exotic and lovely companion that could elevate Sedgwick's political standing. She was born for such a role. *Not for me. Never for me.*

Falconer had to clear his throat before he could manage, "I am most encouraged by your words and your enthusiasm, sir."

"I am reminded of something dear Wilberforce told me my

first weeks in office. 'Parliament is rather like Noah's ark. It contains many beasts and only a few true humans.'" Sedgwick lit up at a thought. "I say, perhaps you might allow me to escort you to the viewers' gallery, where you can see a Parliamentary debate for yourself."

"Thank you, but no. I have seen more than enough of Westminster already." Falconer decided to make it easier for them and spoke around the ache in his heart. "But Miss Gavi should have an opportunity to observe this government at work."

The gentleman brightened immensely. "What an admirable notion! Miss Gavi, would you care to glimpse the inner workings of this great realm?"

She glanced at Falconer with a questioning look. He attempted a smile. Serafina turned back to the gentleman. "You make it sound most appealing, sir."

"It is, Miss Gavi. Especially now, when reform is finally in the air." His enthusiasm had a boyish charm, a fresh eagerness that left Falconer feeling aged and decrepit. Sedgwick leaned forward as he strained to convince her. "Just think, we are debating a measure to rid our empire of a wretched evil. Why, you shall see history being made!"

She pondered a moment longer, then said, "I think I should like that very much."

Falconer had a keen sensation of an invisible fabric tearing. The impression was so strong he thought for a moment he had actually heard the rending. He stood.

Serafina looked up with a question in her eyes.

"Please excuse me for a moment," Falconer managed to say. "I have remembered there is something I must do. . . ."

He walked to the rear of the house and knocked upon the last door in the hallway. When the voice sounded from within, Falconer entered to find Erica seated beside Gareth's daybed. Hannah played with the kitten upon the rug by the glowing fire. Falconer smiled at the image. It was reassuring to see such good and noble people enjoying the loving family they deserved.

"My dear friend," Gareth greeted him. "Join us."

"I went to the market this morning," Erica told him. "I found some chocolate that has only just arrived from the islands."

"It smells like finest perfume," Hannah said.

"Cook is baking us cakes to have with our tea."

Falconer shut the door behind him and came to sit in the chair Erica indicated. He looked at each face and then said, "I have come to take my leave."

No matter how far he might travel or where this road of life might lead, Falconer knew he would carry this moment with him always. How they all looked at him with such sorrow. How they truly cared for him, such that his departure saddened them all. He would hold the image close to his heart like a fire on a frigid night.

"But you can't!" Hannah cried.

"I must, lass. I must."

"But who will look after me?"

He knelt upon the carpet beside her and spoke to her as he would an adult. "The lies they have been weaving have been exposed. And I have delivered my broadside. They have little reason to hunt you after this."

"What of the price on your head?" Erica asked quietly.

"I must risk that and see to my friend's safety back in Trinidad. I cannot wait any longer."

"I have been making some efforts in that regard," Gareth offered. "An official inquiry is about to be launched into the continued slave trafficking within the British realm. And what role a certain banker by the name of Simon Bartholomew might have played. Careful scrutiny will also be given to the action of the Crown's governor. In the meantime, a royal warrant will be issued which protects one John Falconer from prosecution."

Hannah's face was twisted with despair. "You *want* him to leave us?"

"Of course not, my darling. But you knew as well as I that this day would come. Falconer has responsibilities beyond this family."

"But he's my *friend!*" she wailed.

"Aye, that I am," Falconer solemnly agreed. "And wherever I go, I shall hold you three close in my heart and my prayers."

Hannah flung her arms around his neck and burst into tears. "I'll be all alone!"

"Never," Falconer said, patting the soft hair. "You have a mother and a father to whom you are dear as life itself. You have Daniel. You have Ferdinand, who is growing into the finest cat I have ever seen. And you have a household full of people who would make the best of friends if you asked them."

He held her for a time, until the sobbing eased and her mother leaned forward to touch her arm. "Come, dear. Come to me."

Hannah transferred her embrace to her mother but kept her tear-streaked face turned toward Falconer. "Must you go?"

"Aye, lass. I must."

"And Serafina?" Erica asked softly. "What of her?"

Falconer took a hard breath. "She is beginning to recover. She is growing into her own. She is slowly regaining her confidence." Every word fell from his mouth as heavy as bricks. He pressed them carefully into place, forming a wall between himself and a future he knew had never been his to claim. "She will remember who she is soon enough. She will be restored to her family. She will find her future."

Erica examined him with a woman's wisdom. "You must not take the easy road here. You cannot simply leave without a word."

This was precisely what Falconer had intended. His heart quaked at the prospect of facing her.

"You know how fragile she is," Erica continued. "You must be gentle with her. But you must let her hear this from you and not another."

"She will be as sad as I am," Hannah added.

Falconer nodded his acceptance to their words and rose slowly to his feet. "I shall do as you say."

"Falconer." Gareth rose from the daybed and crossed the room. "I wish to share with you something that has been on my heart for some time. We have, all of us, been struck by events which both harmed us and stood in our way. We were all brought to a place where we did not wish to be. We were held there for reasons none of us understood. Yet we have grown from it. And God's work has been furthered by our being there. I for one have found myself enriched by learning to accept God's timing and direction."

"Your words mean a great deal, sir."

Gareth offered his hand. "As we move on from there, we do so with something for which we can all be thankful."

Falconer accepted the handshake and felt the renewed strength within the grip. "New friends."

Chapter 30

Falconer retreated upstairs, for he had no idea what he should say to the young lady still seated with Sedgwick in the front parlor. He knew because he had passed by the open doorway and seen their heads close together. No doubt Sedgwick was describing the intricacies of Parliament. Falconer thumped up the stairs, fighting bitterness at all the twists of heritage and fate that kept him from being seated in the gentleman's place.

Packing his few belongings did not take long. But during that brief period several of the staff stopped by to shake his hand and thank him. They took their leave in the manner of shipmates who had survived foul weather and harsh attacks. Falconer gripped his satchel with his sword and scabbard lashed to its top and faced another trio of faces. He found himself pleased with what saw. The sick old man was well served by this fresh-faced battalion. They were dedicated, aware, and in for the long haul. The future belonged to such as these, God bless them.

Hannah stood at the base of the stairs and watched him descend. "You told them of my departure?" Falconer asked.

"I saw you didn't want to. Friends help each other in the hard times. That's something you taught me. Mama said I could."

"Thank you, Hannah." Though he had planned to just slip away from the household, he saw the moment's rightness. "You did well."

"Besides, you forgot to tell Ferdinand farewell. He would be most upset."

He hefted the cat from her embrace. The animal was a purring bundle of soft golden fur. Falconer nuzzled the cat to his cheek. "The beast is a kitten no longer."

"Mama said you should take Serafina into the back garden." She accepted her kitten back into her arms. "That is a special place for my parents, you know. They fell in love there and decided to travel together back to America, where they got married."

"It makes for a nice tale," Falconer said, knowing there was no such promise to be found there for himself.

He heard a light tread behind him. He knew before turning who it was. He tried to steel himself for what he would surely find, an open gaze in eyes like sunlit smoke.

She looked up at him, and he saw that her expression was still touched with lingering sorrow. But the shattered quality he had seen earlier was gradually fading. He now saw the power of God to restore and heal.

"You're leaving," she said.

Serafina walked alongside Falconer as they traversed the paths that coursed through the rear garden. The gravel was almost lost in places to the weeds. Birds chirped gaily from the surrounding trees. One elm stood out from its neighbors with the first early hint of autumnal colors. Serafina shivered at the thought of life's changing seasons. "Explain to me again, please, this urgency of yours."

"The man who brought me to Christ is a curate on Trinidad. He not only plucked me from the mire of my own making, he gave a direction to my days."

"The fight against slavery, yes?"

"Just so. I acted as Felix's eyes and ears. I must do what I can to ensure his safety."

Serafina knew a moment's desire to argue that such a man

would have many friends. Others who would keep him safe. Others who were not needed by her. But she stopped the thought before it was fully formed. She would show no such selfishness. No matter how much she wished for Falconer to stay and offer her his strength.

All she said was, "I do understand, John Falconer."

His breath flowed out in a constant stream. Serafina sensed that he had readied himself for an argument, and her acceptance had left him finally able to relax. She added quietly, "I shall miss you very much."

"Lass . . ."

She saw how he caught himself then. And knew she could not draw him out. For she was aware of what he yearned to say. Though he fought against revealing himself, she saw his affection for her. The strong features of his face shone with all that remained locked inside his heart.

Finally she said, "I would ask a favor of you, John Falconer."

"You need but say it."

Serafina saw clearly how poised he stood to do her bidding. Whatever she asked, so long as it was in his power. A woman not bound by God's edicts could easily abuse such a gift.

She waited until his eyes met hers. She saw the love there, and the sorrow borne upon his intention to walk away. That was how much he loved her. Enough to declare that she was better off without him.

She knew she did not deserve this love. The fact that her wounded heart was unable to give anything in return only made it worse.

"How long does it take a letter to reach America?" she asked.

"From England?"

"Yes."

He gave it careful thought. "Is the writer a person of authority?"

"Far from it. My aunt at Harrow Hall wrote to my parents in Washington."

"Then it could take months." Falconer spoke with the expertise of one who knew the sea's ways. "Postal commerce is notoriously slow. From Harrow it must go to Bath, then the London sorting house, then postal coach to Portsmouth, and from there await a merchant naval vessel commissioned by the postal service. Four months if all goes perfectly, which it seldom does. More likely twice that."

"And if I requested the help of my new friends here? What then?"

"Even if they appointed a dispatch rider at each end, at least a month—most likely six weeks or more."

"I cannot force my parents to wait that long," she mused aloud.

Falconer's gaze tightened with the awareness of what she was about. "Serafina, it would not be fitting for us to travel together."

"You have just said you would do whatever I asked."

"Aye. But for me to escort you across the Atlantic . . ."

"But if I were to have a woman companion, what then?"

"You must realize, lass, my first port of call is nigh on two thousand miles south of Washington."

"John Falconer . . . I just do not think my own strength is enough. I need to apologize to my mother and my father. I need to beg their forgiveness. Though why they should ever—"

"Put that fear aside," he said. "They already have. Of that I am certain."

"I have hurt them so very badly."

"No doubt. But they love you, and they shall see your remorse, and they will forgive."

His confidence calmed her as nothing had. She started to reach for him again, then realized it was not fitting. She must not take advantage of his openness nor pretend affection that she could not truly fulfill. "This feeling of utter safety you give me is why I would seek to travel with you."

Falconer turned from her and mused to the distant trees, "I have been offered an alliance by Erica's brother, Reginald Langston. He owns merchant ships. I must seek swift passage to Trinidad. I must ensure the safety of my friend the curate. But ship traffic between Trinidad and America's eastern ports is constant. I could act as your manservant—"

"You shall do no such thing!"

Her outburst startled them both. Serafina's hand flew to her mouth. "Forgive me. I should not have spoken as I did."

"Ah, lass." He smiled then. The weight and the shadows lifted. "It is good to see your spirit being restored."

"Your help would be a gift beyond measure. But I should not accept it if you insist upon traveling as a servant. No. I will not."

Falconer's smile did her heart a great deal of good. "I can see that you would be a most difficult adversary in a quarrel."

"And I for one hope that we should never need to confirm that."

"No. Quite." He resumed thinking aloud. "Certainly the folk here could help find you a suitable female companion for the journey."

She studied him with an openness that surprised even herself. For it seemed to her that she could sense a communication between them, one that went far deeper than mere words. "There is one other problem."

"Yes?"

"I have no money."

"Do not concern yourself with that."

"I cannot promise that my father will repay you."

"Coin has never held much importance to me."

Serafina studied this man of humble birth, struck anew by his nobility. "It is not nearly enough to thank you, John Falconer. But it is all I have to offer."

Chapter 31

Falconer stood outside a white stone manor off Pennsylvania Avenue. It was an official sort of residence. A place where someone of Falconer's class would never be welcome.

He had refused to accompany Serafina inside. He had felt cowardly, but he had declined just the same. She had stared at him a long moment, the appeal clear in her gaze. But she had said nothing. And Falconer had been very grateful for that.

The day was crisp but clear, the sky a deep blue. The wind was brisk and tasted faintly of winter. The trees along the boulevard boasted a multitude of autumnal colors. A number of well-heeled ladies and gentlemen passed along the brick sidewalks. The men wore tall hats and high collars, and the women's bright coats and matching hats suggested a genteel way of life. Falconer noticed various accents and languages, confirming that Washington was indeed growing into a citadel of power.

The house before him was designed with classic European flair. Corinthian columns graced the broad façade. Tall windows were framed by gold drapes. Through them Falconer observed men clustering in groups and smoking long clay pipes. Falconer did not need to overhear them to know they spoke of politics and money.

In the distance, a church bell chimed four o'clock. He had been waiting there for over three hours. He glanced up at the driver, who was relaxing in the manner of one who would be paid for his time whether he worked or not. Falconer debated off-loading Serafina's baggage, then decided against it. He was in no hurry either.

He had a place to go, of course. He still had the Langstons' offer of employment. His impression of Reginald and Lillian Langston was that they were people of their word. They had sought him out and made a point of wanting him to return. He should take great satisfaction in having such a future.

Instead, he felt so bereft he could easily have fallen to his knees there in the street. Sooner or later, Serafina would come out that door. She would have made peace with her family. Of that Falconer had no doubt whatsoever. A family in which there was no place for John Falconer.

The young lady seated inside the carriage looked through the window. "Begging your pardon, sir. I was just wondering how much longer we'd be waiting here."

"I have no idea."

Mary Ewes was a likely enough young woman, and she had done well as a traveling companion for Serafina. She had been in service to the Harrow household, widowed early and left childless, and had been seeking a change. "It's just, well, I haven't had a bite since we left the ship this morning."

"Forgive me, Miss Ewes. Of course you haven't." He reached for his coin purse and handed her several pieces of silver. He asked the driver, "Do you know a good place where the lady might find a decent meal at this hour?"

"There's one not three blocks from where we sit."

"Take her and bring her back, that's a good man."

"Shall I bring you something, sir?" Mary asked.

"A capital idea," he agreed, though in truth he doubted very much that he would be able to swallow a mouthful. "A portion of bread and cheese would do me splendidly."

He waved them off, then resumed his slow pacing in front of the mansion. To escape the sorrow his future held, Falconer's mind returned to their Atlantic crossing. It had been as lovely a time as ever in his life. He had spent the days in Serafina's company. They had done everyday things, the same as the other passengers. They had walked the decks beneath a pleasant sky. They had studied the Scriptures. They had spoken about their pasts. But they had not talked about the future. Serafina could not look beyond the painful reunion ahead. And Falconer had wished for no future beyond the days they shared together.

The vessel had off-loaded supplies in Trinidad and taken on a load of cane sugar bound for Baltimore. Falconer had taken three stout seamen along in Trinidad as guards, for he feared the legal documents he kept in his waist pouch would hold little weight that far from London. But he had not been challenged.

In the capital's outskirts he had discovered that Felix was alive, protected by parishioners who had spirited him away at the first hint of danger. Since Falconer was known as both friend and ally, he had been led to the small freehold where Felix now resided. Felix had embraced him and received Falconer's news with tears of joy. Falconer had passed over copies of the pamphlet they had put together, and the Commons edict proposing an outright ban of slavery, and the newspaper articles declaring that it was only a matter of time before the ban was put into force. Falconer had watched the older man gradually comprehend that they had won. He had bowed his head with Felix and given thanks for God's power.

But Falconer had not been tempted to stay. His time in the West Indies was over.

Too soon they had sailed their way north to Baltimore. Too soon the river barge arrived in Georgetown. Too soon the carriage driver located the mansion on Pennsylvania Avenue where the Austrian legate resided. Too soon Serafina gripped his hand and shed tears of pain and dread as he prayed for her reunion with her parents. Too soon she left him behind and walked inside. Too soon.

Falconer looked to the sky above and silently begged his Father in heaven for the strength to let her go.

He could almost wish that he had bade her farewell in England. But even then he had been too much in love to refuse himself as many days in her company as Serafina would grant. Falconer resisted a sudden desire to glance down at his chest. For it felt as though he had taken a cannonball through the heart and now there was nothing but a void through which the cold wind blew.

He wished he had the strength to give thanks for having known such a love. Even though Serafina made no promises nor treated him as anything other than a dear friend. Their most intimate moments had been the times at prayer. Falconer had never known what it would be like for Serafina to look at him in love. He had never known the way her cheek might feel beneath his touch. He had never known the flavor of her kiss.

Still, he counted himself as blessed as any man for every hour he had spent in her company.

The church bells sounded the half hour. As though on signal, the mansion's front door opened. Falconer stiffened as though ordered by an unseen voice to full attention.

Be strong, he told himself. For her and all the days they would not share.

Three of them emerged together. A woman clung to Serafina's shoulders, lovely in middle age, even with her face reddened by the tears she had recently shed. One glance was all it took to know she was Serafina's mother. She stared at Falconer with the desperate disquiet of one recently saved from her own grave.

Serafina's father looked equally spent. He too had clearly been weeping. He held himself erect with great effort. He was dressed like a prince, with an embroidered long coat and shoes bearing silver buckles. But his face bore the stain of deep suffering, along with the anguish of joyful release. "Y-you are John Falconer, is that correct?"

Falconer doffed his hat as an officer should, fitting his fingers into the peak, and swung it down and to his side, bowing deeply. "I am, your lordship."

"My name is Alessandro Gavi." He bowed in reply. "May I present to you my wife, Bettina."

"An honor, madam."

The woman's voice was hoarse and low, and quivered brokenly as she spoke in Italian. Serafina's own voice was unsteady as she translated, "My mother begs your forgiveness, but her English has escaped her."

"I understand, ma'am." And he did. For his own mind seemed to stumble with the slowness of molasses over every word. *O Lord, give me strength to say a proper farewell.*

"Mr. Falconer, to even try and thank you would be a grave error. We are in such debt as we shall never be able to express, much less repay." The man's chin quivered. He coughed deeply and gripped his daughter in a one-armed embrace. "You have brought life again to this old heart."

"Knowing she is safely returned to her family is all the thanks I shall ever need, sir."

The mother broke down then. And the daughter as well. The mother tried to speak, but the words emerged in fragments. Serafina was in no condition to even attempt a translation. Which was just as well.

In that moment, Falconer felt his heart tear in two.

It was over. His time of love upon this earth was done.

Mr. Gavi gestured back toward the manor. "Please, sir. Please to come inside."

But not even the temptation of one more hour with Serafina could grant Falconer the strength to enter. "Thank you, but I must be off."

All three of the Gavis looked at him with genuine despair. "But, sir!" The gentleman waved feebly. "At least grant me—"

"Serafina." Speaking her name was almost enough to open the floodgates. But a lifetime of hardship served John Falconer well. He would not weep in public. He granted himself the chance to say the word once more. The loveliest word in all the languages of all the world. "Serafina."

"Yes?"

"It is time."

"No. You can't—"

"I must."

He started to turn away, forced by the sorrow welling up inside him, as hot and strong as lava. He would walk away now and make the end of the street, and turn the corner, and give himself over to the lifetime of loneliness that awaited.

Serafina stepped away from her parents' embrace and took hold of his hand.

He looked down at the soft fingers. He did not have the strength to tear himself away. "Serafina. Please."

But she did not release him. His entire universe was centered upon the hand that held his own. He was helpless. He knew he was scarce moments away from weeping. And unable to do a thing except stand there.

Then a second hand touched his arm. One that was not Serafina's but rather her mother's.

"Please, good sir. You will listen to my husband, yes?"

His mind had to make a huge effort to make sense of the words. English. Serafina's mother had spoken to him in English. And her words held an appeal that was mirrored by her gaze and that of her daughter's.

"My daughter has spoken of you in words that I cannot repeat without weeping," Mr. Gavi said. "It is a silly thing for a man to admit. But it is the truth, sir. And that is what she has told us. Of a man who has spoken to her in truth and truth alone. Who has protected her and brought her home. Time and again keeping her safe. A man of honesty and integrity."

"Sir—"

"Wait, John Falconer." Serafina pressed his hand more tightly still. "Listen."

"Mr. Falconer, you have answered many prayers this day."

"So many," Bettina Gavi agreed in her deep-throated voice. "Many times many."

"I would speak of this inside, but since you insist . . ." He waved it aside as unimportant. "Sir, I have been sent to America on a matter of utmost secrecy. I have prayed for someone I could trust, who counts money beneath dignity, who would accept great risk. A man I could trust, sir, with my life and my family's honor."

Falconer found himself drawing back from the brink. The internal motion was almost against his will. For he had found the strength to do what he must, which was turn and walk away. Now that he knew the pain that lay in store, he was uncertain that he could find the strength again.

If Serafina's father noticed Falconer's distress, he gave no sign. "A grave responsibility has been laid upon me, sir. I must trust my instincts and speak openly. I am a stranger in this land. Since arriving here, I have heard many promises of loyalty. But who to trust with these grave duties? I can only look at what is here before me. A man has restored to me my most precious possession, my daughter. He has kept her honor intact. He has asked nothing in return. In fact, I see that he is now willing to turn and walk away."

"No," Mrs. Gavi murmured. "You must not."

"I-I don't understand," Falconer stammered.

The gentleman lowered his voice. "The merchants of Venice loaned a coalition of American merchants a great sum of money, sir. In secrecy. There was a run upon your banks, in New York and in Boston. The merchants and their banks were overextended."

"Sir, such matters are beyond my comprehension."

"No matter. The crisis has passed, but the banks still do not have the money to repay us. So we have been offered ownership of . . . Excuse me, I have lost the words." He turned and spoke to his daughter in Italian.

"Mines," Serafina translated. "And a stamping mill."

"Mines, yes. For gold. In hills to the south and east. In a place called Carolina. There are problems. Immense problems."

Falconer found his mind becoming clear once more. This was what he knew. This was the only work he had ever known. The sort of work that others would shy from. Dangerous work. Tasks that cried aloud with peril.

Falconer said, "You must travel and see if the claims about these mines are true."

"Precisely!" The man's anxiety drew sweat from his brow, despite the chill wind. "If the mines exist, I will accept ownership in repayment for the sum that is owed us. This gold is very important to us. The Venice jewelers, Mr. Falconer, now they must buy all their gold from the Austrian crown and pay a terrible tax. If we can find and manage a source of our own, it would mean a very great deal. But the risk, sir. The risk!"

Falconer looked at the young woman standing between the two anxious parents. He saw the serene assurance with which Serafina regarded him.

No, he wanted to shout. *I cannot.*

"What I wish to ask you, Mr. Falconer, is this. Will you be the man I have prayed to find? A man who can be trusted to take us safely to these mountains? A man who will deliver us and my funds safely home? Will you be our . . . I am sorry. My daughter told me the word, but already I have forgotten." He turned to Serafina. "What was it you called this fine gentleman?"

Serafina replied calmly. For once her gaze was truly intact. "A leader and warrior with a servant's heart."

Book Four/HEIRS OF ACADIA
The Night Angel

The dramatic story of Serafina and Falconer continues . . .

Serafina, reunited with her parents, quickly adjusts to life in bustling Washington. The painful memories of betrayal in Venice soften with her growing fondness for John Falconer, who has now joined her father in a new commercial venture. His work thrusts him into America's first gold rush in the Carolina mountains.

When Falconer fails to return from a month-long enterprise as planned, the rumors begin to swirl. He has sailed back to his ruthless life in the Caribbean. He has been shot dead in a gambling dispute. He is rotting in prison for robbery. Serafina seeks hope from yet another tale: a mysterious figure is purchasing slaves throughout the South and secretly setting them free. He is called the Night Angel, and he pays their ransom in freshly-minted gold!

An unexpected visitor leaves Serafina even more unsettled. How does this woman know Falconer, and can her warning be trusted? Serafina, with her father's help, sets out to determine Falconer's fate. But is she prepared for her own destiny to be revolutionized if Falconer is indeed revealed as . . .

The Night Angel

*Watch for this powerful combination
of romance and redemption coming
in early fall 2006!*

Do You Believe in
Love *at* First Fight?

Lady Constance Morrow
finds herself in the American
colonies, taken against her will
to become a farmer's bride.
Nearly as headstrong as
Constance, Drew O'Connor
wins her as his bride but soon
realizes their marriage of
convenience has become most
inconvenient indeed. Gist's
witty dialogue and humorous
descriptions make this novel
compulsively readable.

A Bride Most Begrudging
by DEEANNE GIST

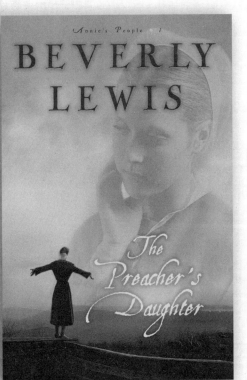